the LOST BOY

GREG RUTH

graphix

An Imprint of

SCHOLASTIC

For David Saylor, who kept this book afloat
through foul, fair, and furious weather. And for Adam
Rau, who brought it in to harbor at last.

Copyright © 2013 by Greg Ruth

All rights reserved. Published by Graphix, an imprint of Scholastic Inc.,
Publishers since 1920. SCHOLASTIC, GRAPHIX, and associated logos are
trademarks and/or registered trademarks of Scholastic Inc.

No part of this publication may be reproduced, stored in a retrieval system,
or transmitted in any form or by any means, electronic, mechanical, photo-
copying, recording, or otherwise, without written permission of the publisher.
For information regarding permission, write to Scholastic Inc., Attention:
Permissions Department, 557 Broadway, New York, NY 10012.

Library of Congress Control Number: 2013937147

ISBN 978-0-439-82331-9 (hardcover)
ISBN 978-0-439-82332-6 (paperback)
12 11 10 9 8 7 6 5 4 3 2 1   13 14 15 16 17
Printed in China   38

First edition, September 2013
Edited by Adam Rau
Book design by Phil Falco
Creative Director: David Saylor

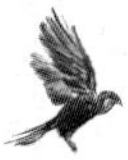

Part One

Walt

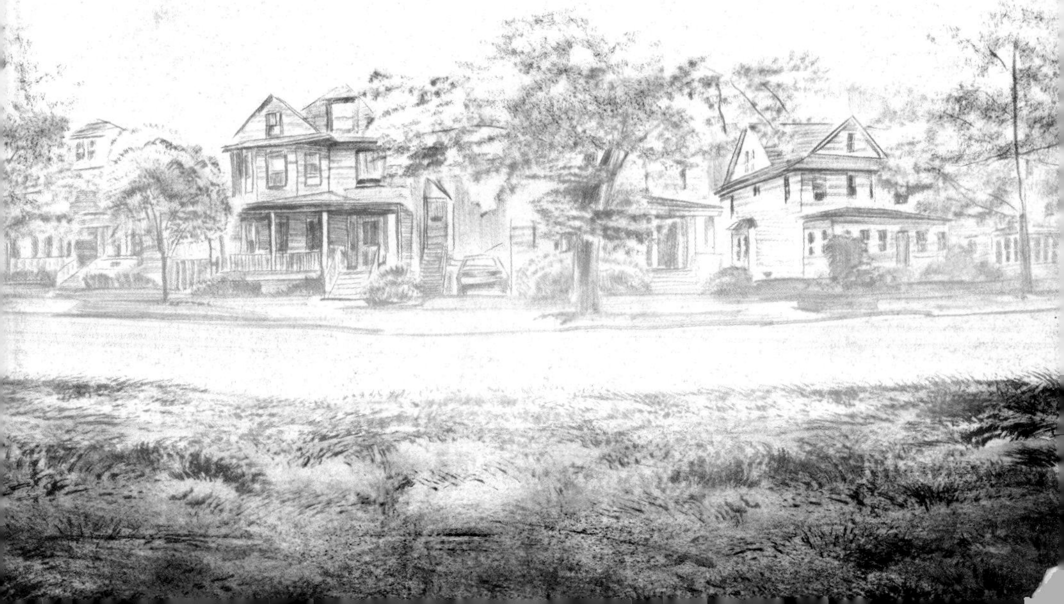

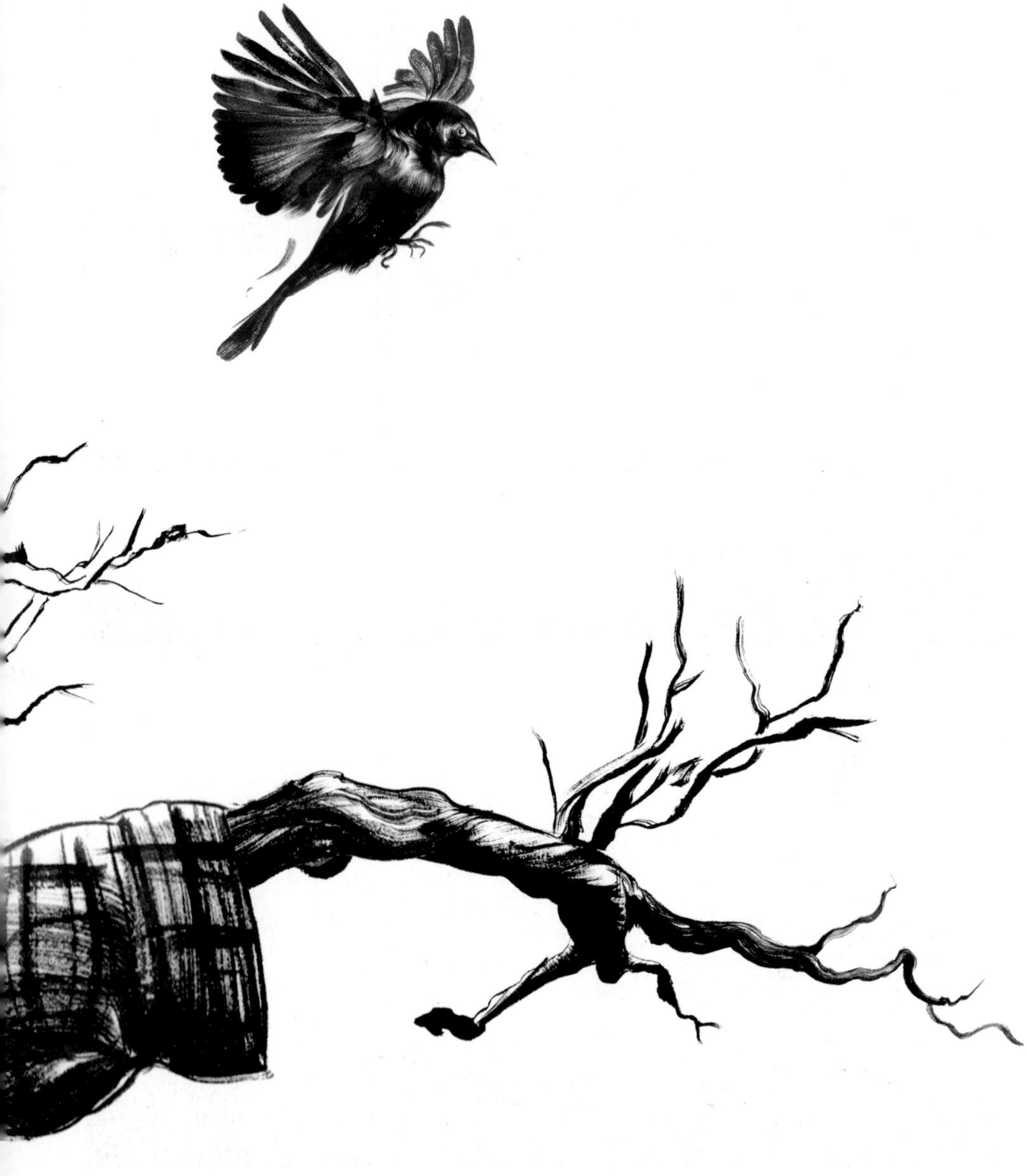

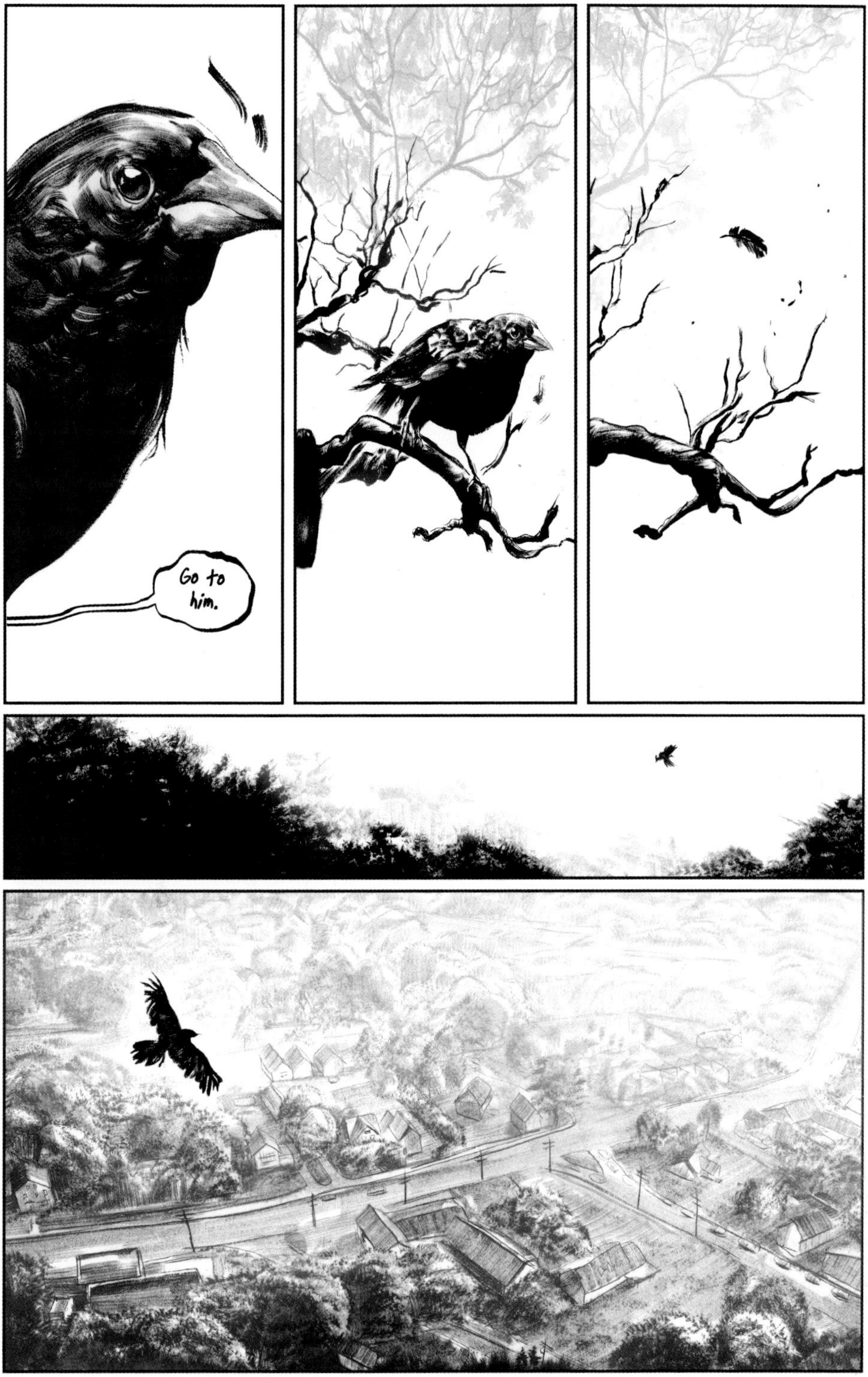
Go to him.

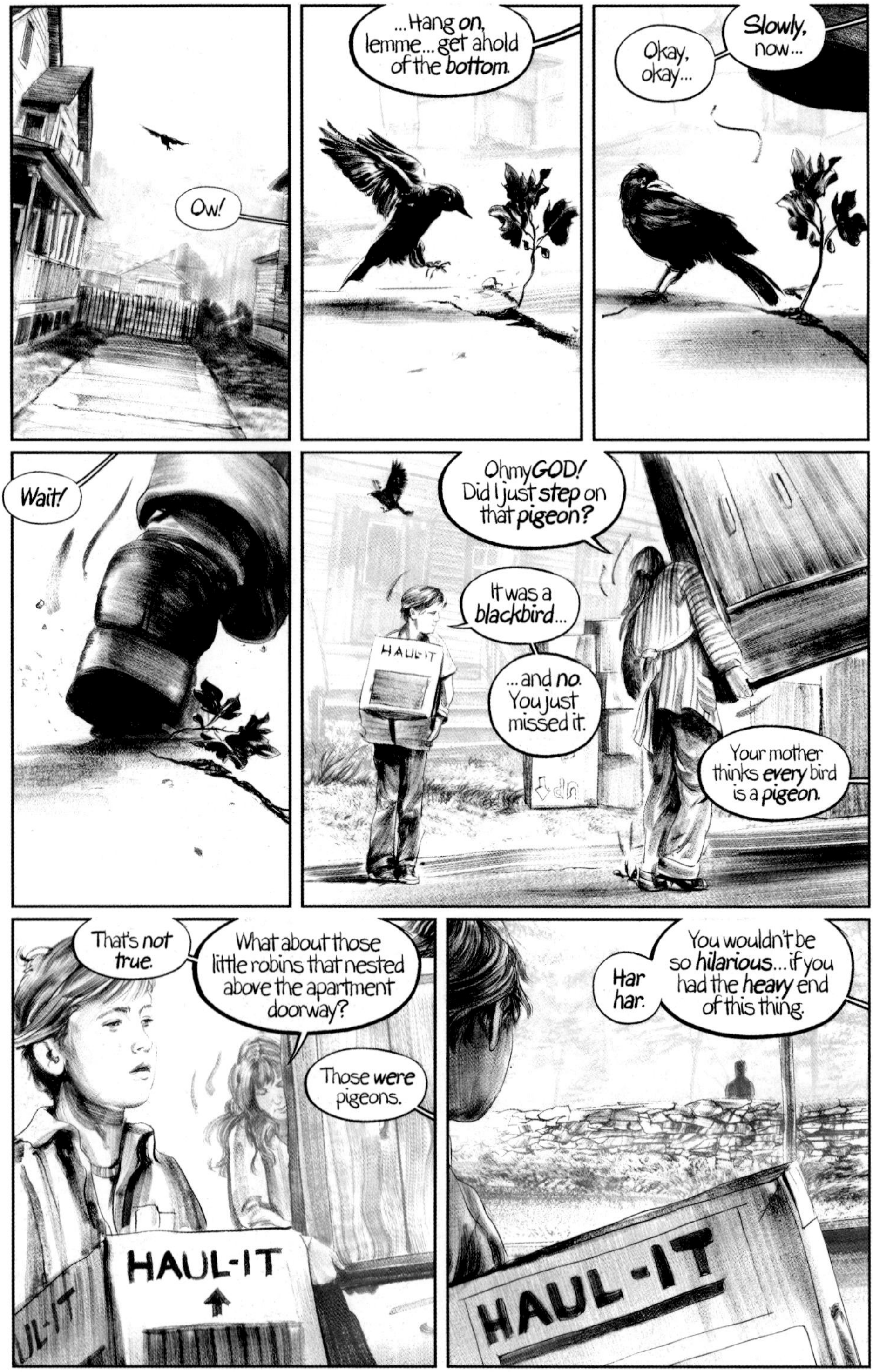
Ow!
...Hang on, lemme... get ahold of the bottom.
Okay, okay...
Slowly, now...
Wait!
OhmyGOD! Did I just step on that pigeon?
It was a blackbird...
HAUL-IT
...and no. You just missed it.
Your mother thinks every bird is a pigeon.
That's not true.
What about those little robins that nested above the apartment doorway?
Those were pigeons.
HAUL-IT
Har har.
You wouldn't be so hilarious... if you had the heavy end of this thing.
HAUL-IT

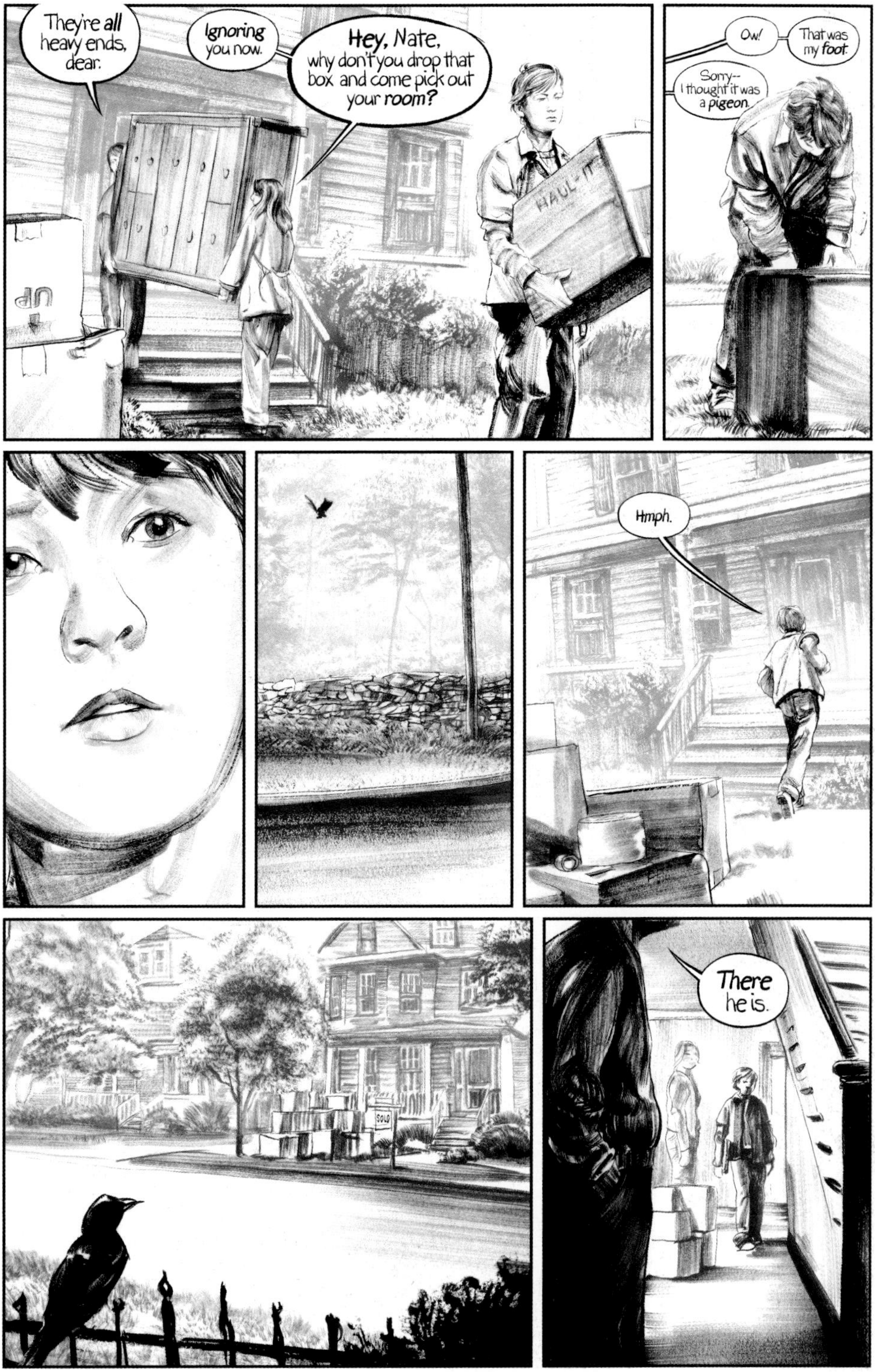
They're all heavy ends, dear.
Ignoring you now.
Hey, Nate, why don't you drop that box and come pick out your room?
HAUL-IT
Ow!
That was my foot.
Sorry-- I thought it was a pigeon.
Hmph.
SOLD
There he is.

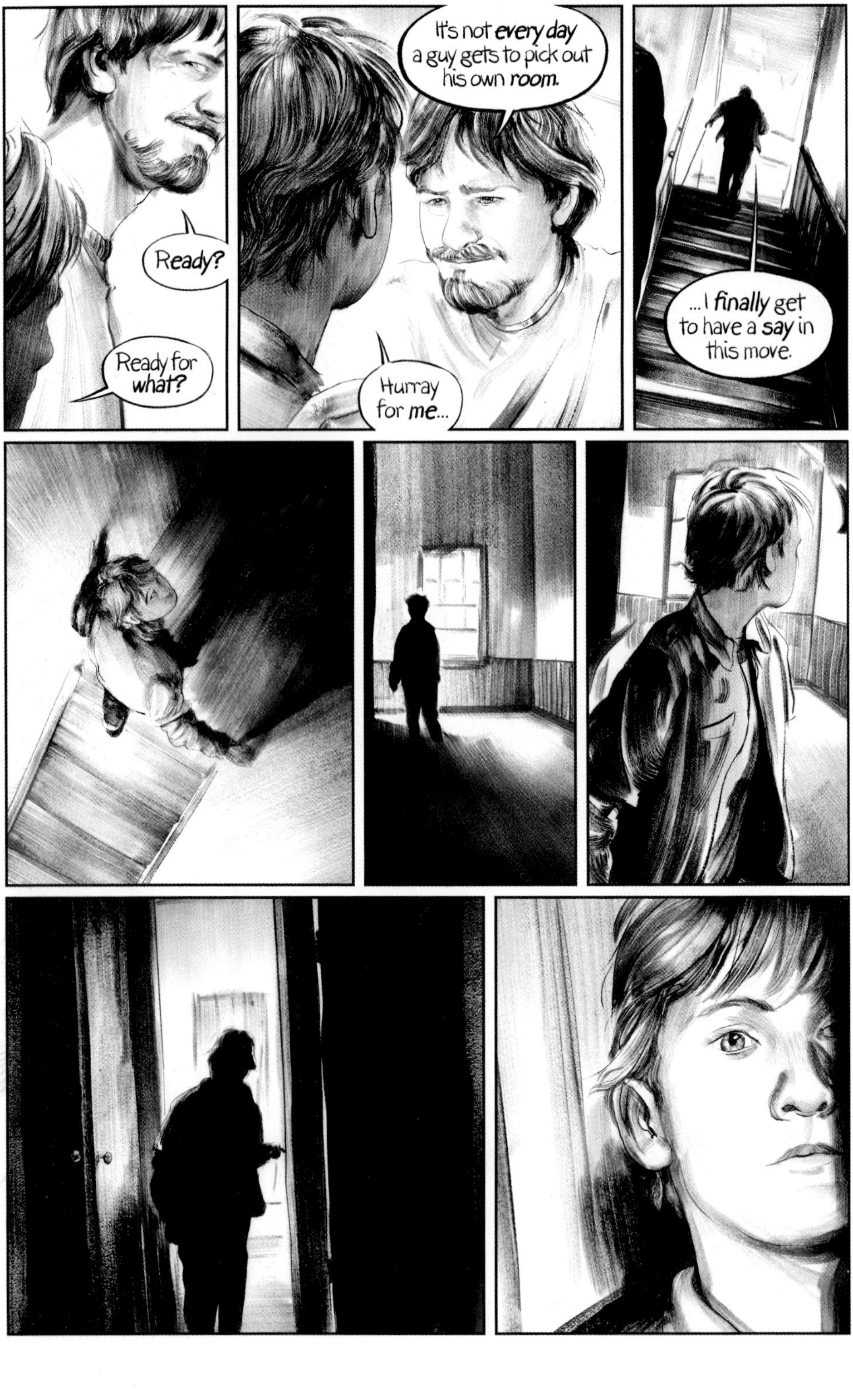
Ready?
Ready for what?
It's not every day a guy gets to pick out his own room.
Hurray for me...
...I finally get to have a say in this move.

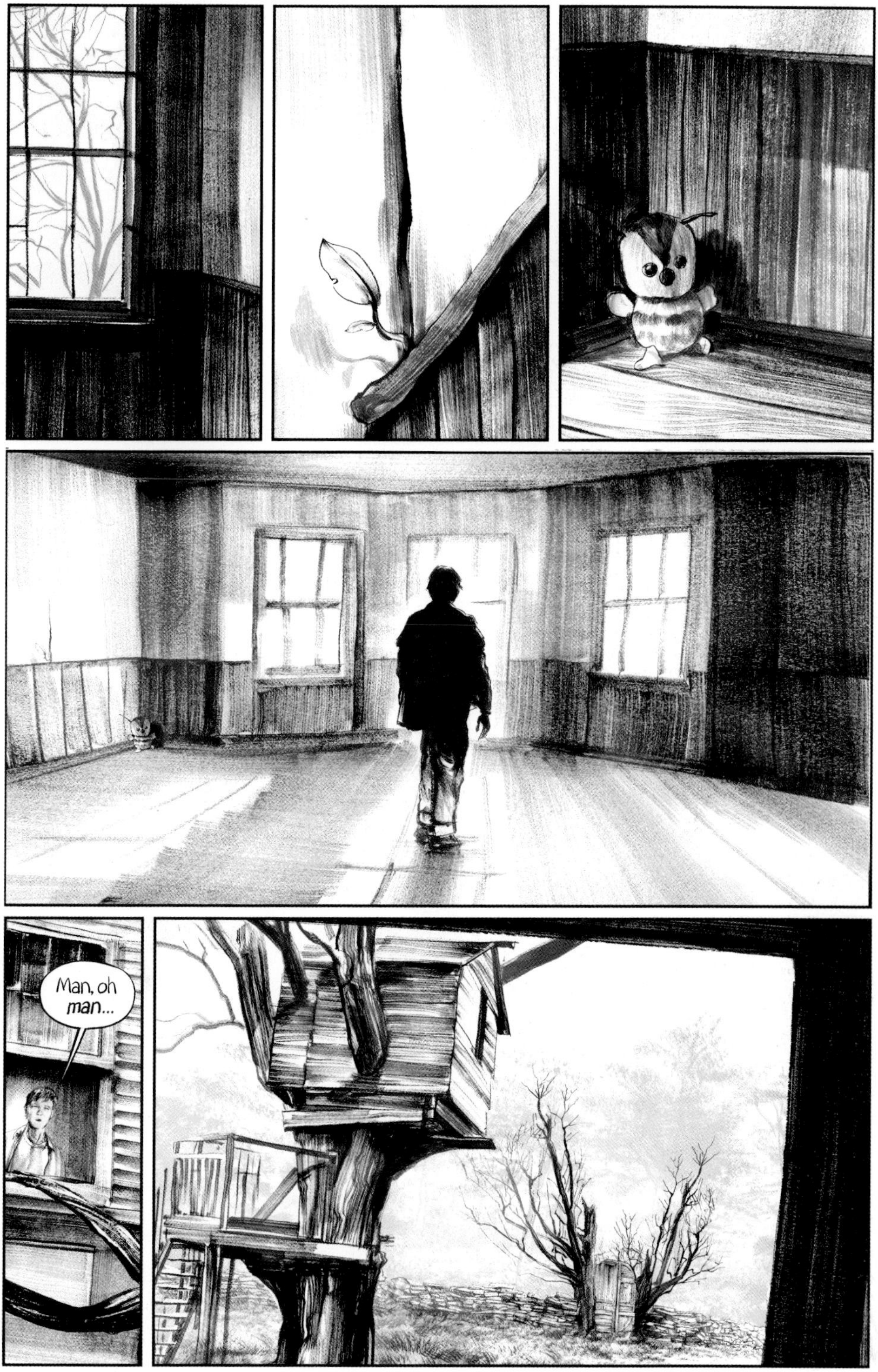
Man, oh
man...

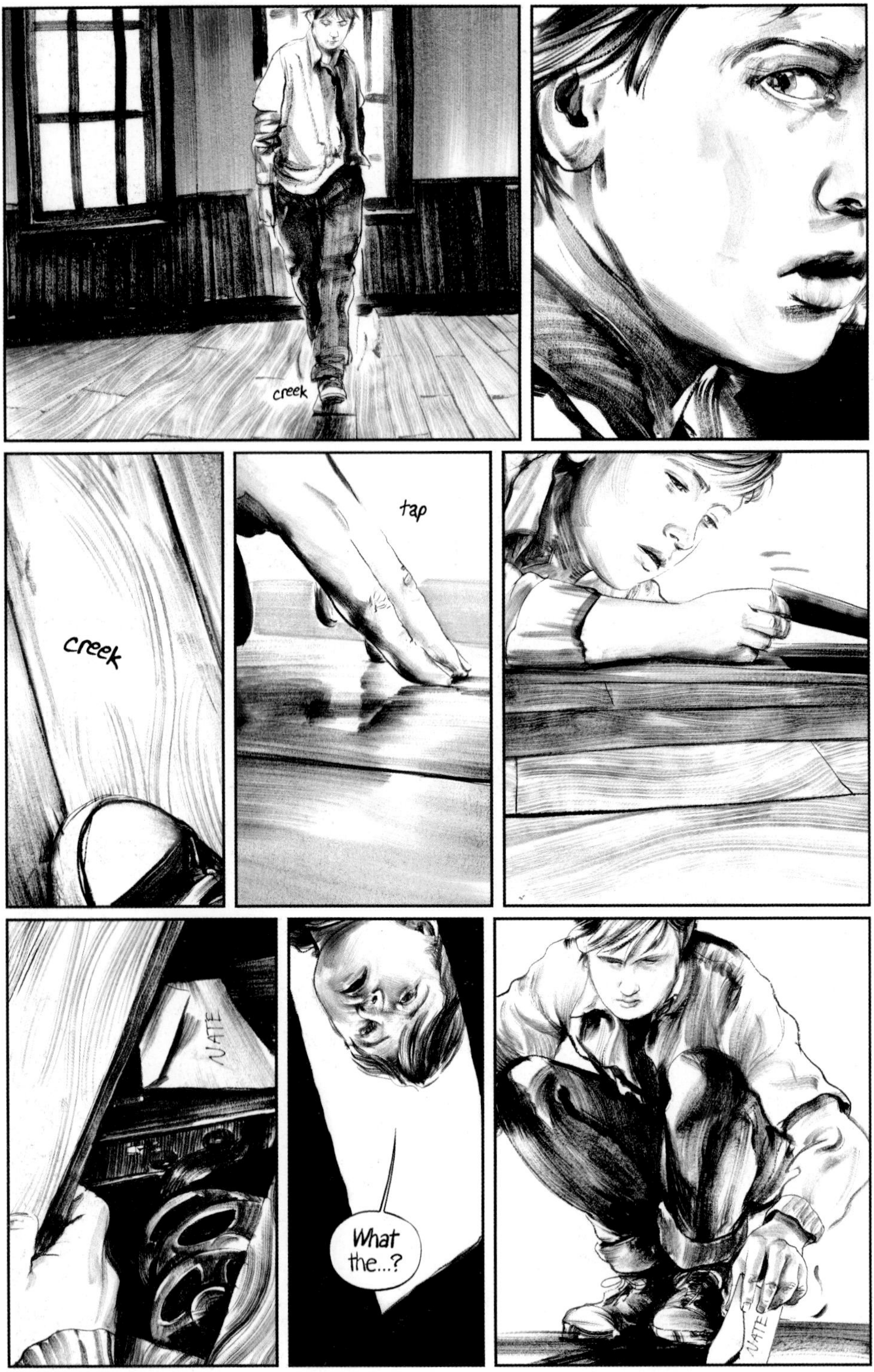
creek
creek
tap
NATE
What the...?
NATE

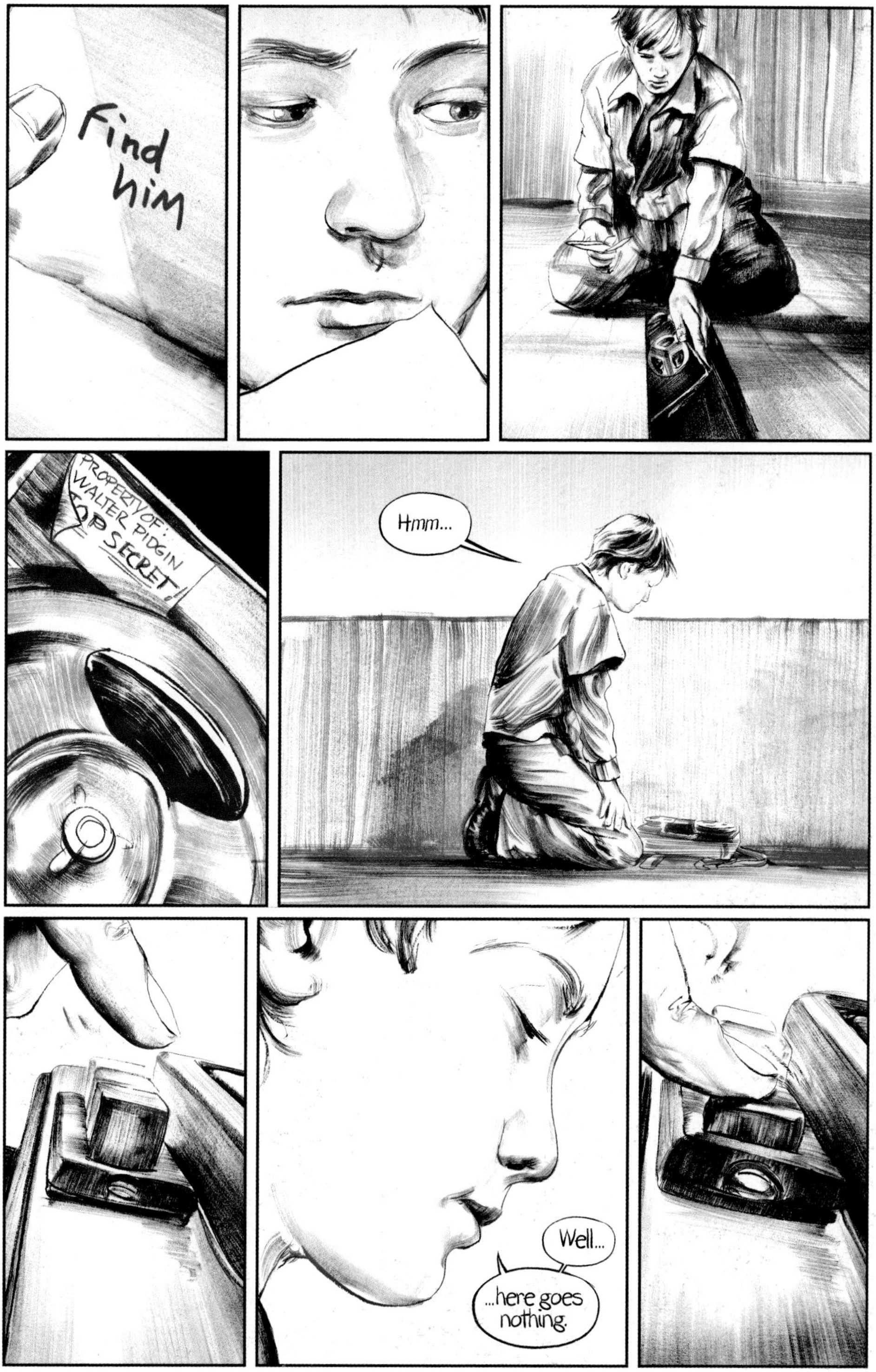
find him
PROPERTY OF: WALTER PIDGIN TOP SECRET
Hmm...
Well...
...here goes nothing.

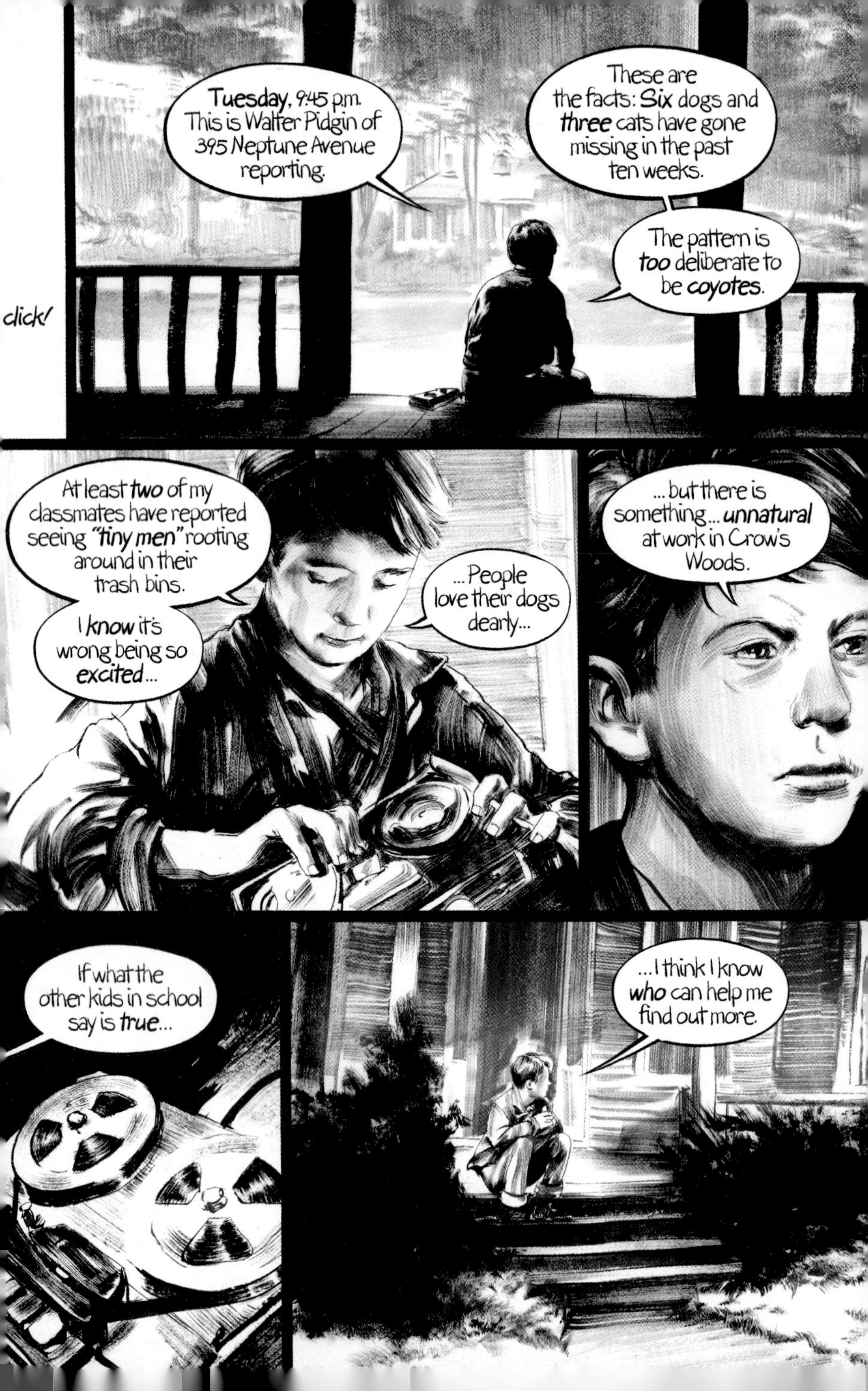
Tuesday, 9:45 p.m. This is Walter Pidgin of 395 Neptune Avenue reporting.
These are the facts: Six dogs and three cats have gone missing in the past ten weeks.
The pattern is too deliberate to be coyotes.
click!
At least two of my classmates have reported seeing "tiny men" rooting around in their trash bins.
I know it's wrong being so excited...
...People love their dogs dearly...
...but there is something... unnatural at work in Crow's Woods.
If what the other kids in school say is true...
...I think I know who can help me find out more.

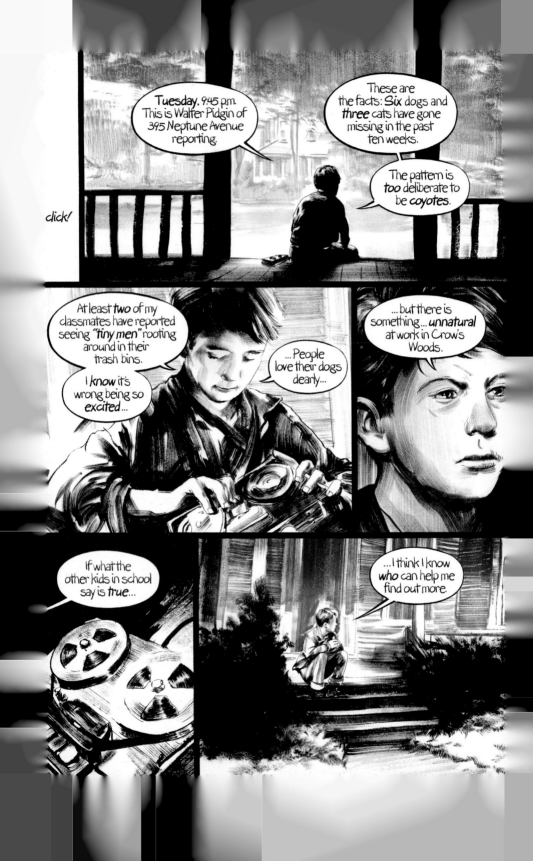

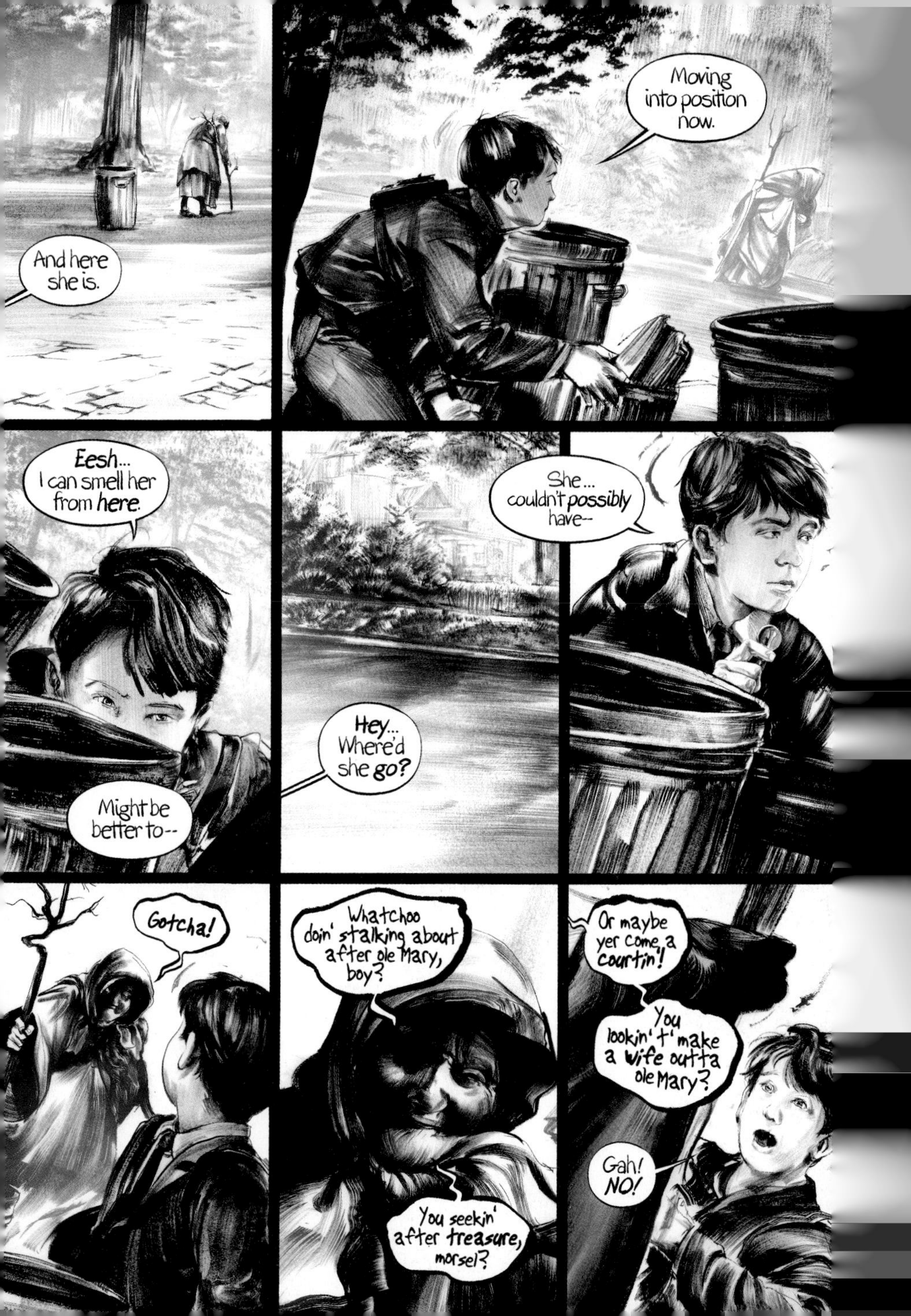
And here she is.
Moving into position now.
Eesh... I can smell her from here.
Might be better to--
Hey... Where'd she go?
She... couldn't possibly have--
Gotcha!
Whatchoo doin' stalking about after ole Mary, boy?
You seekin' after treasure, morsel?
Or maybe yer come a courtin'!
You lookin' t' make a wife outta ole Mary?
Gah! NO!

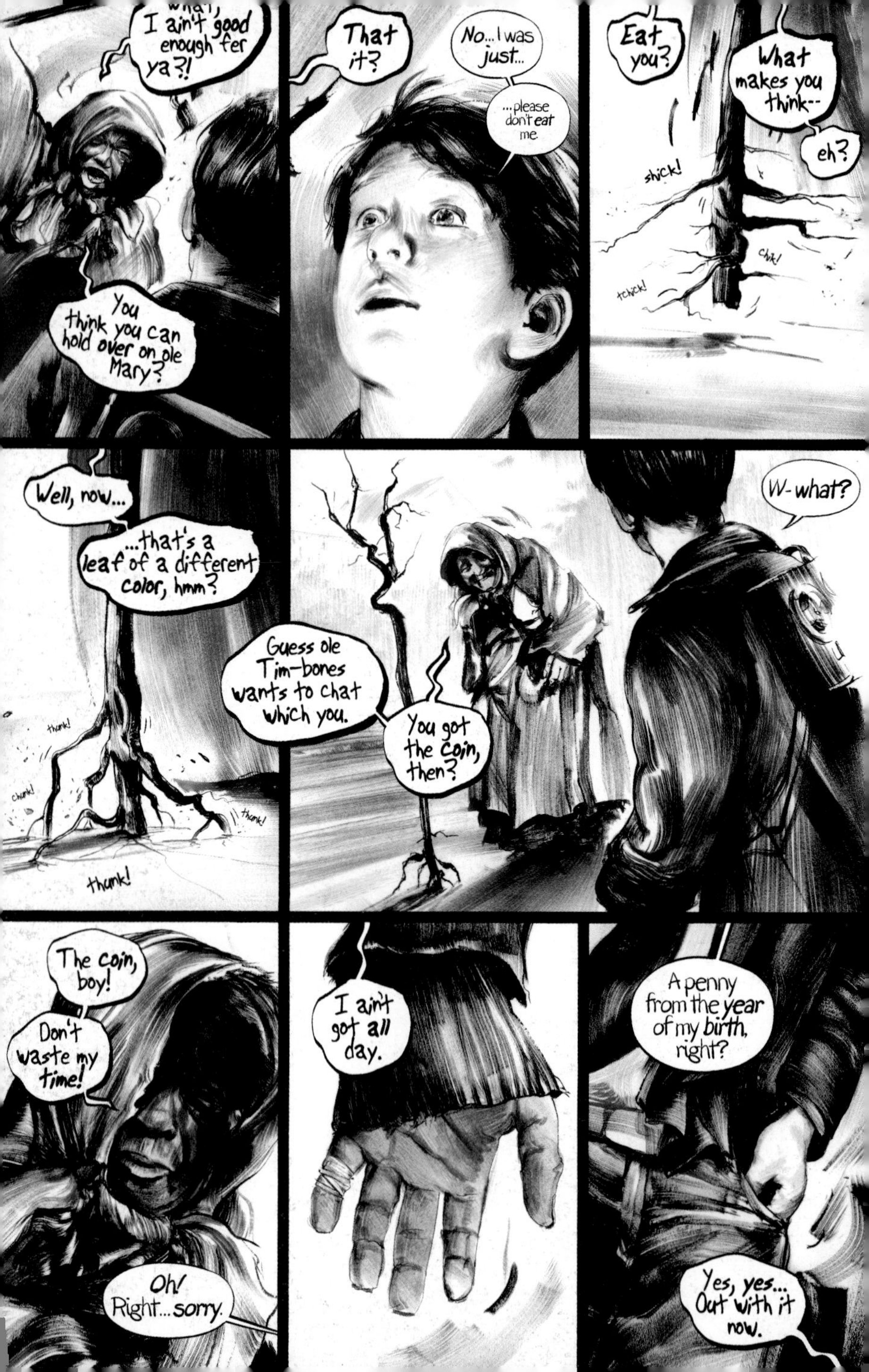

I ain't good enough fer ya?!
You think you can hold over on ole Mary?
That it?
No... I was just...
...please don't eat me.
Eat you?
What makes you think--
eh?
shick!
chik!
tchick!
Well, now...
...that's a leaf of a different color, hmm?
thunk!
chunk!
thunk!
thunk!
Guess ole Tim-bones wants to chat which you.
You got the coin, then?
W-what?
The coin, boy!
Don't waste my time!
Oh! Right...sorry.
I ain't got all day.
A penny from the year of my birth, right?
Yes, yes... Out with it now.

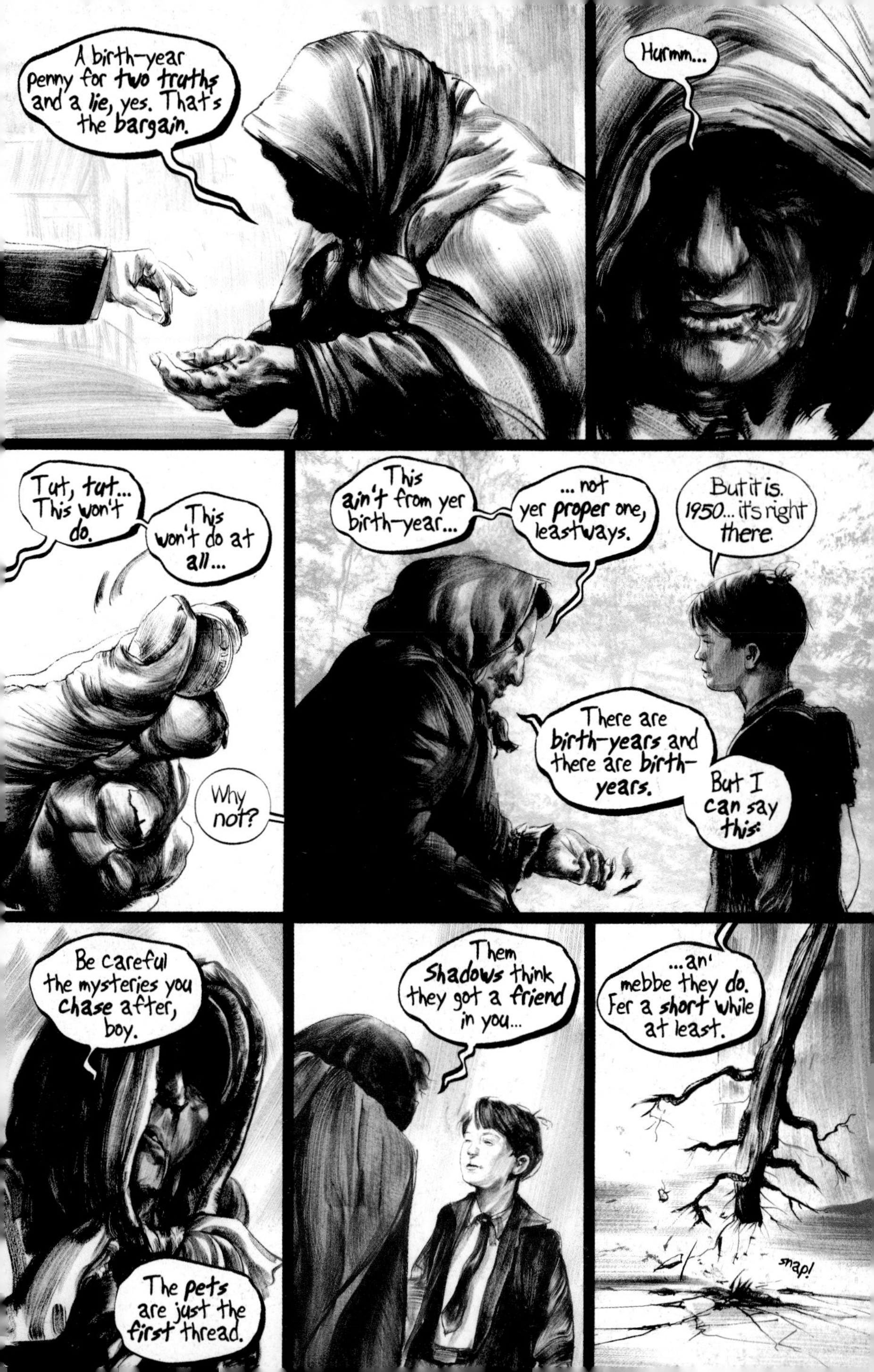
A birth-year penny for two truths and a lie, yes. That's the bargain.
Hurmm...
Tut, tut... This won't do.
This won't do at all...
Why not?
This ain't from yer birth-year...
... not yer proper one, leastways.
But it is. 1950... it's right there.
There are birth-years and there are birth-years.
But I can say this:
Be careful the mysteries you chase after, boy.
The pets are just the first thread.
Them Shadows think they got a friend in you...
...an' mebbe they do. Fer a short while at least.
snap!

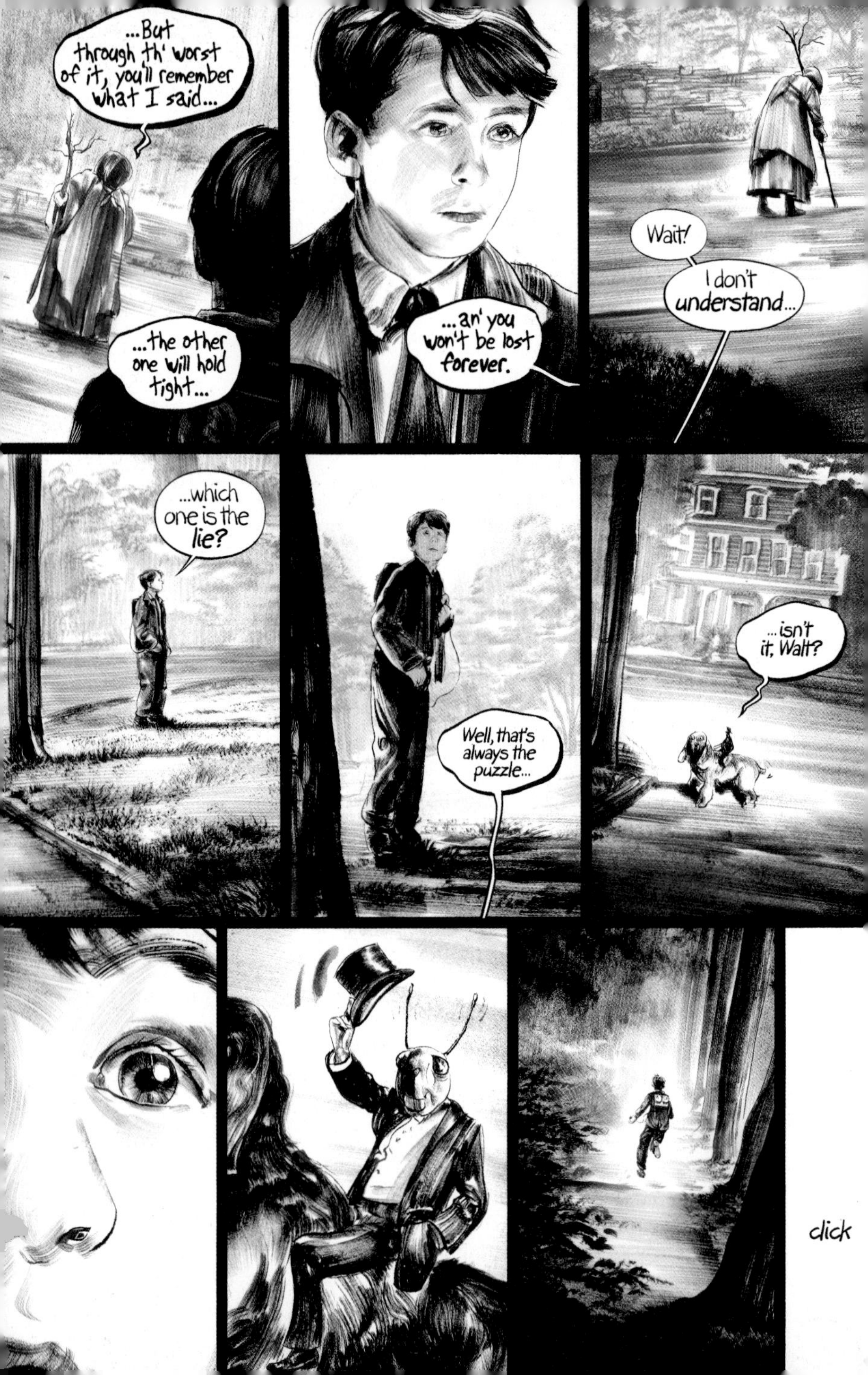
...But through th' worst of it, you'll remember what I said...
...the other one will hold tight...
...an' you won't be lost forever.
Wait!
I don't understand...
...which one is the lie?
Well, that's always the puzzle...
...isn't it, Walt?
click

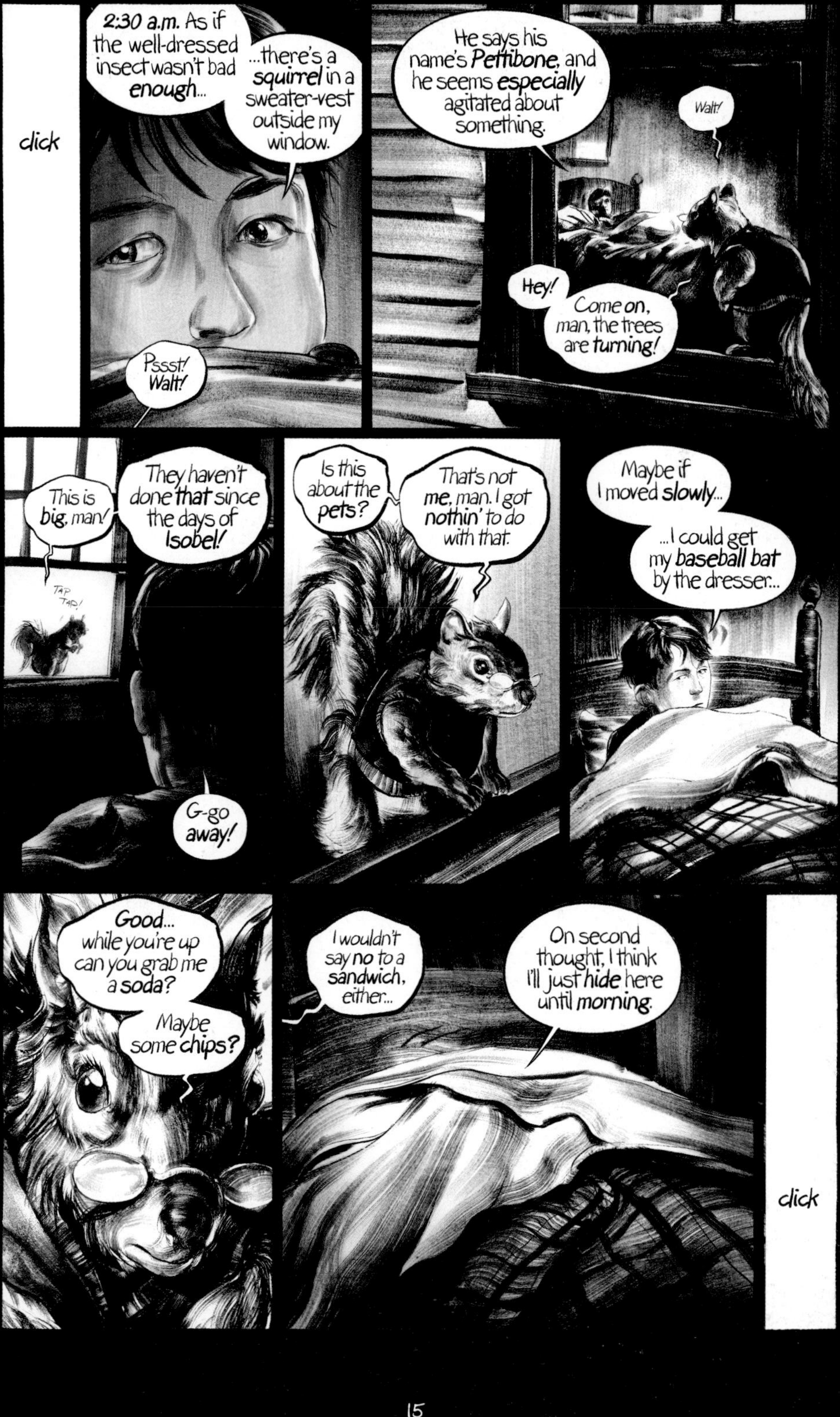
click
2:30 a.m. As if the well-dressed insect wasn't bad enough...
...there's a squirrel in a sweater-vest outside my window.
Pssst! Walt!
He says his name's Pettibone, and he seems especially agitated about something.
Walt!
Hey!
Come on, man, the trees are turning!
This is big, man!
They haven't done that since the days of Isobel!
TAP TAP!
G-go away!
Is this about the pets?
That's not me, man. I got nothin' to do with that.
Maybe if I moved slowly...
...I could get my baseball bat by the dresser...
Good... while you're up can you grab me a soda?
Maybe some chips?
I wouldn't say no to a sandwich, either...
On second thought, I think I'll just hide here until morning.
click

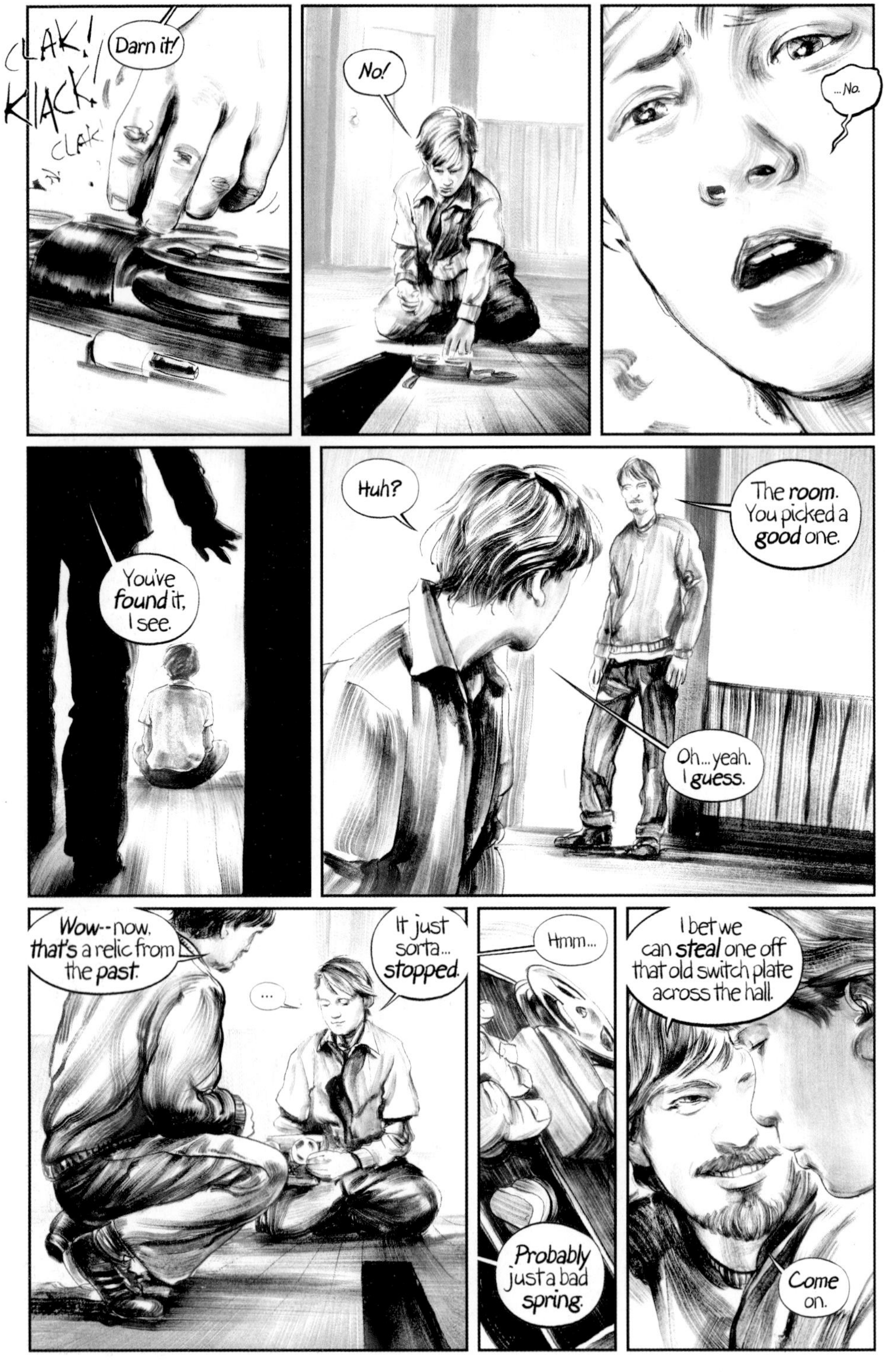
CLAK! KLACK! CLAK!
Darn it!
No!
...No.
You've found it, I see.
Huh?
The room. You picked a good one.
Oh... yeah. I guess.
Wow--now, that's a relic from the past.
...
It just sorta... stopped.
Hmm...
Probably just a bad spring.
I bet we can steal one off that old switch plate across the hall.
Come on.

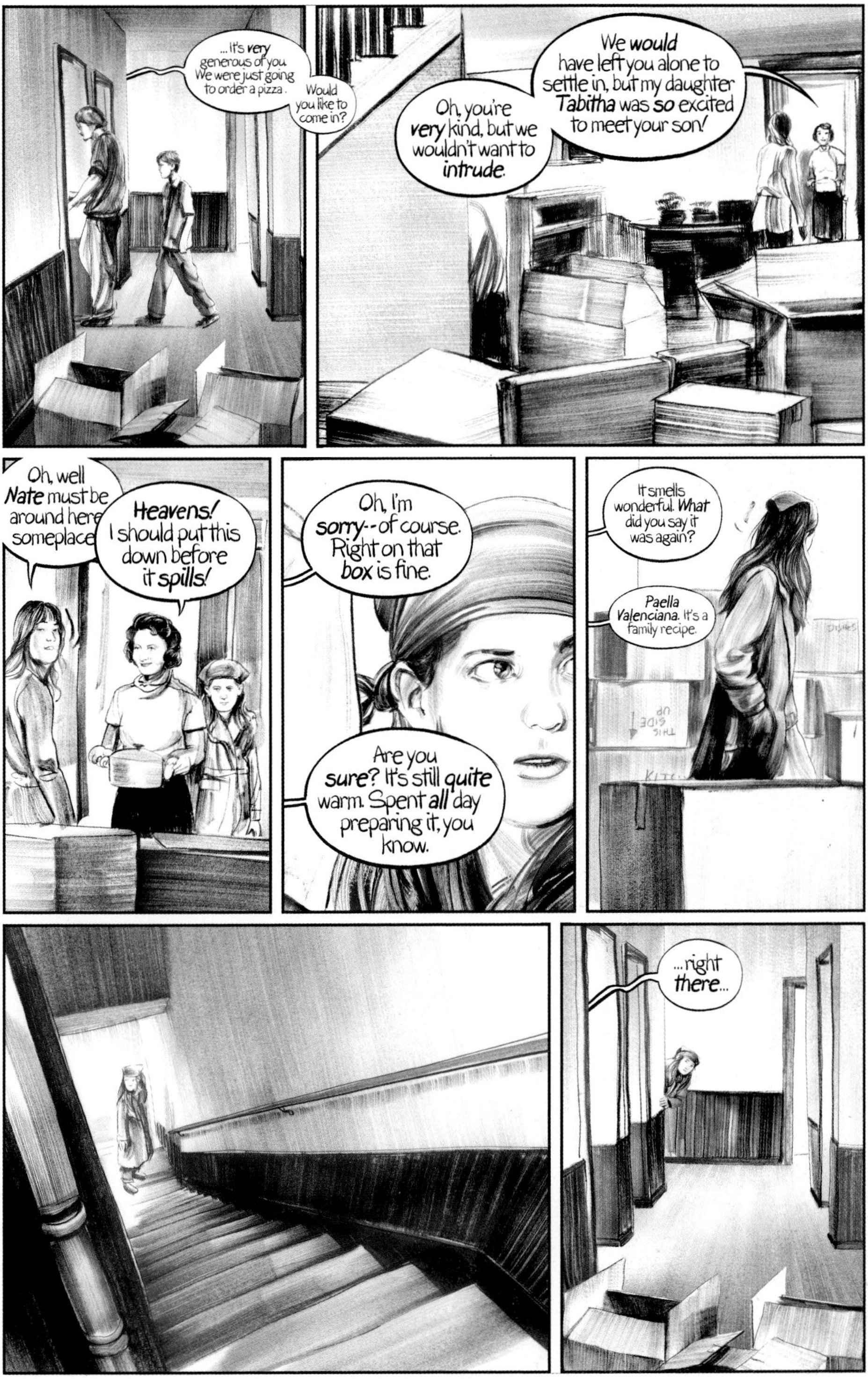
...It's very generous of you. We were just going to order a pizza.
Would you like to come in?
Oh, you're very kind, but we wouldn't want to intrude.
We would have left you alone to settle in, but my daughter Tabitha was so excited to meet your son!
Oh, well Nate must be around here someplace.
Heavens! I should put this down before it spills!
Oh, I'm sorry--of course. Right on that box is fine.
Are you sure? It's still quite warm. Spent all day preparing it, you know.
It smells wonderful. What did you say it was again?
Paella Valenciana. It's a family recipe.
...right there...

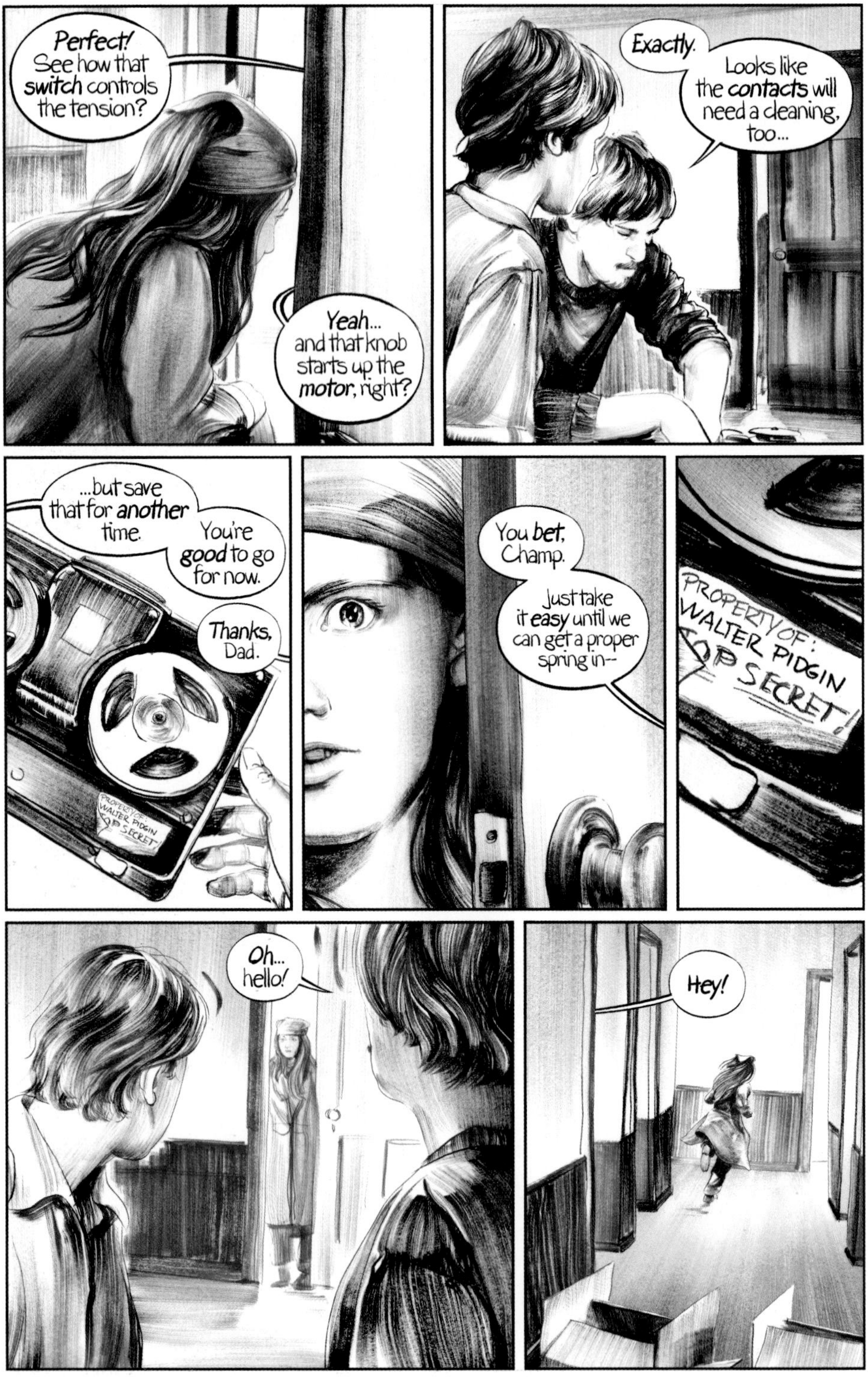
Perfect! See how that switch controls the tension?
Yeah... and that knob starts up the motor, right?
Exactly.
Looks like the contacts will need a cleaning, too...
...but save that for another time.
You're good to go for now.
Thanks, Dad.
PROPERTY OF: WALTER PIDGIN
You bet, Champ.
Just take it easy until we can get a proper spring in--
PROPERTY OF: WALTER PIDGIN
Oh... hello!
Hey!

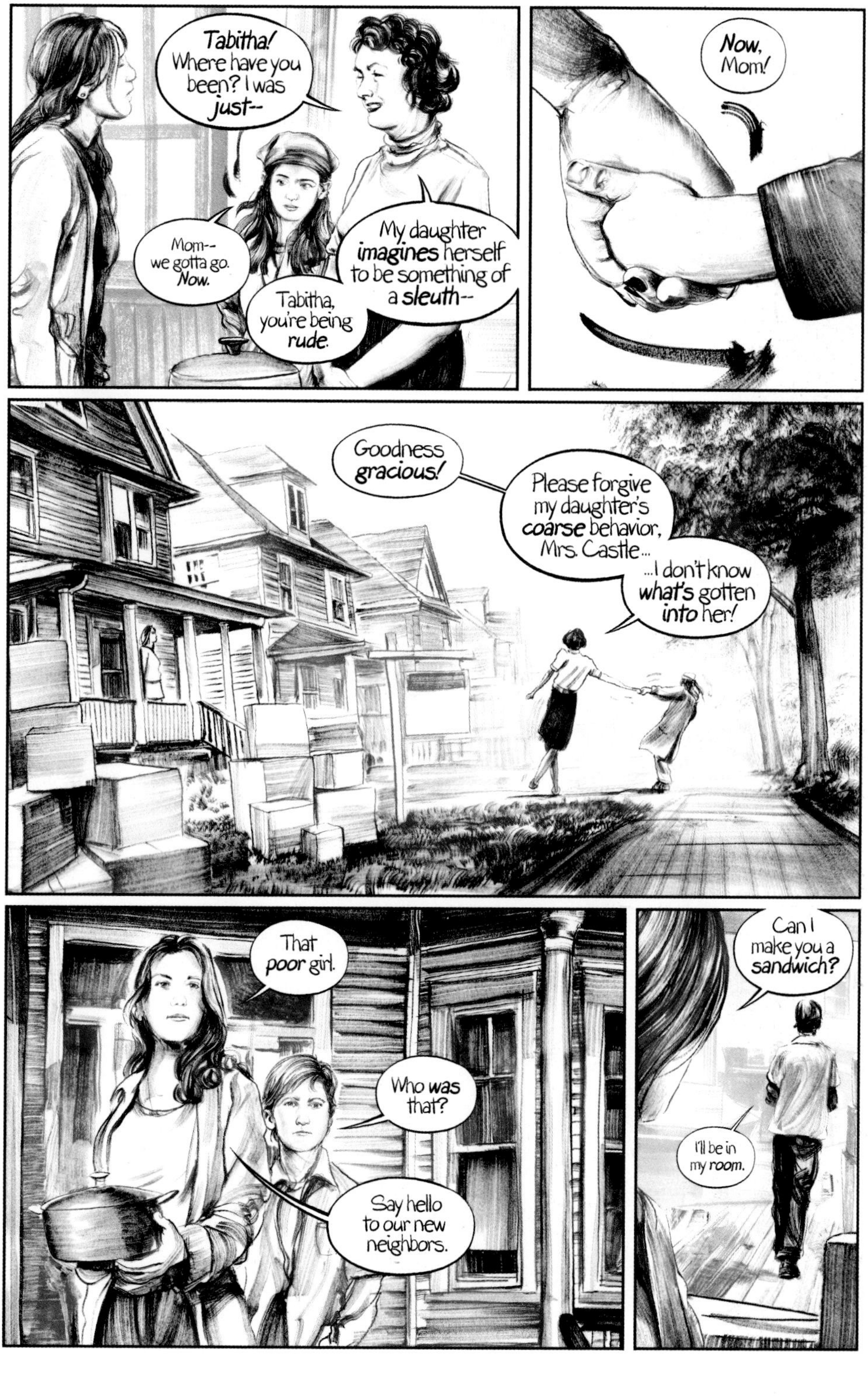
Tabitha! Where have you been? I was just--
Mom-- we gotta go. Now.
My daughter imagines herself to be something of a sleuth--
Tabitha, you're being rude.
Now, Mom!
Goodness gracious!
Please forgive my daughter's coarse behavior, Mrs. Castle...
...I don't know what's gotten into her!
That poor girl.
Who was that?
Say hello to our new neighbors.
Can I make you a sandwich?
I'll be in my room.

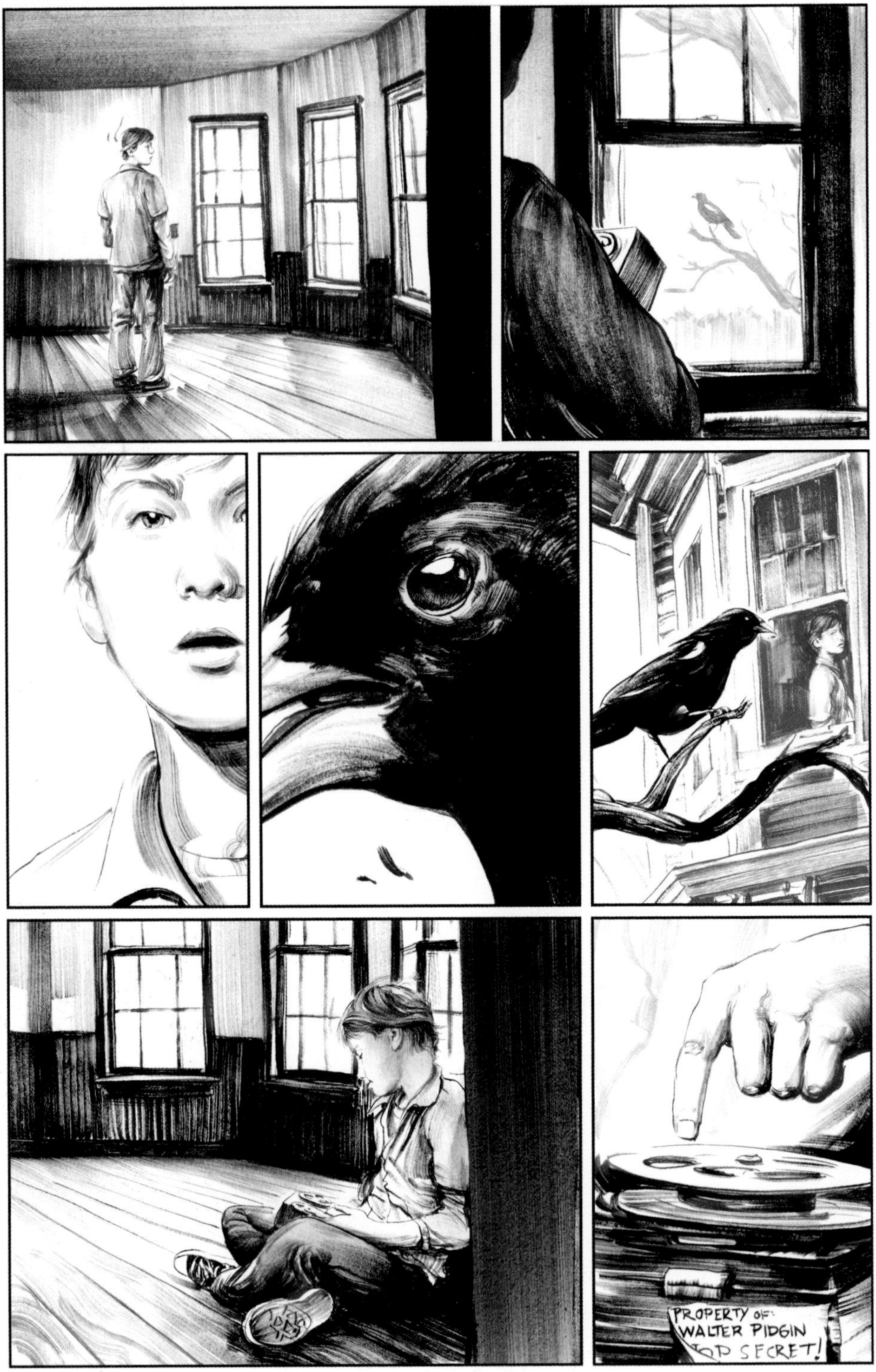
PROPERTY OF:
WALTER PIDGIN
TOP SECRET!

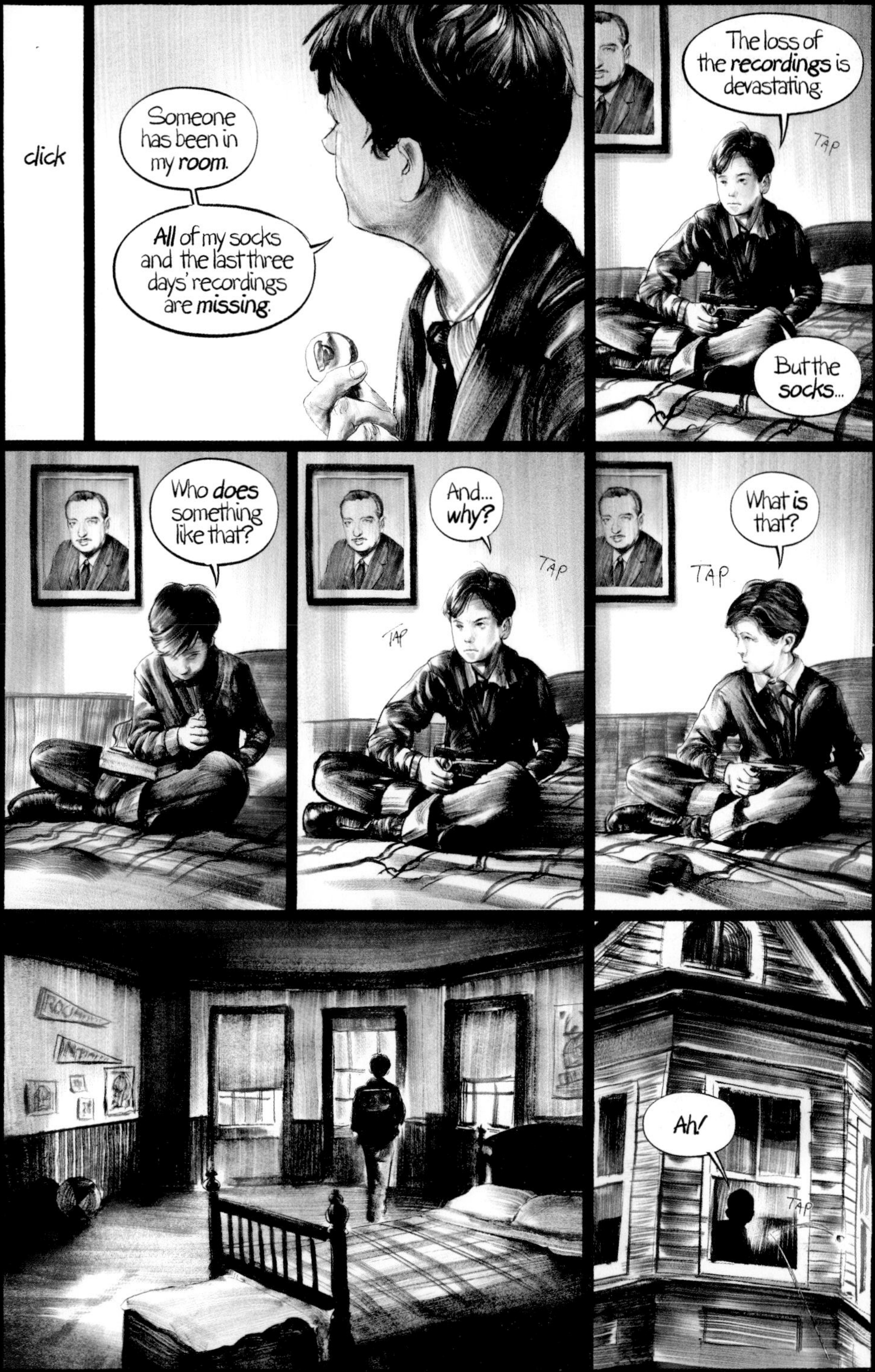
click
Someone has been in my room.
All of my socks and the last three days' recordings are missing.
The loss of the recordings is devastating.
TAP
But the socks...
Who does something like that?
And... why?
TAP
TAP
What is that?
TAP
Ah!
TAP

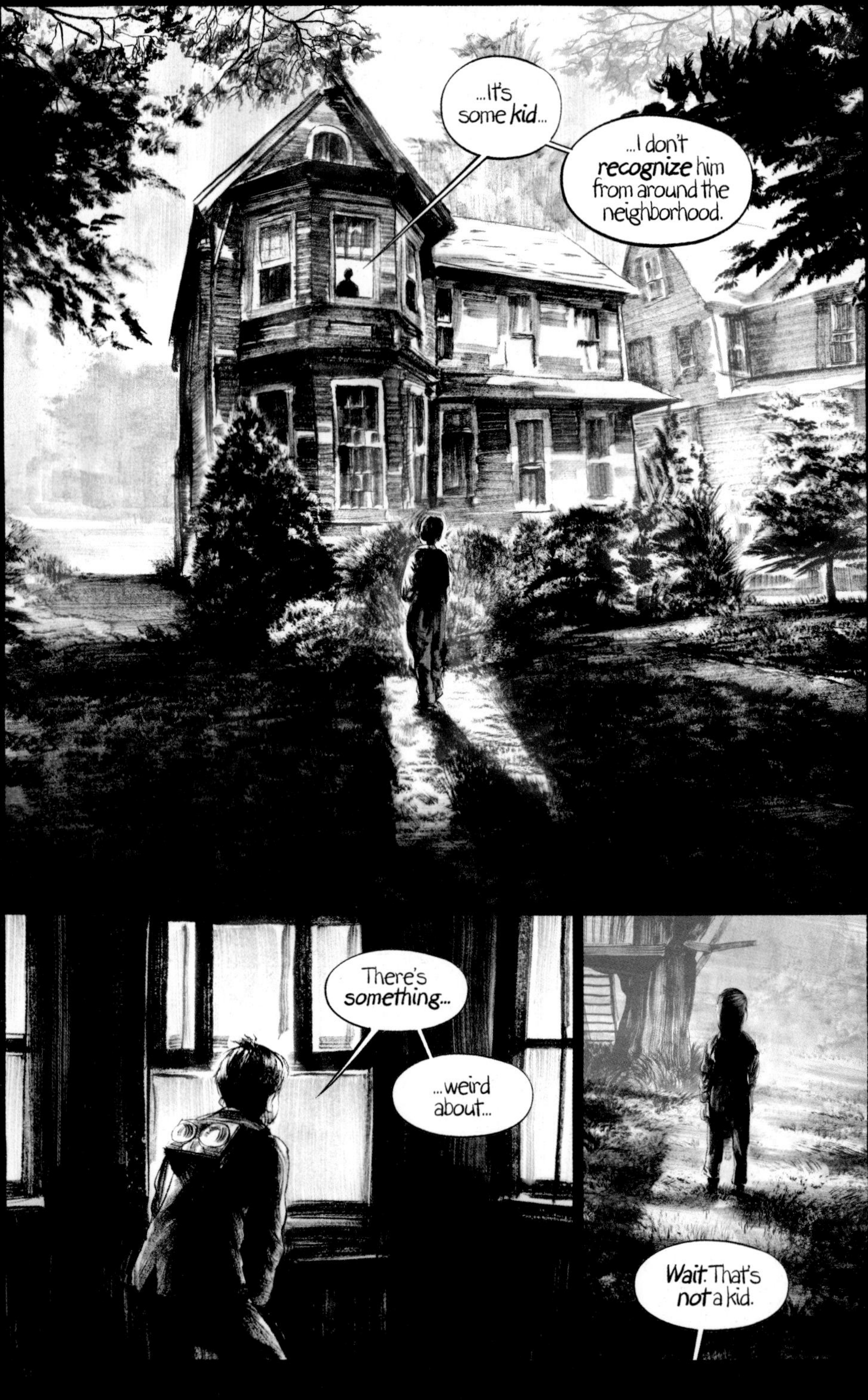
...It's some kid...
...I don't recognize him from around the neighborhood.
There's something...
...weird about...
Wait. That's not a kid.

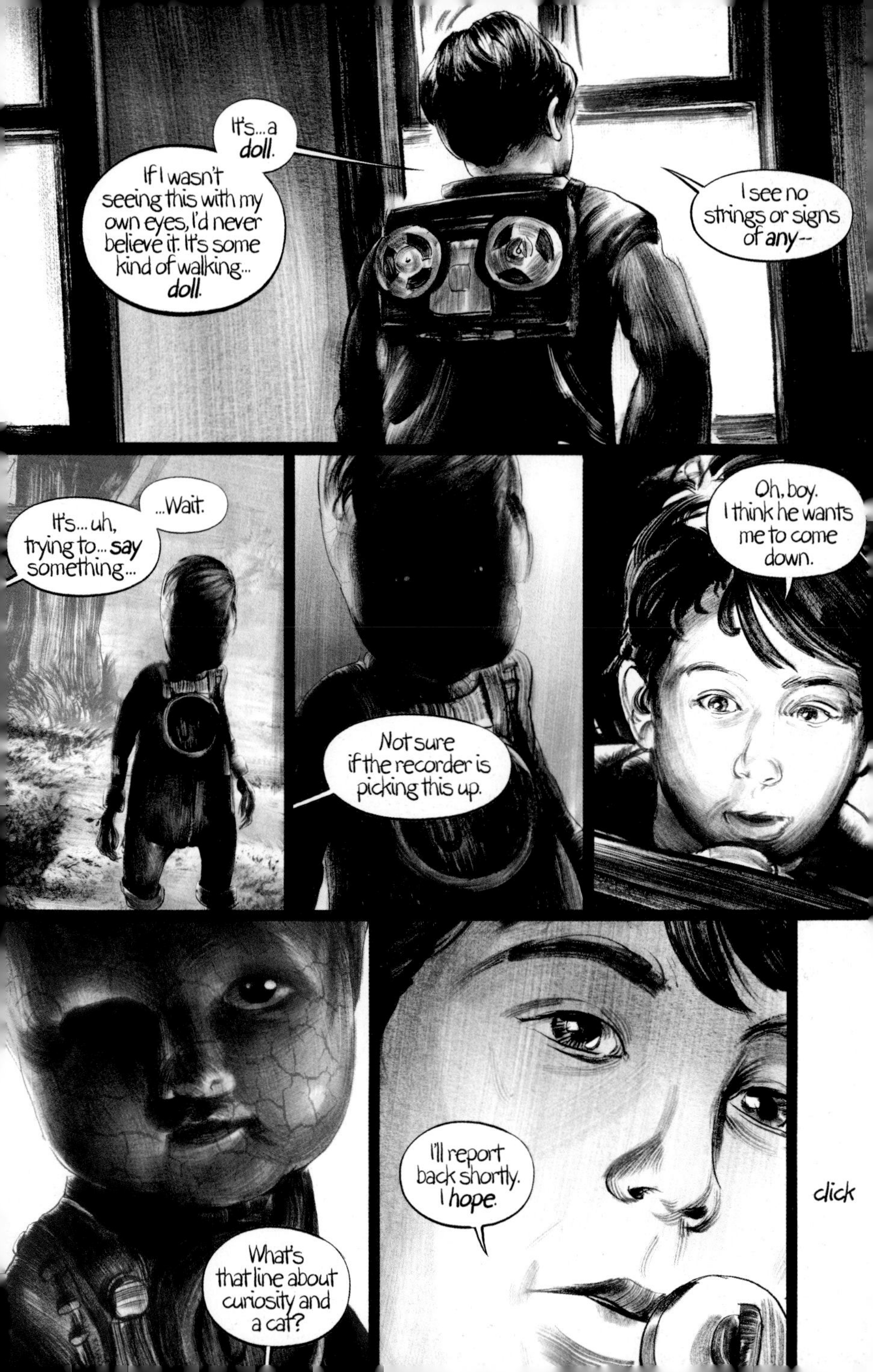
It's...a doll.
If I wasn't seeing this with my own eyes, I'd never believe it. It's some kind of walking... doll.
I see no strings or signs of any--
...Wait.
It's... uh, trying to... say something...
Not sure if the recorder is picking this up.
Oh, boy. I think he wants me to come down.
What's that line about curiosity and a cat?
I'll report back shortly. I hope.
click

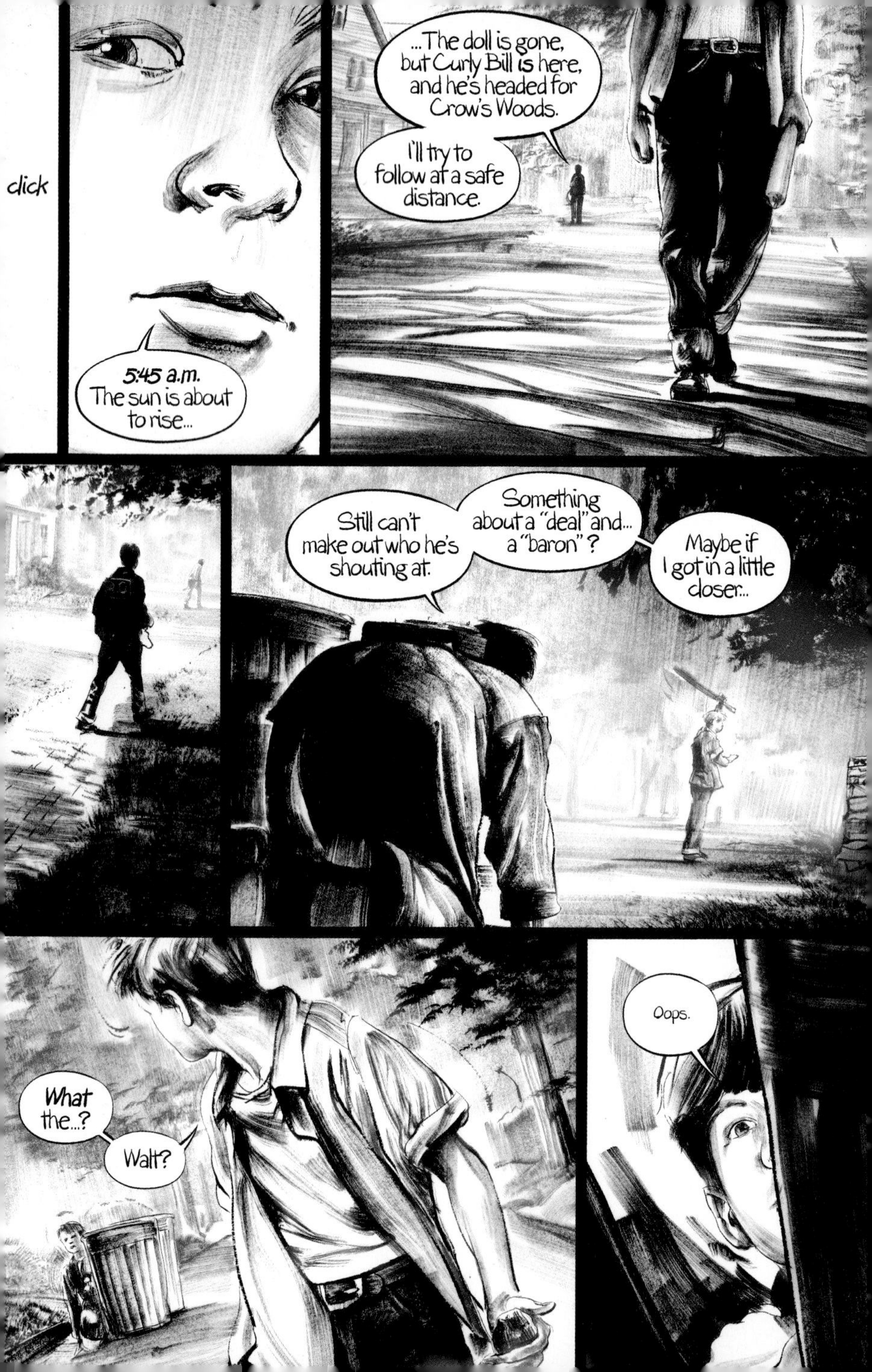
click
5:45 a.m. The sun is about to rise...
...The doll is gone, but Curly Bill is here, and he's headed for Crow's Woods.
I'll try to follow at a safe distance.
Still can't make out who he's shouting at.
Something about a "deal" and... a "baron"?
Maybe if I got in a little closer...
What the...?
Walt?
Oops.

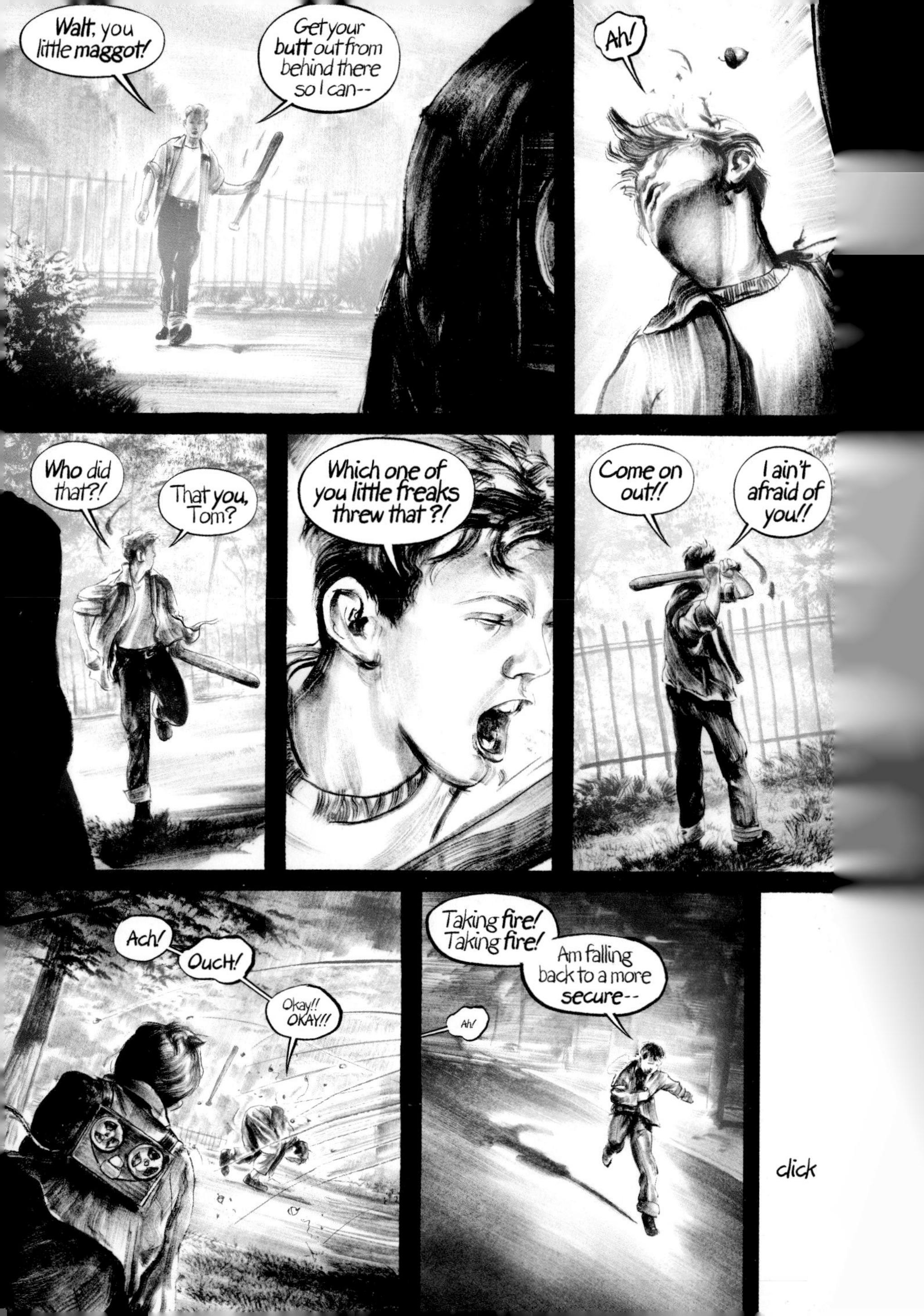
Walt, you little maggot!
Get your butt out from behind there so I can--
Ah!
Who did that?!
That you, Tom?
Which one of you little freaks threw that?!
Come on out!!
I ain't afraid of you!!
Ach!
OucH!
Okay!! OKAY!!
Taking fire! Taking fire!
Am falling back to a more secure--
Ah!
click

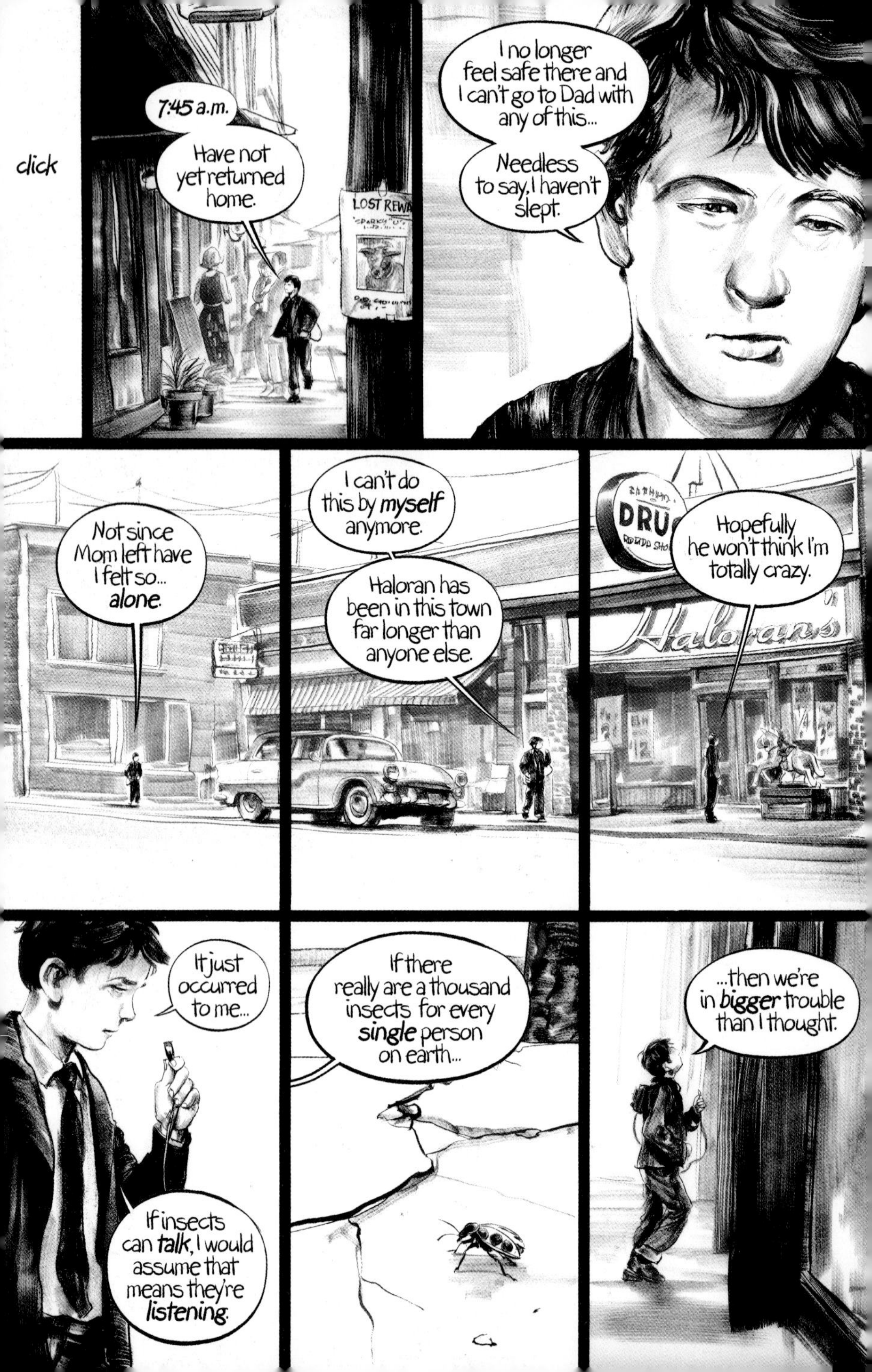
click
7:45 a.m.
Have not yet returned home.
LOST REWA
I no longer feel safe there and I can't go to Dad with any of this...
Needless to say, I haven't slept.
Not since Mom left have I felt so... alone.
I can't do this by myself anymore.
Haloran has been in this town far longer than anyone else.
DRU
Hopefully he won't think I'm totally crazy.
Halorans
It just occurred to me...
If insects can talk, I would assume that means they're listening.
If there really are a thousand insects for every single person on earth...
...then we're in bigger trouble than I thought.

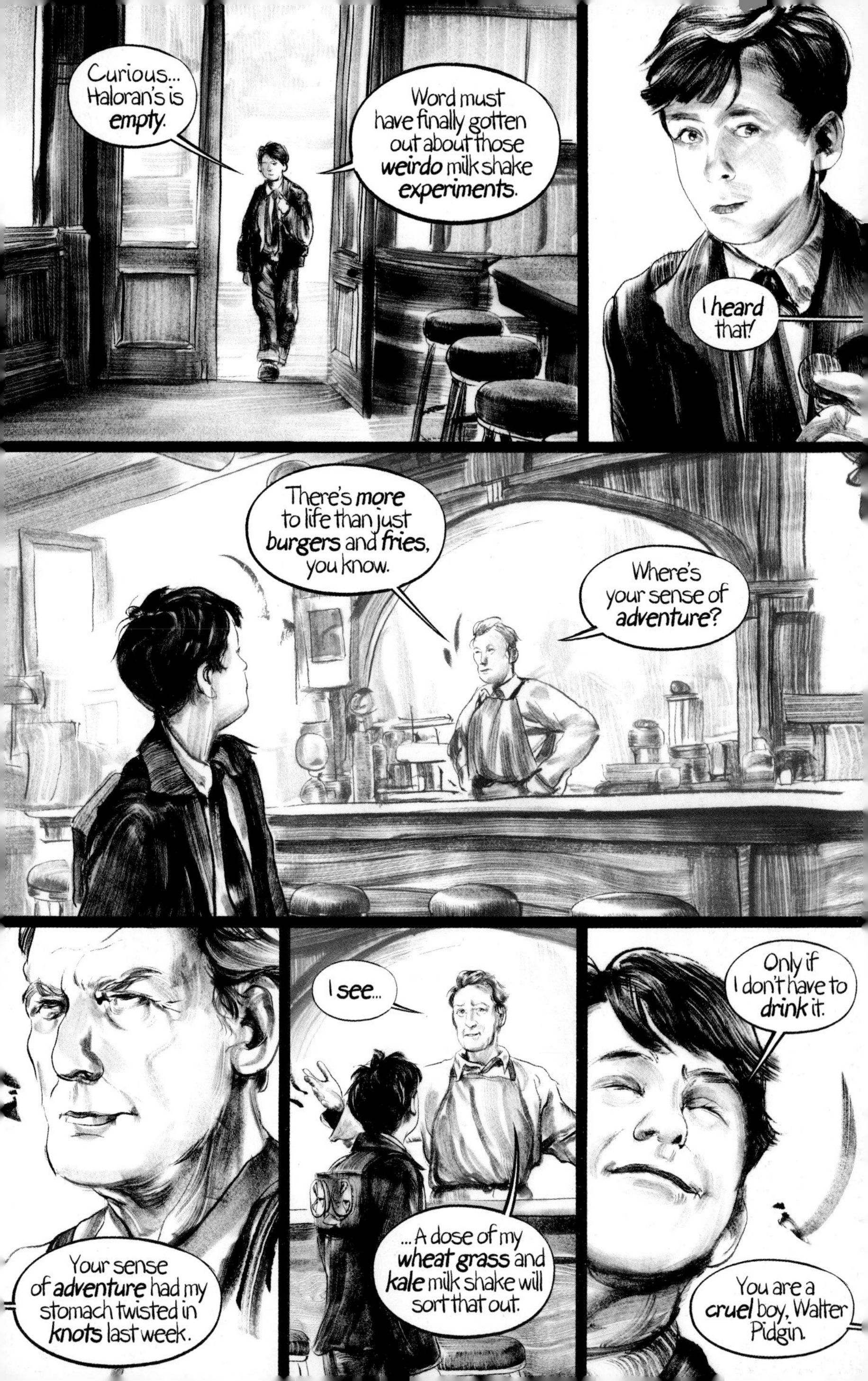
Curious... Haloran's is empty.
Word must have finally gotten out about those weirdo milk shake experiments.
I heard that!
There's more to life than just burgers and fries, you know.
Where's your sense of adventure?
Your sense of adventure had my stomach twisted in knots last week.
I see...
...A dose of my wheat grass and kale milk shake will sort that out.
Only if I don't have to drink it.
You are a cruel boy, Walter Pidgin.

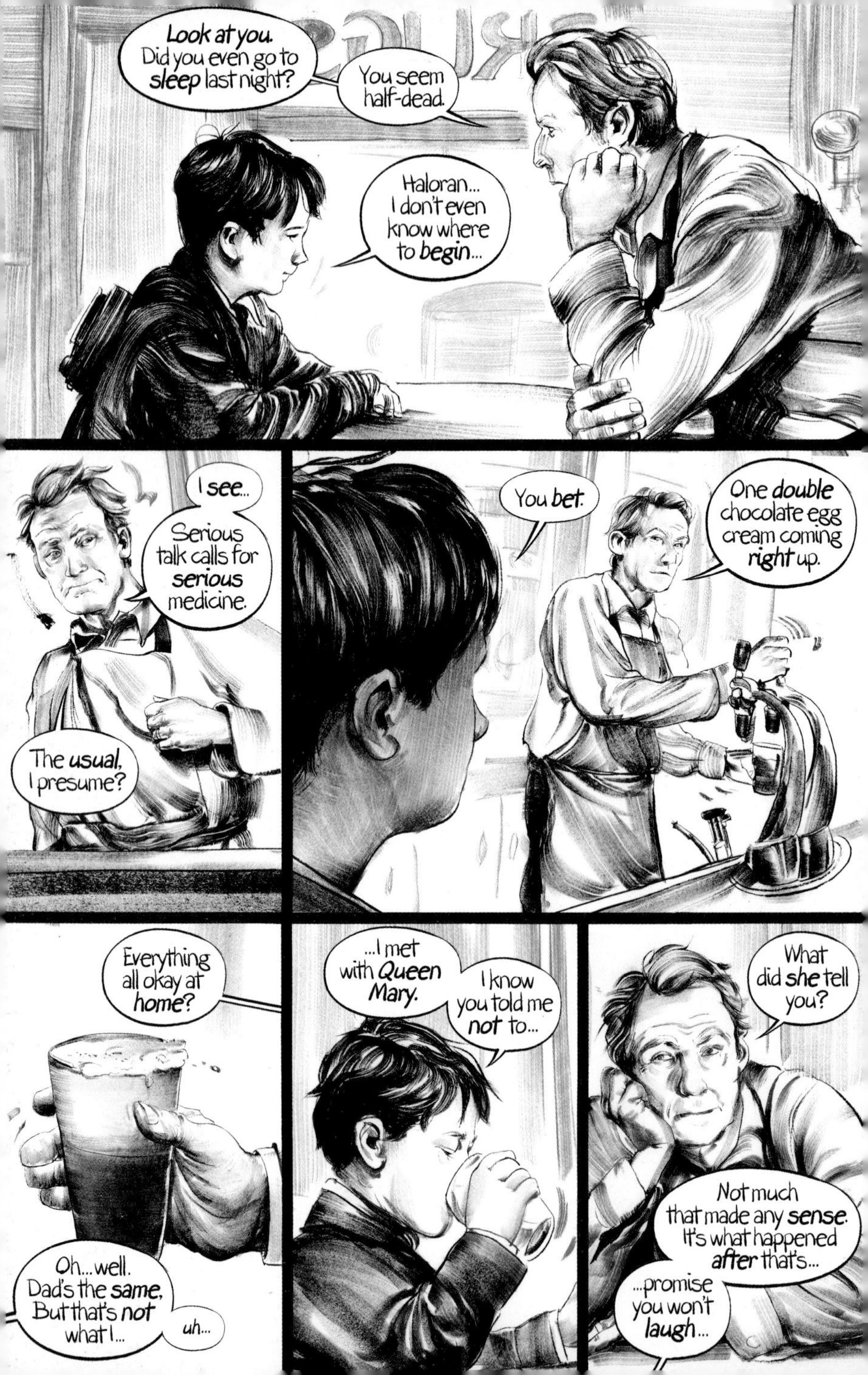
Look at you. Did you even go to sleep last night?
You seem half-dead.
Haloran... I don't even know where to begin...
I see...
Serious talk calls for serious medicine.
The usual, I presume?
You bet.
One double chocolate egg cream coming right up.
Everything all okay at home?
Oh...well. Dad's the same, But that's not what I...
uh...
...I met with Queen Mary.
I know you told me not to...
What did she tell you?
Not much that made any sense. It's what happened after that's...
...promise you won't laugh...

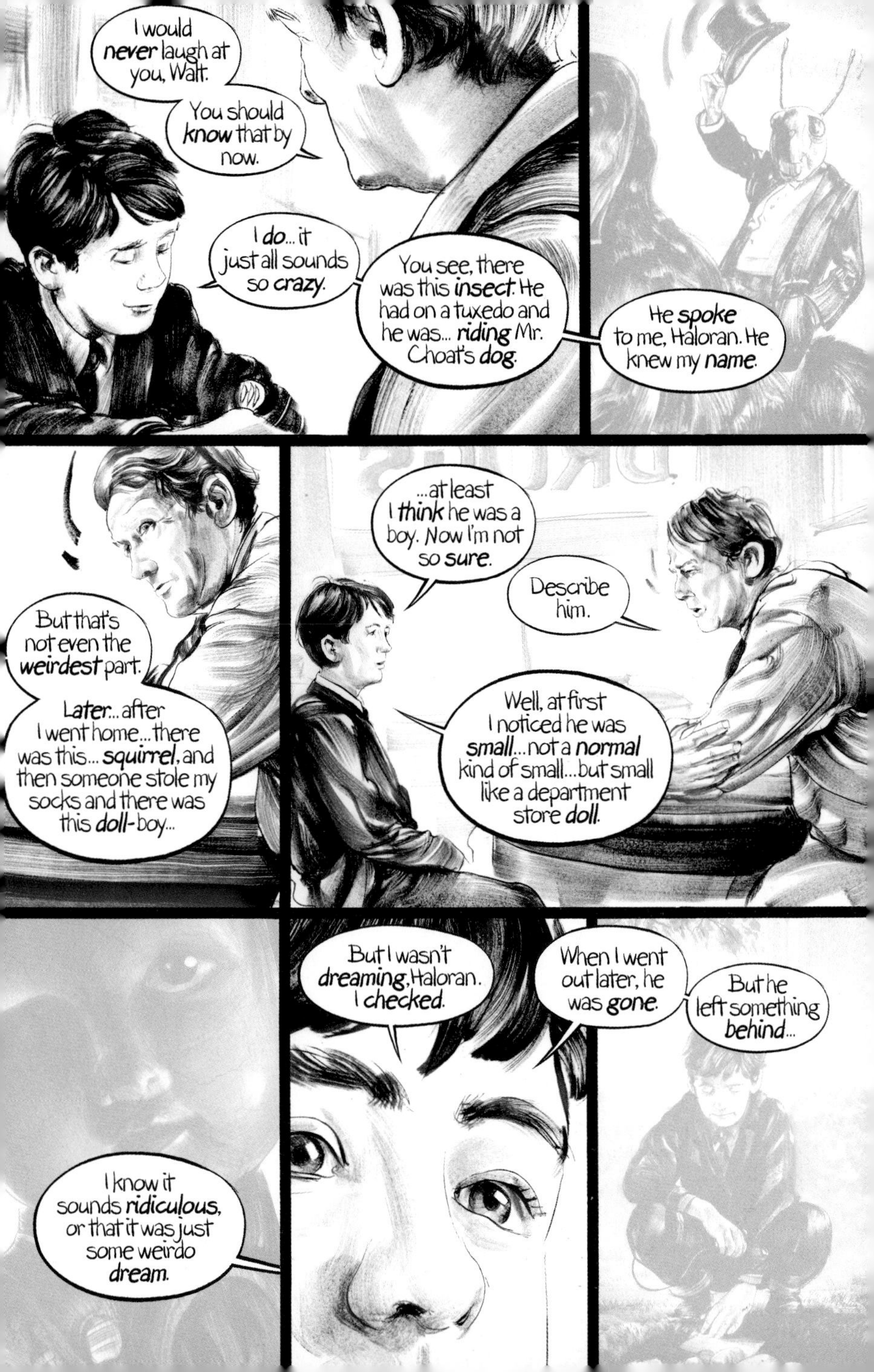
I would **never** laugh at you, Walt.
You should **know** that by now.
I **do**... it just all sounds so **crazy**.
You see, there was this **insect**. He had on a tuxedo and he was... **riding** Mr. Choat's **dog**.
He **spoke** to me, Haloran. He knew my **name**.
But that's not even the **weirdest** part.
Later... after I went home... there was this... **squirrel**, and then someone stole my socks and there was this **doll**-boy...
...at least I **think** he was a boy. Now I'm not so **sure**.
Describe him.
Well, at first I noticed he was **small**... not a **normal** kind of small... but small like a department store **doll**.
I know it sounds **ridiculous**, or that it was just some weirdo **dream**.
But I wasn't **dreaming**, Haloran. I **checked**.
When I went out later, he was **gone**.
But he left something **behind**...

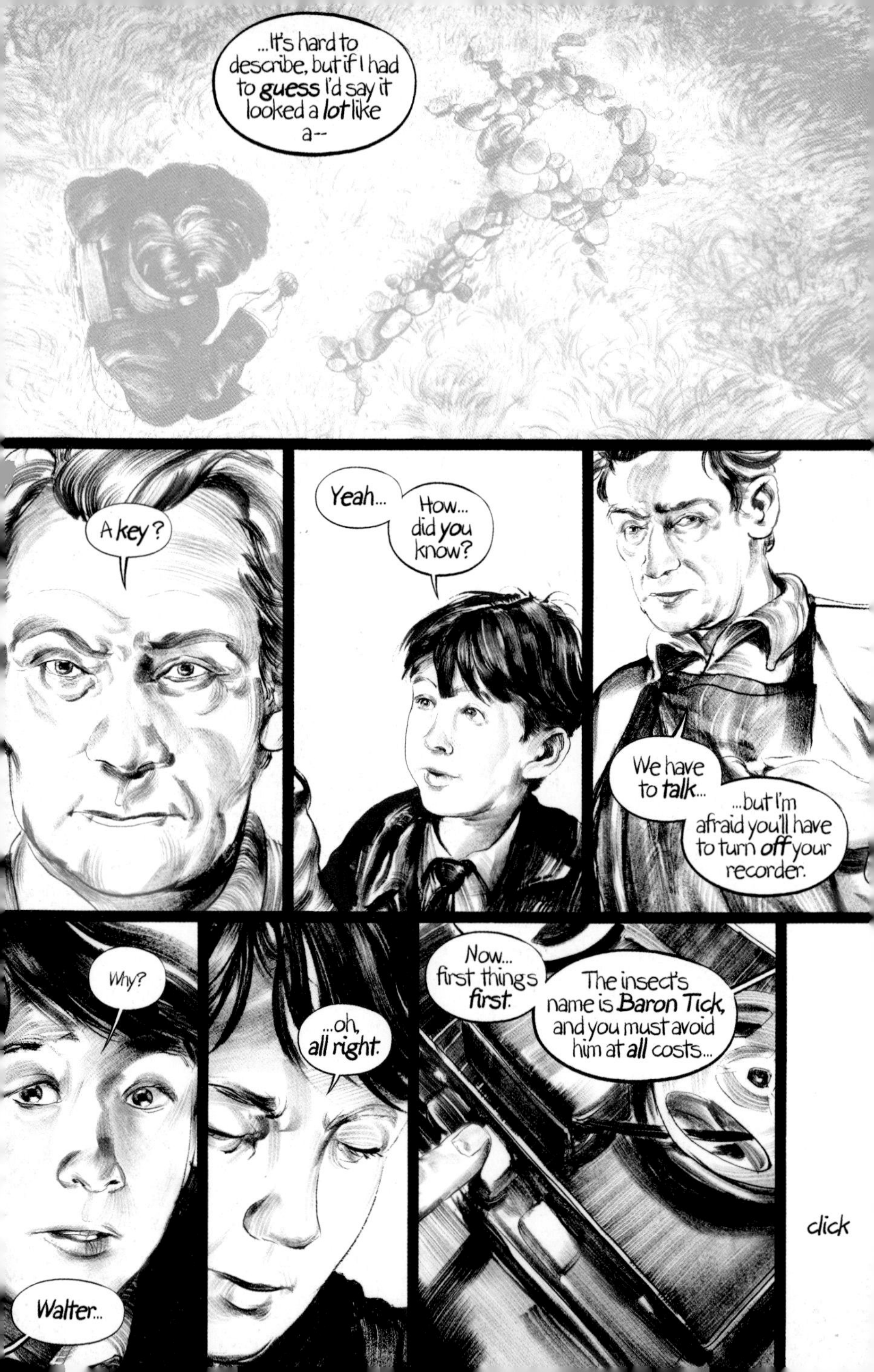
...It's hard to describe, but if I had to **guess** I'd say it looked a **lot** like a--
A **key**?
Yeah...
How... did **you** know?
We have to **talk**...
...but I'm afraid you'll have to turn **off** your recorder.
Why?
Walter...
...oh, **all right**.
Now... first things **first**.
The insect's name is **Baron Tick**, and you must avoid him at **all** costs...
click

Click

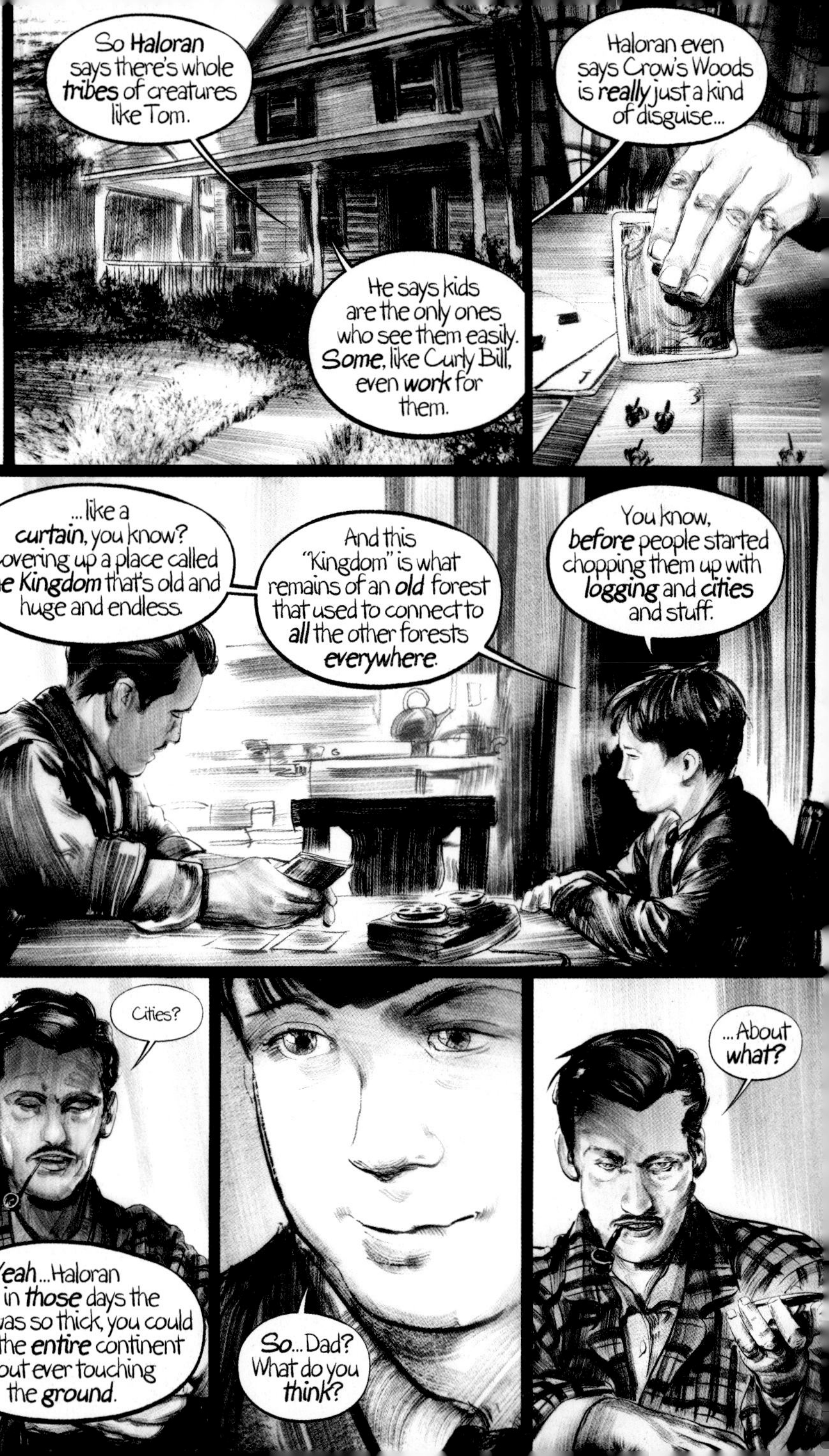
So Haloran says there's whole tribes of creatures like Tom.
He says kids are the only ones who see them easily. Some, like Curly Bill, even work for them.
Haloran even says Crow's Woods is really just a kind of disguise...
...like a curtain, you know? Covering up a place called The Kingdom that's old and huge and endless.
And this "Kingdom" is what remains of an old forest that used to connect to all the other forests everywhere.
You know, before people started chopping them up with logging and cities and stuff.
Cities?
Yeah...Haloran says in those days the forest was so thick, you could cross the entire continent without ever touching the ground.
So...Dad? What do you think?
...About what?

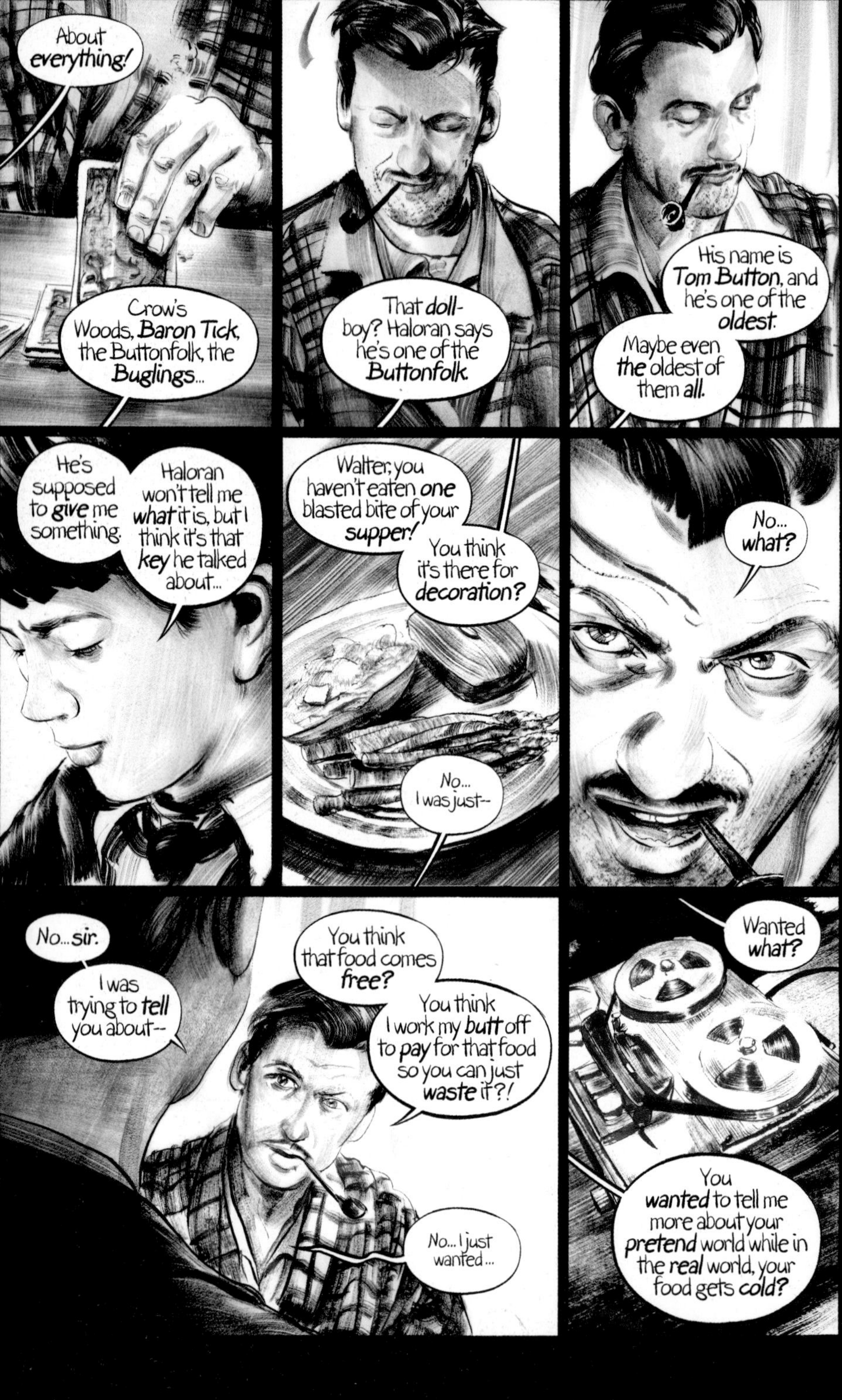
About everything!
Crow's Woods, Baron Tick, the Buttonfolk, the Buglings...
That doll-boy? Haloran says he's one of the Buttonfolk.
His name is Tom Button, and he's one of the oldest.
Maybe even the oldest of them all.
He's supposed to give me something.
Haloran won't tell me what it is, but I think it's that key he talked about...
Walter, you haven't eaten one blasted bite of your supper!
You think it's there for decoration?
No... I was just--
No... what?
No... sir.
I was trying to tell you about--
You think that food comes free?
You think I work my butt off to pay for that food so you can just waste it?!
No... I just wanted...
Wanted what?
You wanted to tell me more about your pretend world while in the real world, your food gets cold?

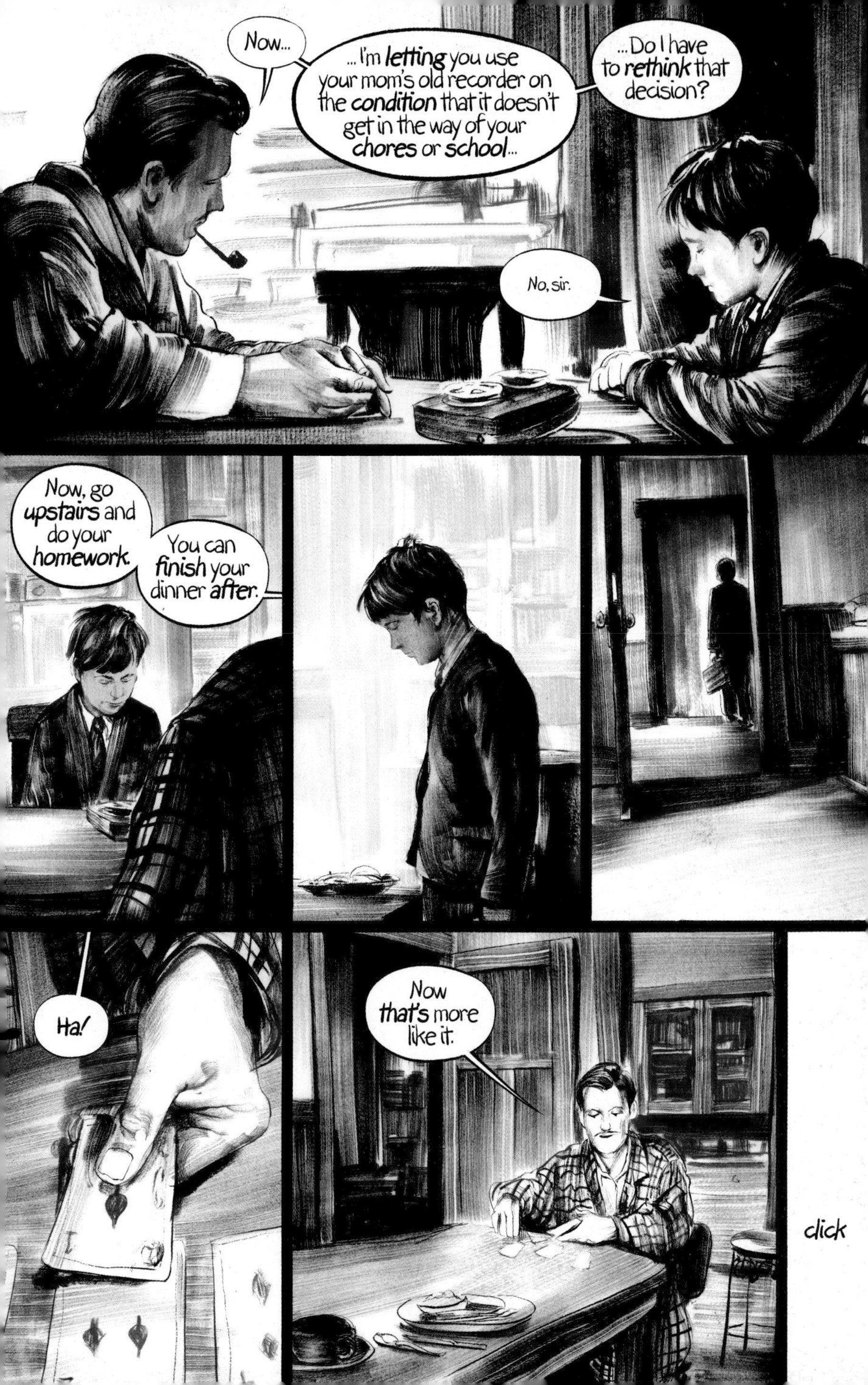

Now...
... I'm letting you use your mom's old recorder on the condition that it doesn't get in the way of your chores or school...
... Do I have to rethink that decision?
No, sir.
Now, go upstairs and do your homework.
You can finish your dinner after.
Ha!
Now that's more like it.
click

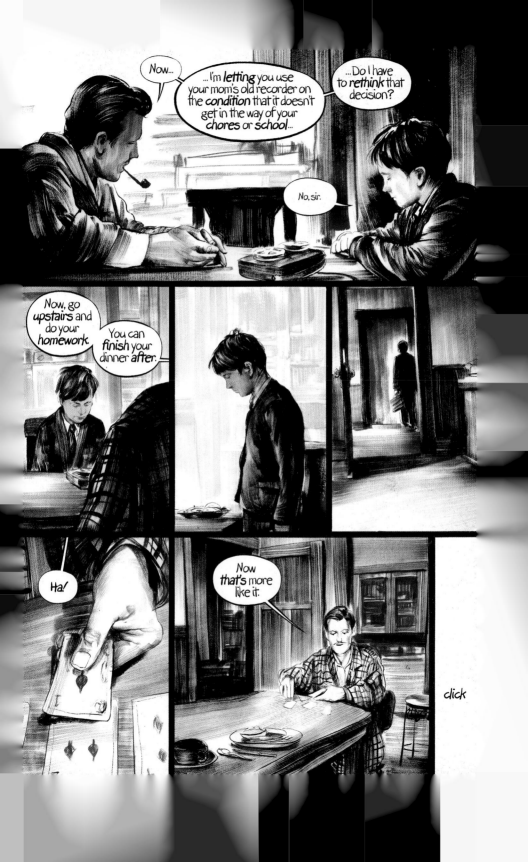

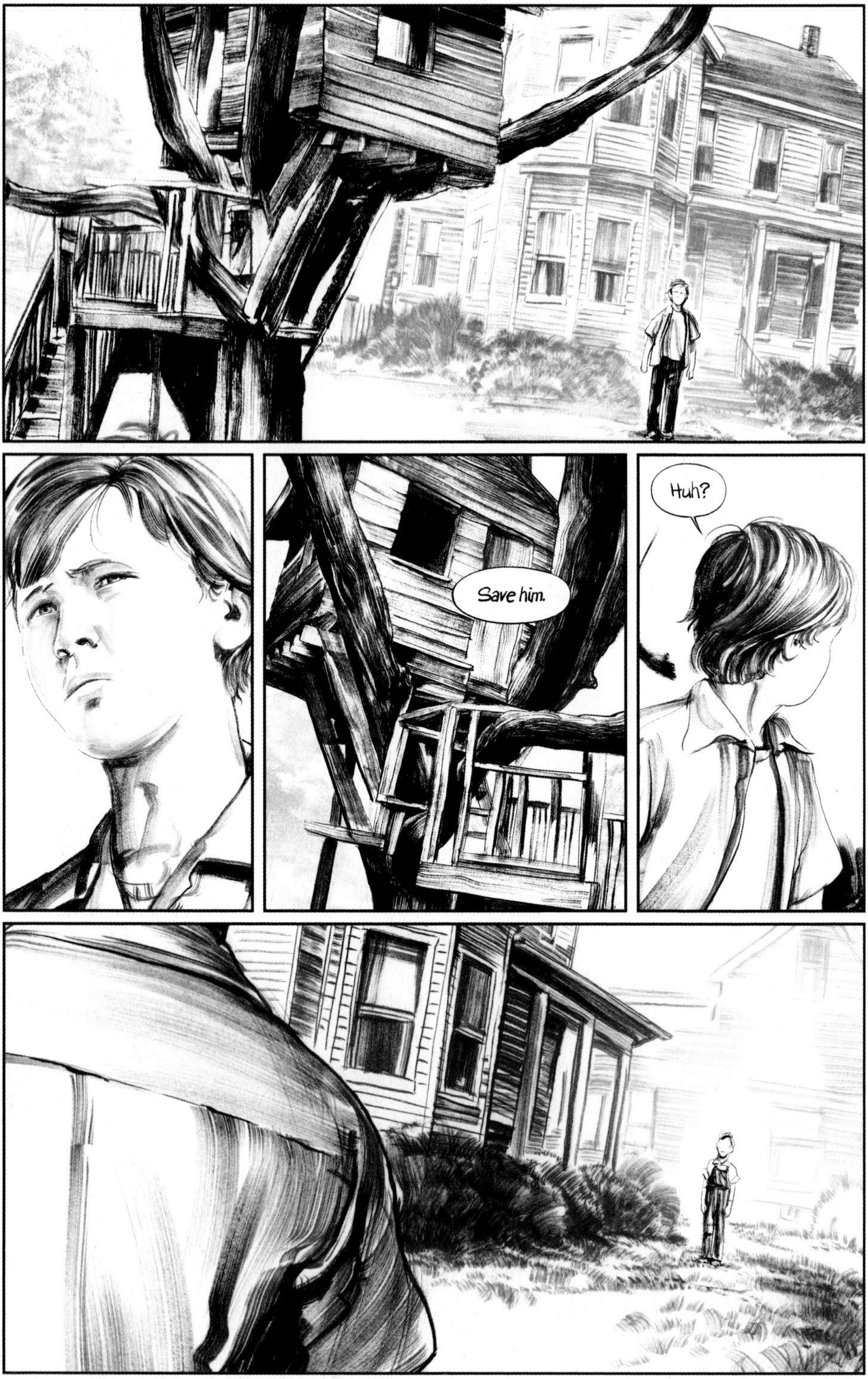
Save him.
Huh?

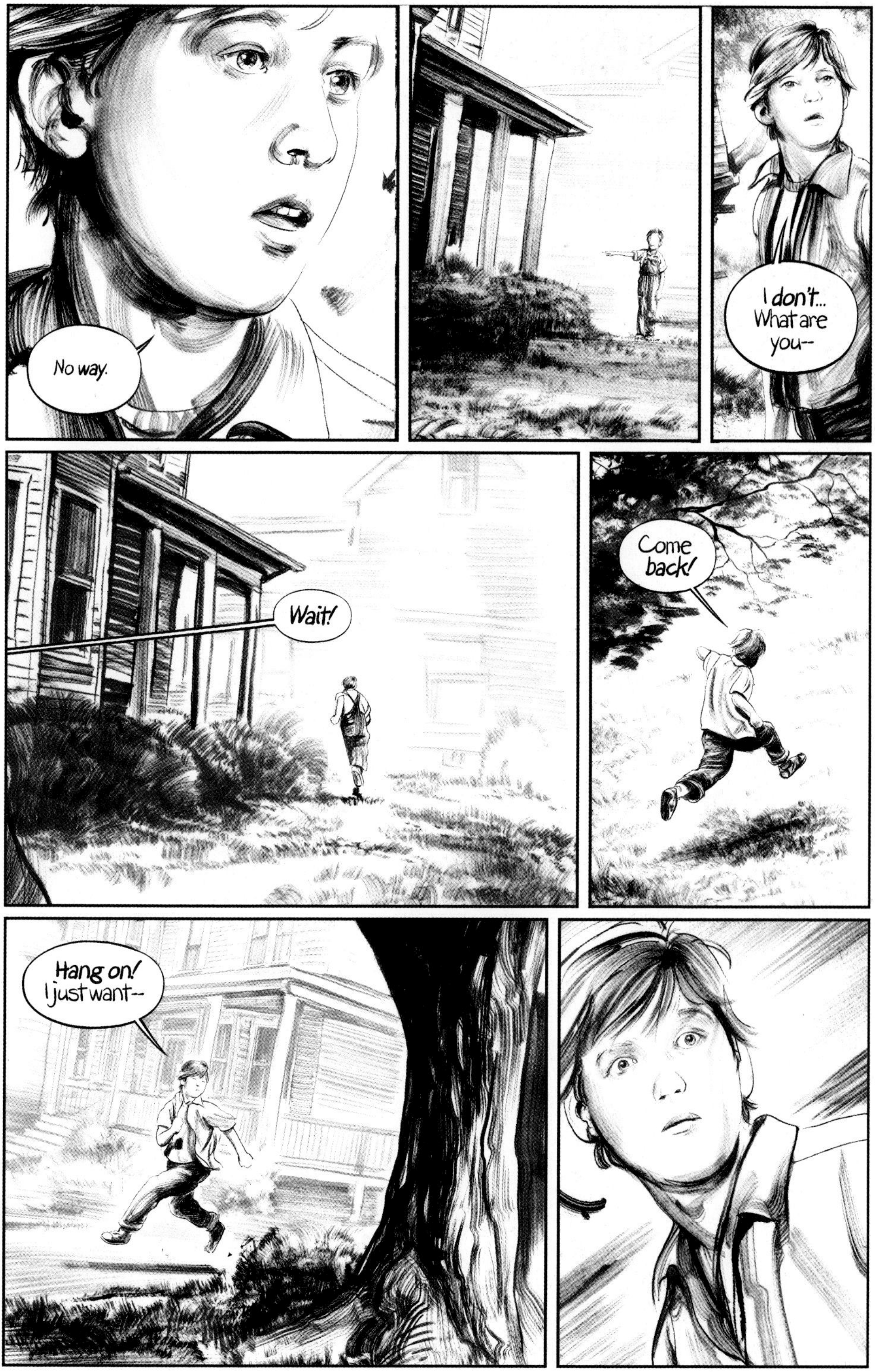
No way.
I don't... What are you--
Wait!
Come back!
Hang on! I just want--

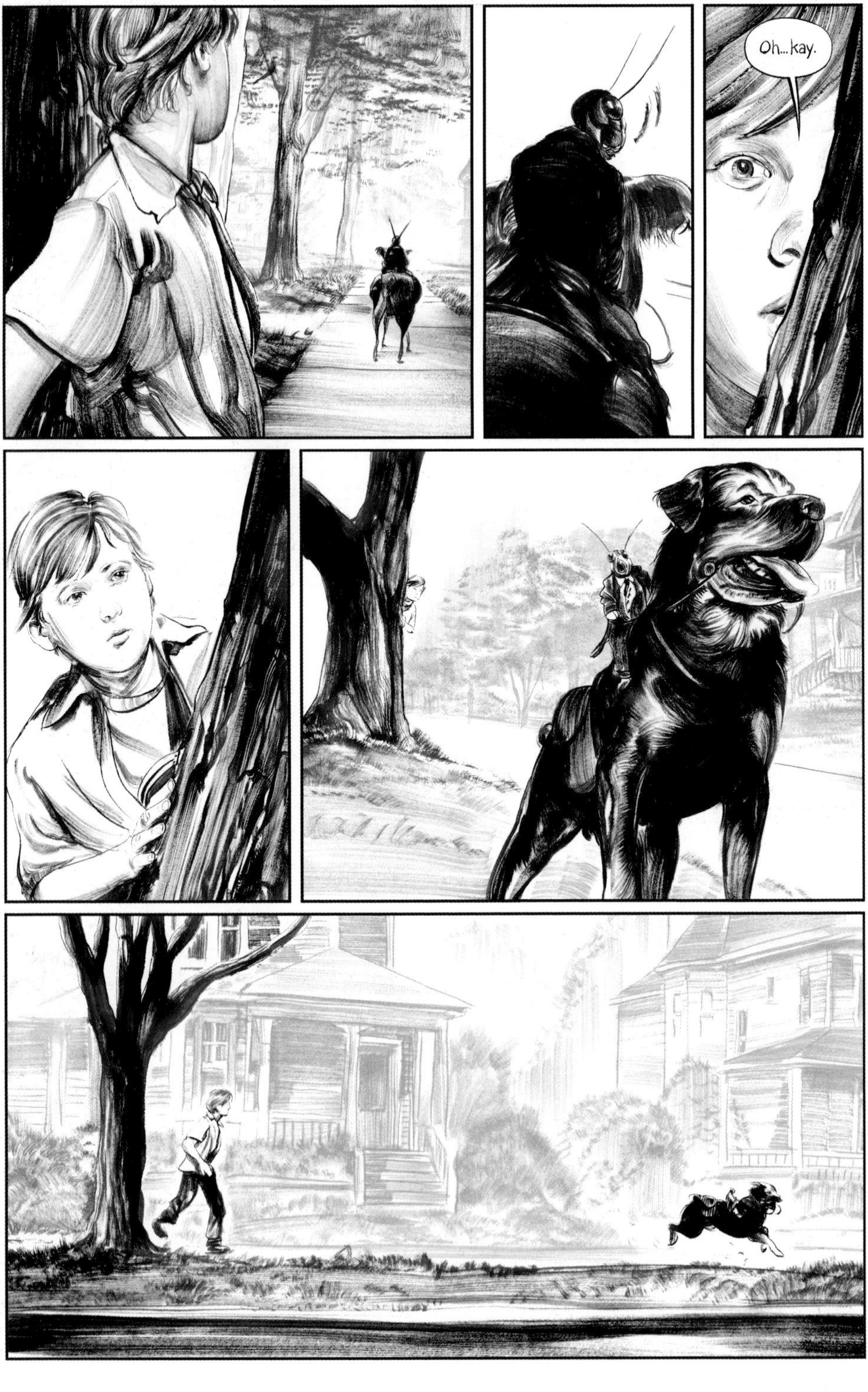
Oh...kay.

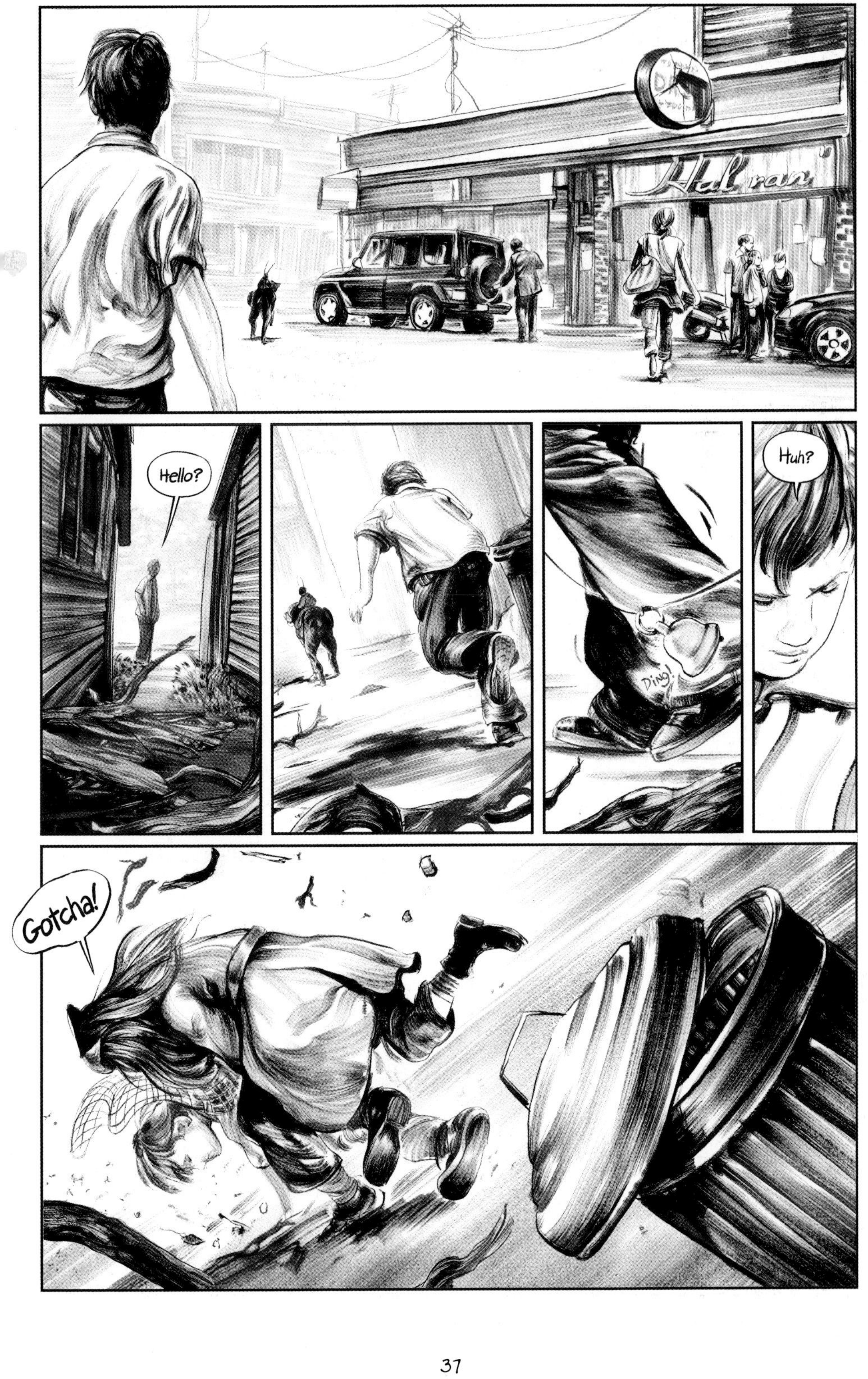
Hal ran
Hello?
Ding!
Huh?
Gotcha!

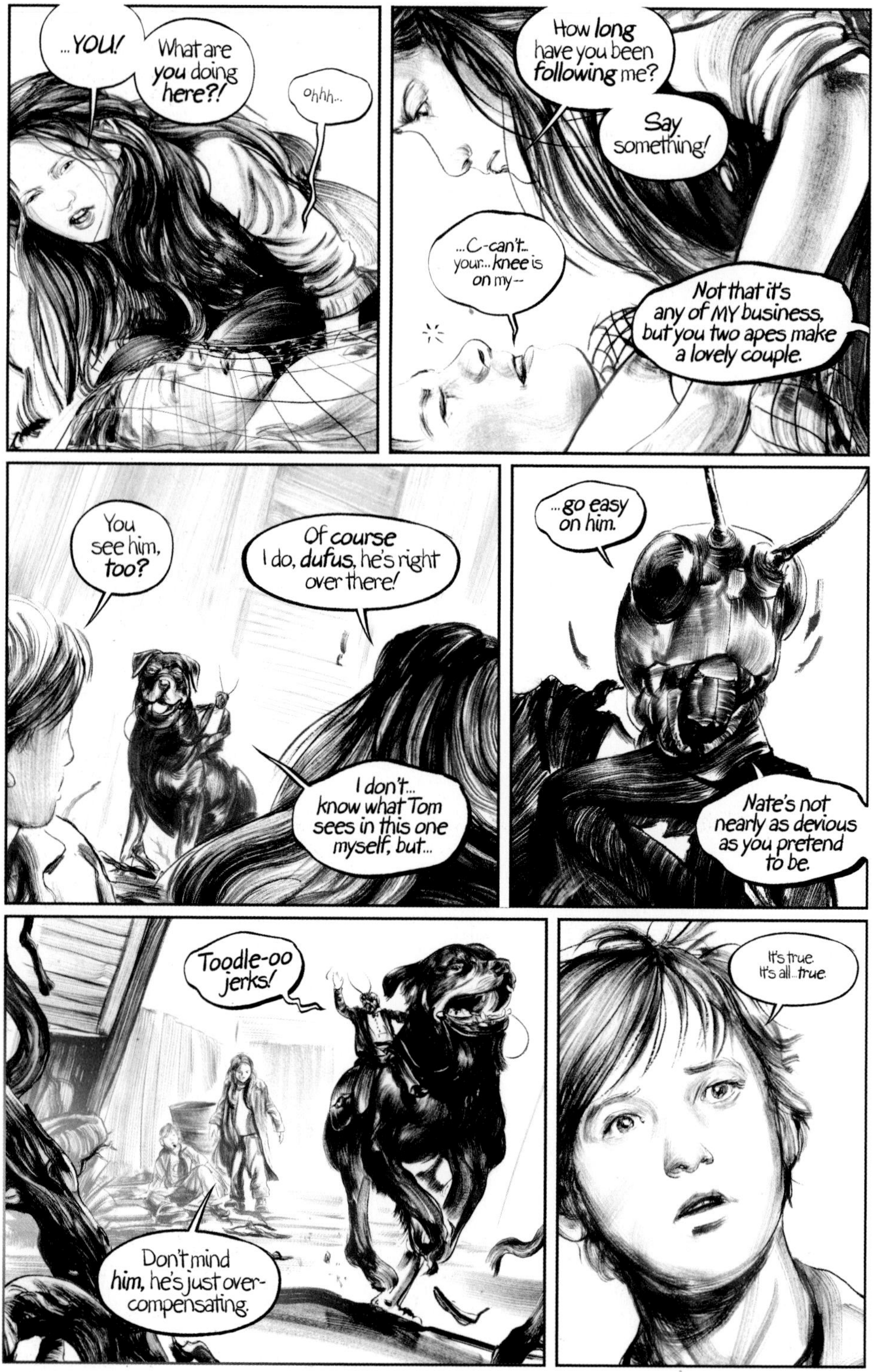
...YOU!
What are you doing here?!
ohhh...
How long have you been following me?
Say something!
...C-can't... your... knee is on my--
Not that it's any of MY business, but you two apes make a lovely couple.
You see him, too?
Of course I do, dufus, he's right over there!
I don't... know what Tom sees in this one myself, but...
...go easy on him.
Nate's not nearly as devious as you pretend to be.
Toodle-oo jerks!
Don't mind him, he's just over-compensating.
It's true. It's all...true.

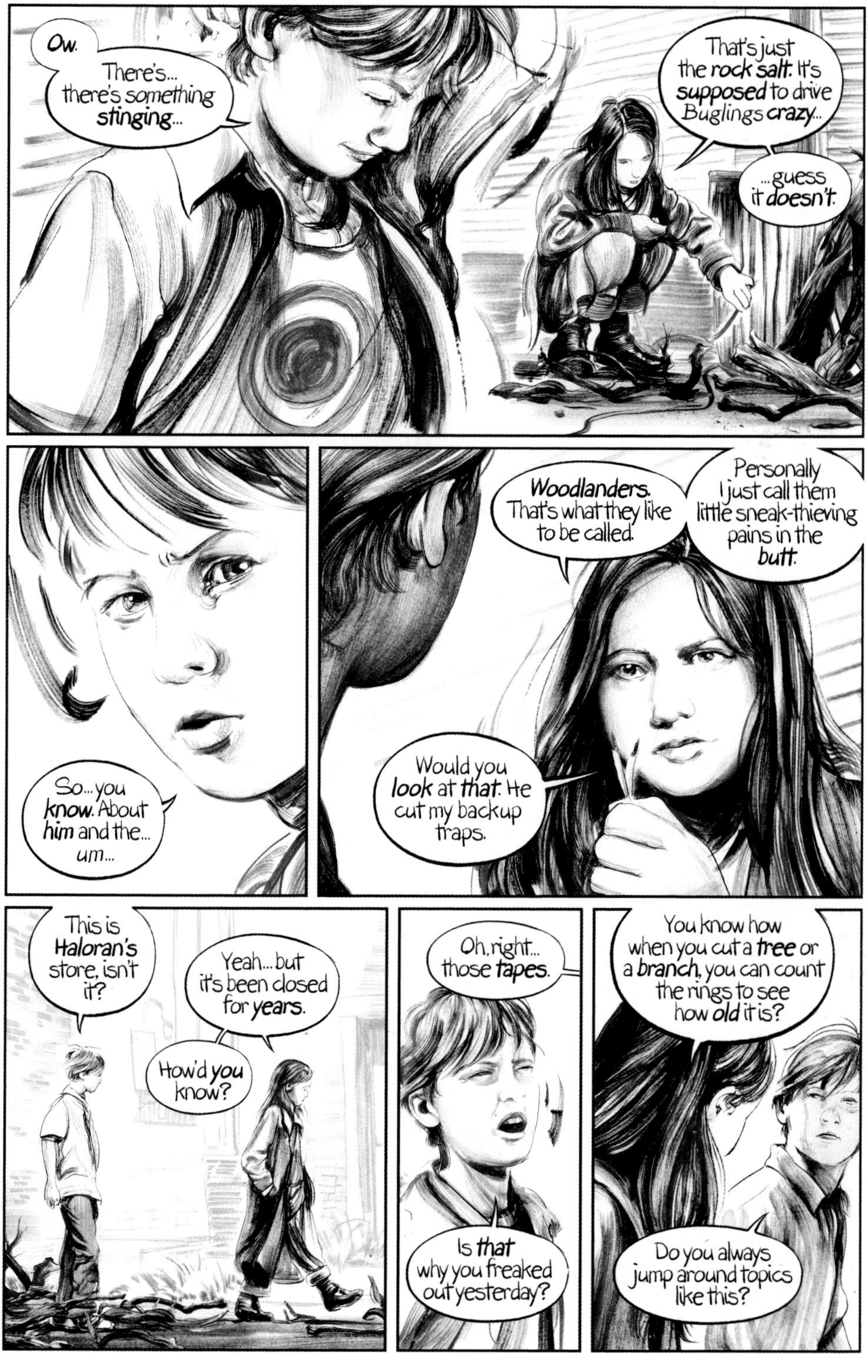
Ow.
There's... there's something stinging...
That's just the rock salt. It's supposed to drive Buglings crazy...
...guess it doesn't.
Woodlanders. That's what they like to be called.
Personally I just call them little sneak-thieving pains in the butt.
So... you know. About him and the... um...
Would you look at that. He cut my backup traps.
This is Haloran's store, isn't it?
Yeah... but it's been closed for years.
How'd you know?
Oh, right... those tapes.
Is that why you freaked out yesterday?
You know how when you cut a tree or a branch, you can count the rings to see how old it is?
Do you always jump around topics like this?

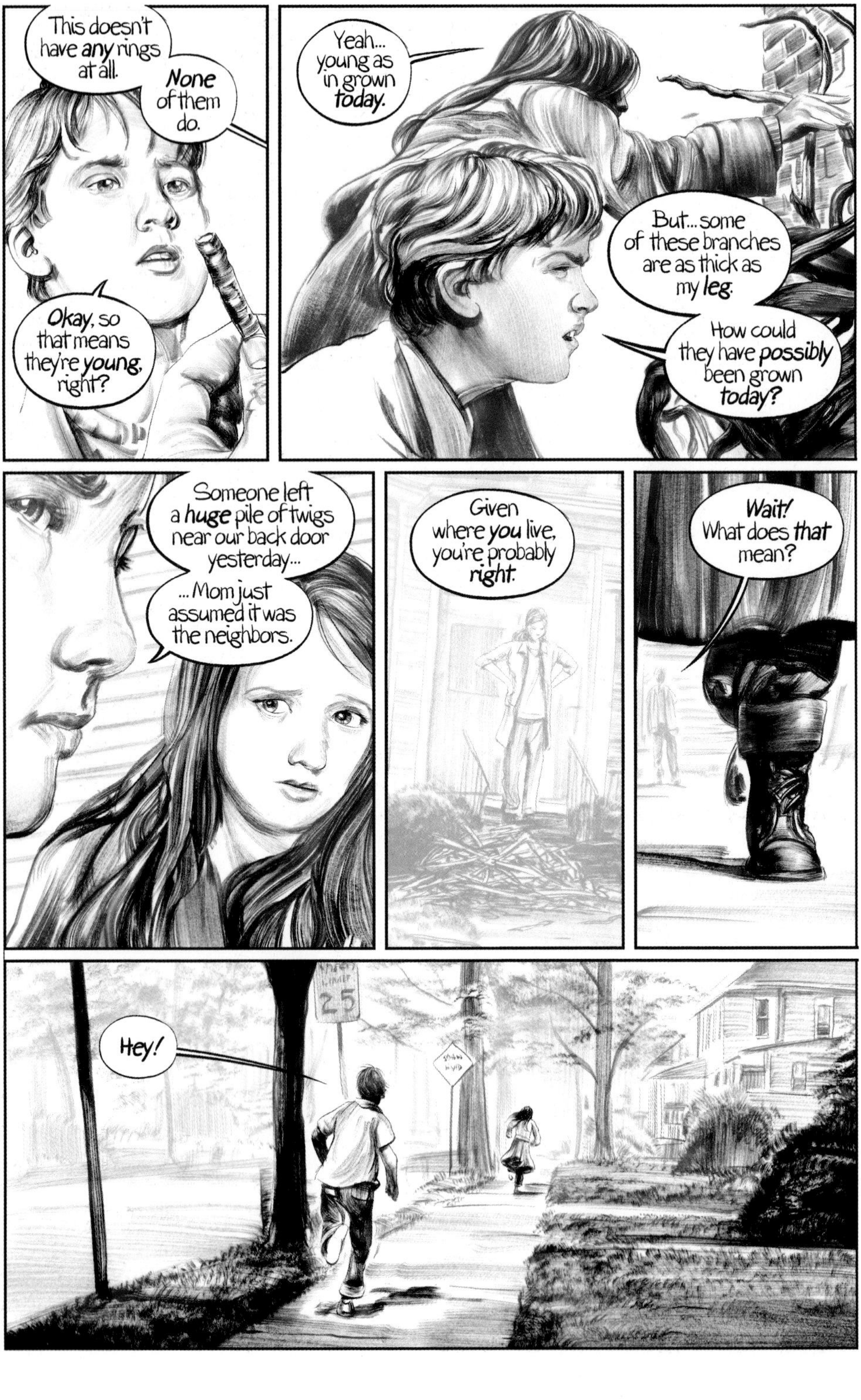
This doesn't have any rings at all.
None of them do.
Okay, so that means they're young, right?
Yeah... young as in grown today.
But... some of these branches are as thick as my leg.
How could they have possibly been grown today?
Someone left a huge pile of twigs near our back door yesterday...
...Mom just assumed it was the neighbors.
Given where you live, you're probably right.
Wait! What does that mean?
25
Hey!

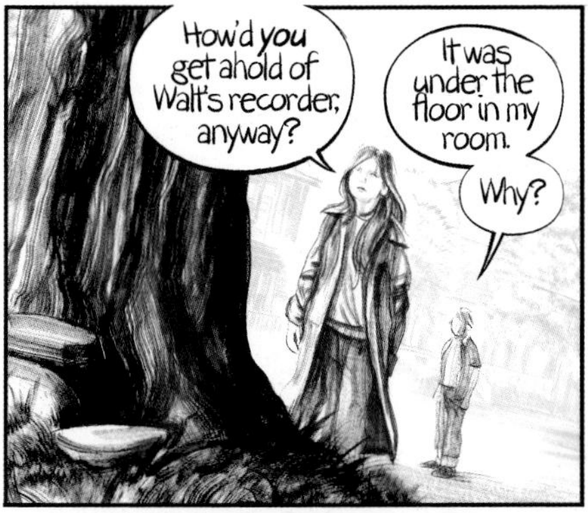
How'd you get ahold of Walt's recorder, anyway?
It was under the floor in my room.
Why?

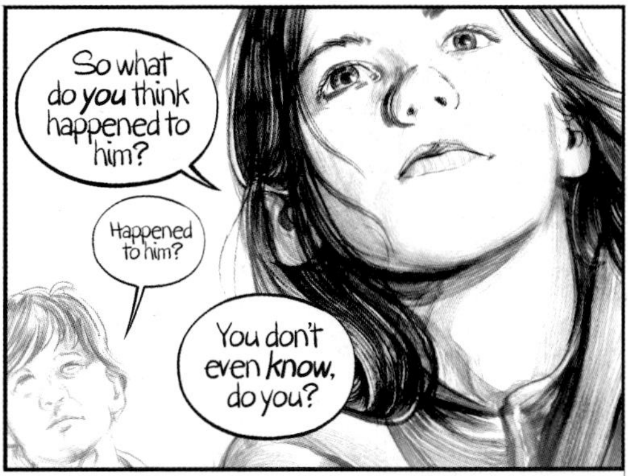
So what do you think happened to him?
Happened to him?
You don't even know, do you?

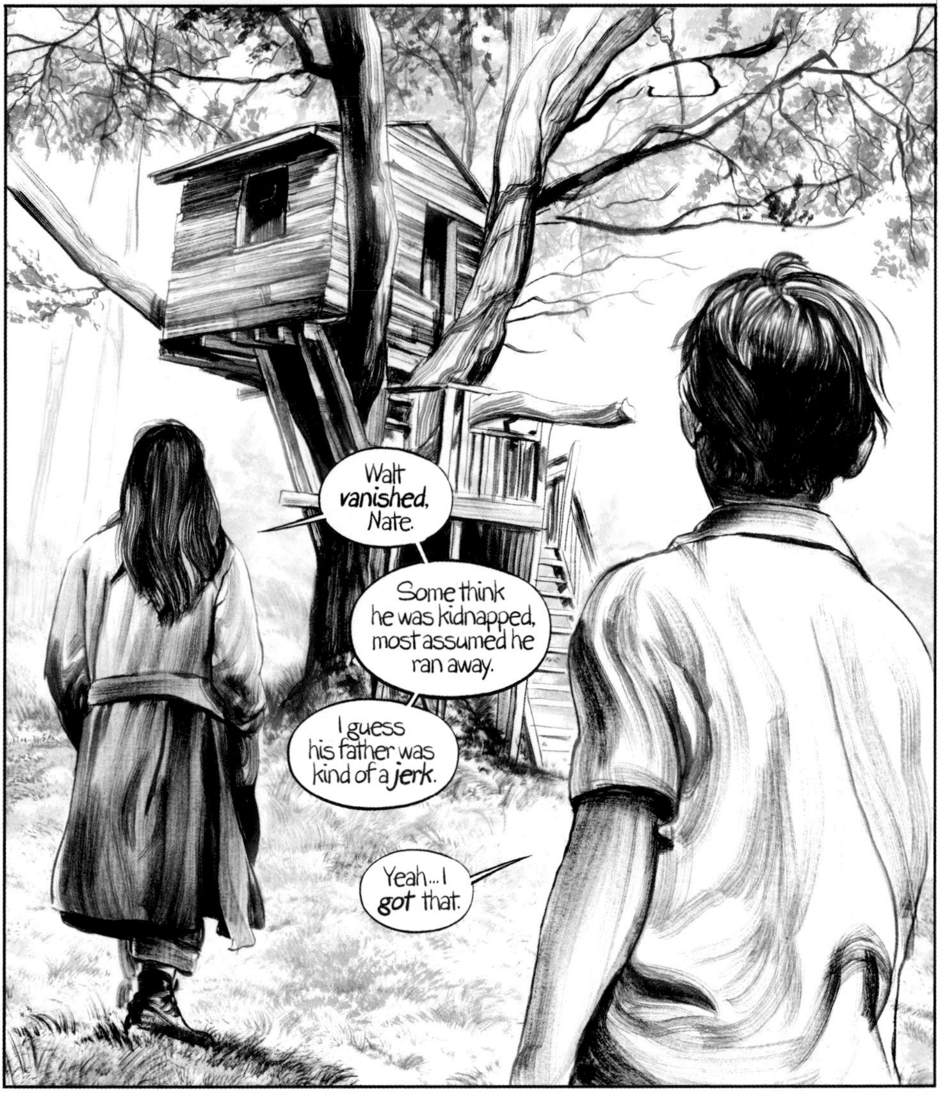
Walt vanished, Nate.
Some think he was kidnapped, most assumed he ran away.
I guess his father was kind of a jerk.
Yeah... I got that.

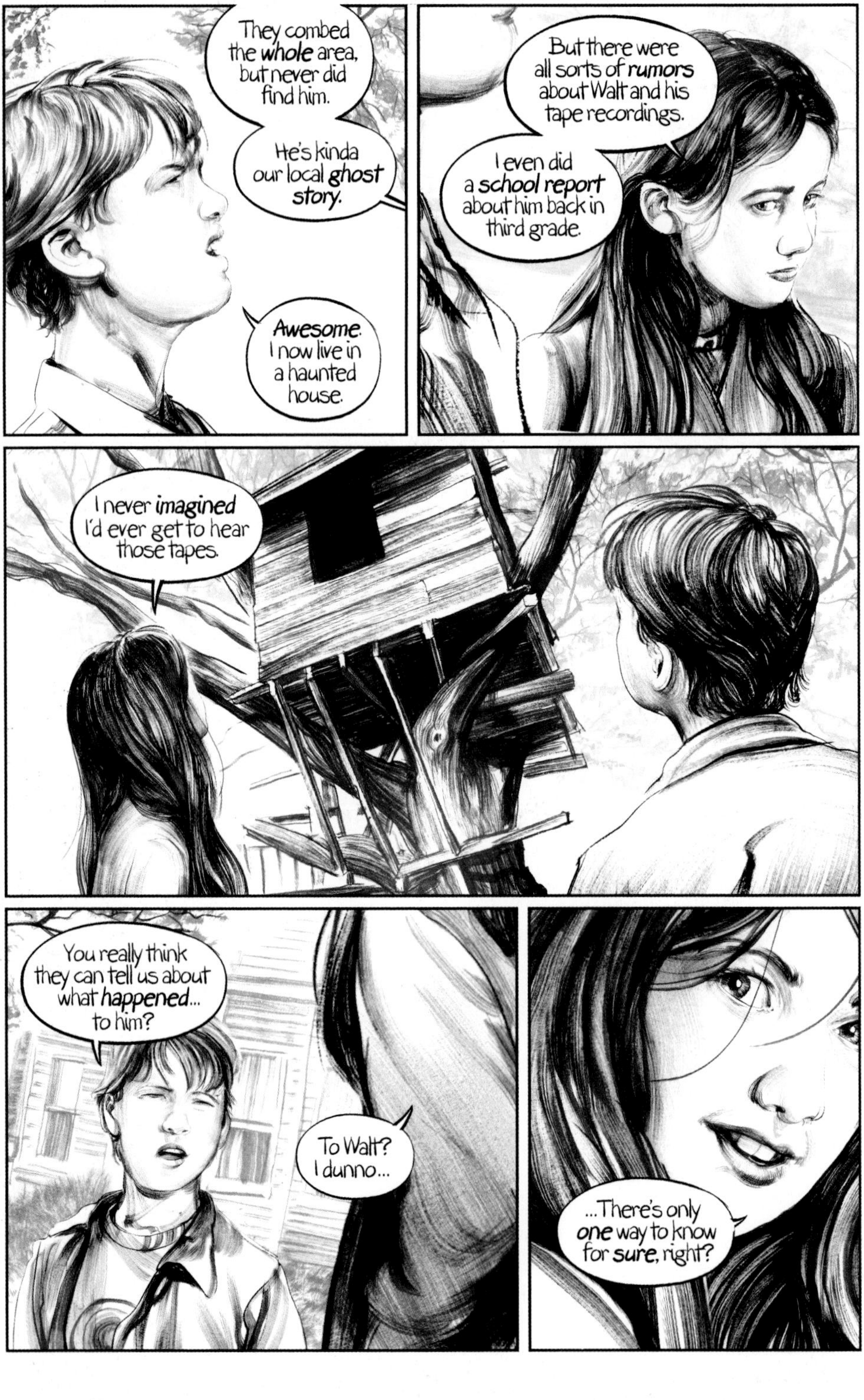
They combed the whole area, but never did find him.
He's kinda our local ghost story.
Awesome. I now live in a haunted house.
But there were all sorts of rumors about Walt and his tape recordings.
I even did a school report about him back in third grade.
I never imagined I'd ever get to hear those tapes.
You really think they can tell us about what happened... to him?
To Walt? I dunno...
...There's only one way to know for sure, right?

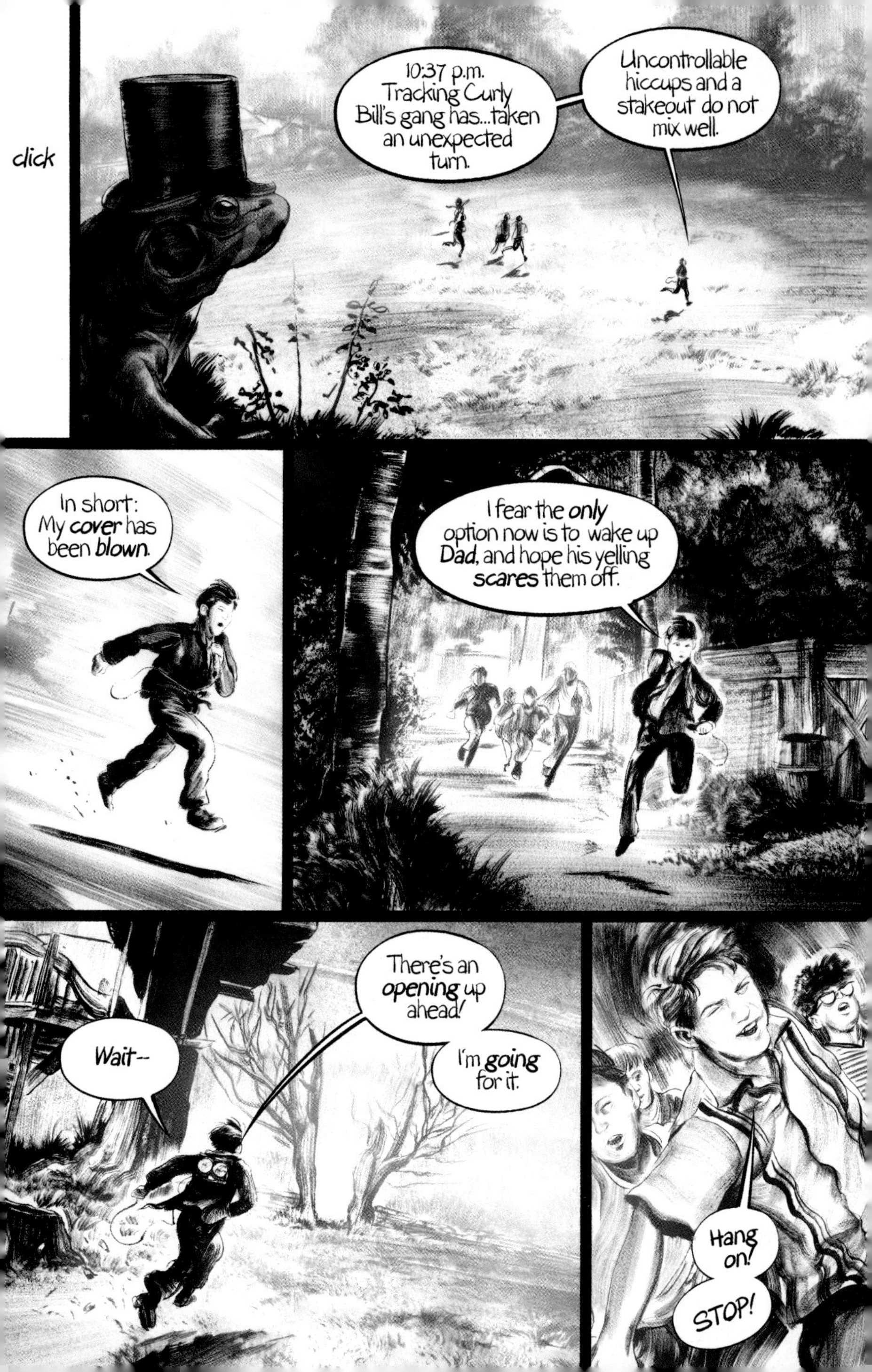
click
10:37 p.m. Tracking Curly Bill's gang has...taken an unexpected turn.
Uncontrollable hiccups and a stakeout do not mix well.
In short: My **cover** has been **blown**.
I fear the **only** option now is to wake up **Dad**, and hope his yelling **scares** them off.
There's an **opening** up ahead!
I'm **going** for it.
Wait--
Hang on!
STOP!

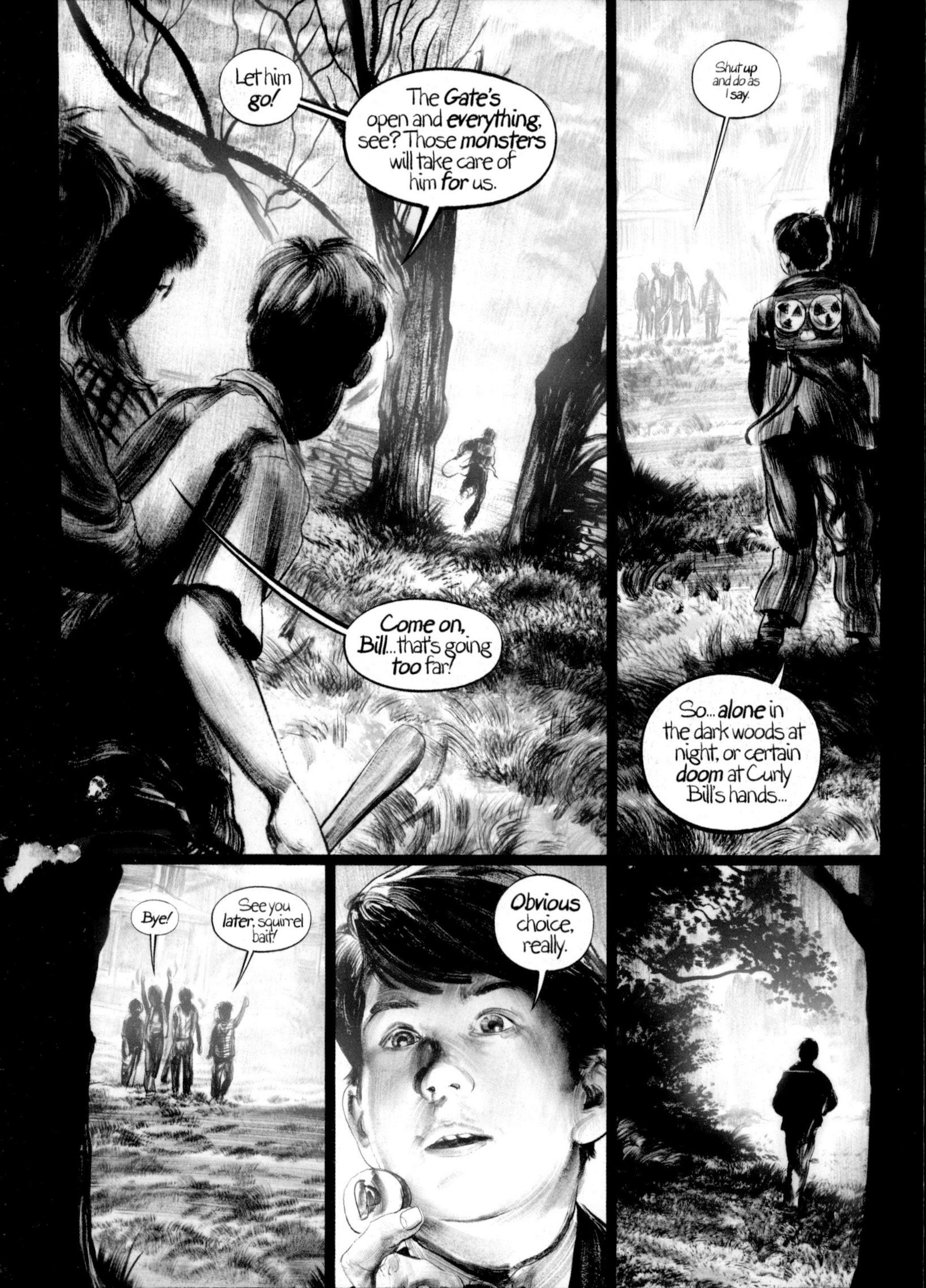
Let him go!
The Gate's open and everything, see? Those monsters will take care of him for us.
Come on, Bill...that's going too far!
Shut up and do as I say.
So...alone in the dark woods at night, or certain doom at Curly Bill's hands...
Bye!
See you later, squirrel bait!
Obvious choice, really.

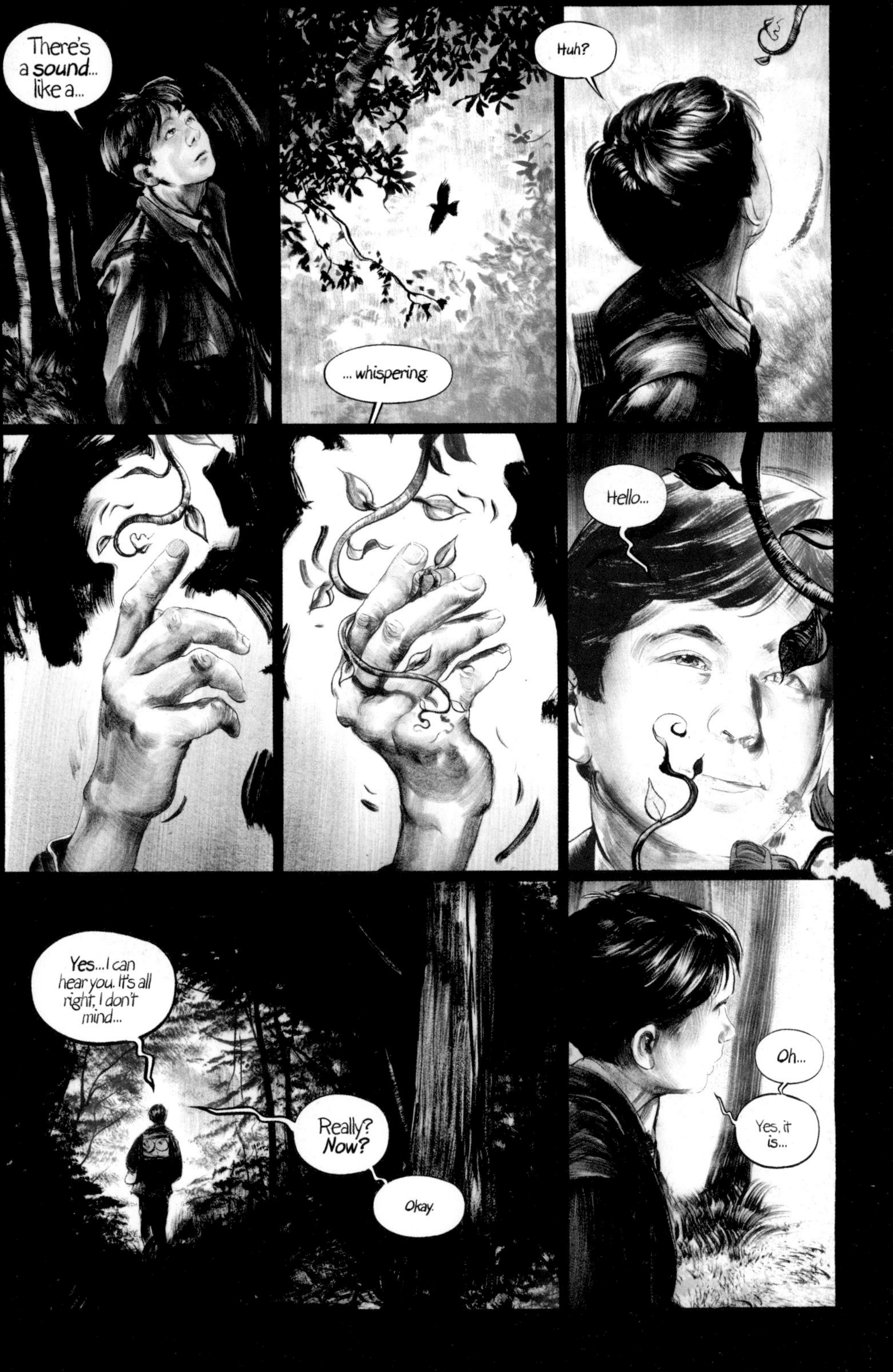
There's a sound... like a...
... whispering.
Huh?
Hello...
Yes... I can hear you. It's all right, I don't mind...
Really? Now?
Okay.
Oh...
Yes, it is...

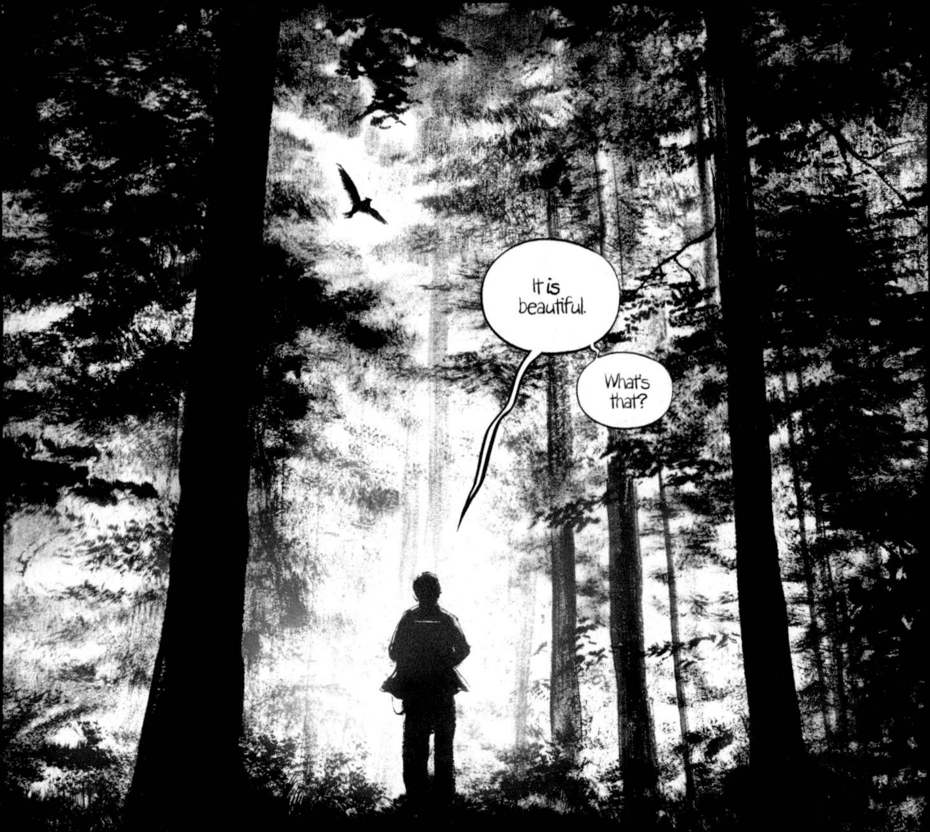
It is beautiful.
What's that?

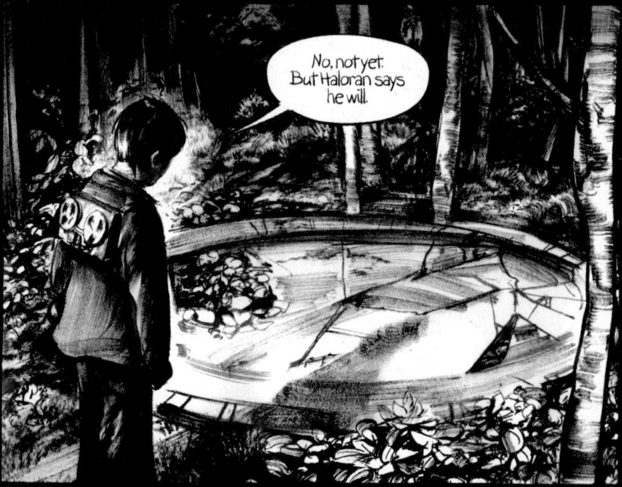
No, not yet. But Haloran says he will.

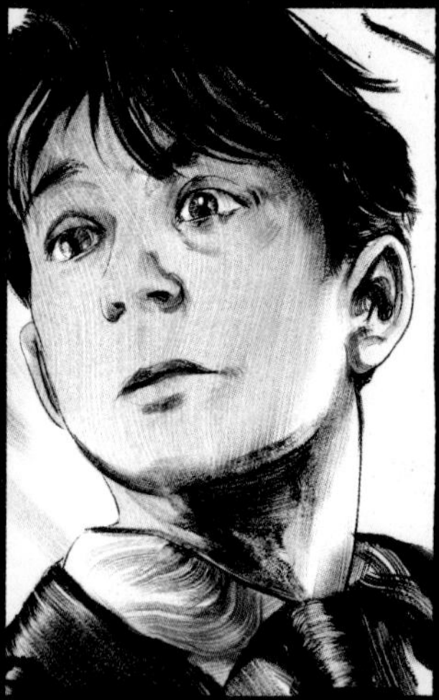

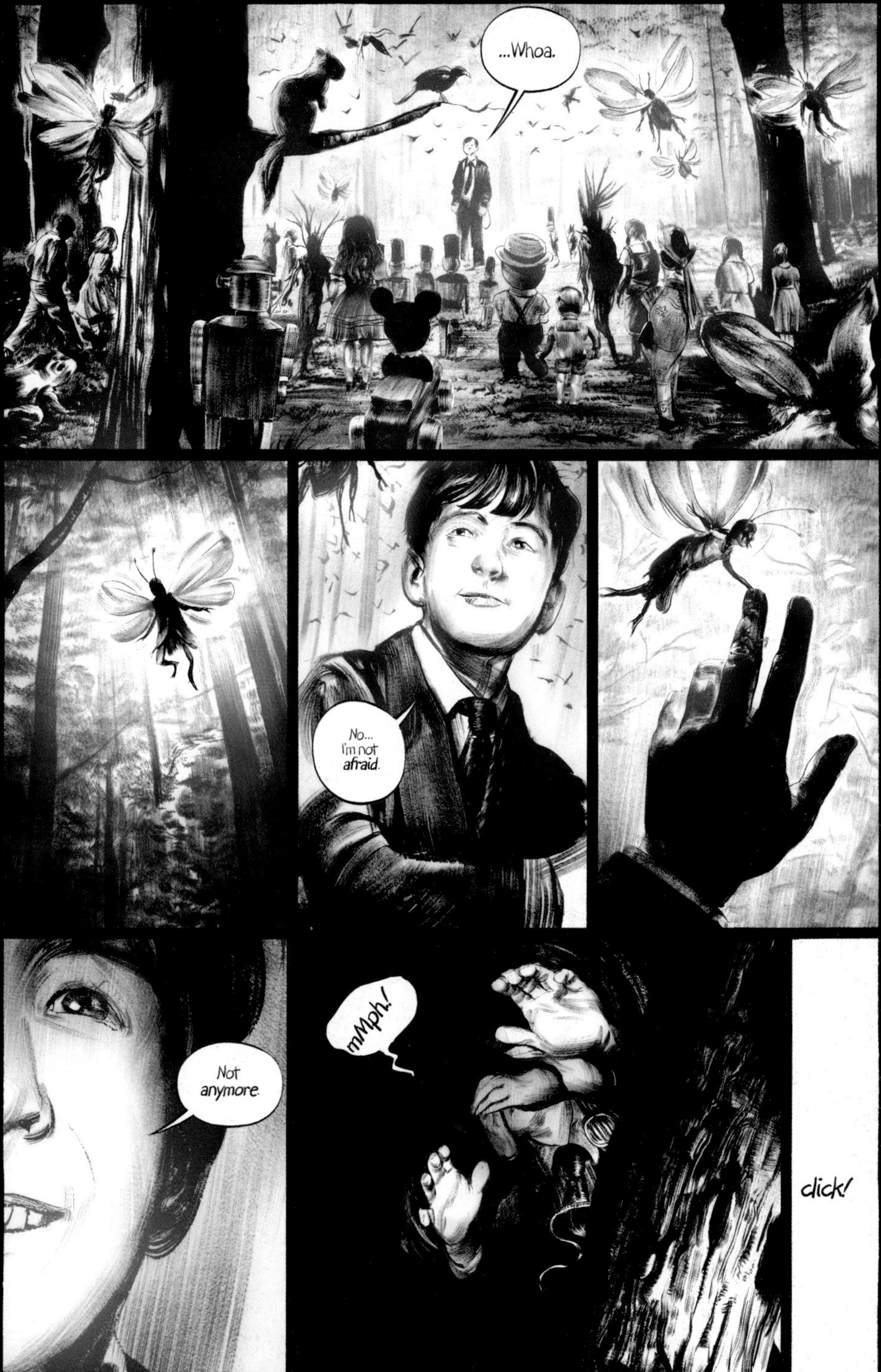
...Whoa.
No... I'm not afraid.
Not anymore.
mMph!
click!

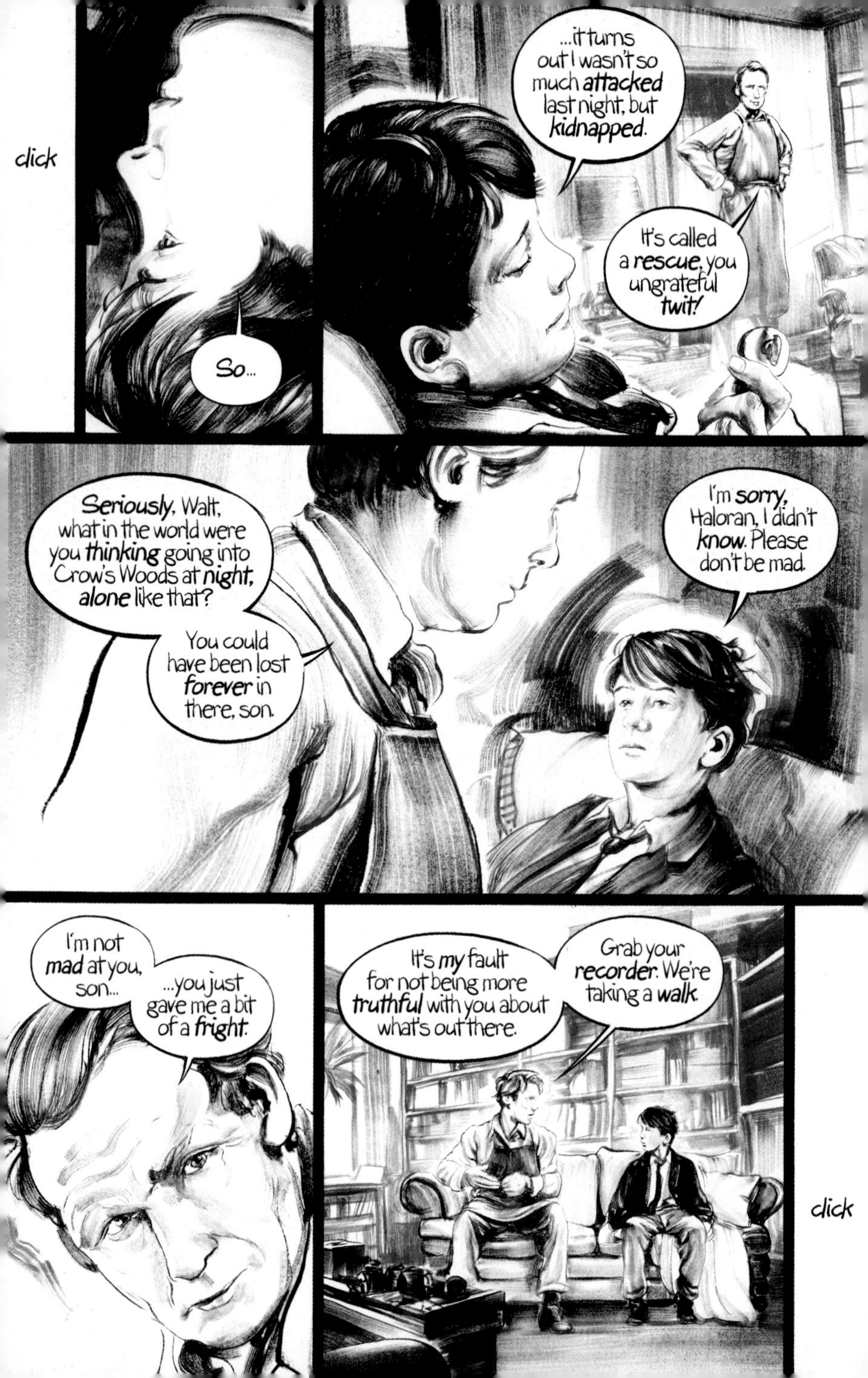
click
So...
...it turns out I wasn't so much attacked last night, but kidnapped.
It's called a rescue, you ungrateful twit!
Seriously, Walt, what in the world were you thinking going into Crow's Woods at night, alone like that?
You could have been lost forever in there, son.
I'm sorry, Haloran, I didn't know. Please don't be mad.
I'm not mad at you, son...
...you just gave me a bit of a fright.
It's my fault for not being more truthful with you about what's out there.
Grab your recorder. We're taking a walk.
click

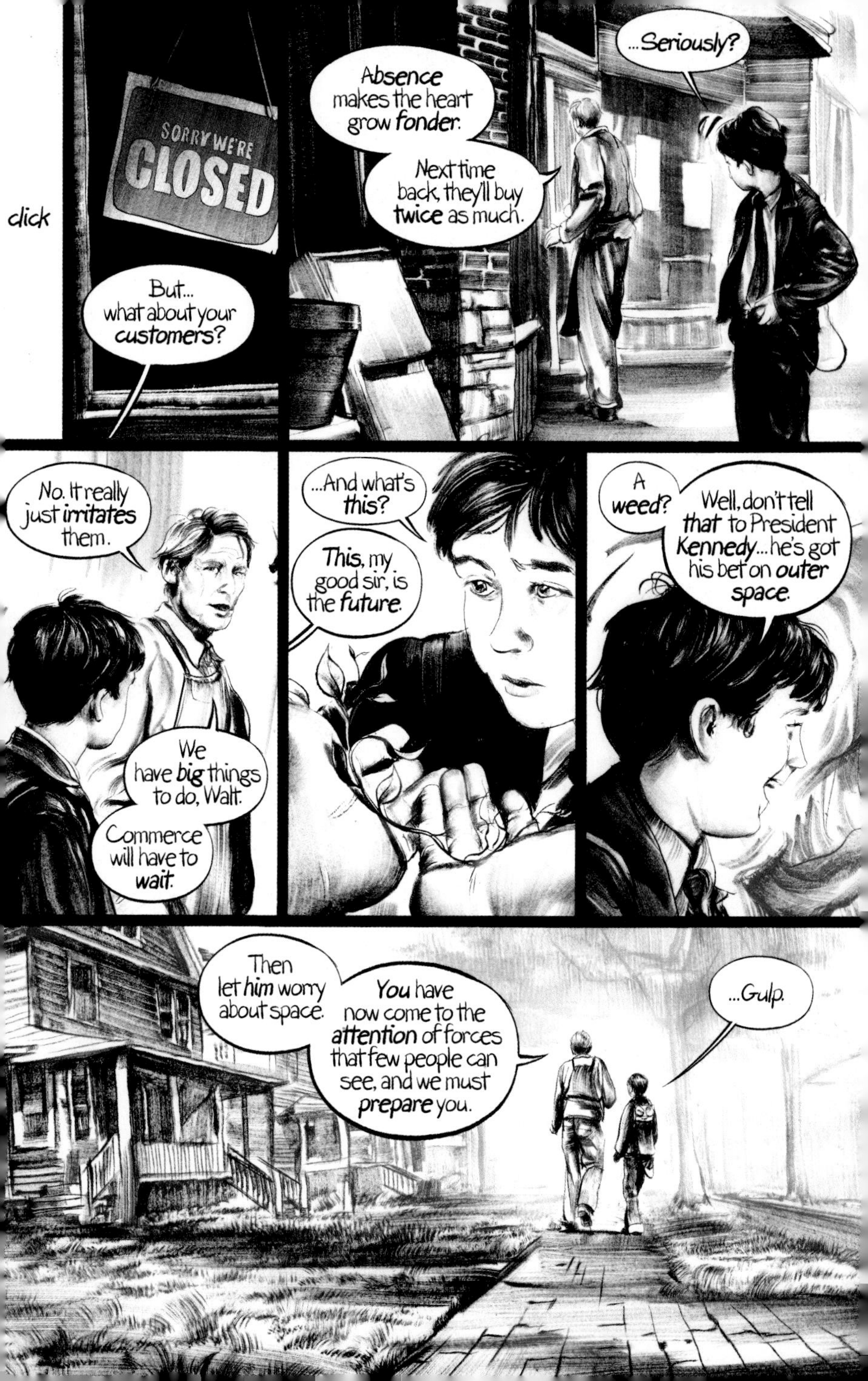
click
SORRY WE'RE CLOSED
But... what about your customers?
Absence makes the heart grow fonder.
Next time back, they'll buy twice as much.
...Seriously?
No. It really just irritates them.
We have big things to do, Walt.
Commerce will have to wait.
...And what's this?
This, my good sir, is the future.
A weed?
Well, don't tell that to President Kennedy...he's got his bet on outer space.
Then let him worry about space.
You have now come to the attention of forces that few people can see, and we must prepare you.
...Gulp.

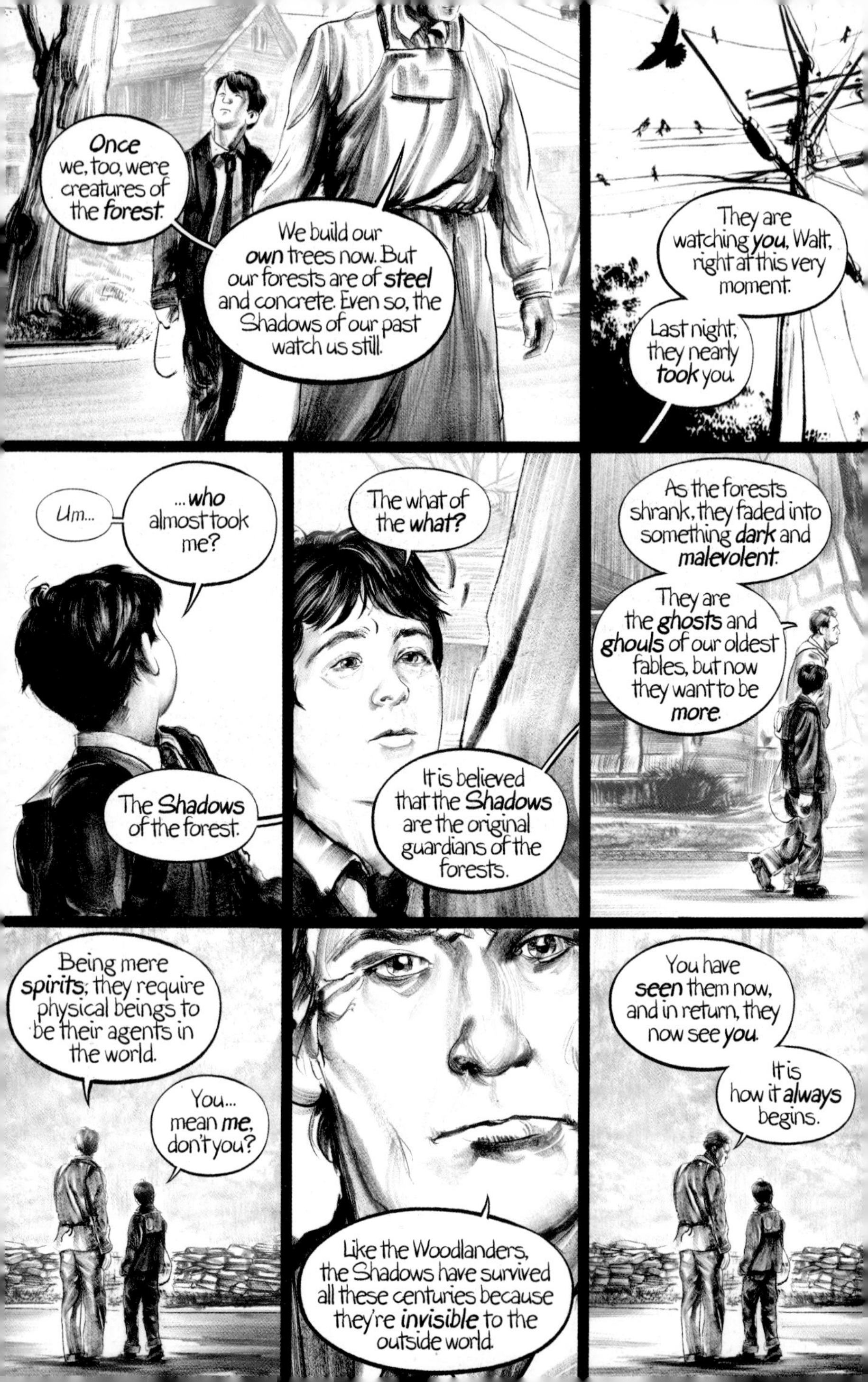
Once we, too, were creatures of the forest.
We build our own trees now. But our forests are of steel and concrete. Even so, the Shadows of our past watch us still.
They are watching you, Walt, right at this very moment.
Last night, they nearly took you.
Um...
...who almost took me?
The Shadows of the forest.
The what of the what?
It is believed that the Shadows are the original guardians of the forests.
As the forests shrank, they faded into something dark and malevolent.
They are the ghosts and ghouls of our oldest fables, but now they want to be more.
Being mere spirits, they require physical beings to be their agents in the world.
You... mean me, don't you?
Like the Woodlanders, the Shadows have survived all these centuries because they're invisible to the outside world.
You have seen them now, and in return, they now see you.
It is how it always begins.

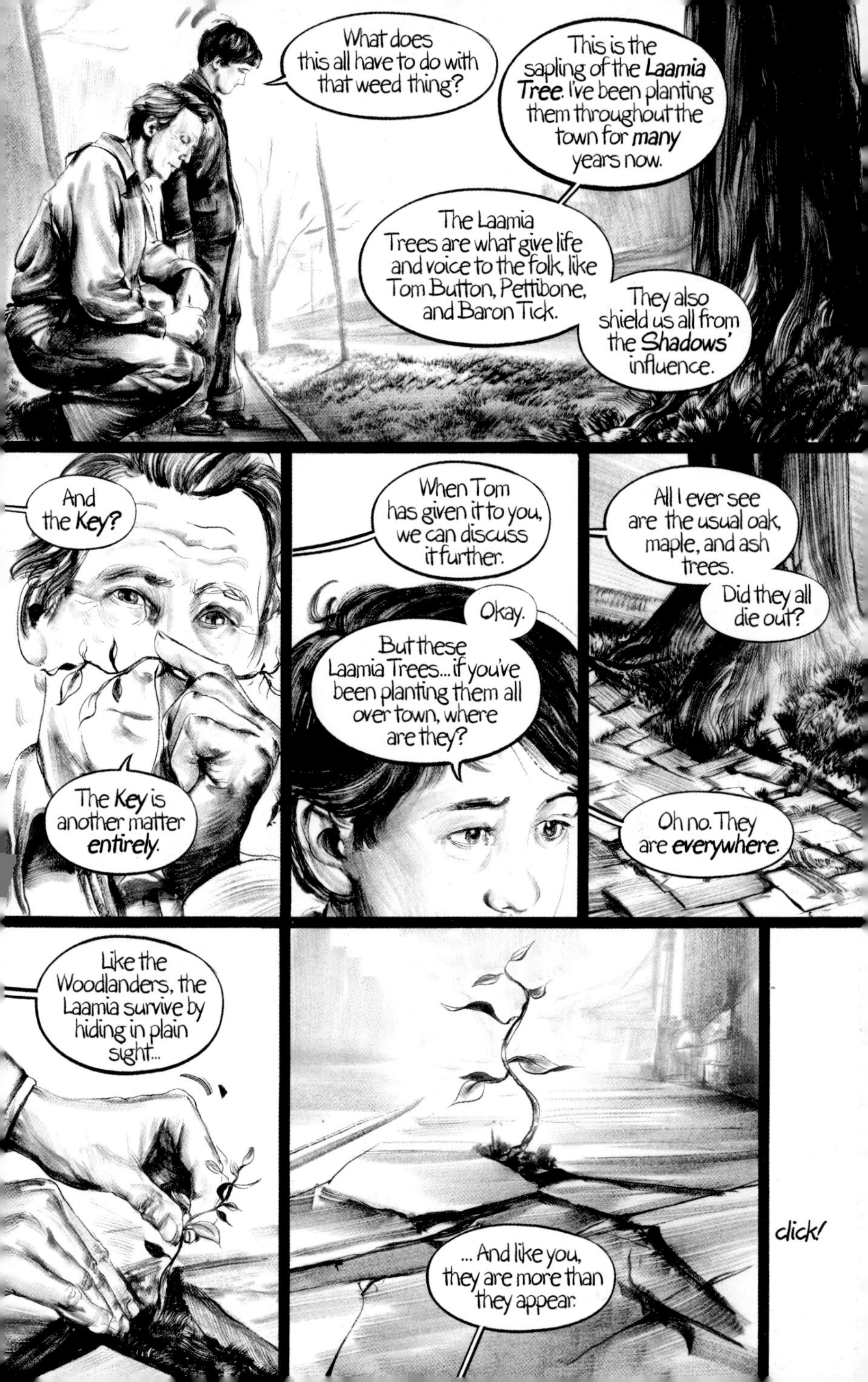
What does this all have to do with that weed thing?
This is the sapling of the **Laamia Tree**. I've been planting them throughout the town for *many* years now.
The Laamia Trees are what give life and voice to the folk, like Tom Button, Pettibone, and Baron Tick.
They also shield us all from the *Shadows'* influence.
And the *Key?*
The *Key* is another matter *entirely*.
When Tom has given it to you, we can discuss it further.
Okay.
But these Laamia Trees... if you've been planting them all over town, where are they?
All I ever see are the usual oak, maple, and ash trees.
Did they all die out?
Oh no. They are *everywhere*.
Like the Woodlanders, the Laamia survive by hiding in plain sight...
... And like you, they are more than they appear.
click!

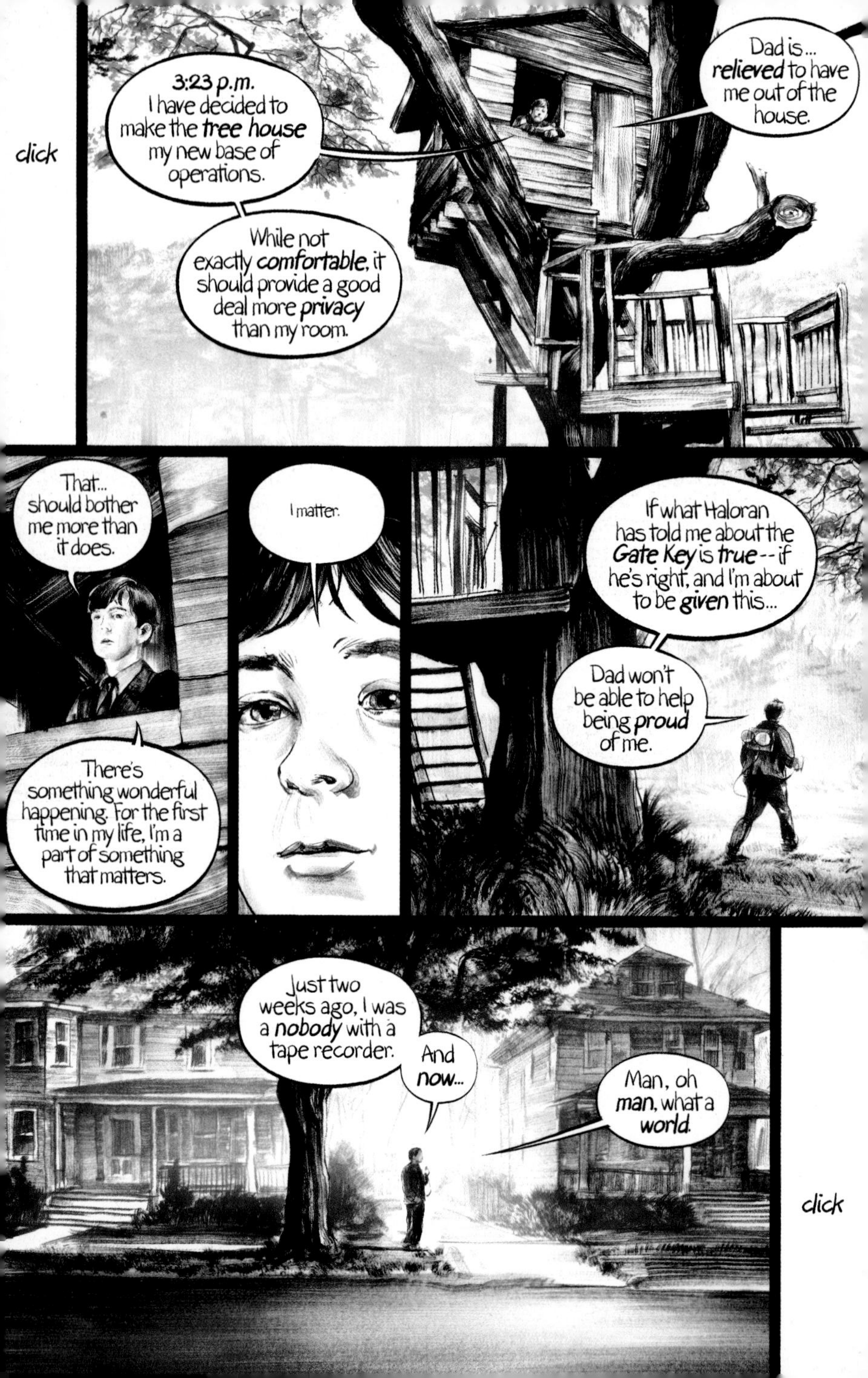

click
3:23 p.m. I have decided to make the tree house my new base of operations.
While not exactly comfortable, it should provide a good deal more privacy than my room.
Dad is... relieved to have me out of the house.
That... should bother me more than it does.
There's something wonderful happening. For the first time in my life, I'm a part of something that matters.
I matter.
If what Haloran has told me about the Gate Key is true--if he's right, and I'm about to be given this...
Dad won't be able to help being proud of me.
Just two weeks ago, I was a nobody with a tape recorder.
And now...
Man, oh man, what a world.
click

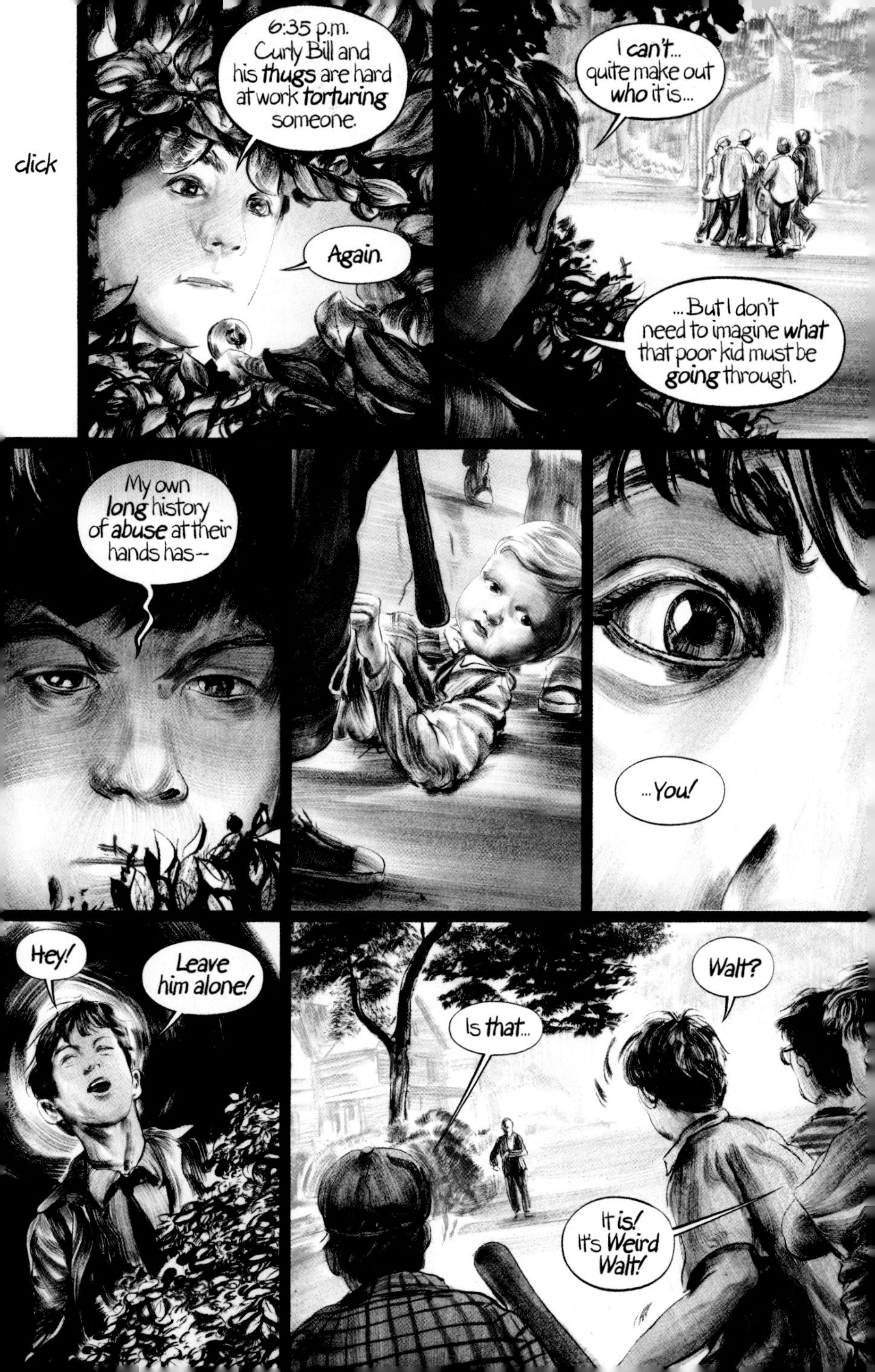
click
6:35 p.m. Curly Bill and his thugs are hard at work torturing someone.
Again.
I can't... quite make out who it is...
...But I don't need to imagine what that poor kid must be going through.
My own long history of abuse at their hands has--
...You!
Hey!
Leave him alone!
Walt?
Is that...
It is! It's Weird Walt!

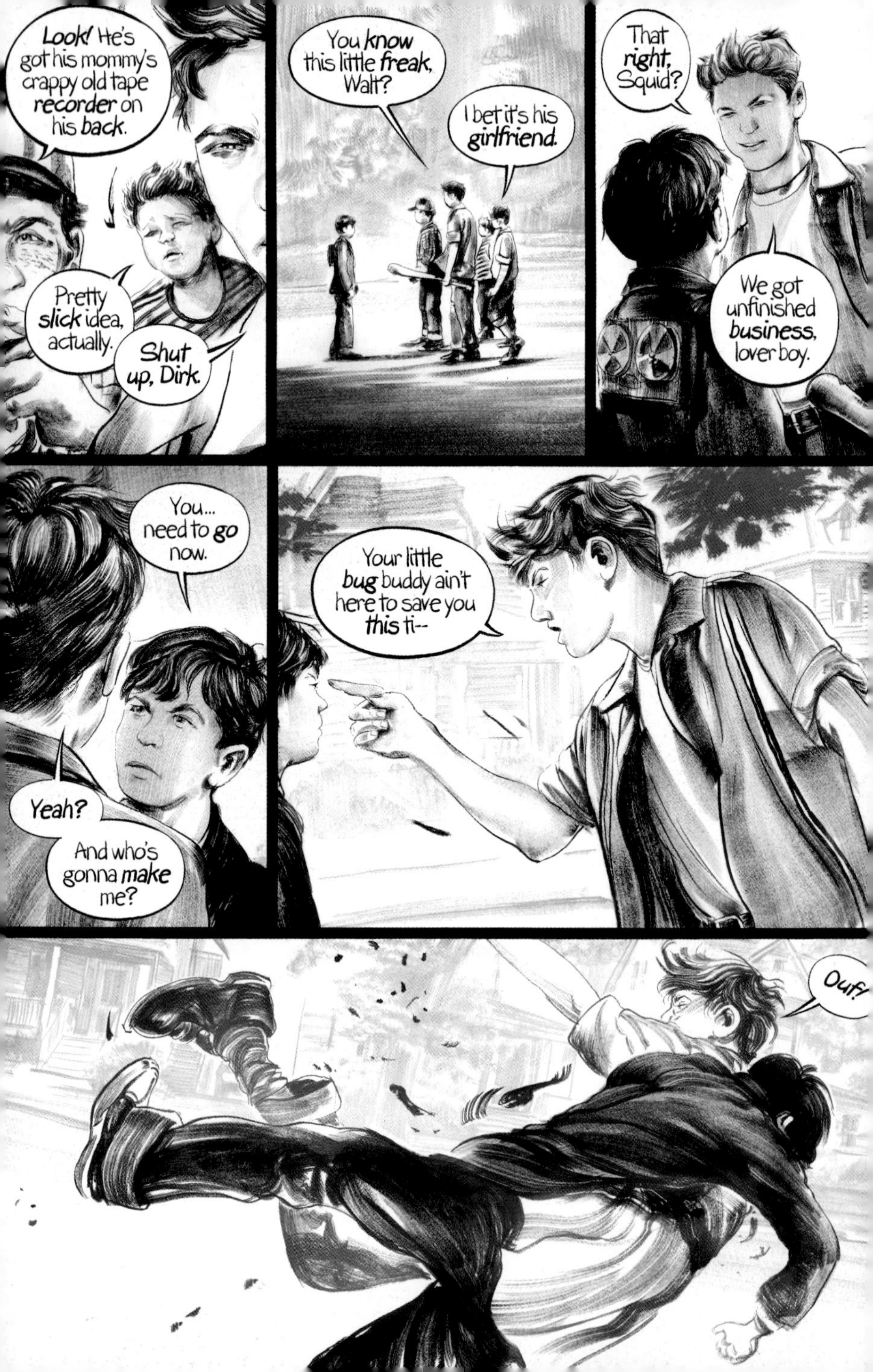
Look! He's got his mommy's crappy old tape recorder on his back.
Pretty slick idea, actually.
Shut up, Dirk.
You know this little freak, Walt?
I bet it's his girlfriend.
That right, Squid?
We got unfinished business, lover boy.
You... need to go now.
Yeah?
And who's gonna make me?
Your little bug buddy ain't here to save you this ti--
Ouf!

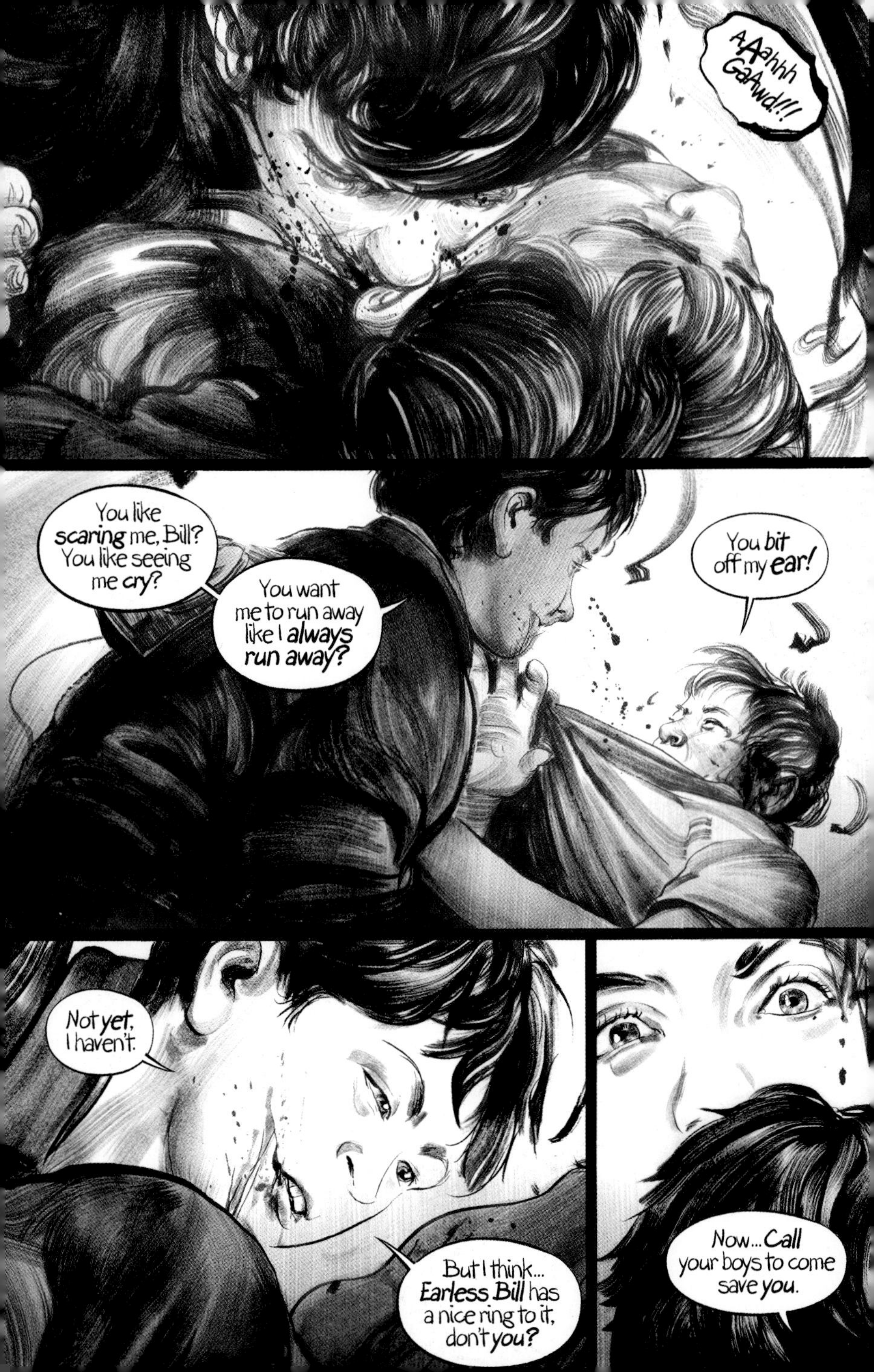

AAahhh GaAwd!!!
You like **scaring** me, Bill? You like seeing me *cry*?
You want me to run away like I **always run away**?
You *bit* off my **ear**!
Not *yet*, I haven't.
But I think... **Earless Bill** has a nice ring to it, don't *you*?
Now... **Call** your boys to come save *you*.

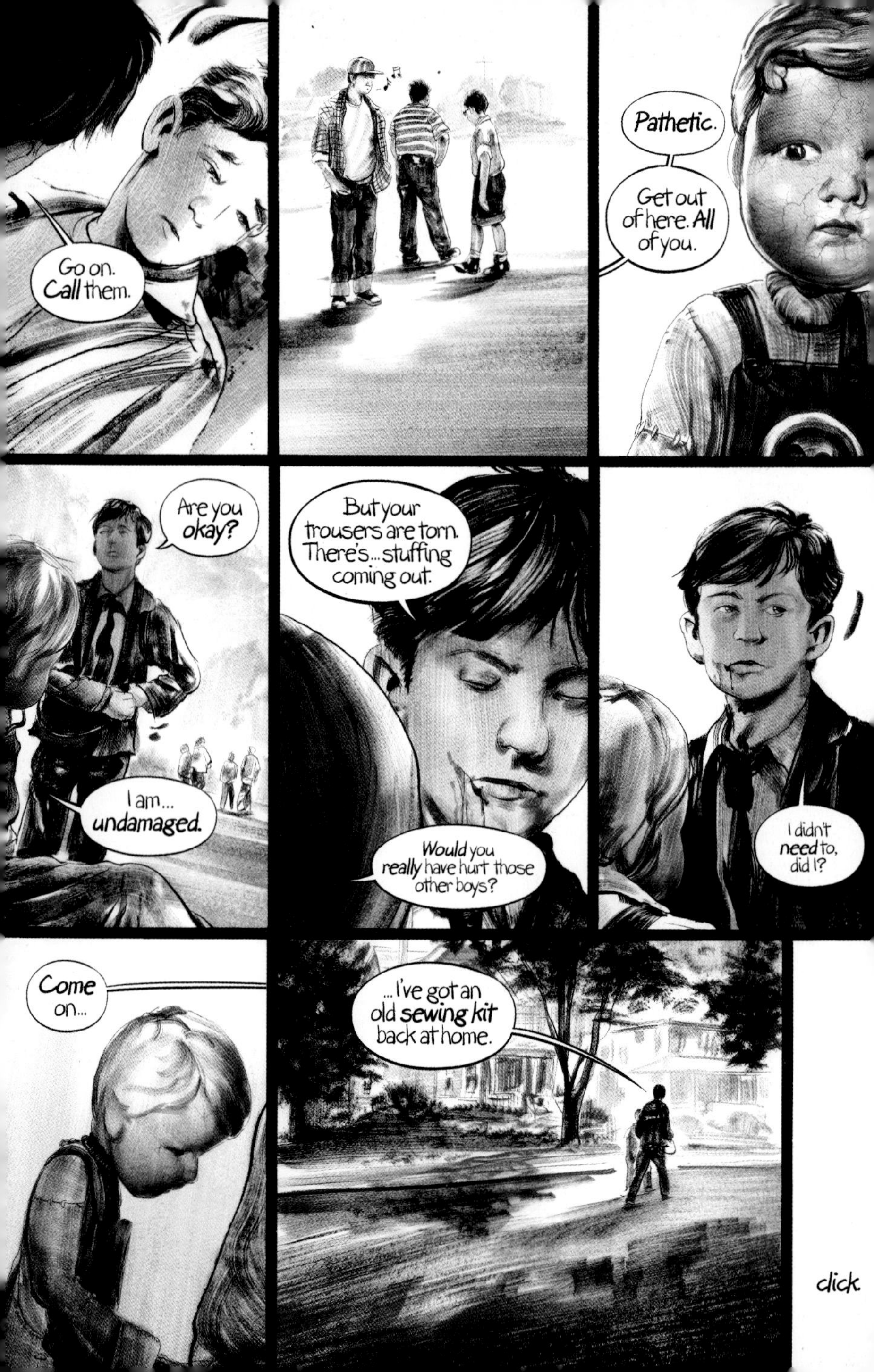
Go on. Call them.
Pathetic.
Get out of here. All of you.
Are you okay?
I am... undamaged.
But your trousers are torn. There's... stuffing coming out.
Would you really have hurt those other boys?
I didn't need to, did I?
Come on...
... I've got an old sewing kit back at home.
click.

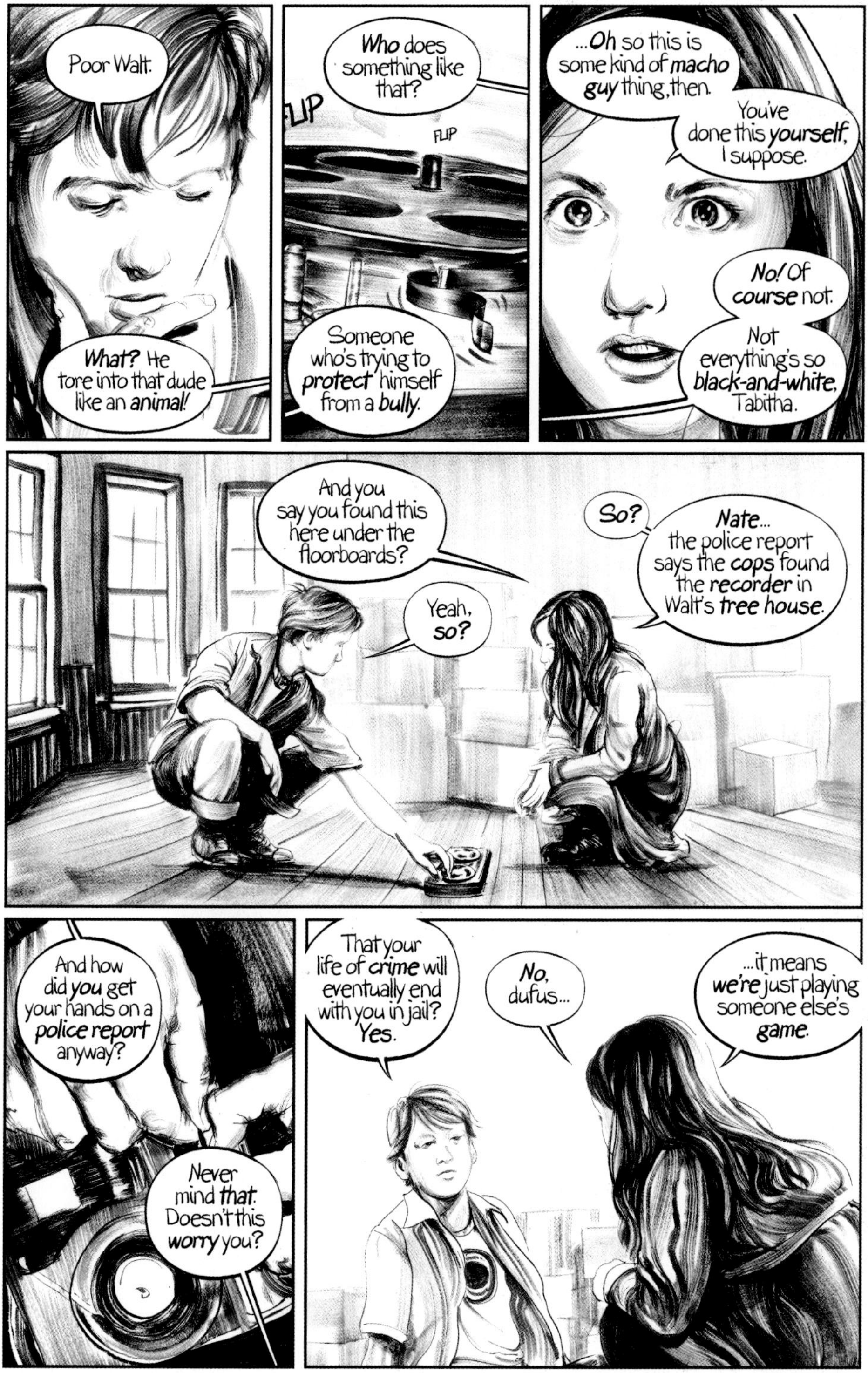
Poor Walt.
What? He tore into that dude like an animal!
Who does something like that?
FLIP
FLIP
Someone who's trying to protect himself from a bully.
...Oh so this is some kind of macho guy thing, then.
You've done this yourself, I suppose.
No! Of course not.
Not everything's so black-and-white, Tabitha.
And you say you found this here under the floorboards?
Yeah, so?
So?
Nate... the police report says the cops found the recorder in Walt's tree house.
And how did you get your hands on a police report anyway?
Never mind that. Doesn't this worry you?
That your life of crime will eventually end with you in jail? Yes.
No, dufus...
...it means we're just playing someone else's game.

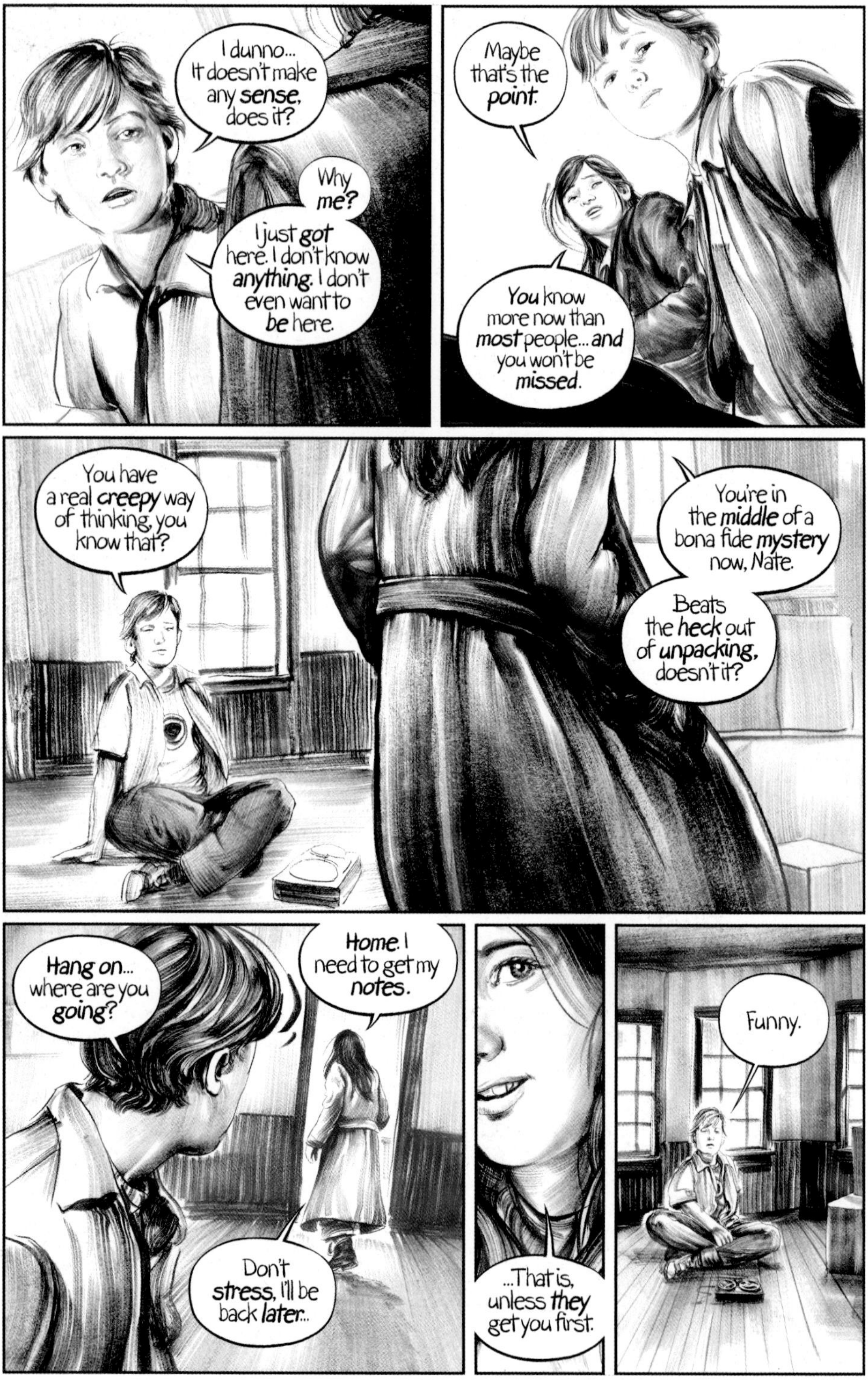
I dunno... It doesn't make any **sense**, does it?
Why **me?**
I just **got** here. I don't know **anything**. I don't even want to **be** here.
Maybe that's the **point**.
You know more now than **most** people... **and** you won't be **missed**.
You have a real **creepy** way of thinking, you know that?
You're in the **middle** of a bona fide **mystery** now, Nate.
Beats the **heck** out of **unpacking**, doesn't it?
Hang on... where are you **going**?
Home. I need to get my **notes**.
Don't **stress**, I'll be back **later**...
...That is, unless **they** get you first.
Funny.

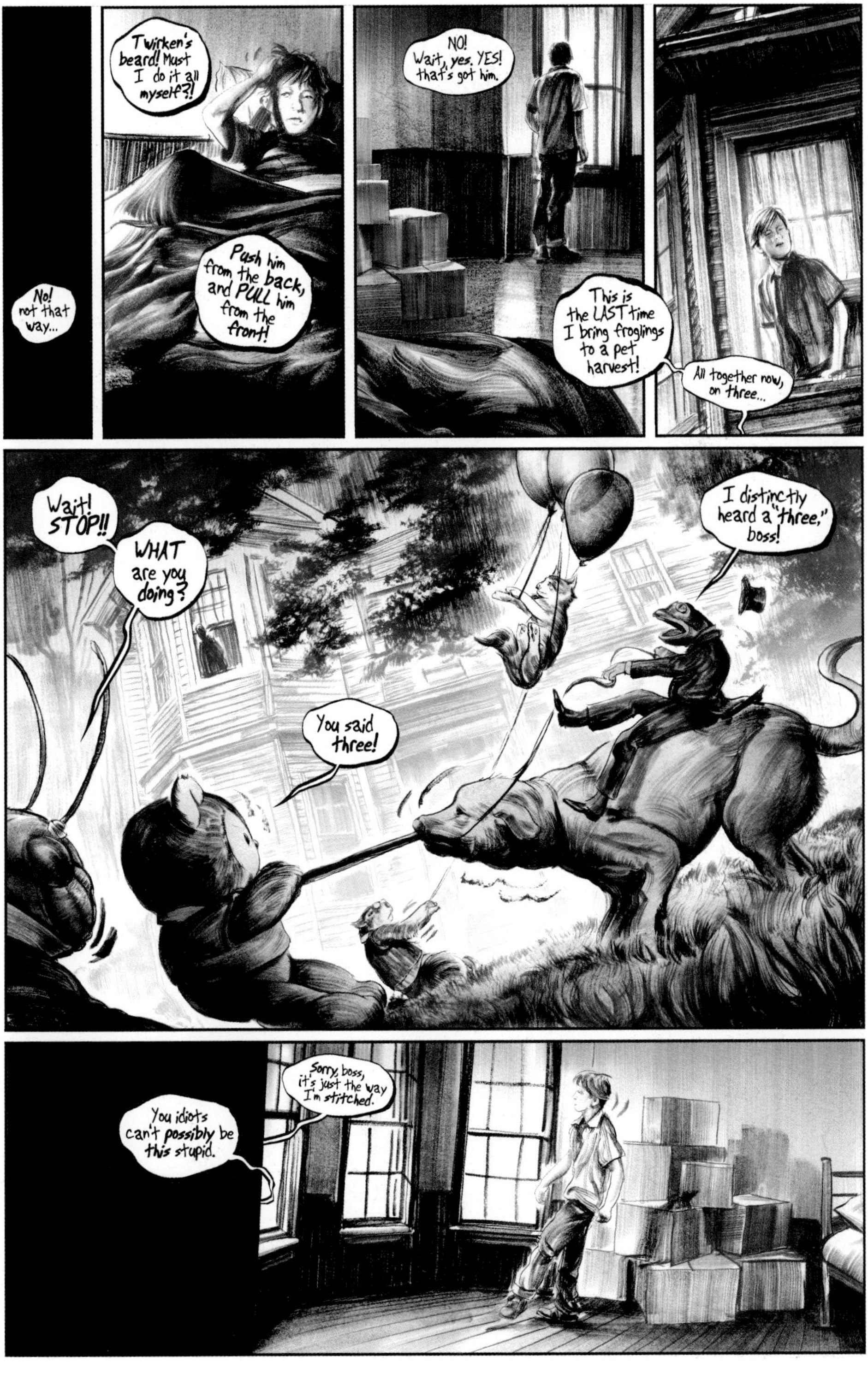
No! not that way...
Twirken's beard! Must I do it all myself?!
Push him from the back, and PULL him from the front!
NO! Wait, yes. YES! that's got him.
This is the LAST time I bring froglings to a pet harvest!
All together now, on three...
Wait! STOP!!
WHAT are you doing?
I distinctly heard a "three," boss!
You said three!
You idiots can't possibly be this stupid.
Sorry, boss, it's just the way I'm stitched.

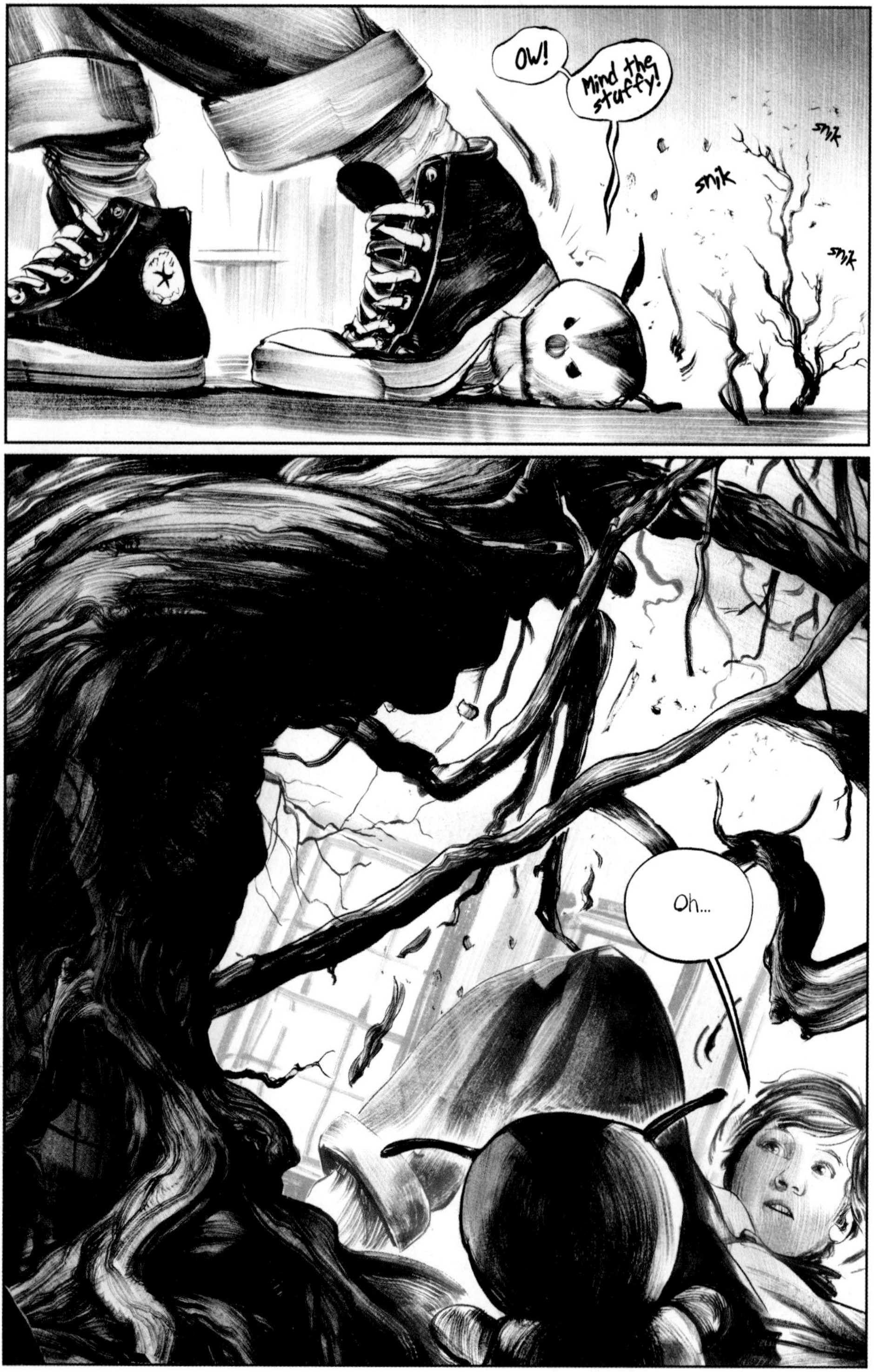
OW!
Mind the stuffy!
snik
snik
snik
Oh...

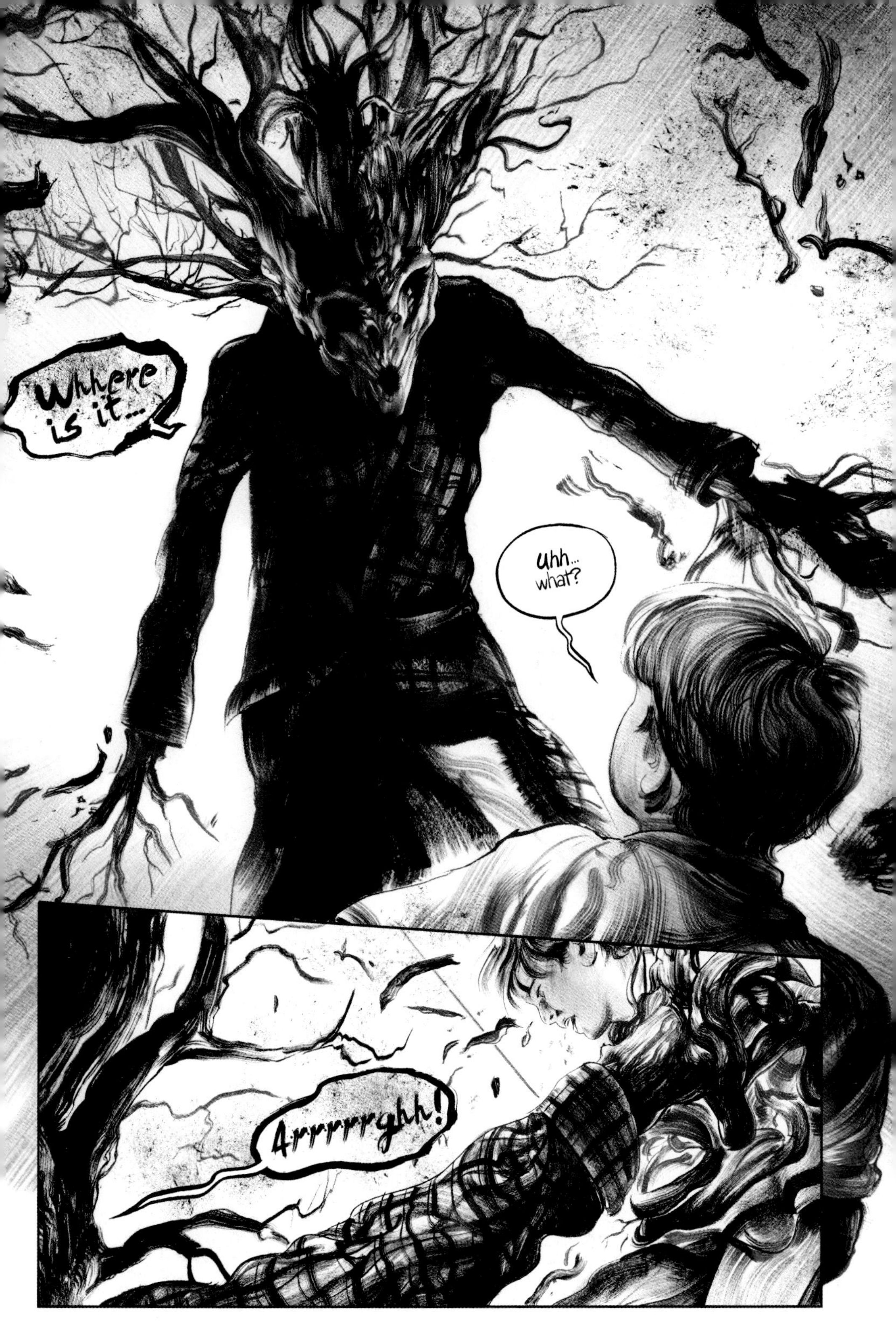
Whhere is it...
uhh... what?
Arrrrrrghh!

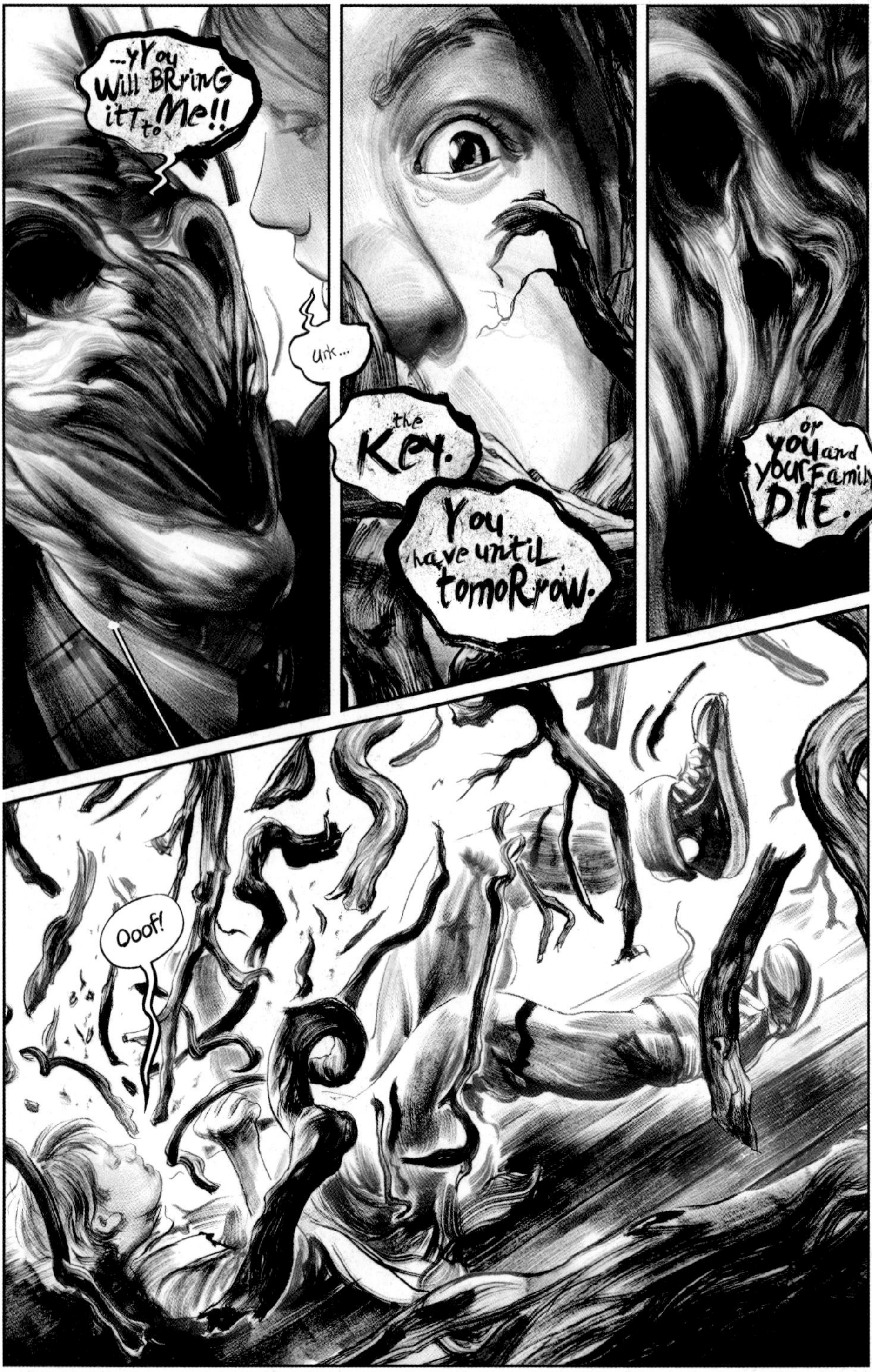
...yYou Will BRring itT to Me!!
urk...
the Key.
You have until tomoRrow.
or you and your Family DIE.
Ooof!

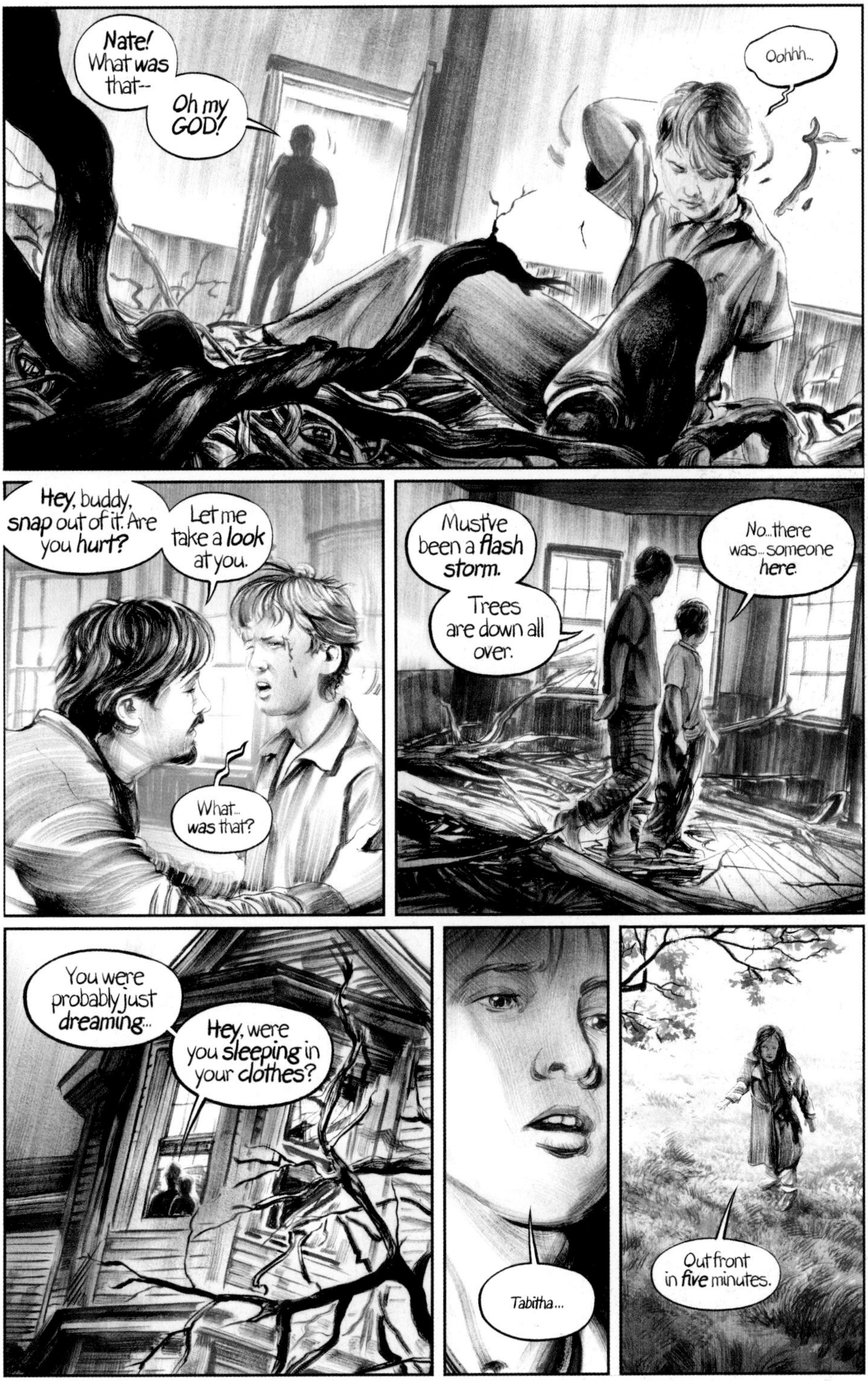

Nate! What was that--
Oh my GOD!
Oohhh...
Hey, buddy, snap out of it. Are you hurt?
Let me take a look at you.
What... was that?
Must've been a flash storm.
Trees are down all over.
No...there was...someone here.
You were probably just dreaming...
Hey, were you sleeping in your clothes?
Tabitha...
Out front in five minutes.

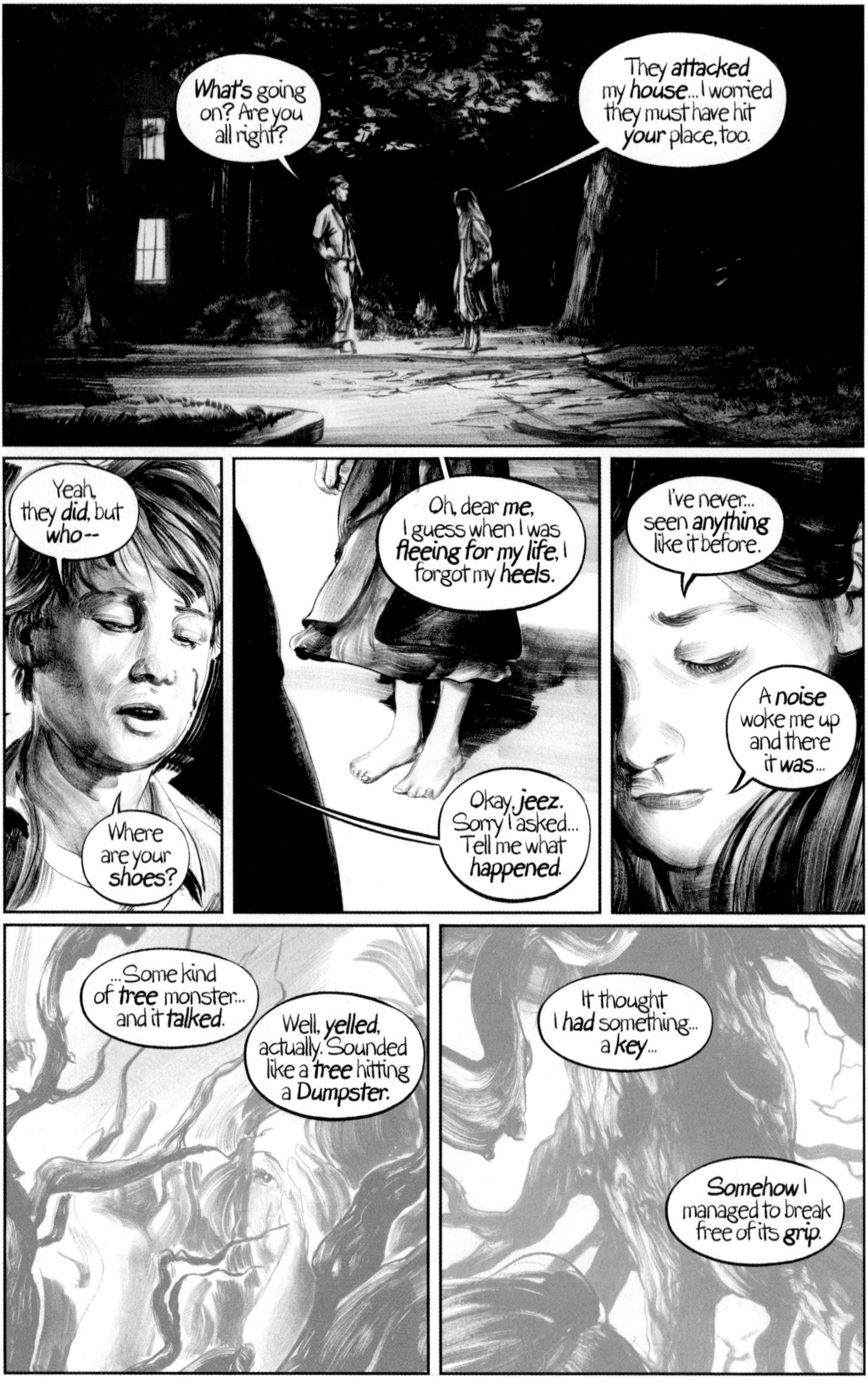
What's going on? Are you all right?
They attacked my house... I worried they must have hit your place, too.
Yeah, they did, but who--
Where are your shoes?
Oh, dear me, I guess when I was fleeing for my life, I forgot my heels.
Okay, jeez. Sorry I asked... Tell me what happened.
I've never... seen anything like it before.
A noise woke me up and there it was...
...Some kind of tree monster... and it talked.
Well, yelled, actually. Sounded like a tree hitting a Dumpster.
It thought I had something... a key...
Somehow I managed to break free of its grip.

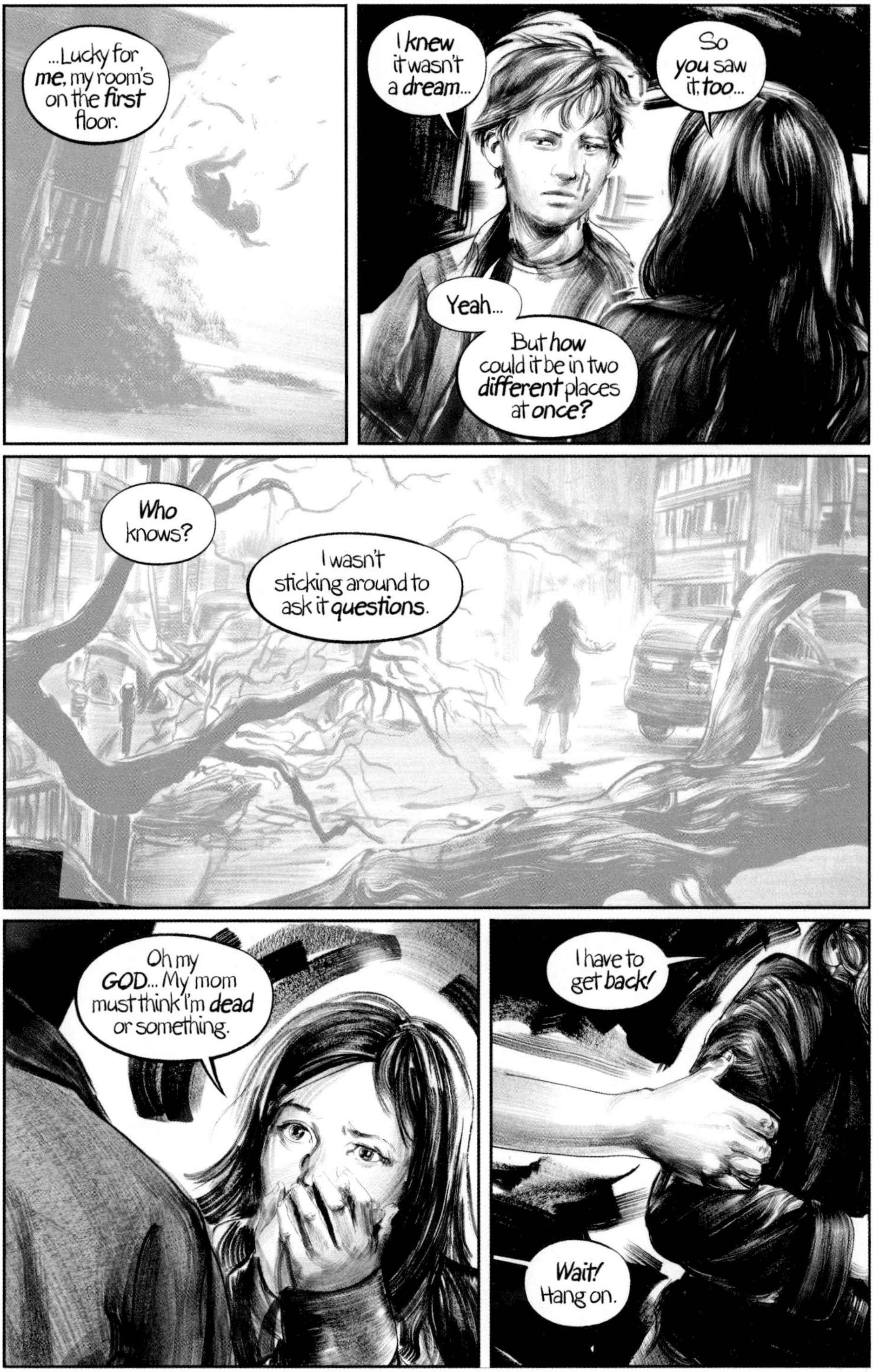
...Lucky for me, my room's on the first floor.
I knew it wasn't a dream...
So you saw it, too...
Yeah...
But how could it be in two different places at once?
Who knows?
I wasn't sticking around to ask it questions.
Oh my GOD... My mom must think I'm dead or something.
I have to get back!
Wait! Hang on.

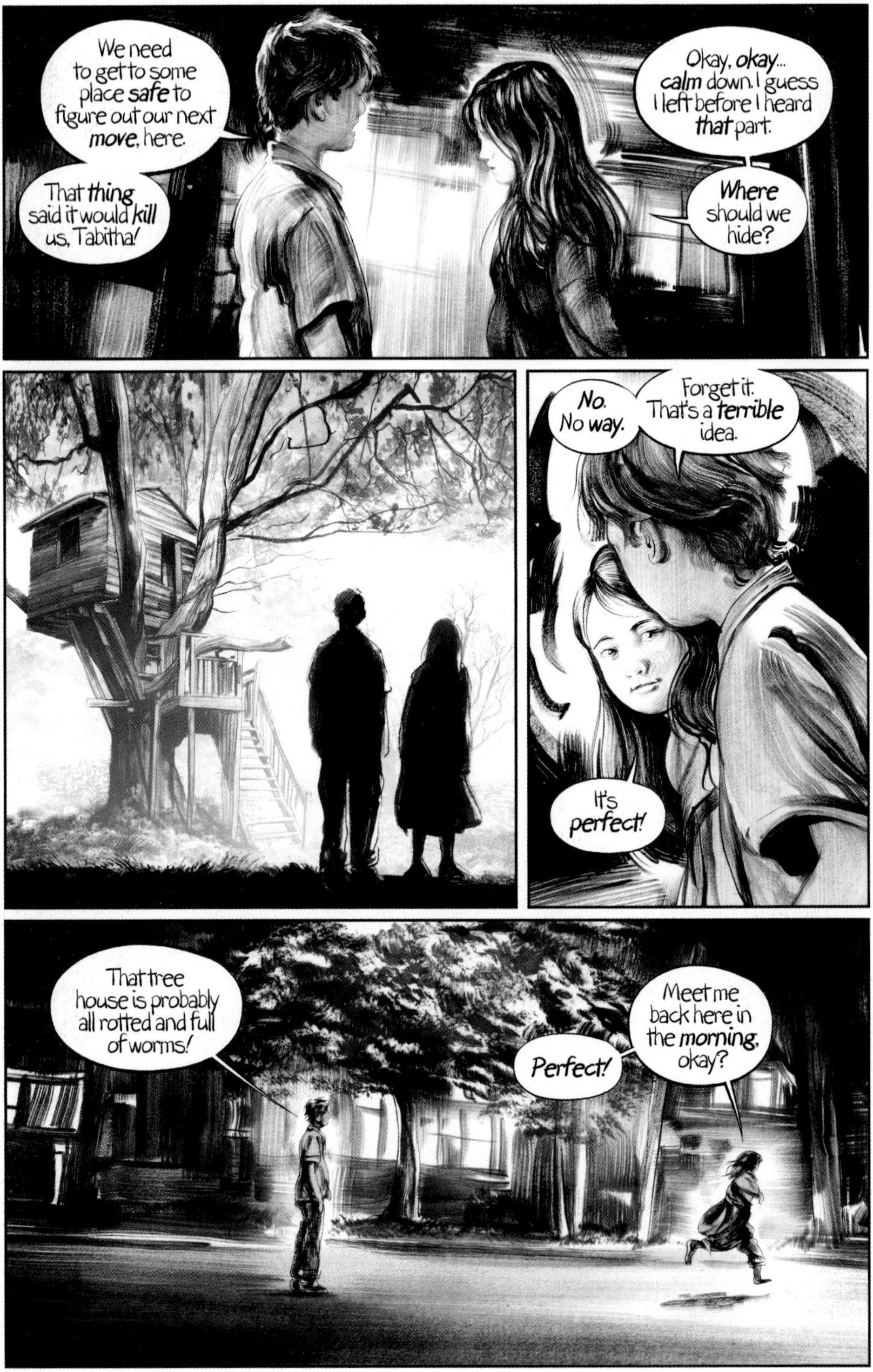
We need to get to some place *safe* to figure out our next *move*, here.
That *thing* said it would *kill* us, Tabitha!
Okay, *okay*... *calm* down. I guess I left before I heard *that* part.
Where should we hide?
No. No *way.*
Forget it. That's a *terrible* idea.
It's *perfect!*
That tree house is probably all rotted and full of worms!
Perfect!
Meet me back here in the *morning*, okay?

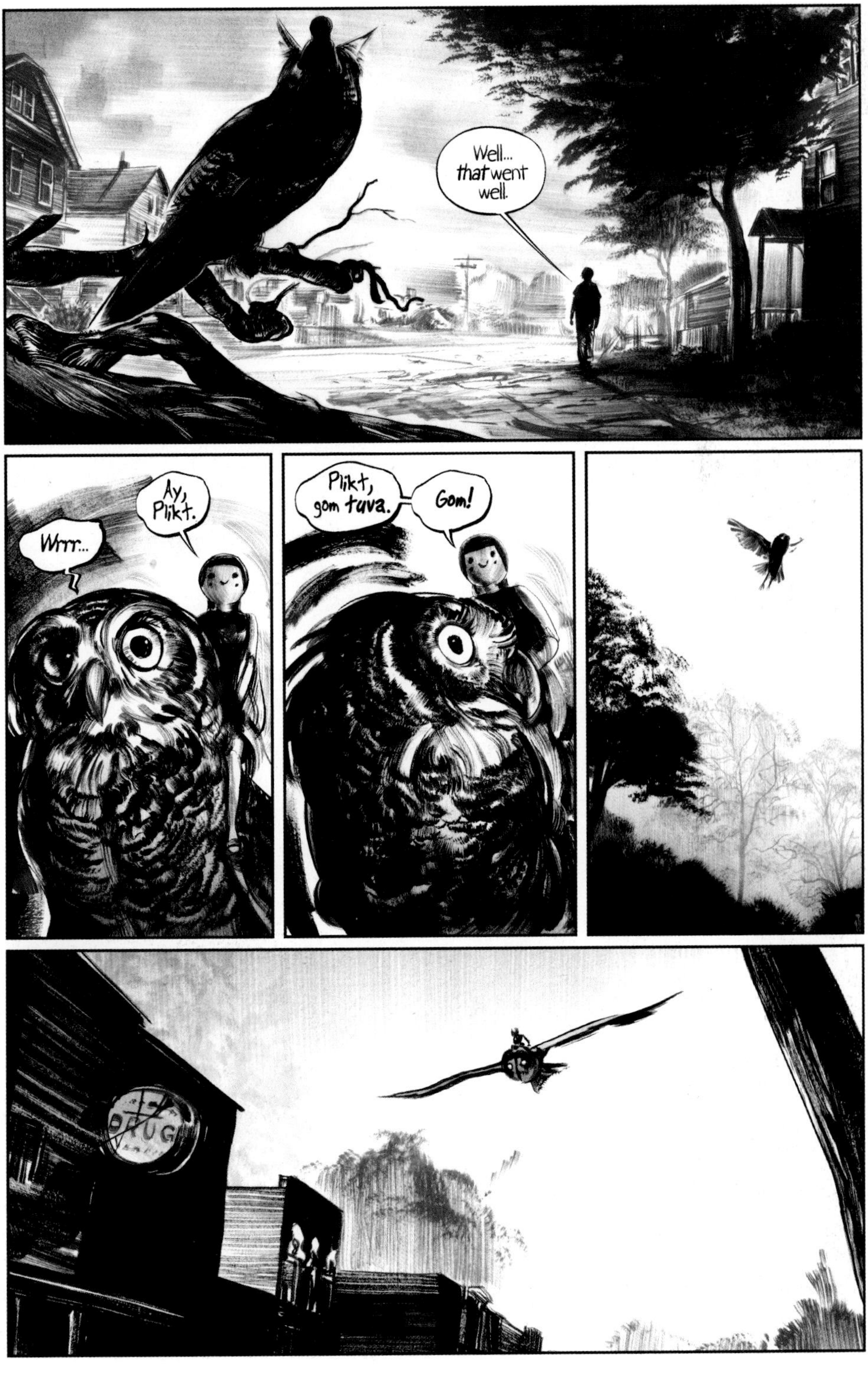
Well...
that went
well.
Wrrr...
Ay,
Plikt.
Plikt,
gom tuva.
Gom!

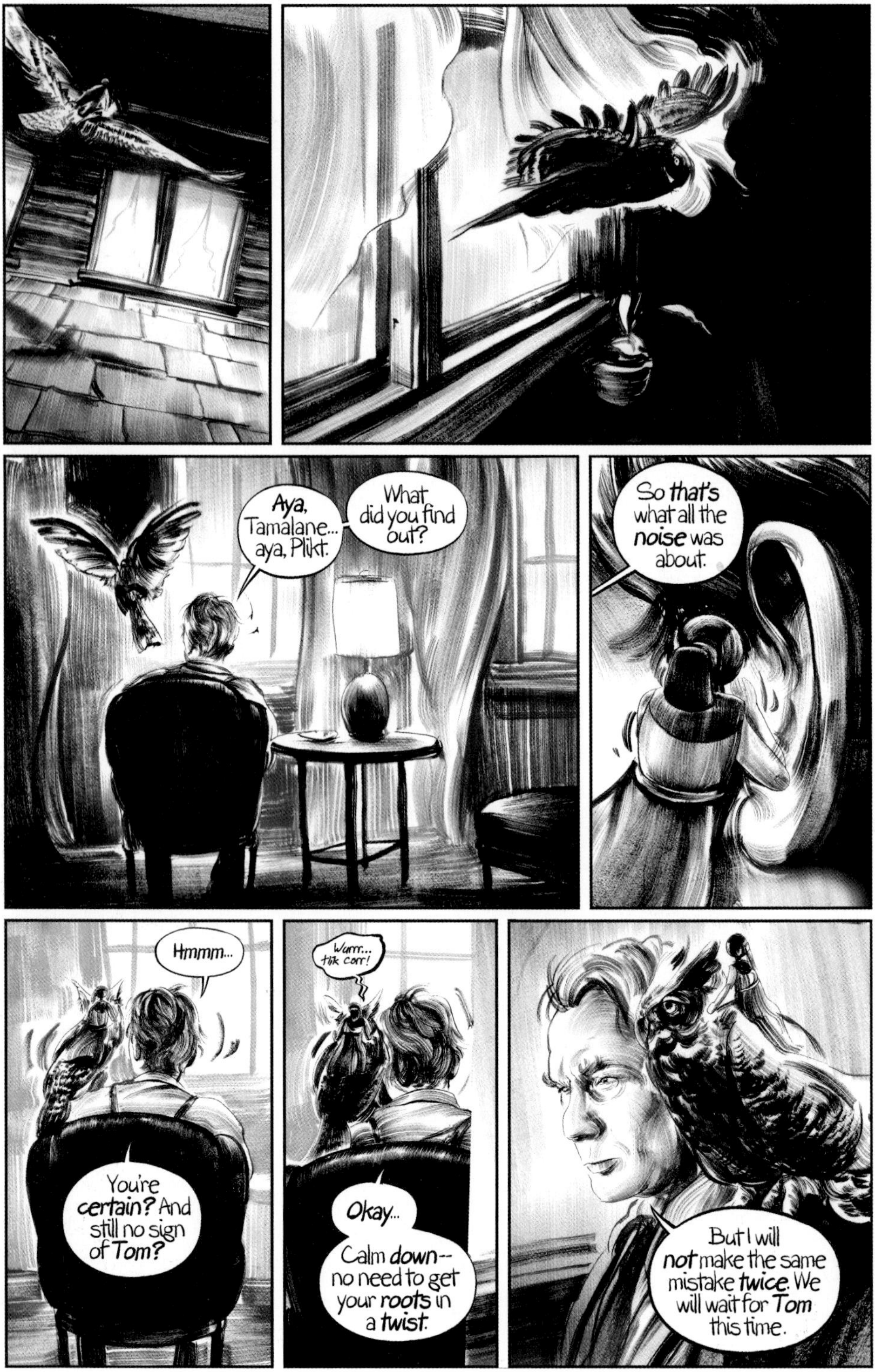
Aya, Tamalane... aya, Plikt.
What did you find out?
So that's what all the noise was about.
Hmmm...
You're certain? And still no sign of Tom?
Warrr... tik corr!
Okay...
Calm down-- no need to get your roots in a twist.
But I will not make the same mistake twice. We will wait for Tom this time.

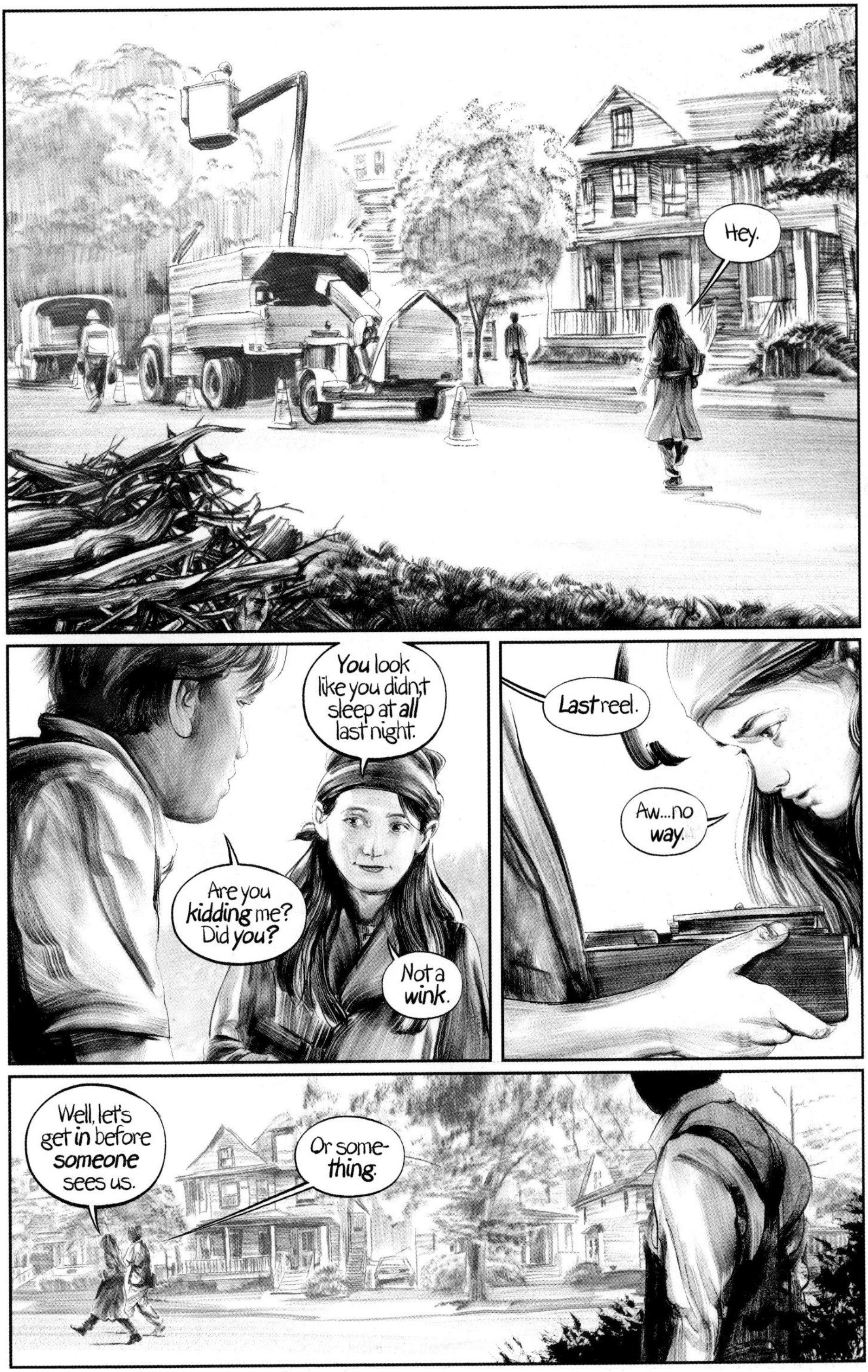
Hey.
You look like you didn't sleep at *all* last night.
Are you *kidding* me? Did *you?*
Not a *wink*.
Last reel.
Aw...no *way*.
Well, let's get *in* before *someone* sees us.
Or some-*thing*.

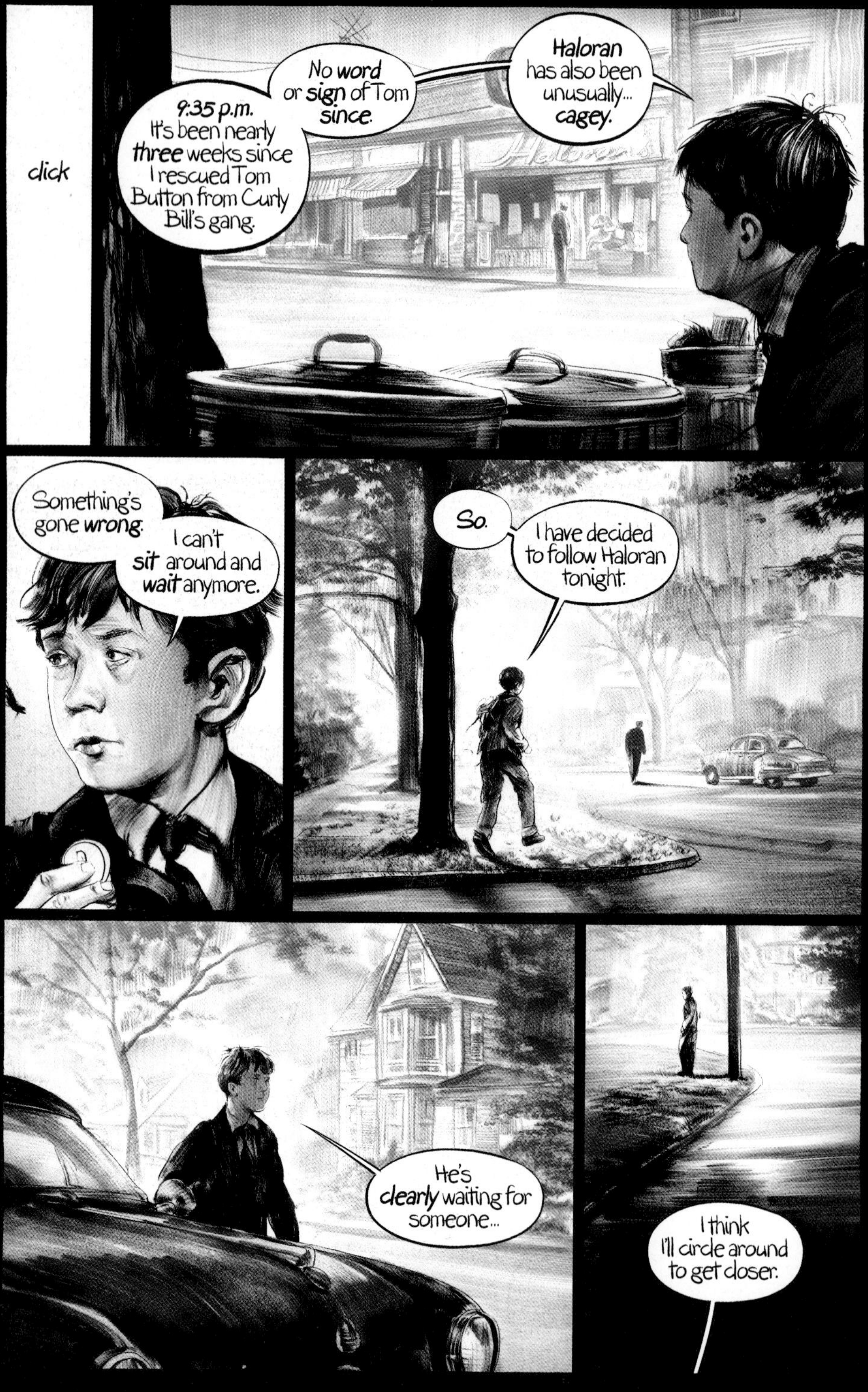
click
9:35 p.m.
It's been nearly three weeks since I rescued Tom Button from Curly Bill's gang.
No word or sign of Tom since.
Haloran has also been unusually... cagey.
Something's gone wrong.
I can't sit around and wait anymore.
So.
I have decided to follow Haloran tonight.
He's clearly waiting for someone...
I think I'll circle around to get closer.

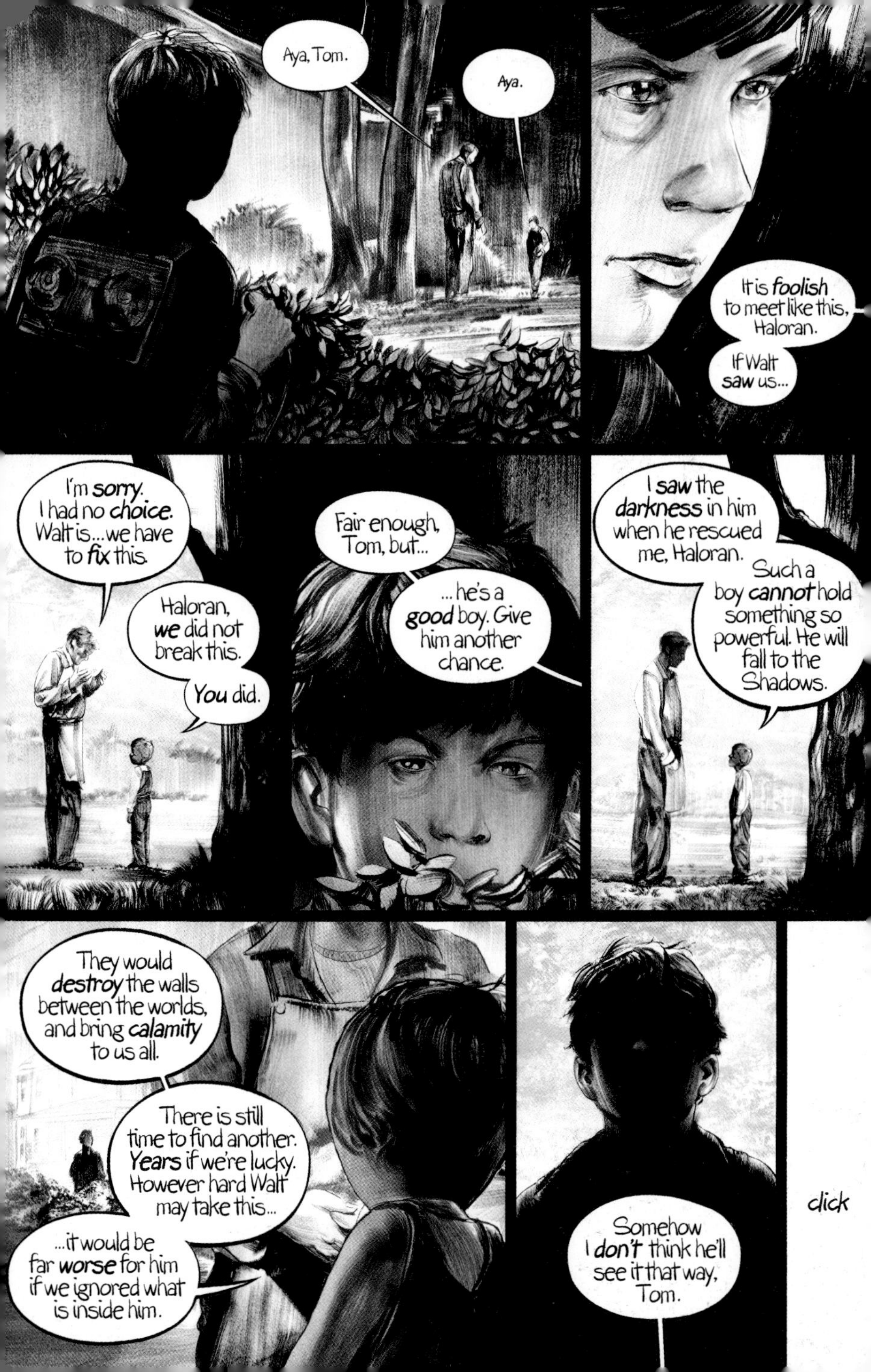
Aya, Tom.
Aya.
It is foolish to meet like this, Haloran.
If Walt saw us...
I'm sorry. I had no choice. Walt is... we have to fix this.
Haloran, we did not break this.
You did.
Fair enough, Tom, but...
...he's a good boy. Give him another chance.
I saw the darkness in him when he rescued me, Haloran.
Such a boy cannot hold something so powerful. He will fall to the Shadows.
They would destroy the walls between the worlds, and bring calamity to us all.
There is still time to find another. Years if we're lucky. However hard Walt may take this...
...it would be far worse for him if we ignored what is inside him.
Somehow I don't think he'll see it that way, Tom.
click

click

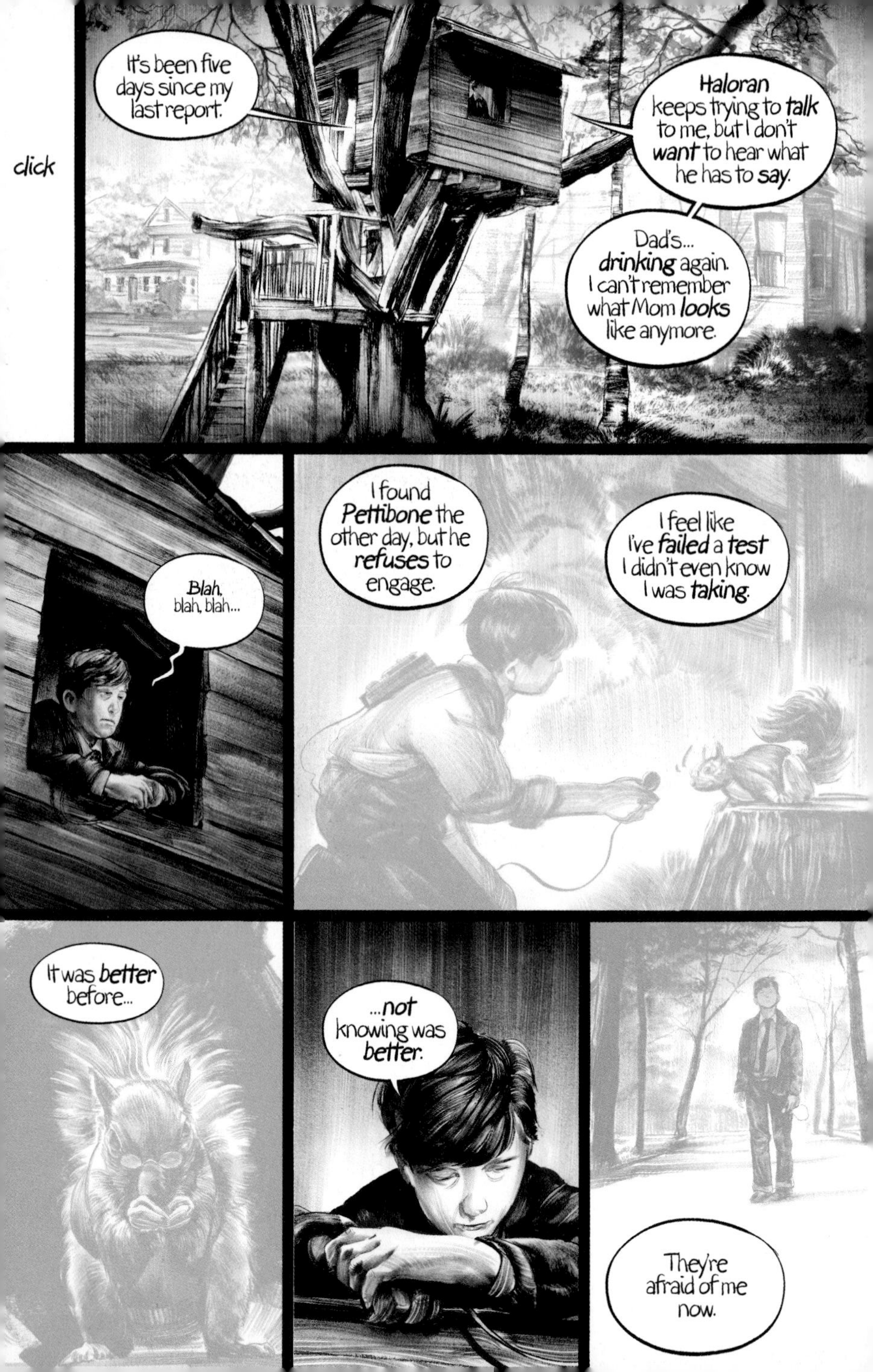

It's been five days since my last report.
Haloran keeps trying to talk to me, but I don't want to hear what he has to say.
Dad's... drinking again. I can't remember what Mom looks like anymore.
Blah, blah, blah...
I found Pettibone the other day, but he refuses to engage.
I feel like I've failed a test I didn't even know I was taking.
It was better before...
...not knowing was better.
They're afraid of me now.

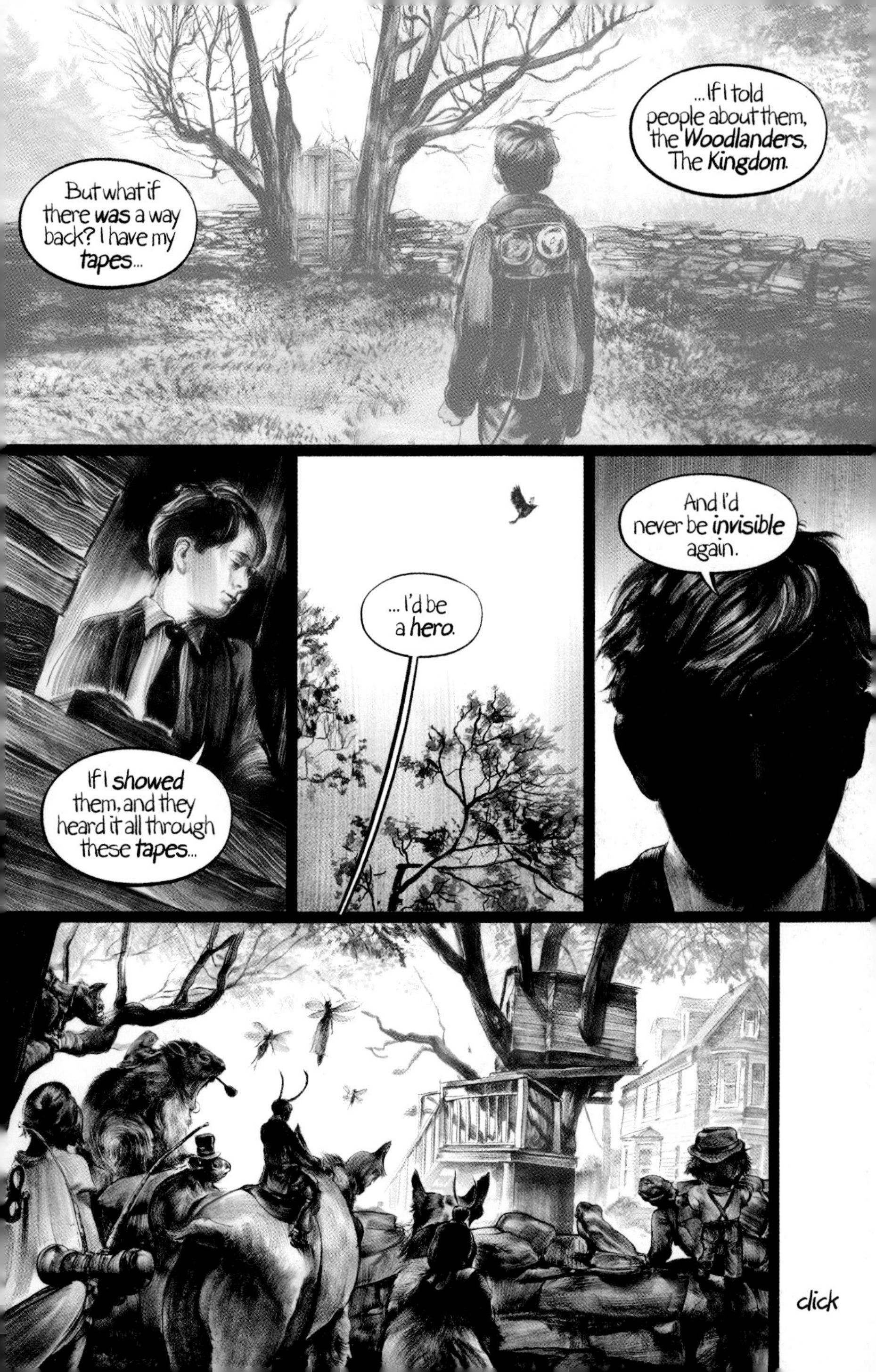
But what if there was a way back? I have my tapes...
...If I told people about them, the Woodlanders, The Kingdom.
If I showed them, and they heard it all through these tapes...
...I'd be a hero.
And I'd never be invisible again.
click

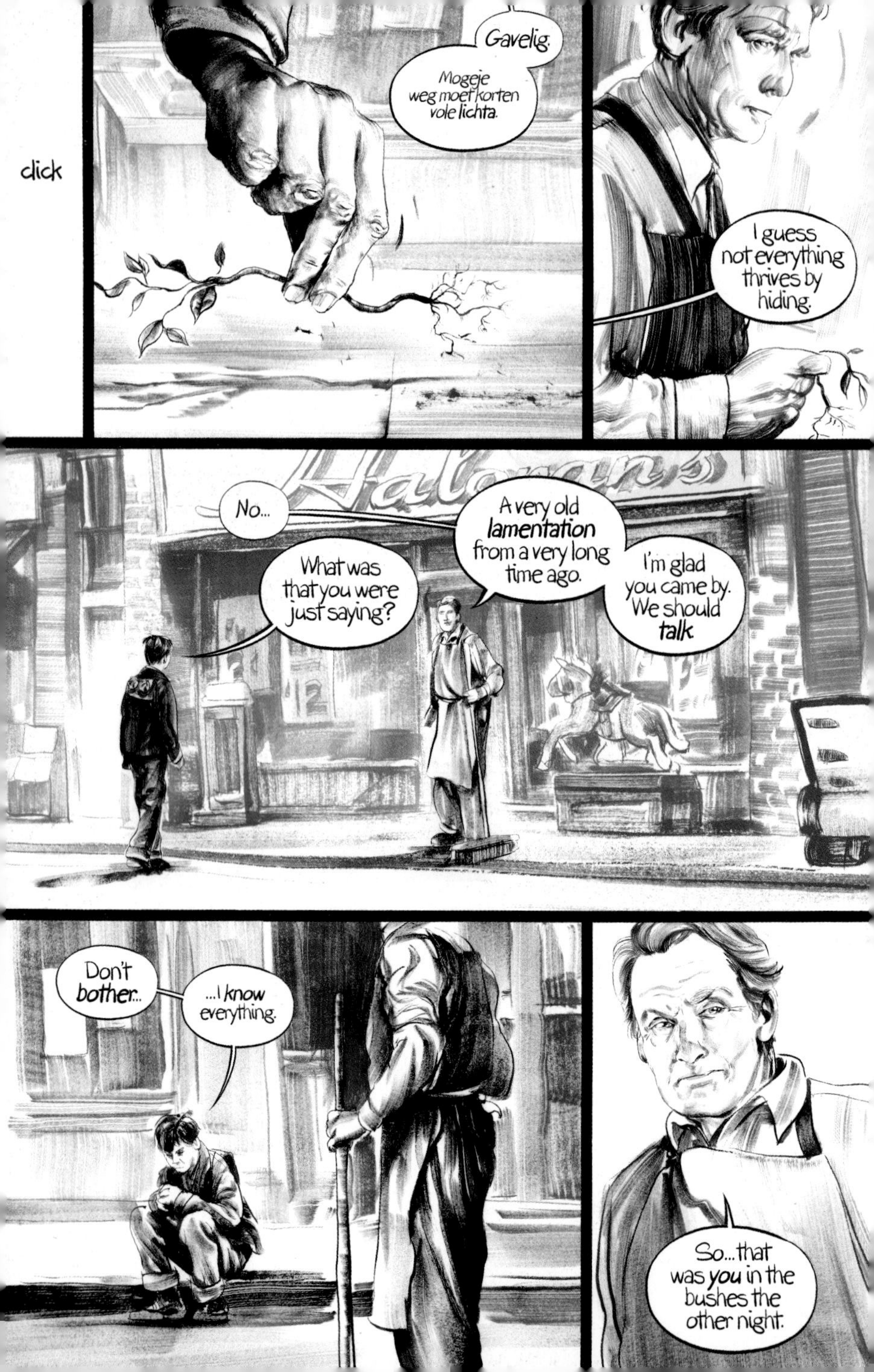

click
Gavelig.
Mogeje weg moet korten vole lichta.
I guess not everything thrives by hiding.
No...
What was that you were just saying?
A very old lamentation from a very long time ago.
I'm glad you came by. We should talk.
Don't bother...
...I know everything.
So... that was you in the bushes the other night.

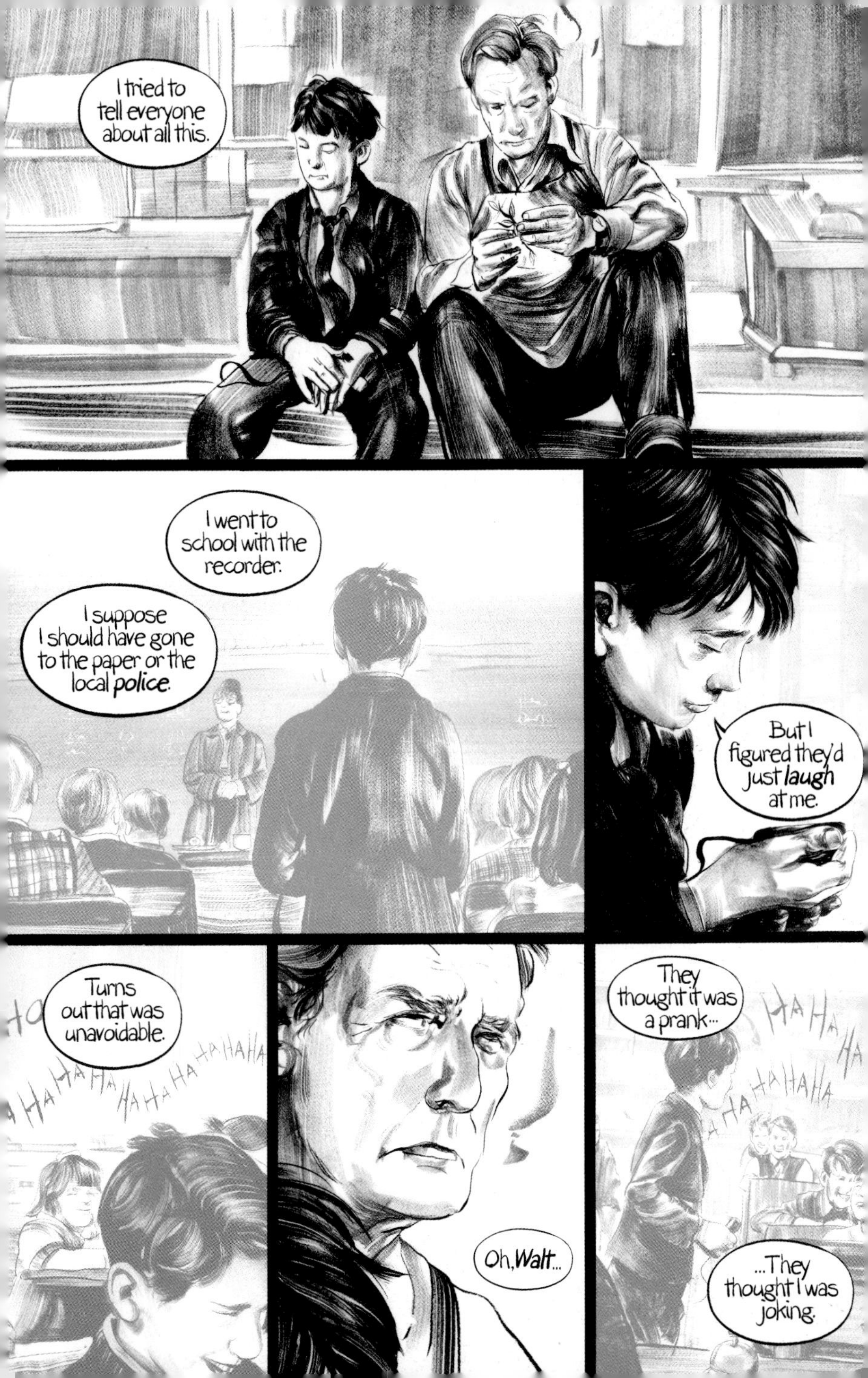
I tried to tell everyone about all this.
I went to school with the recorder.
I suppose I should have gone to the paper or the local *police*.
But I figured they'd just *laugh* at me.
Turns out that was unavoidable.
HA HA HA HA HA HA HA HA HA HA HA HA
Oh, *Walt*...
They thought it was a prank...
HA HA HA HA HA HA HA HA HA
...They thought I was joking.

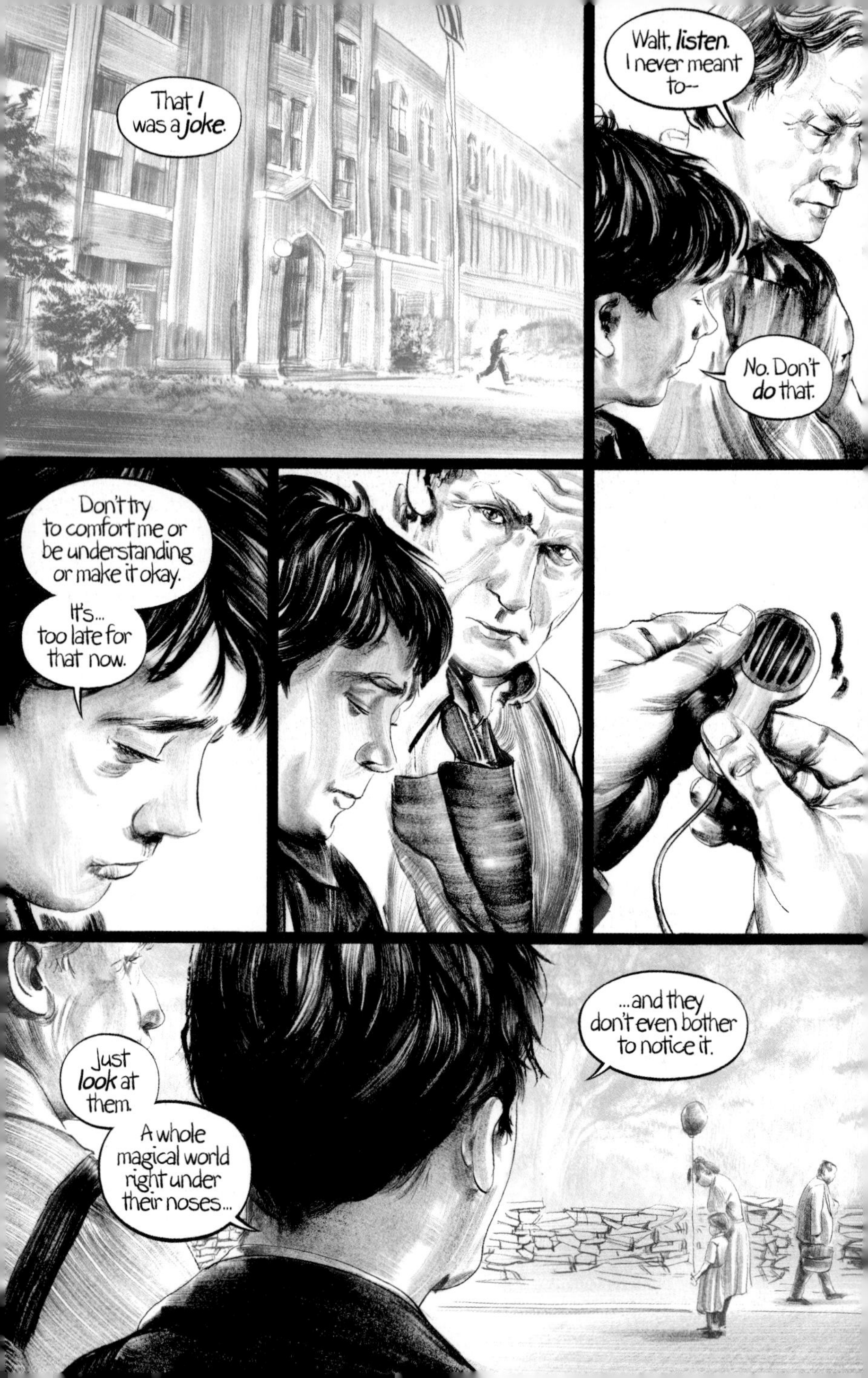
That I was a joke.
Walt, listen. I never meant to--
No. Don't do that.
Don't try to comfort me or be understanding or make it okay.
It's... too late for that now.
!
Just look at them.
A whole magical world right under their noses...
...and they don't even bother to notice it.

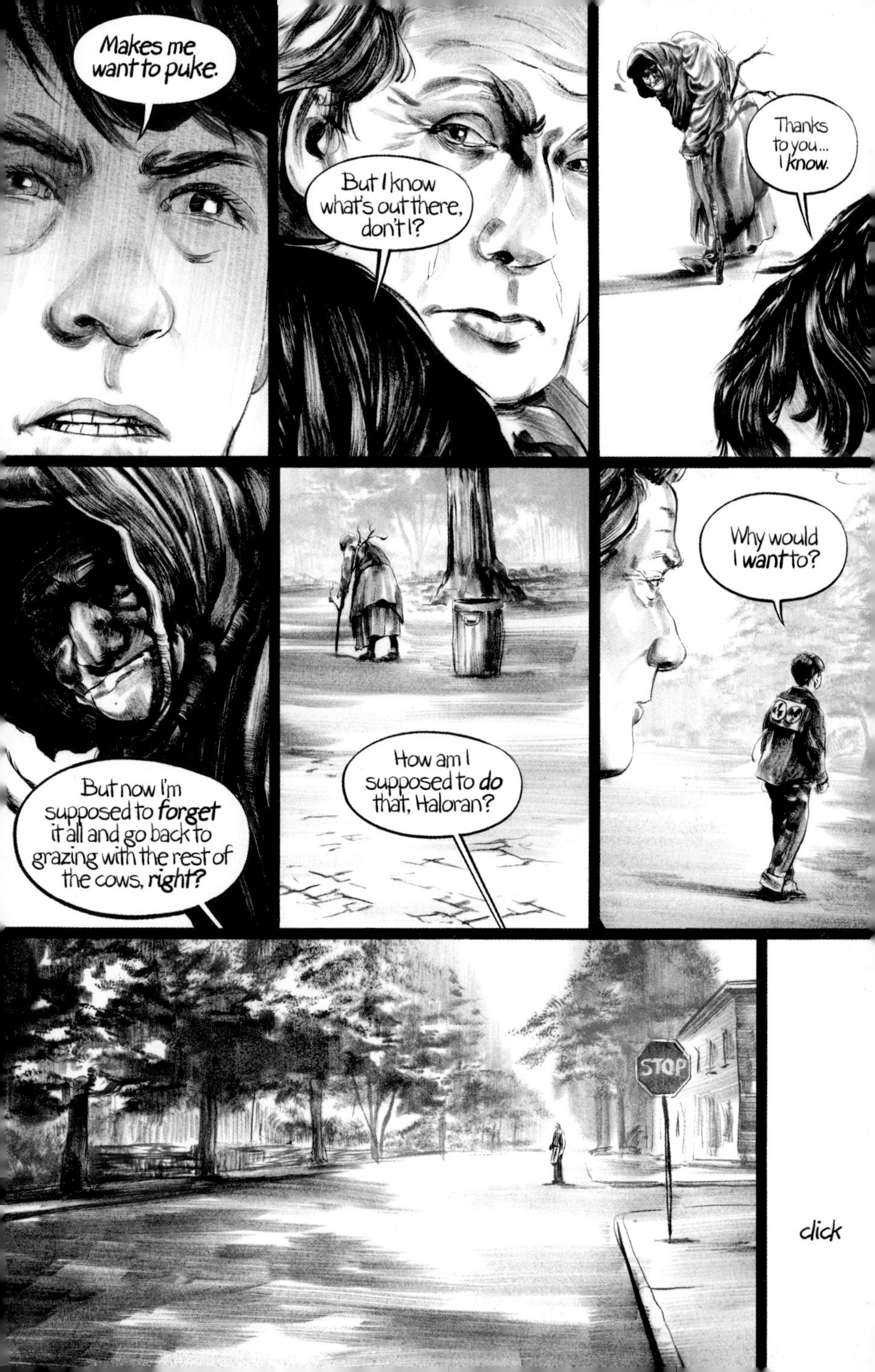
Makes me want to puke.
But I know what's out there, don't I?
Thanks to you... I know.
But now I'm supposed to forget it all and go back to grazing with the rest of the cows, right?
How am I supposed to do that, Haloran?
Why would I want to?
STOP
click

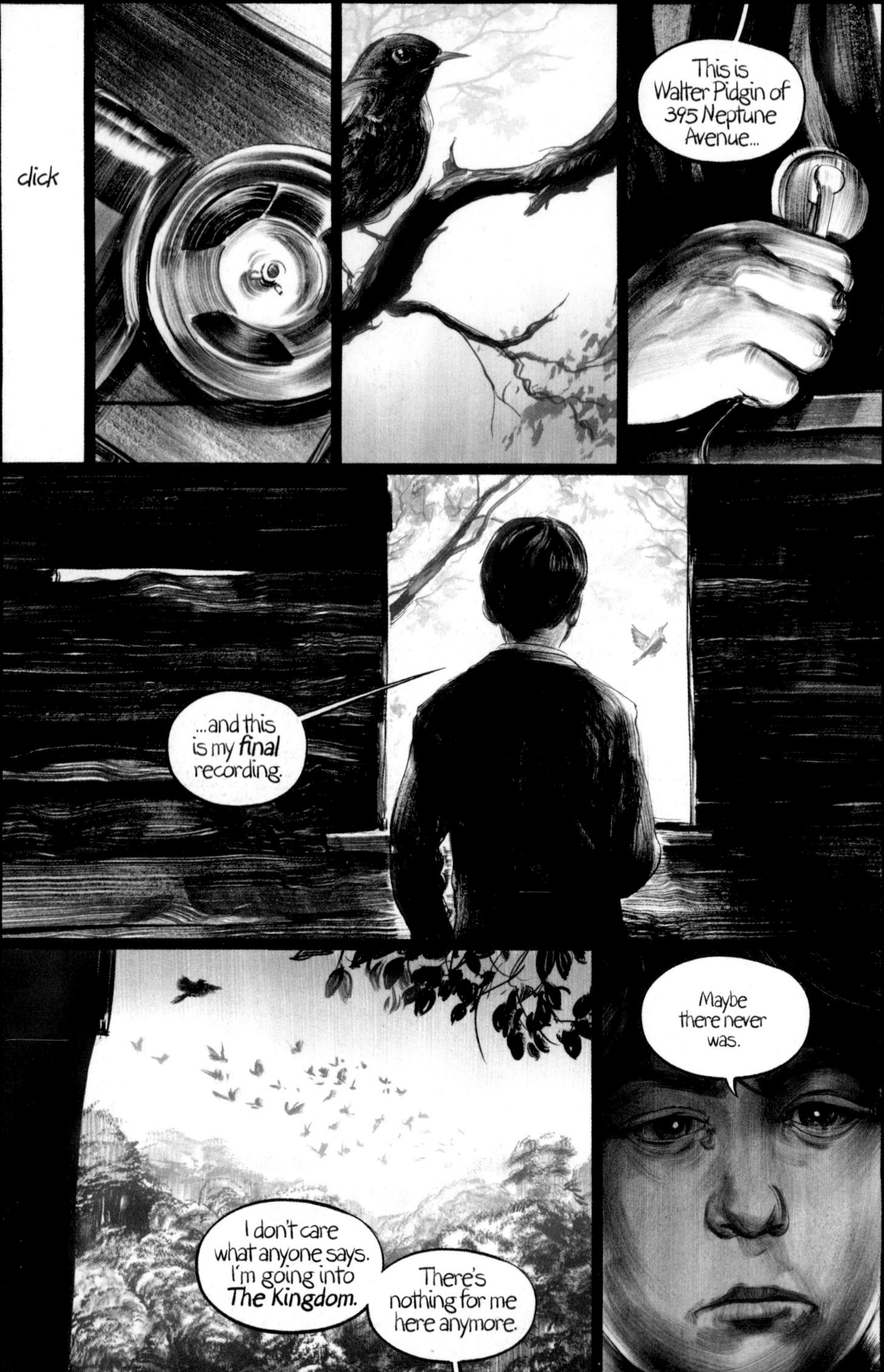
click
This is Walter Pidgin of 395 Neptune Avenue...
...and this is my final recording.
I don't care what anyone says. I'm going into The Kingdom.
There's nothing for me here anymore.
Maybe there never was.

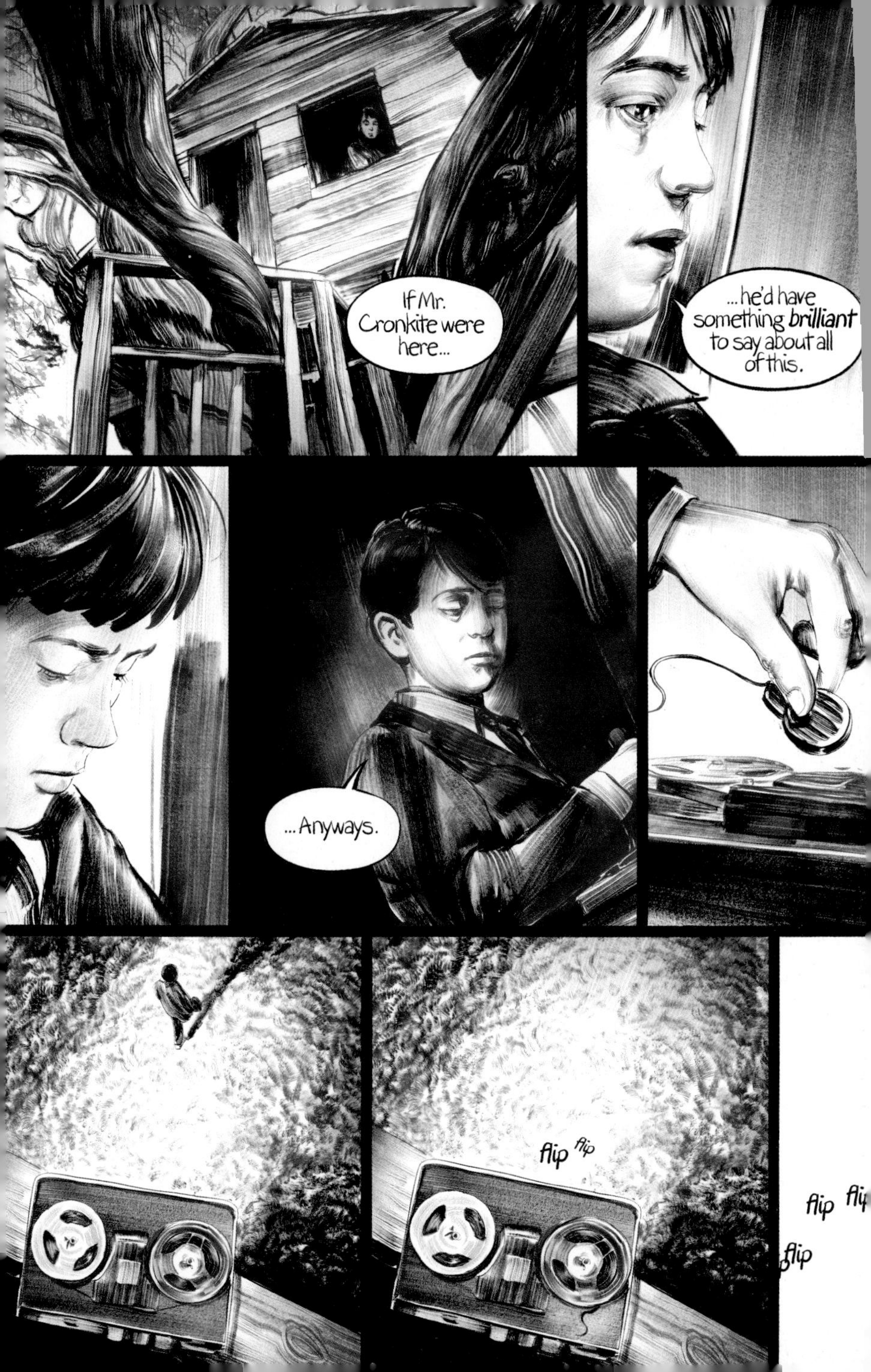
If Mr. Cronkite were here...
...he'd have something **brilliant** to say about all of this.
...Anyways.
flip flip
flip flip
flip

Part Two

Nate & Tabitha

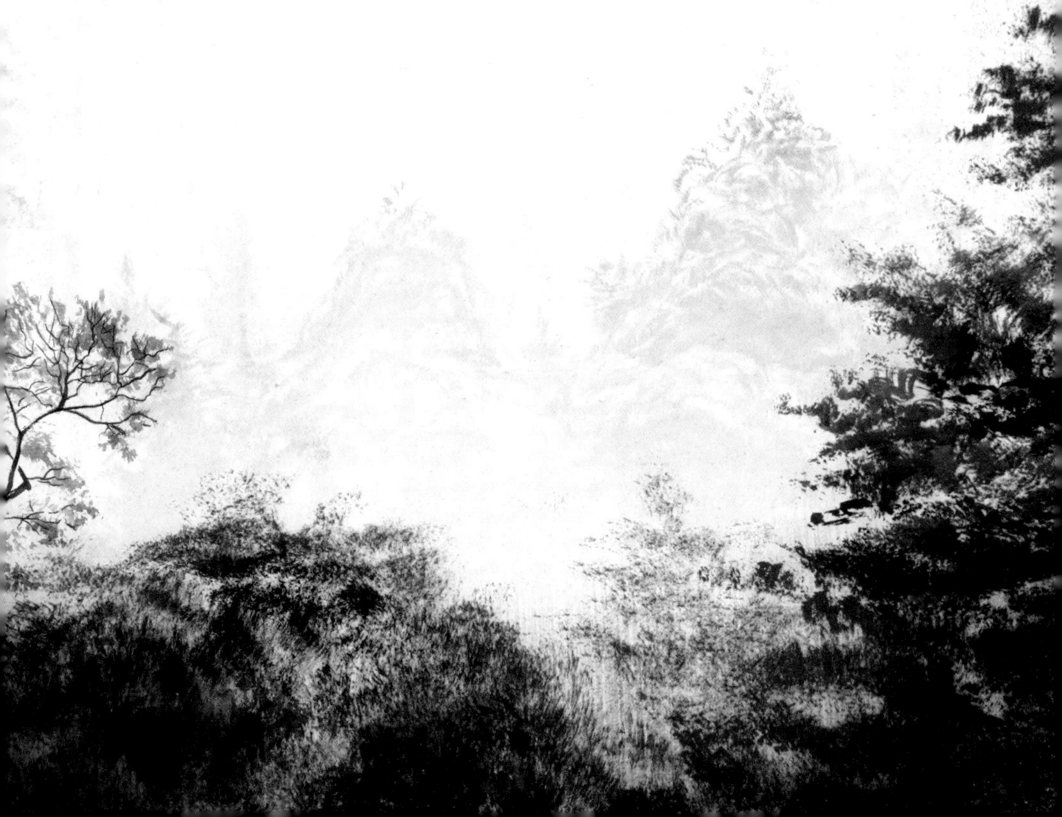

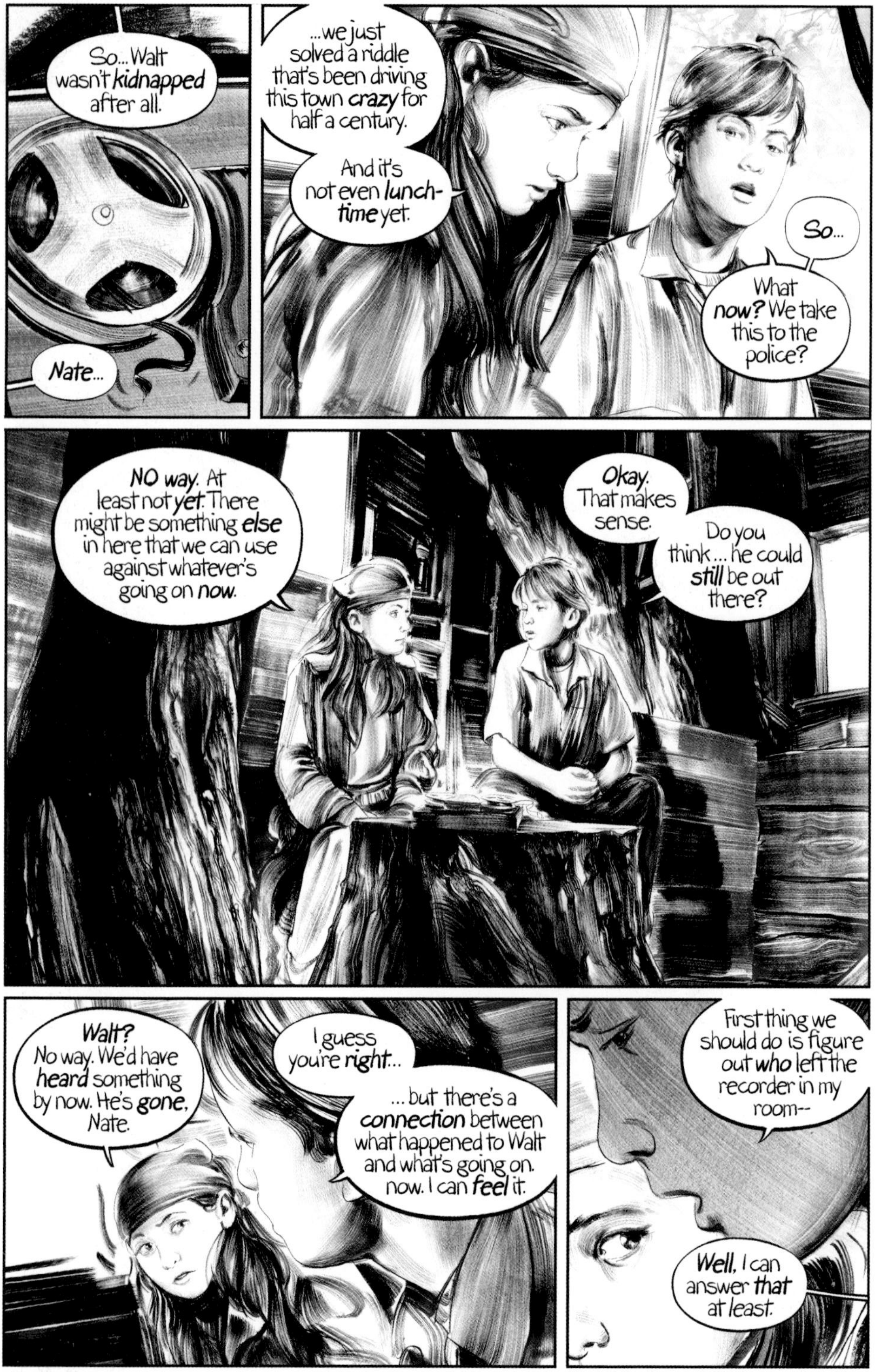
So... Walt wasn't kidnapped after all.
Nate...
...we just solved a riddle that's been driving this town crazy for half a century.
And it's not even lunch-time yet.
So...
What now? We take this to the police?
NO way. At least not yet. There might be something else in here that we can use against whatever's going on now.
Okay. That makes sense.
Do you think... he could still be out there?
Walt? No way. We'd have heard something by now. He's gone, Nate.
I guess you're right...
... but there's a connection between what happened to Walt and what's going on. now. I can feel it.
First thing we should do is figure out who left the recorder in my room--
Well, I can answer that at least.

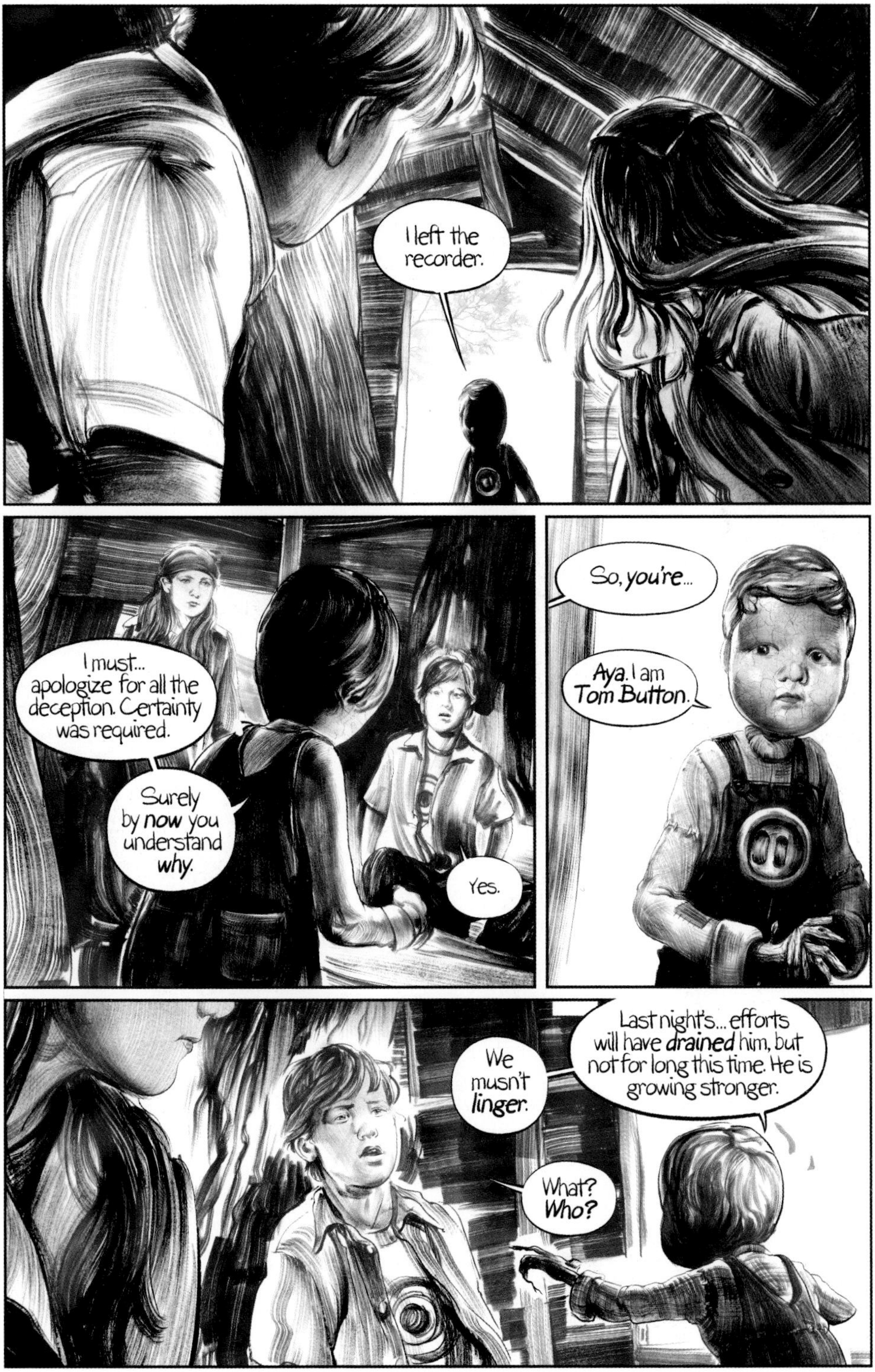
I left the recorder.
I must... apologize for all the deception. Certainty was required.
Surely by now you understand why.
Yes.
So, you're...
Aya. I am Tom Button.
We musn't linger.
Last night's... efforts will have drained him, but not for long this time. He is growing stronger.
What? Who?

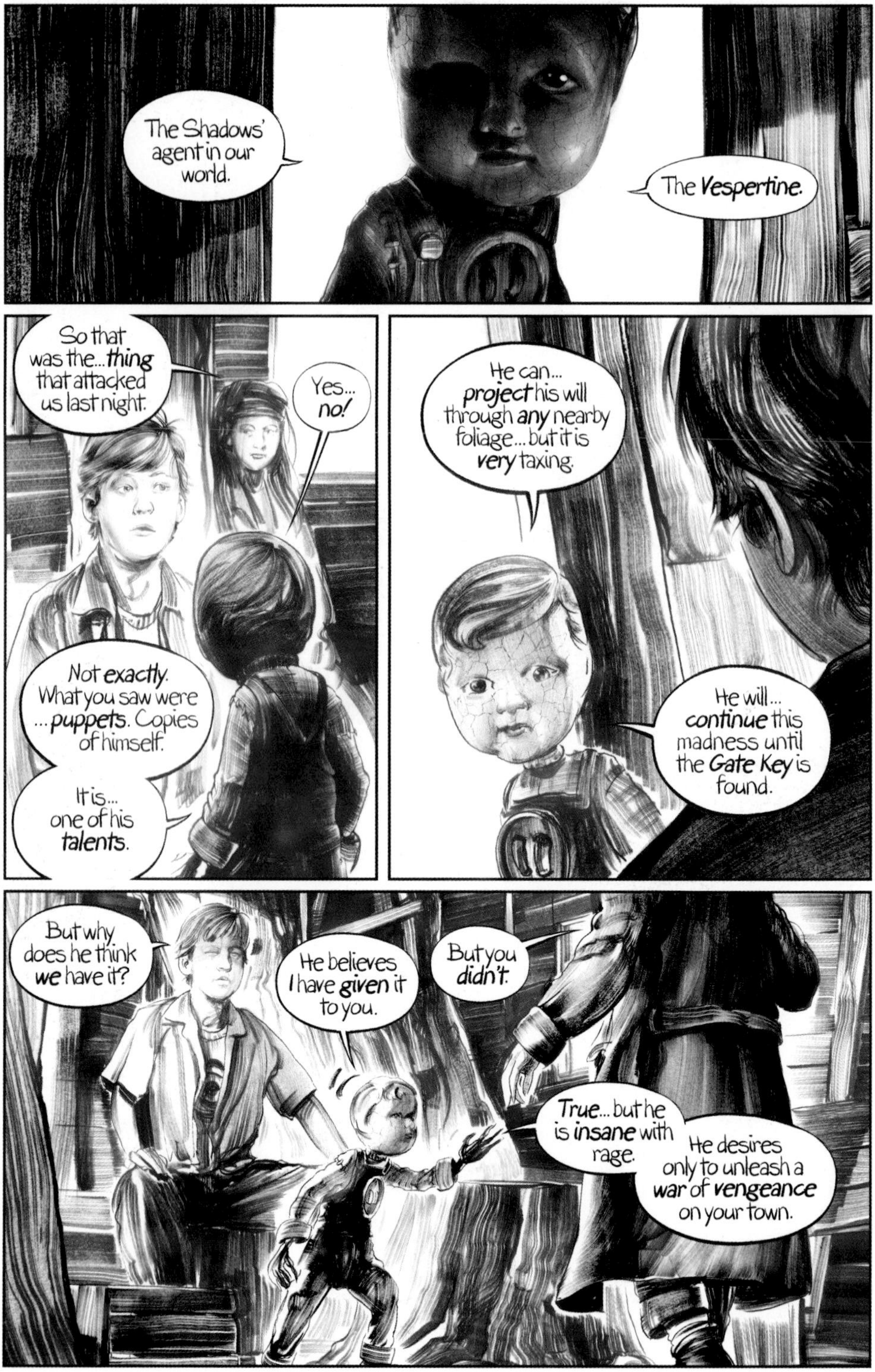
The Shadows' agent in our world.
The *Vespertine.*
So that was the... *thing* that attacked us last night.
Yes... *no!*
Not *exactly*. What you saw were ... *puppets*. Copies of himself.
It is... one of his *talents*.
He can... *project* his will through *any* nearby foliage... but it is *very* taxing.
He will... *continue* this madness until the *Gate Key* is found.
But why does he think *we* have it?
He believes I have *given* it to you.
But you *didn't*.
True... but he is *insane* with rage.
He desires only to unleash a *war* of *vengeance* on your town.

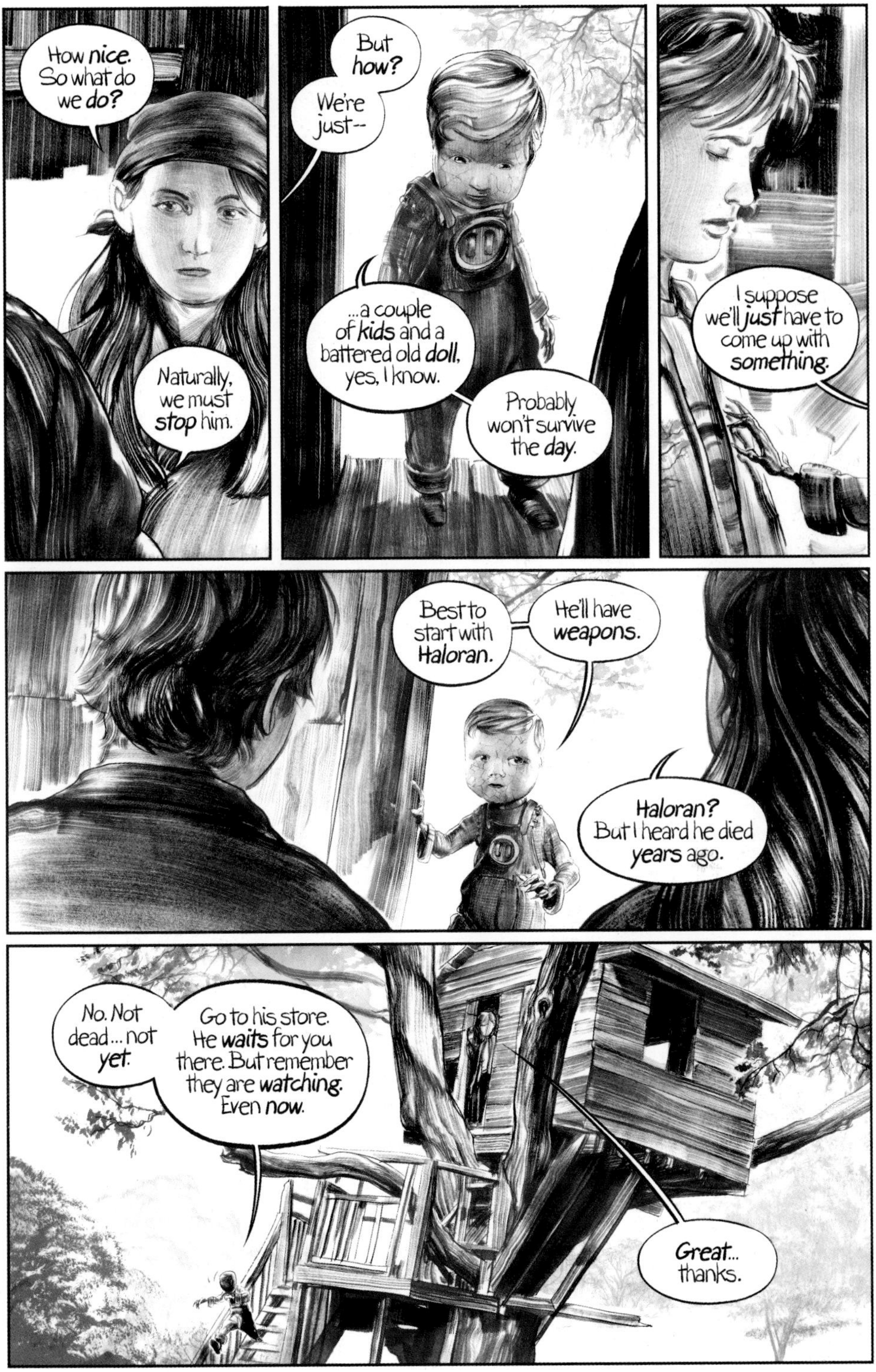
How nice. So what do we do?
Naturally, we must stop him.
But how?
We're just--
...a couple of kids and a battered old doll, yes, I know.
Probably won't survive the day.
I suppose we'll just have to come up with something.
Best to start with Haloran.
He'll have weapons.
Haloran? But I heard he died years ago.
No. Not dead... not yet.
Go to his store. He waits for you there. But remember they are watching. Even now.
Great... thanks.

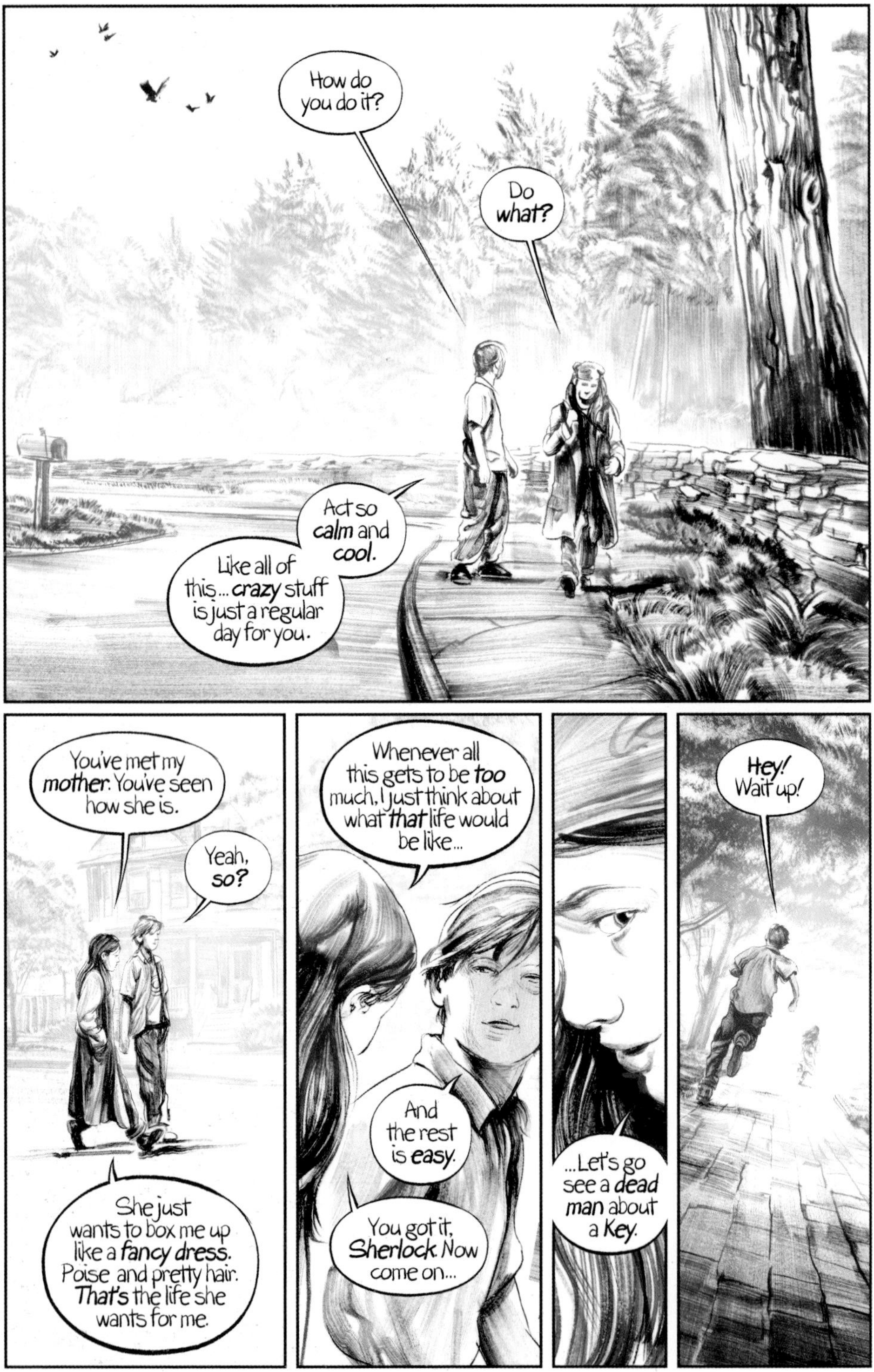
How do you do it?
Do what?
Act so calm and cool.
Like all of this... crazy stuff is just a regular day for you.
You've met my mother. You've seen how she is.
Yeah, so?
She just wants to box me up like a fancy dress. Poise and pretty hair. That's the life she wants for me.
Whenever all this gets to be too much, I just think about what that life would be like...
And the rest is easy.
You got it, Sherlock. Now come on...
...Let's go see a dead man about a Key.
Hey! Wait up!

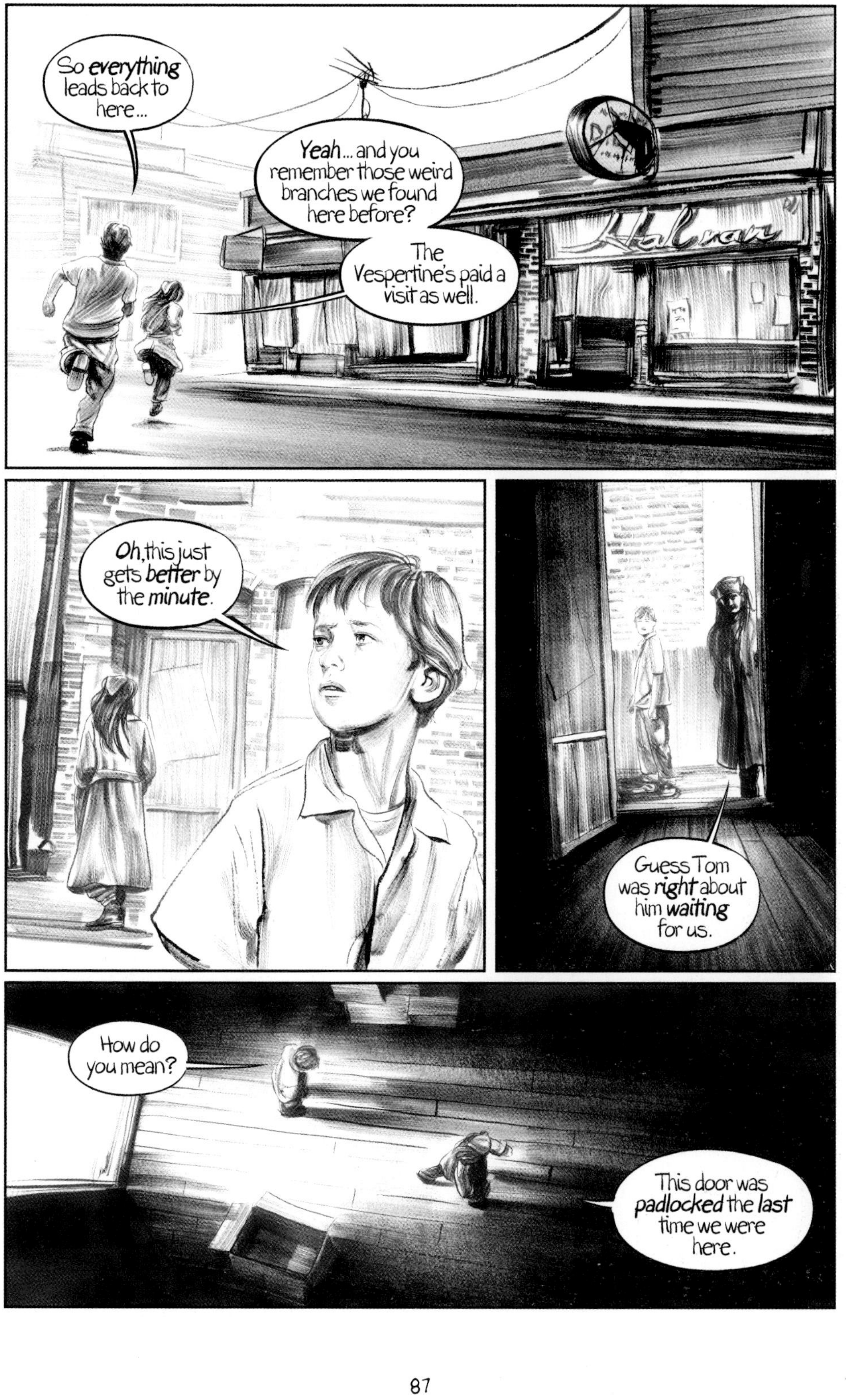
So everything leads back to here...
Yeah... and you remember those weird branches we found here before?
The Vespertine's paid a visit as well.
Oh, this just gets better by the minute.
Guess Tom was right about him waiting for us.
How do you mean?
This door was padlocked the last time we were here.

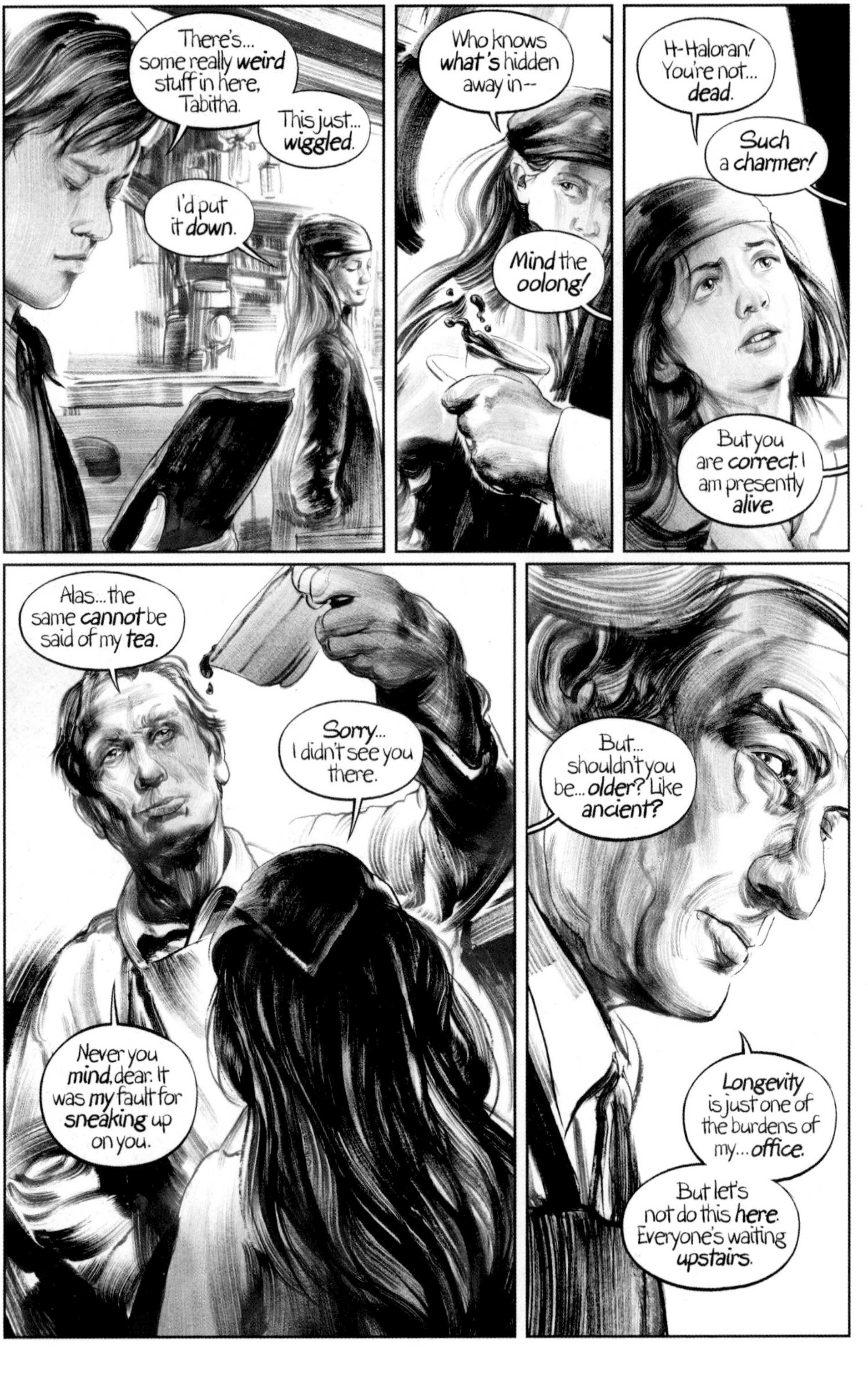
There's... some really weird stuff in here, Tabitha.
This just... wiggled.
I'd put it down.
Who knows what's hidden away in--
Mind the oolong!
H-Haloran! You're not... dead.
Such a charmer!
But you are correct. I am presently alive.
Alas... the same cannot be said of my tea.
Sorry... I didn't see you there.
Never you mind, dear. It was my fault for sneaking up on you.
But... shouldn't you be... older? Like ancient?
Longevity is just one of the burdens of my... office.
But let's not do this here. Everyone's waiting upstairs.

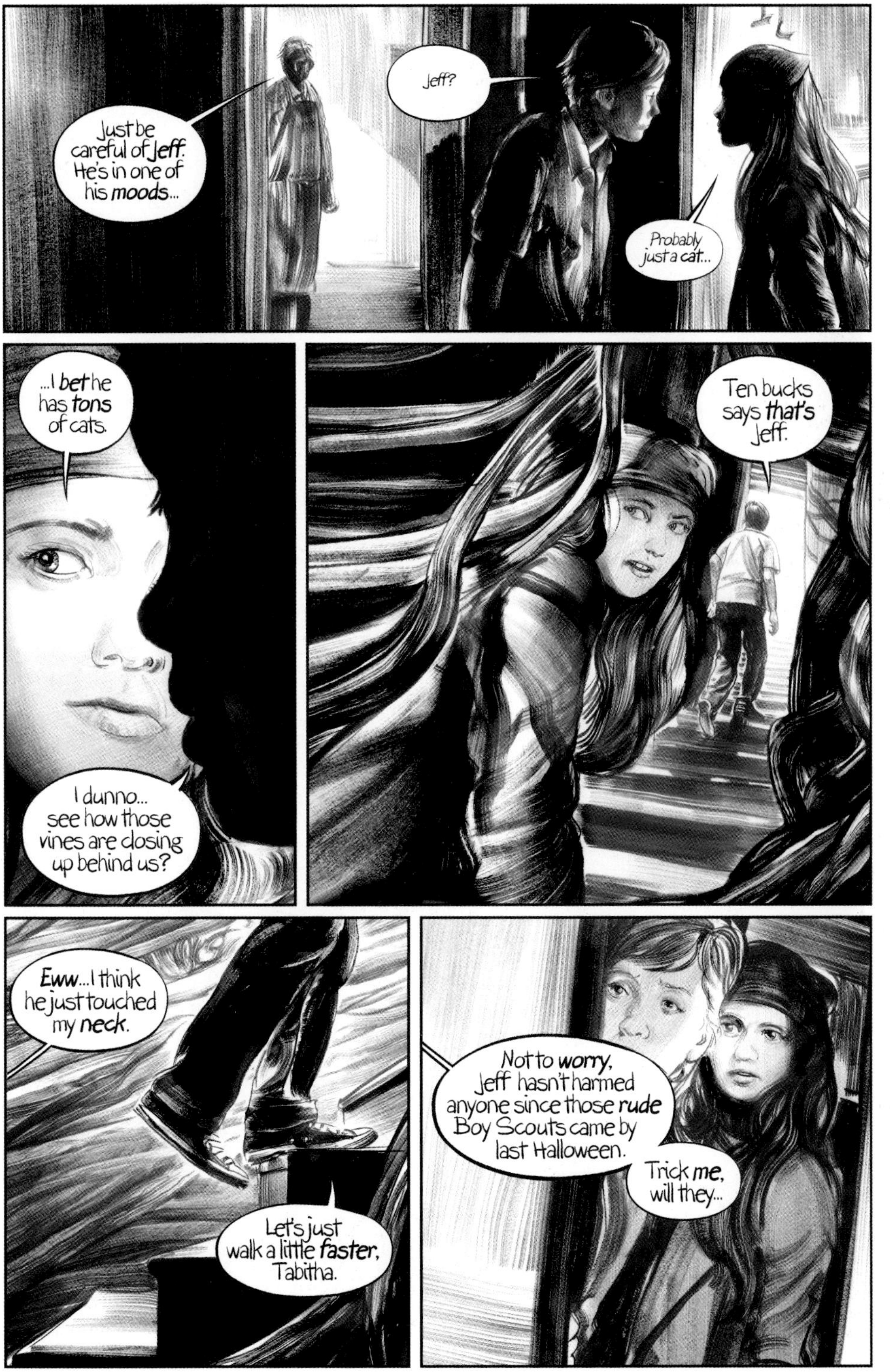
Just be careful of Jeff. He's in one of his moods...
Jeff?
Probably just a cat...
...I bet he has tons of cats.
I dunno... see how those vines are closing up behind us?
Ten bucks says that's Jeff.
Eww...I think he just touched my neck.
Let's just walk a little faster, Tabitha.
Not to worry, Jeff hasn't harmed anyone since those rude Boy Scouts came by last Halloween.
Trick me, will they...

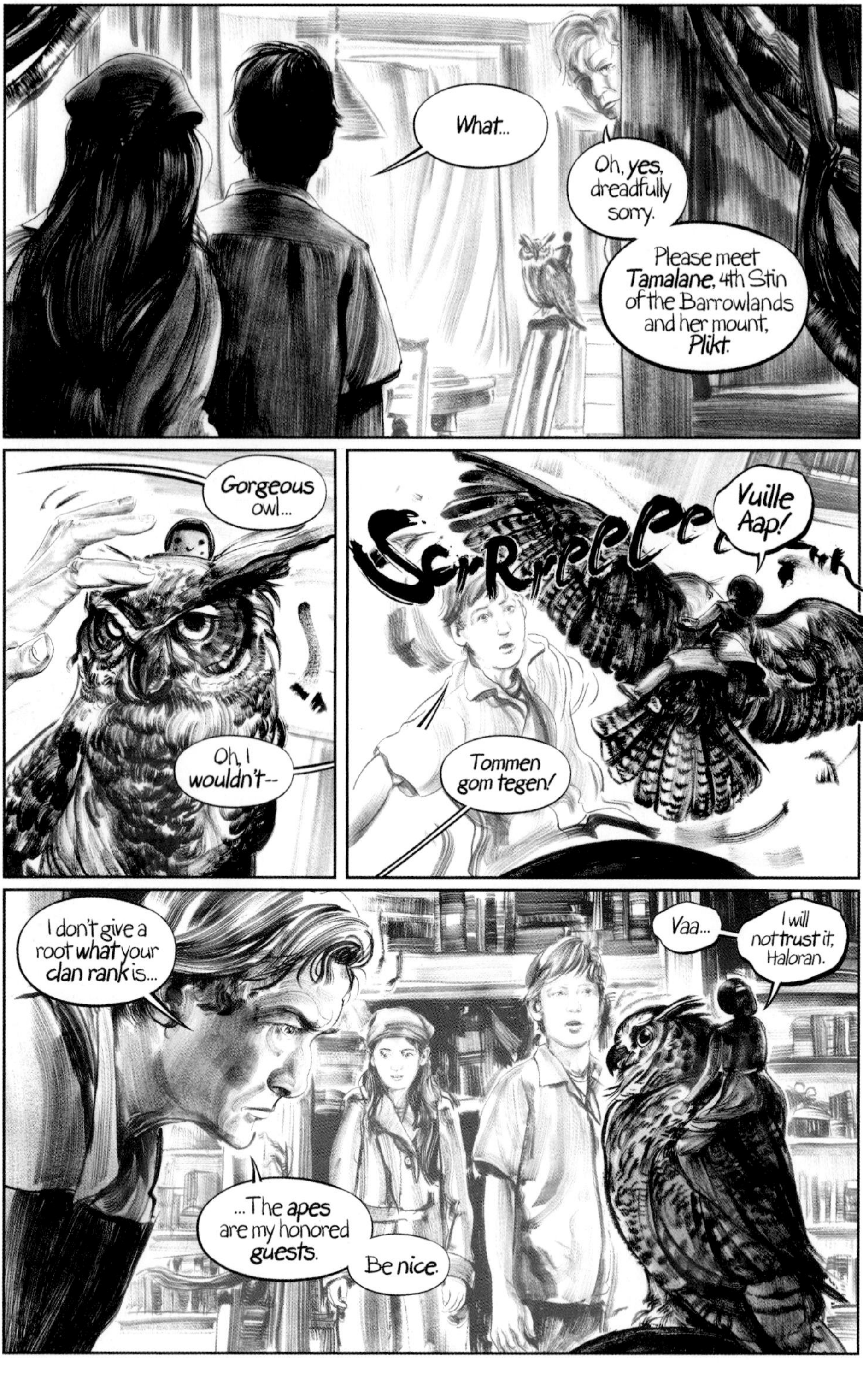
What...
Oh, yes, dreadfully sorry.
Please meet Tamalane, 4th Stin of the Barrowlands and her mount, Plikt.
Gorgeous owl...
Oh, I wouldn't--
Vuille Aap!
Tommen gom tegen!
I don't give a root what your clan rank is...
...The apes are my honored guests.
Be nice.
Vaa...
I will not trust it, Haloran.

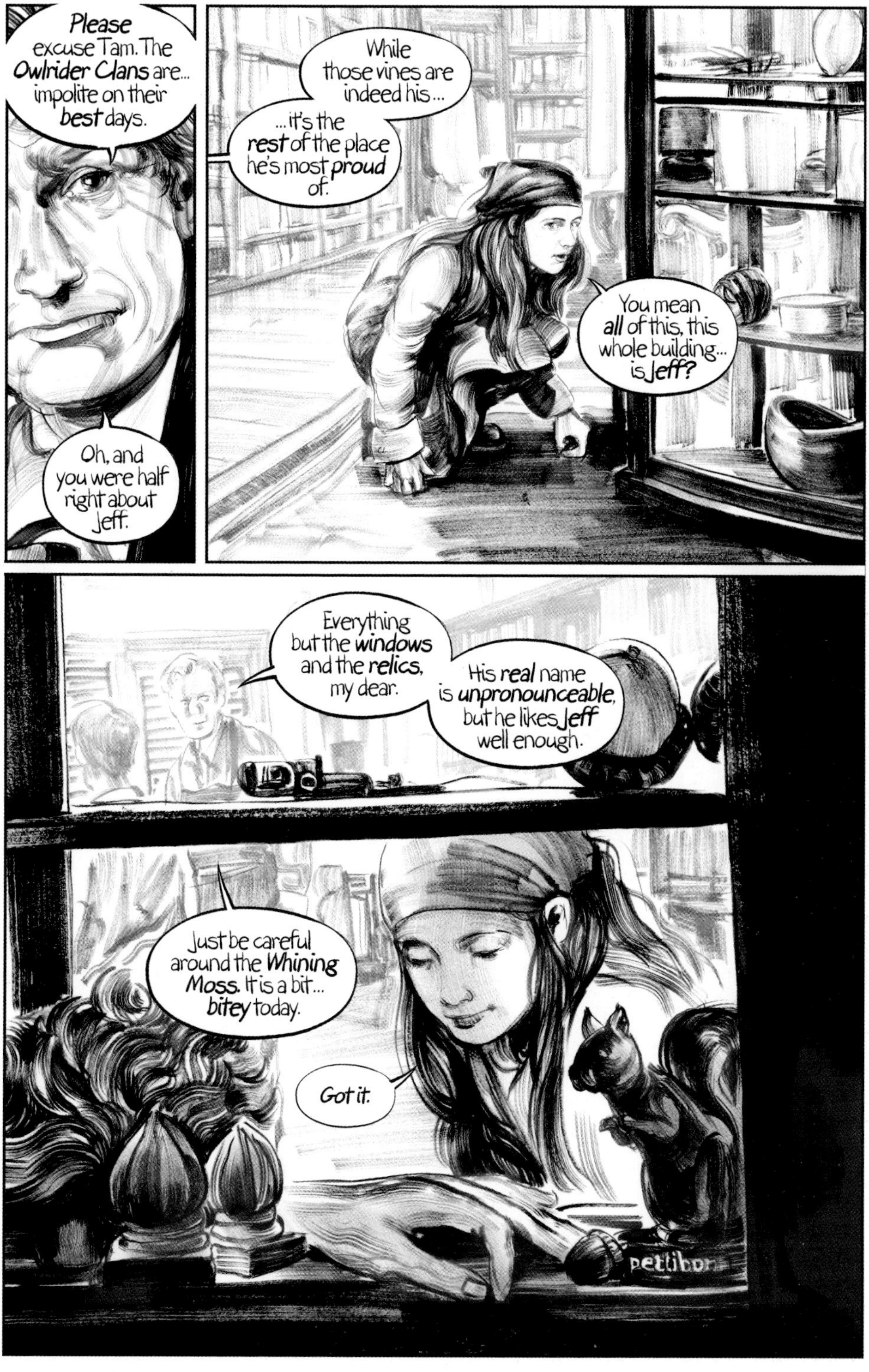

Please excuse Tam. The Owlrider Clans are... impolite on their best days.
While those vines are indeed his...
...it's the rest of the place he's most proud of.
You mean all of this, this whole building... is Jeff?
Oh, and you were half right about Jeff.
Everything but the windows and the relics, my dear.
His real name is unpronounceable, but he likes Jeff well enough.
Just be careful around the Whining Moss. It is a bit... bitey today.
Got it.
pettibon

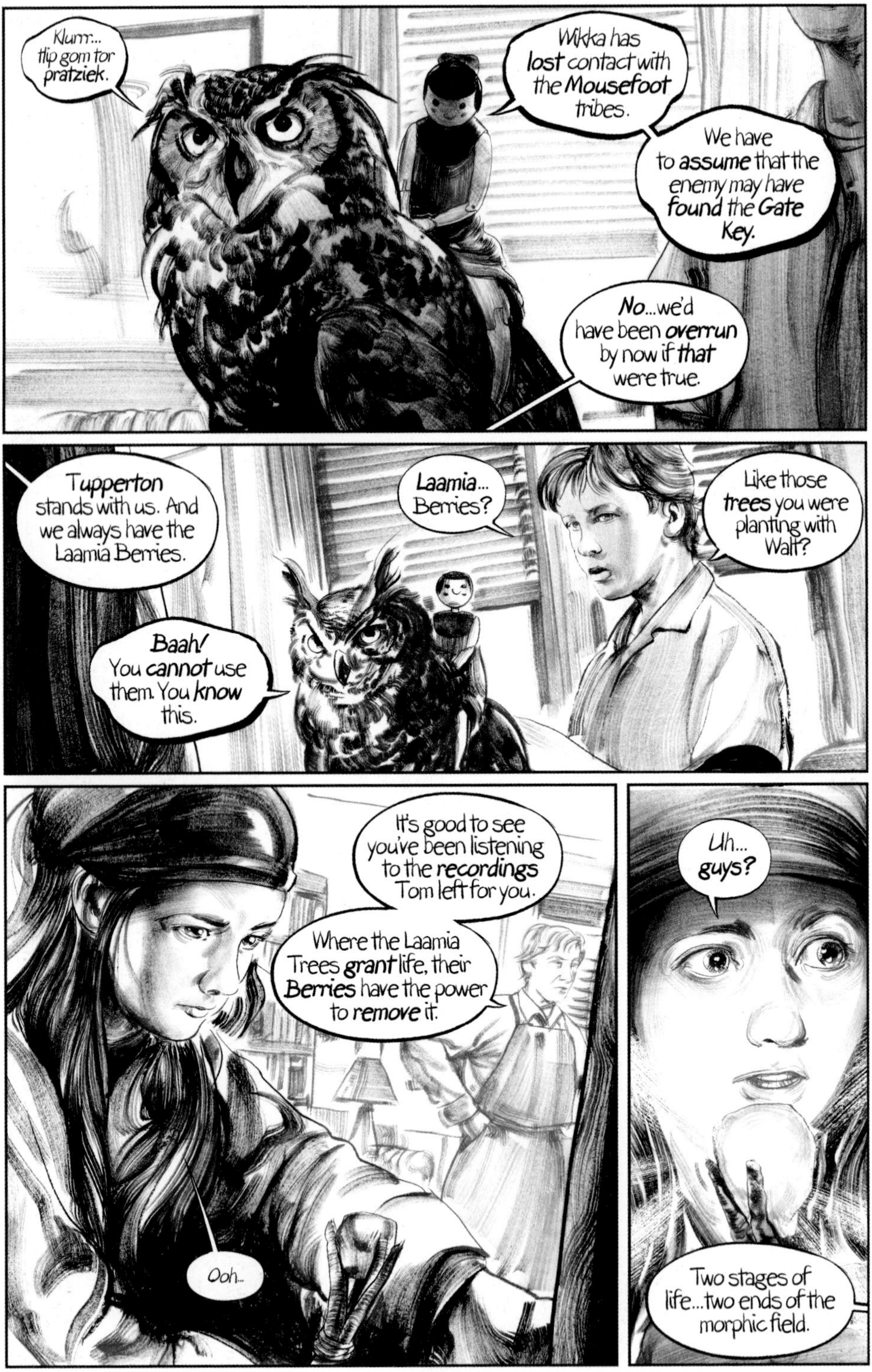
Klurrr... tlip gom tor pratziek.
Wikka has lost contact with the Mousefoot tribes.
We have to assume that the enemy may have found the Gate Key.
No...we'd have been overrun by now if that were true.
Tupperton stands with us. And we always have the Laamia Berries.
Baah! You cannot use them. You know this.
Laamia... Berries?
Like those trees you were planting with Walt?
It's good to see you've been listening to the recordings Tom left for you.
Where the Laamia Trees grant life, their Berries have the power to remove it.
Ooh...
Uh... guys?
Two stages of life...two ends of the morphic field.

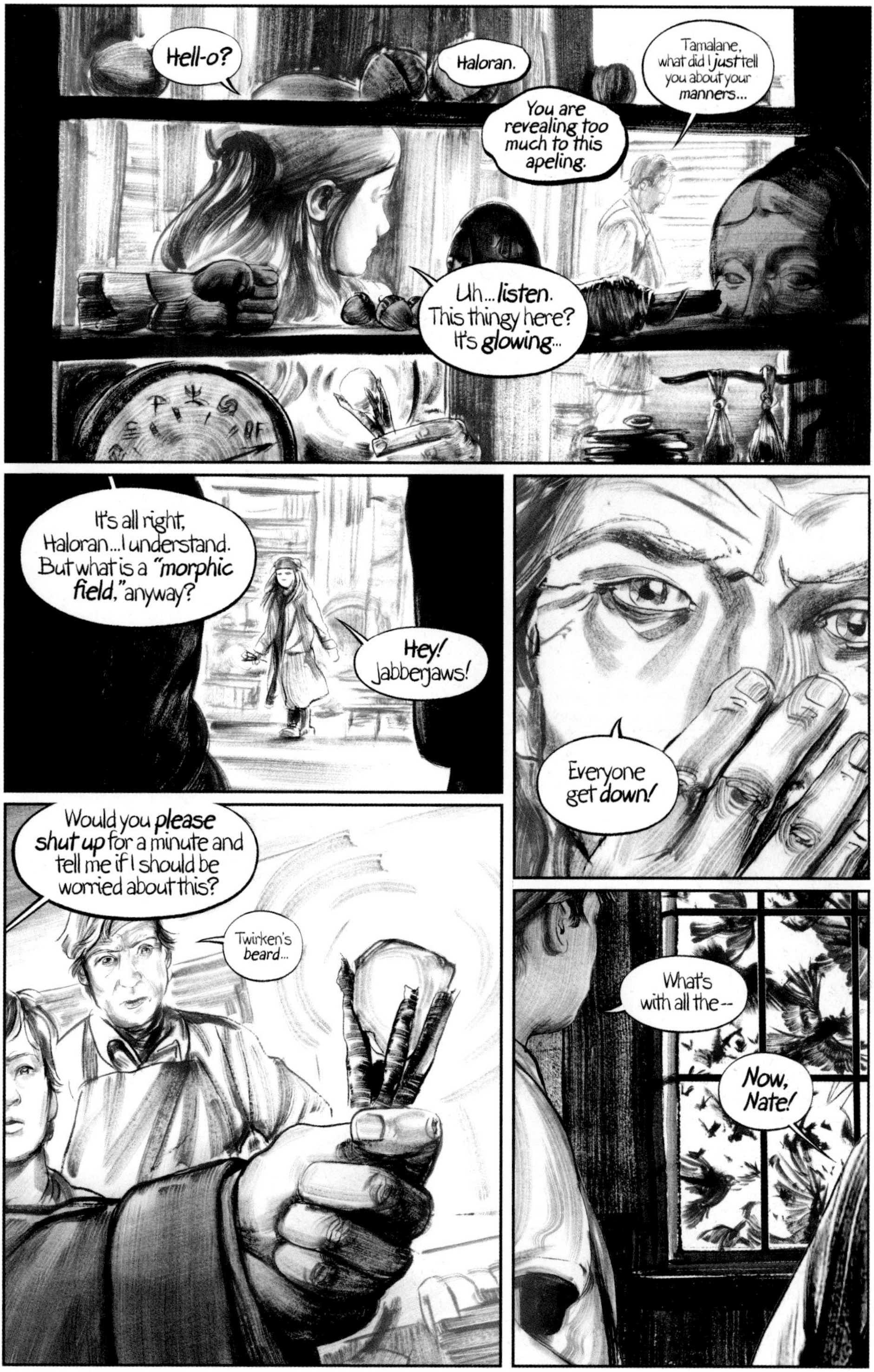
Hell-o?
Haloran.
Tamalane, what did I just tell you about your manners...
You are revealing too much to this apeling.
Uh... listen. This thingy here? It's glowing...
It's all right, Haloran... I understand. But what is a "morphic field," anyway?
Hey! Jabberjaws!
Everyone get down!
Would you please shut up for a minute and tell me if I should be worried about this?
Twirken's beard...
What's with all the --
Now, Nate!

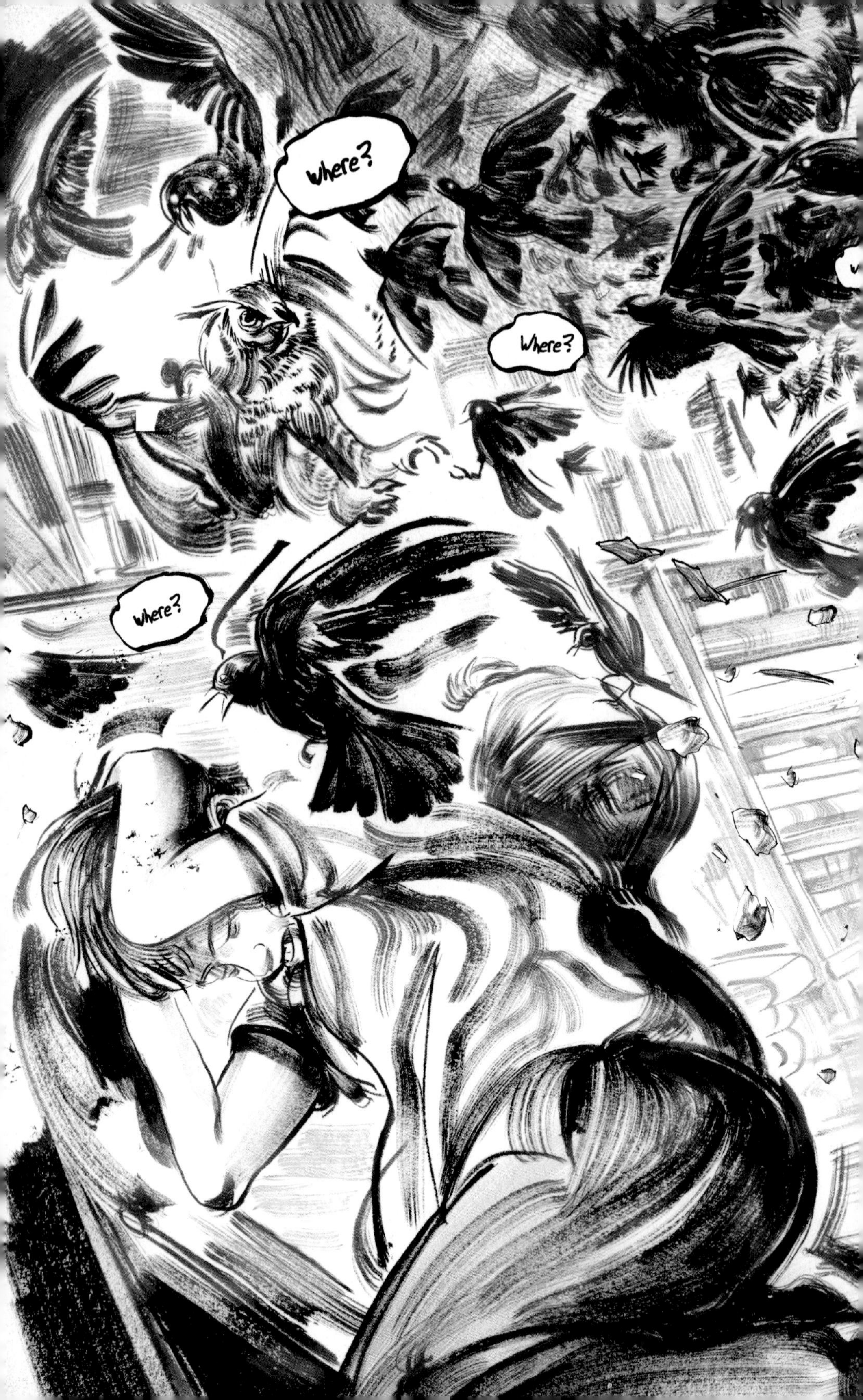
where?
Where?
where?

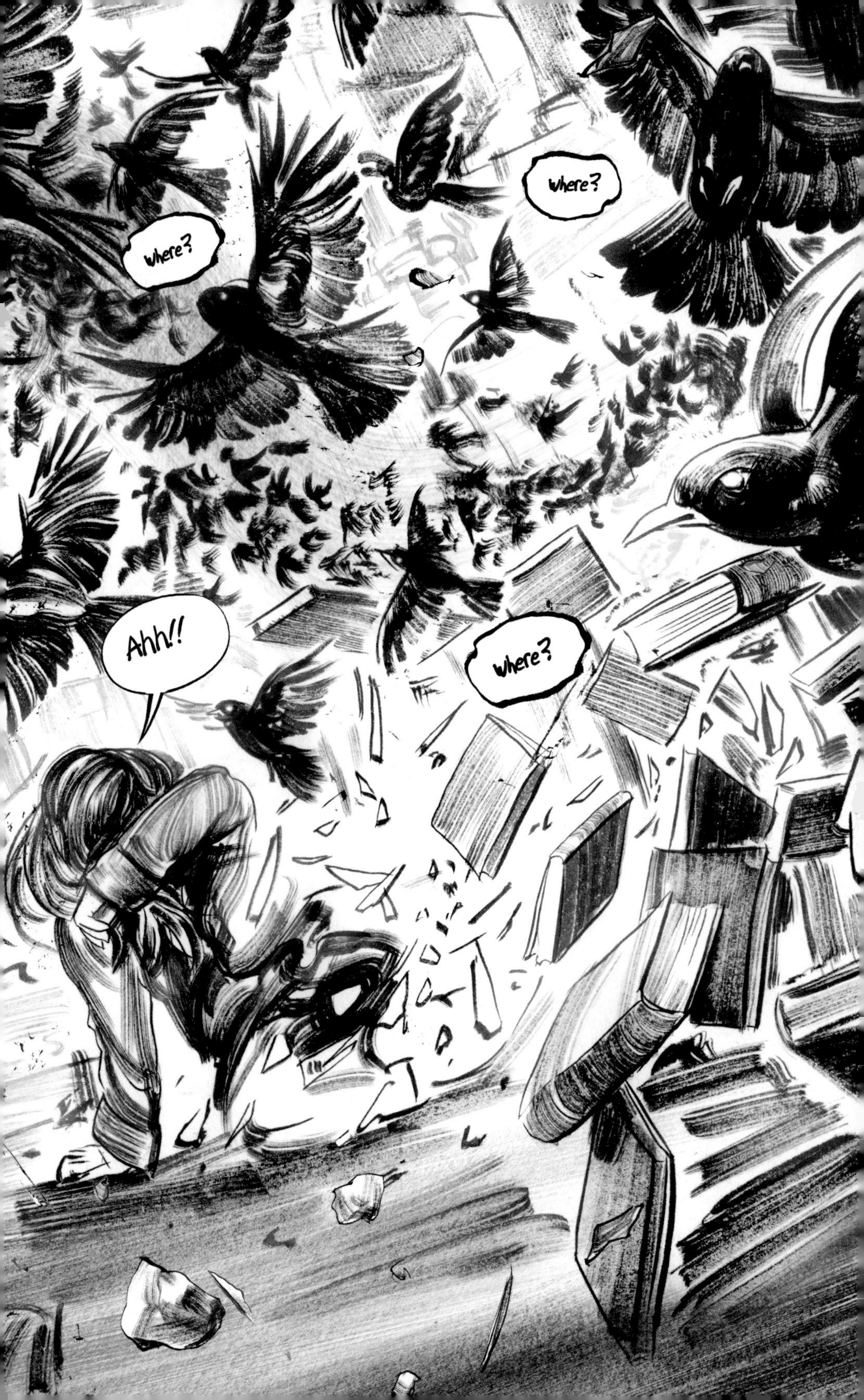
where?
where?
Ahh!!
where?

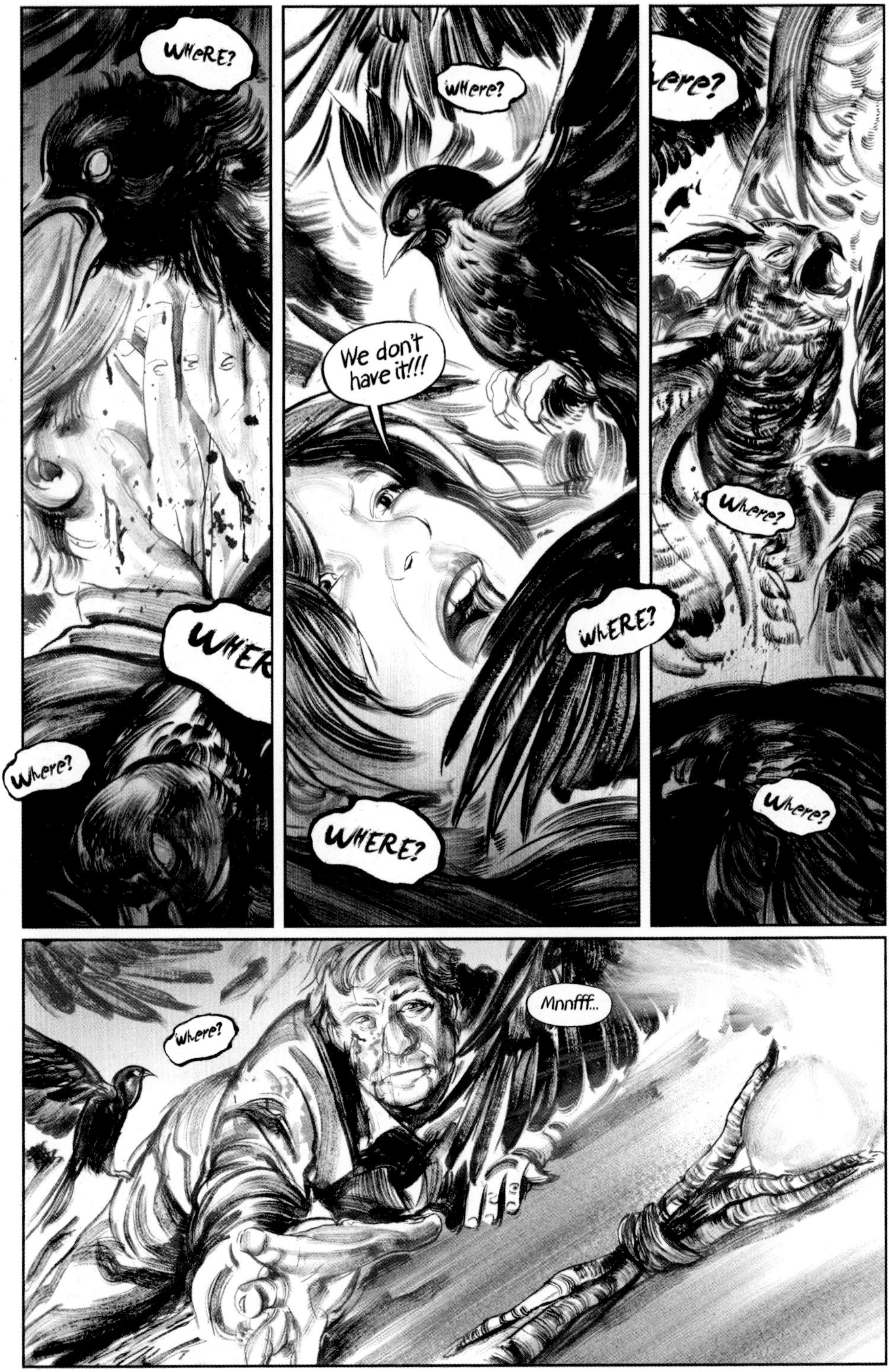
WHERE?
WHER
Where?
where?
We don't have it!!!
WHERE?
WHERE?
ere?
Where?
Where?
where?
Mnnfff...

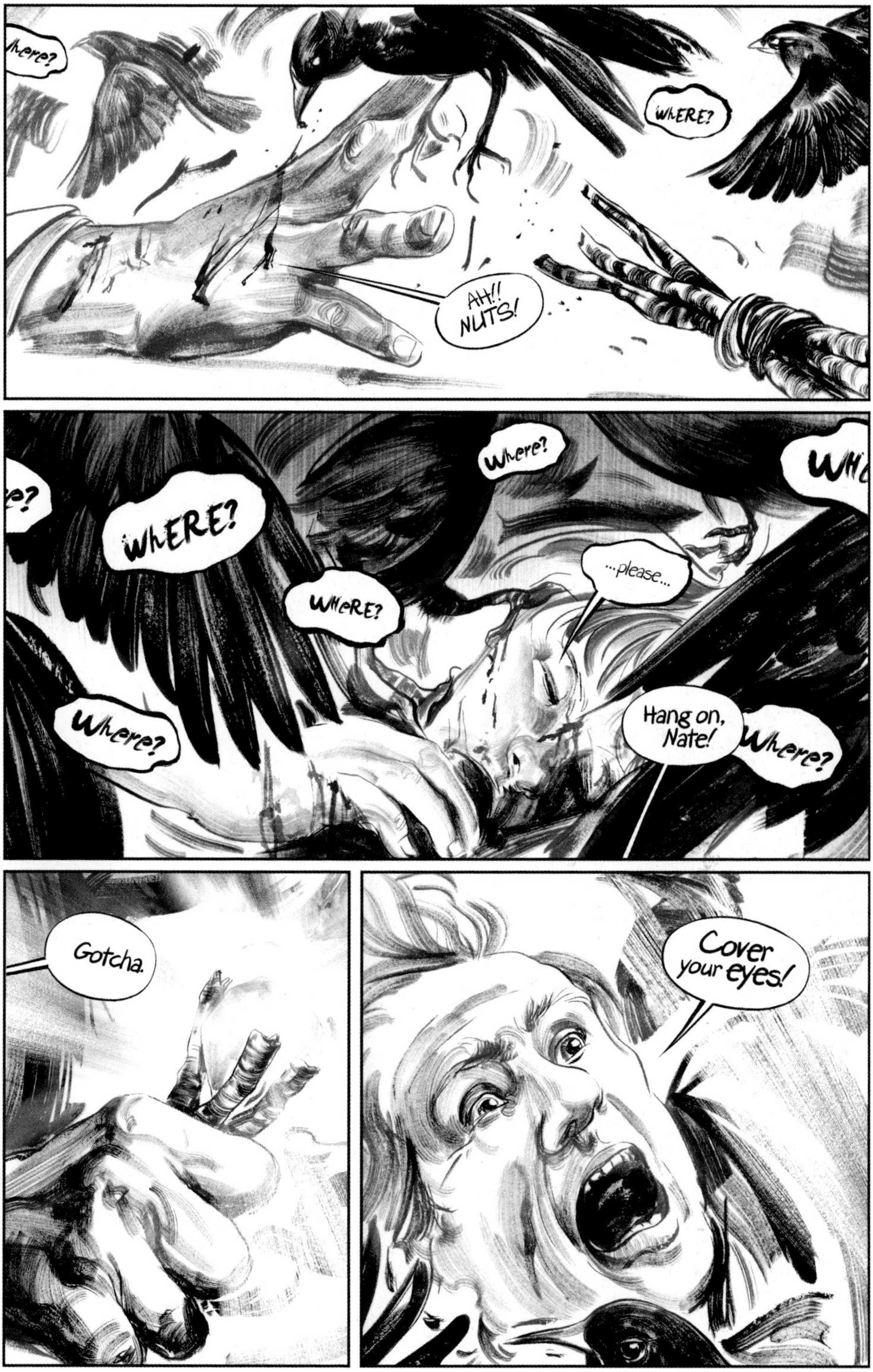

Where?
WHERE?
AH!! NUTS!
Where?
WHERE?
Where?
...please...
WHERE?
Where?
Hang on, Nate!
Where?
Gotcha.
Cover your eyes!

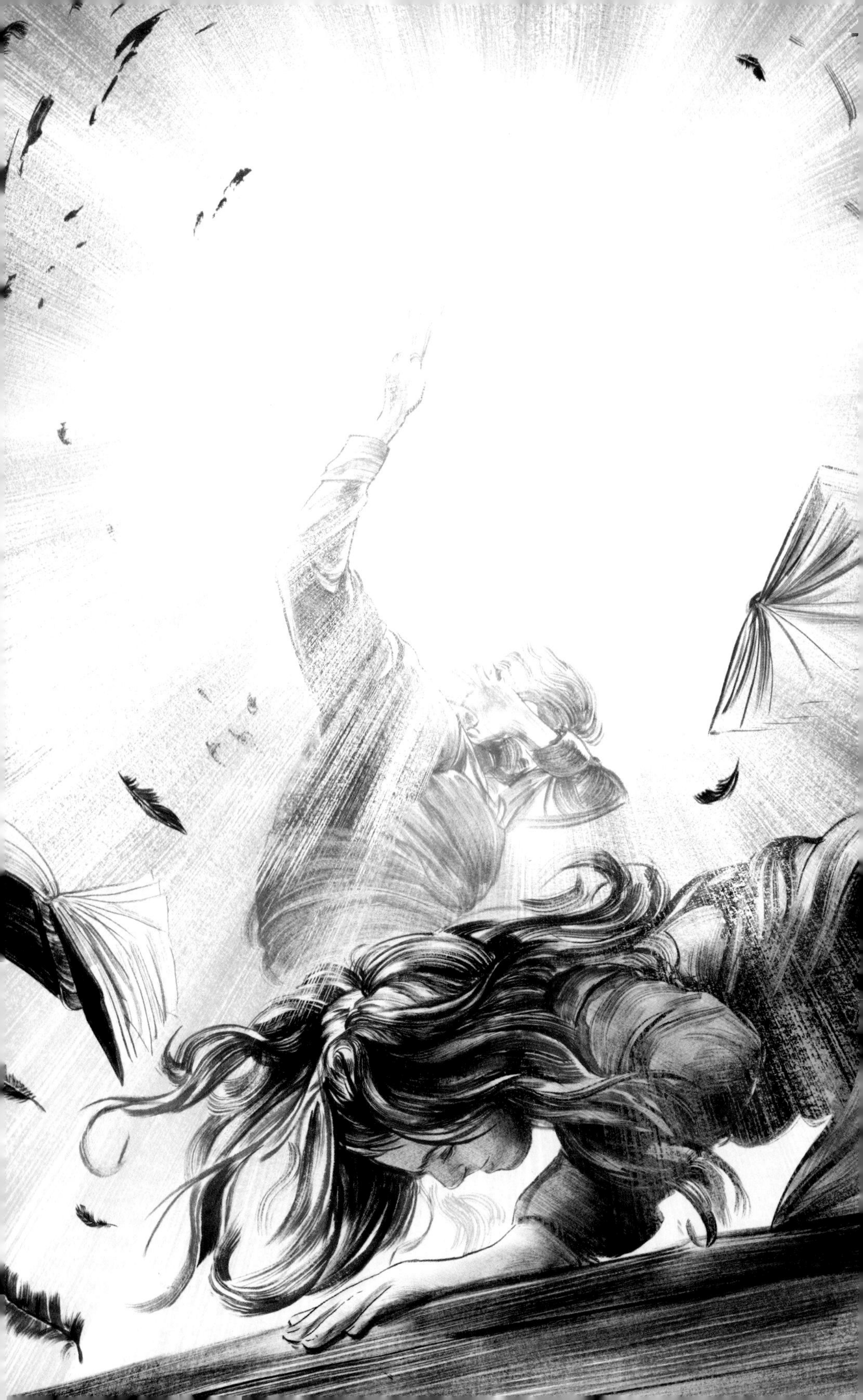

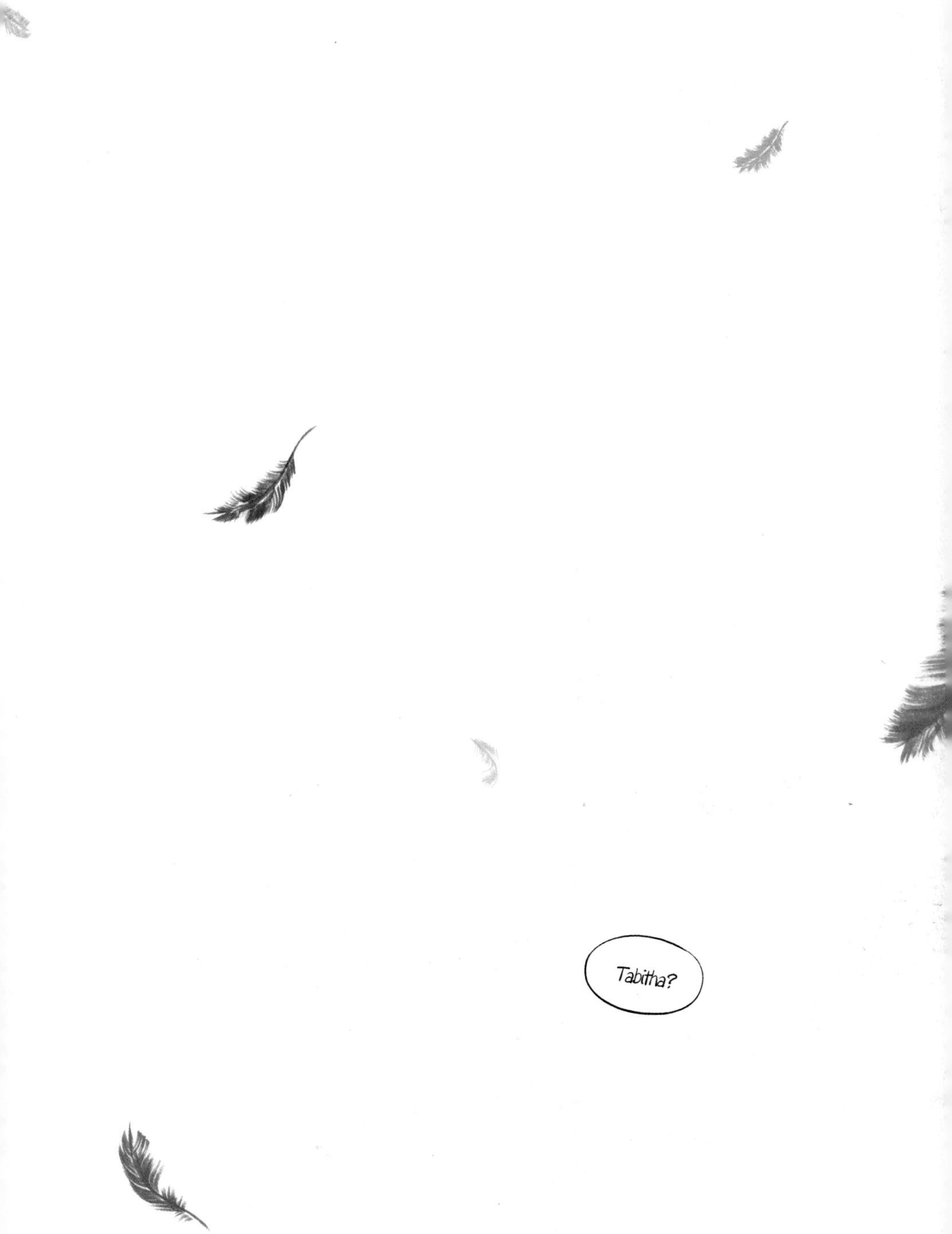
Tabitha?

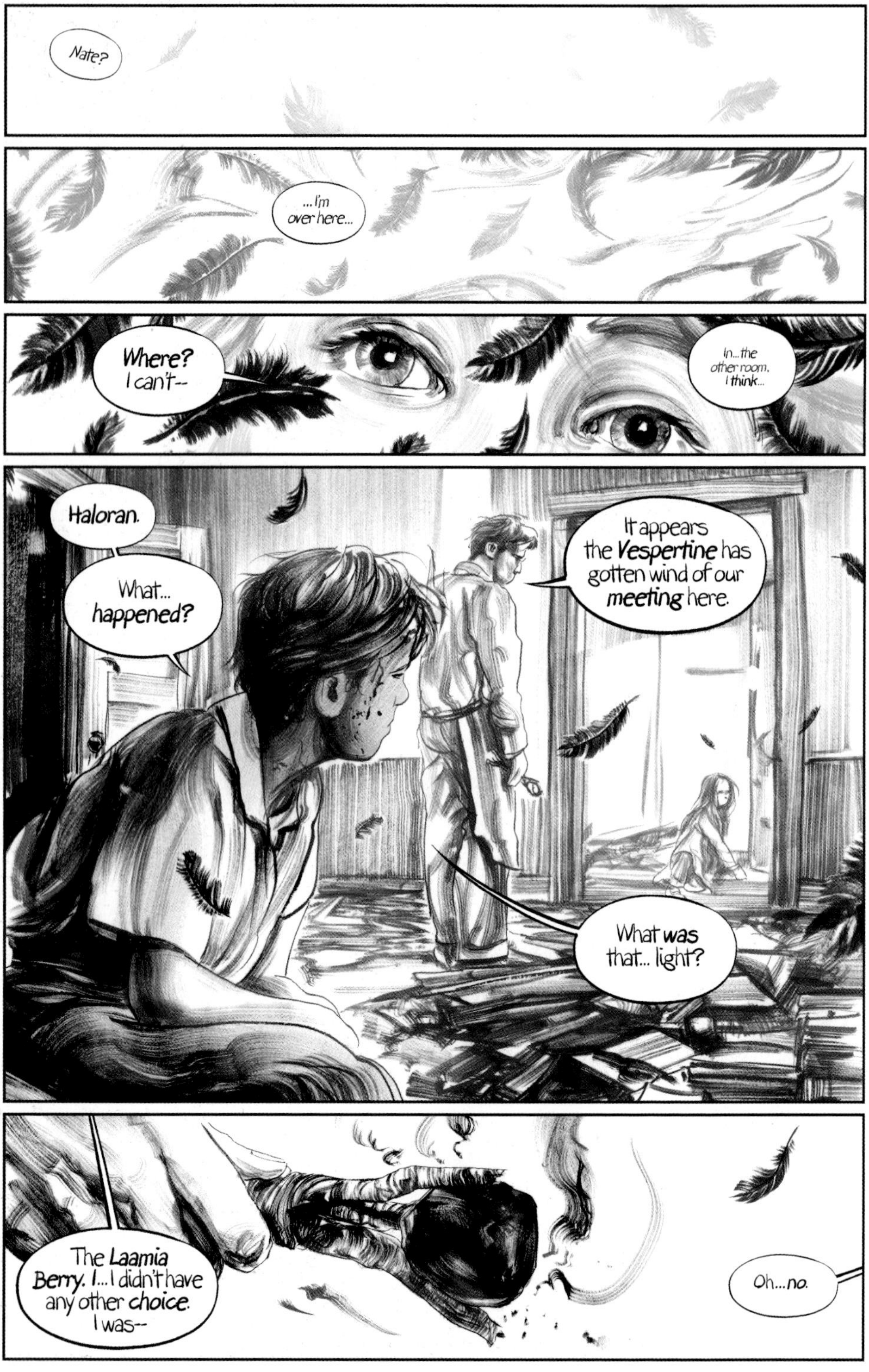
Nate?
...I'm over here...
Where? I can't--
In...the other room. I think...
Haloran.
What... happened?
It appears the Vespertine has gotten wind of our meeting here.
What was that... light?
The Laamia Berry. I...I didn't have any other choice. I was--
Oh...no.

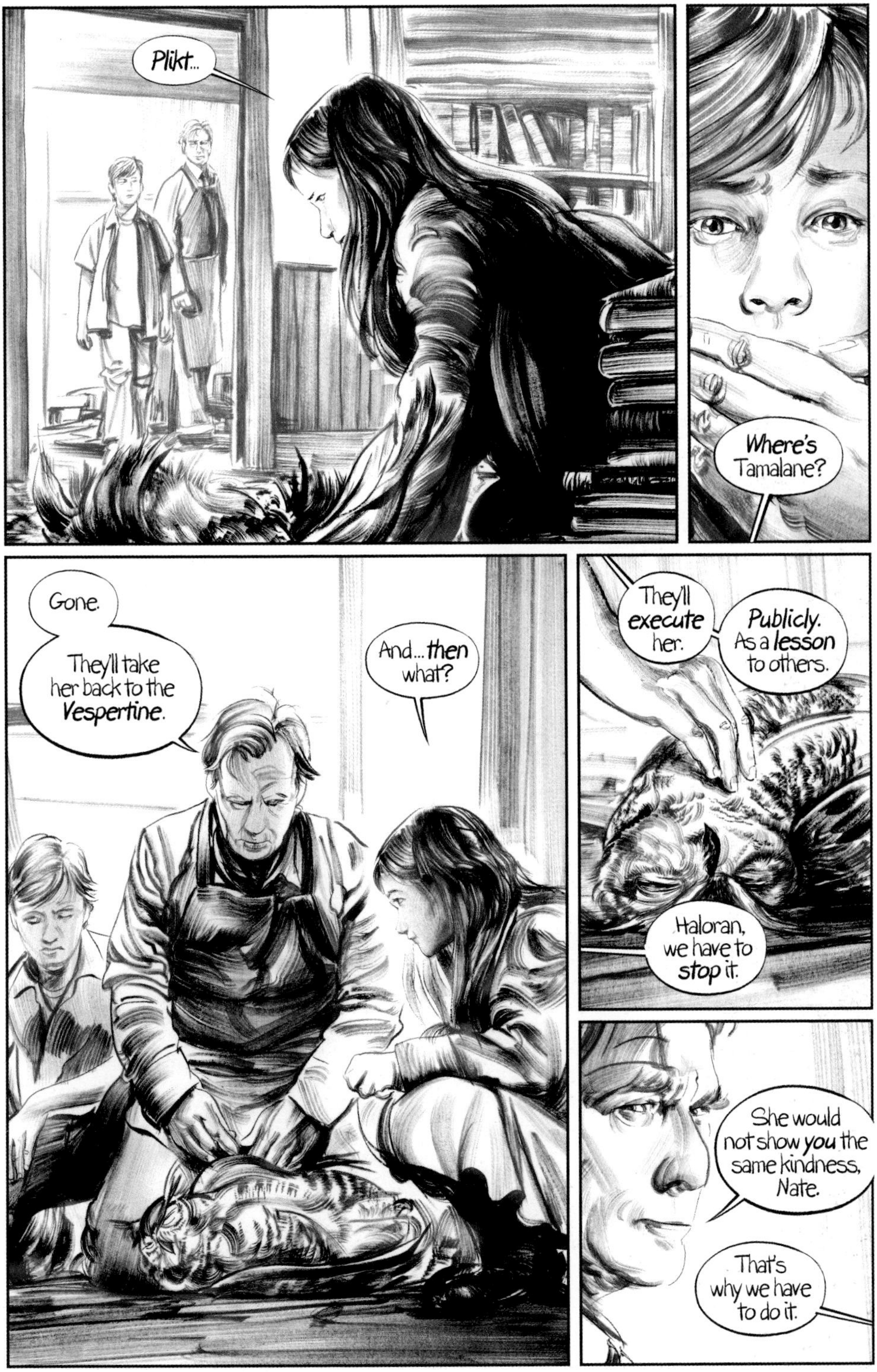

Plikt...
Where's Tamalane?
Gone.
They'll take her back to the Vespertine.
And... then what?
They'll execute her.
Publicly. As a lesson to others.
Haloran, we have to stop it.
She would not show you the same kindness, Nate.
That's why we have to do it.

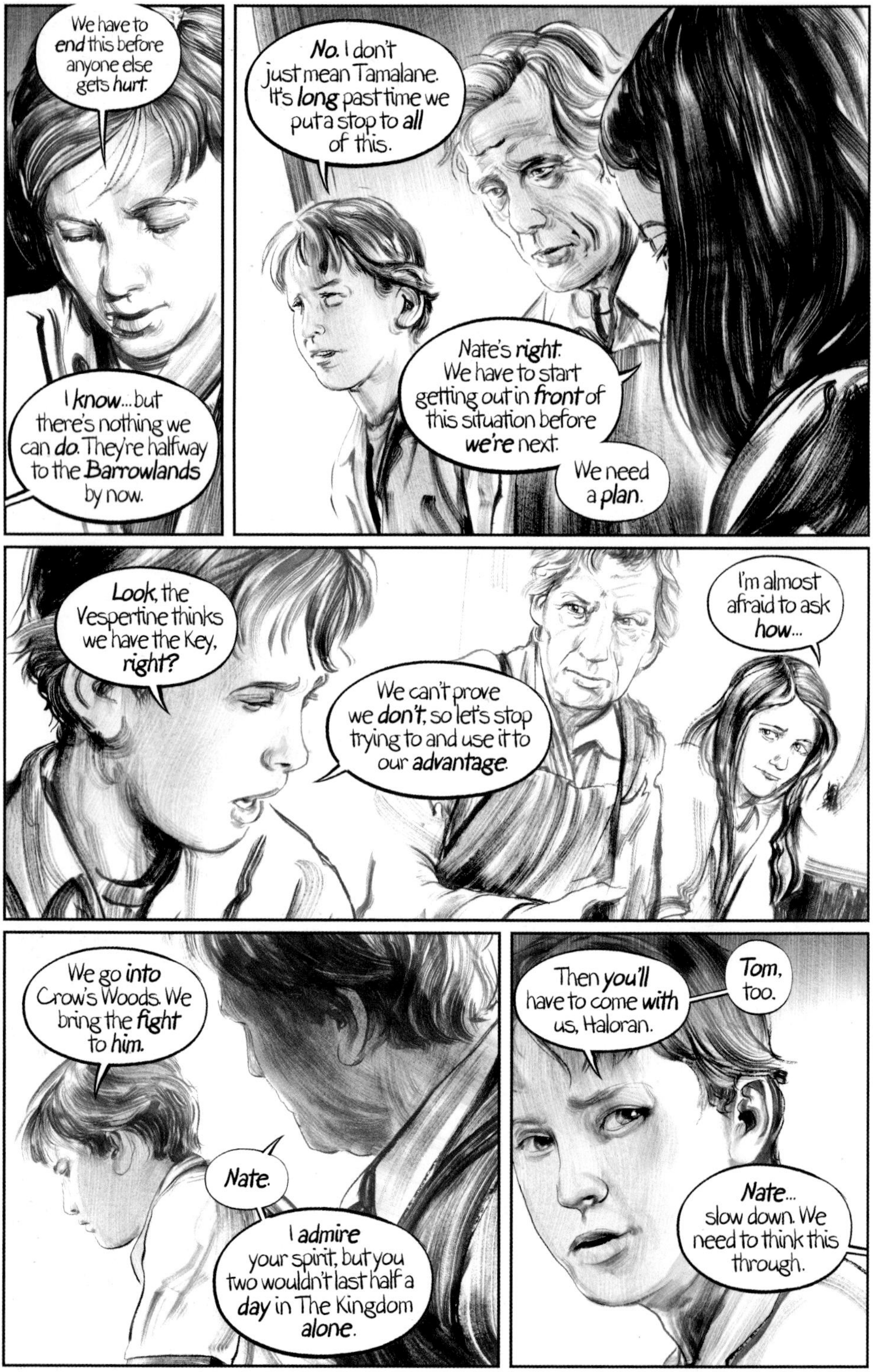
We have to end this before anyone else gets hurt.
No. I don't just mean Tamalane. It's long past time we put a stop to all of this.
I know... but there's nothing we can do. They're halfway to the Barrowlands by now.
Nate's right. We have to start getting out in front of this situation before we're next.
We need a plan.
Look, the Vespertine thinks we have the Key, right?
We can't prove we don't, so let's stop trying to and use it to our advantage.
I'm almost afraid to ask how...
We go into Crow's Woods. We bring the fight to him.
Nate.
I admire your spirit, but you two wouldn't last half a day in The Kingdom alone.
Then you'll have to come with us, Haloran.
Tom, too.
Nate... slow down. We need to think this through.

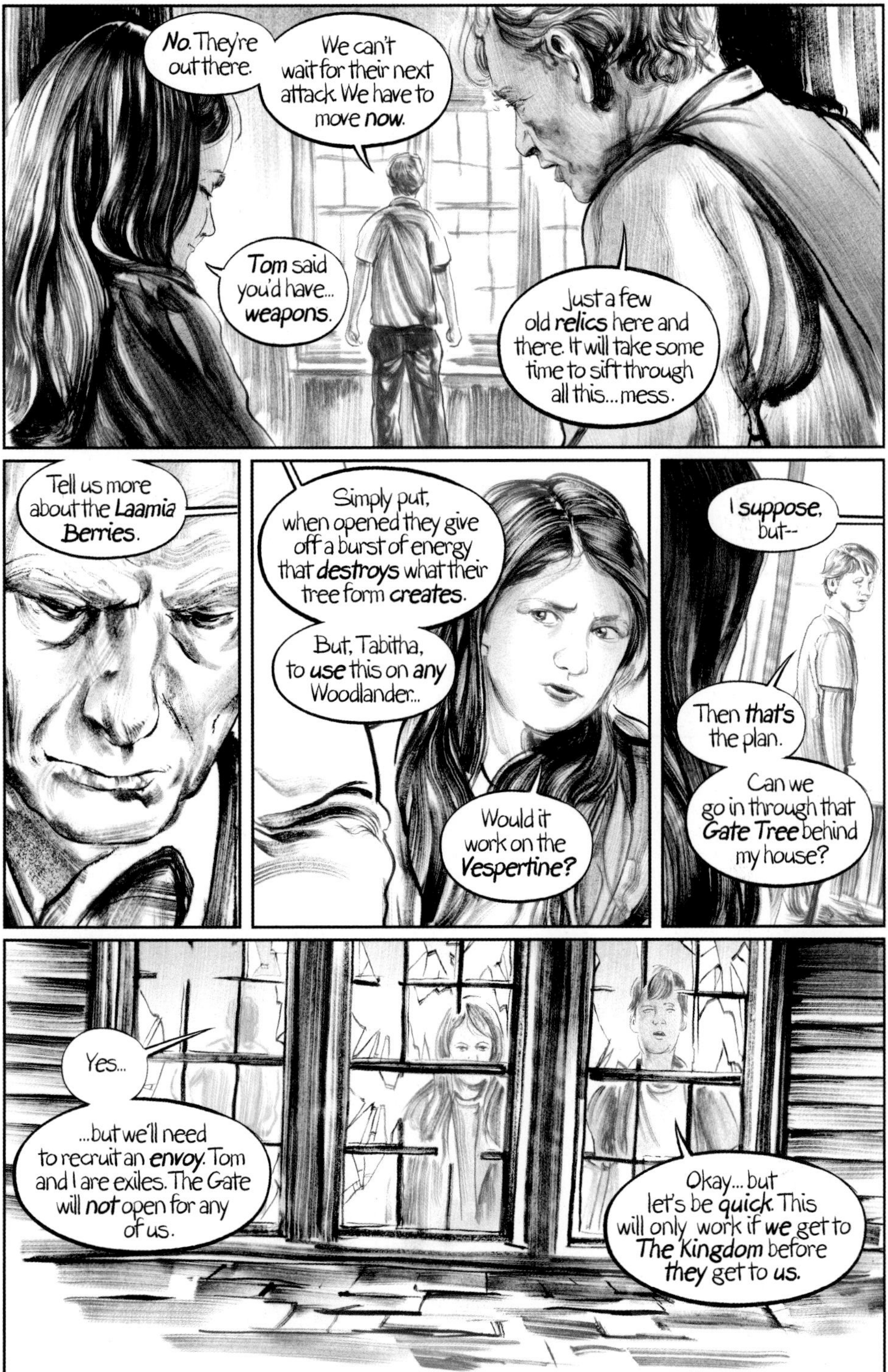
No. They're out there.
We can't wait for their next attack. We have to move now.
Tom said you'd have... weapons.
Just a few old relics here and there. It will take some time to sift through all this... mess.
Tell us more about the Laamia Berries.
Simply put, when opened they give off a burst of energy that destroys what their tree form creates.
But, Tabitha, to use this on any Woodlander...
Would it work on the Vespertine?
I suppose, but--
Then that's the plan.
Can we go in through that Gate Tree behind my house?
Yes...
...but we'll need to recruit an envoy. Tom and I are exiles. The Gate will not open for any of us.
Okay... but let's be quick. This will only work if we get to The Kingdom before they get to us.

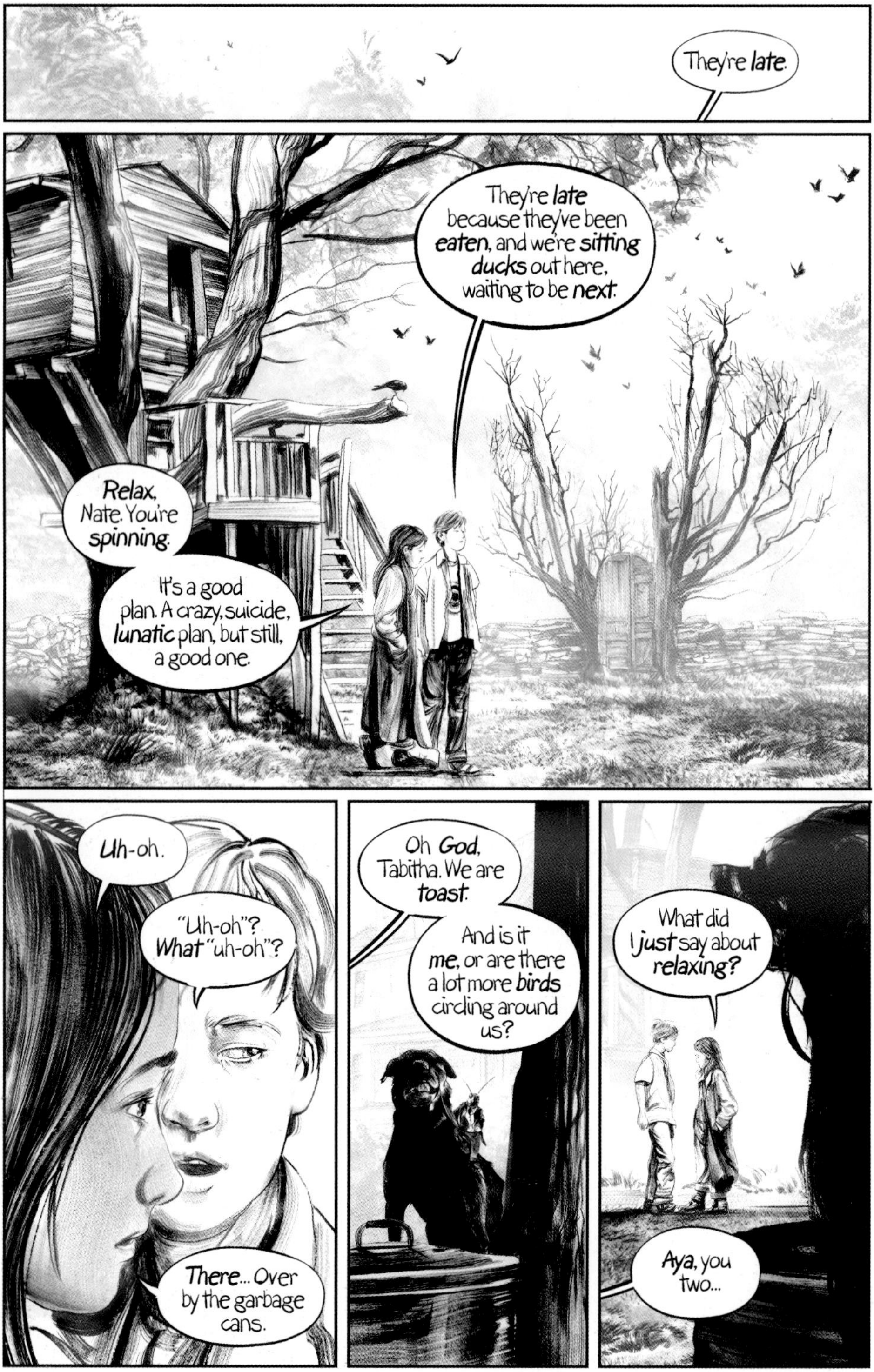
They're late.
They're late because they've been eaten, and we're sitting ducks out here, waiting to be next.
Relax, Nate. You're spinning.
It's a good plan. A crazy, suicide, lunatic plan, but still, a good one.
Uh-oh.
"Uh-oh"? What "uh-oh"?
There... Over by the garbage cans.
Oh God, Tabitha. We are toast.
And is it me, or are there a lot more birds circling around us?
What did I just say about relaxing?
Aya, you two...

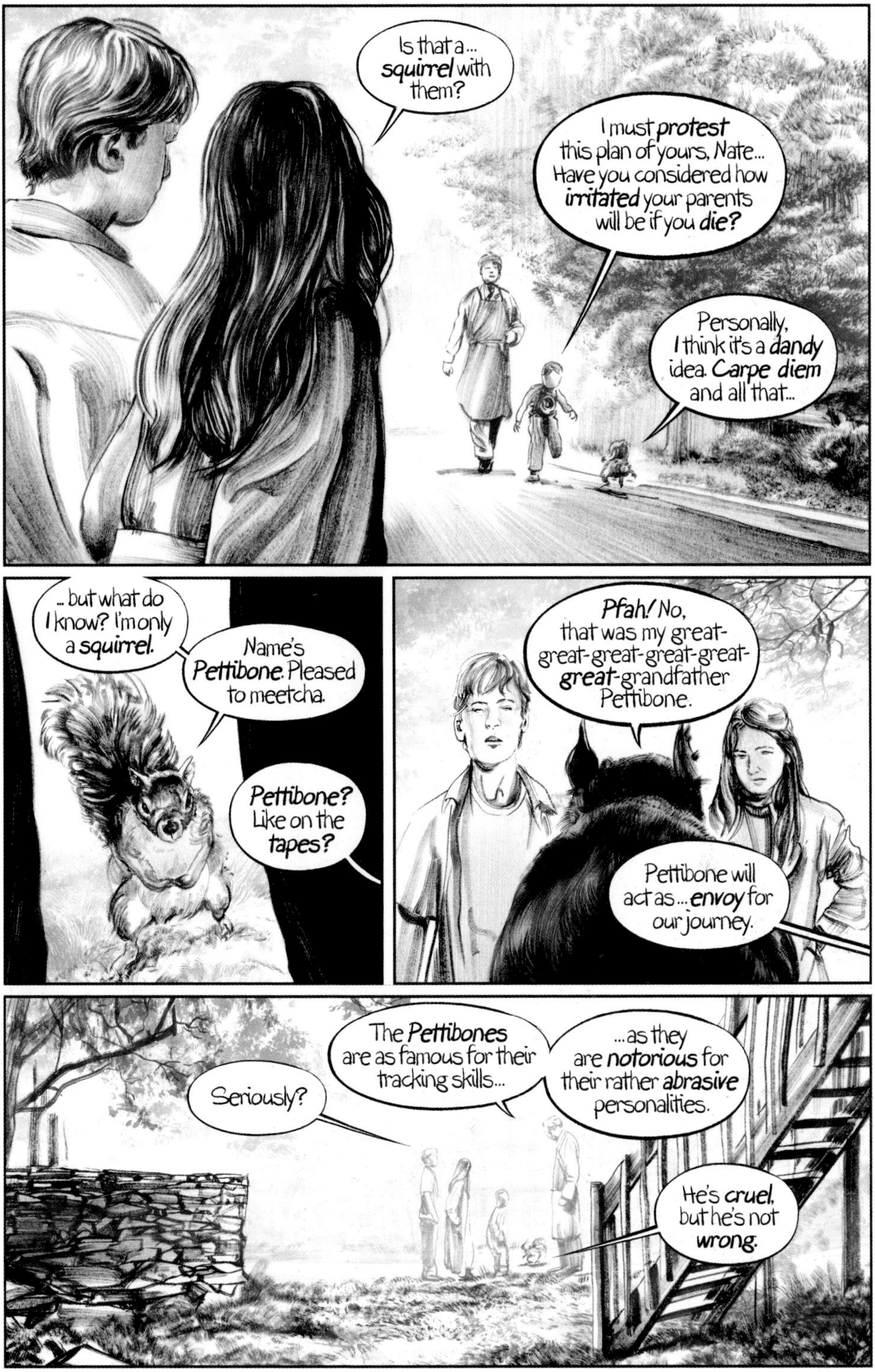
Is that a... squirrel with them?
I must protest this plan of yours, Nate... Have you considered how irritated your parents will be if you die?
Personally, I think it's a dandy idea. Carpe diem and all that...
... but what do I know? I'm only a squirrel.
Name's Pettibone. Pleased to meetcha.
Pettibone? Like on the tapes?
Pfah! No, that was my great-great-great-great-great-great-grandfather Pettibone.
Pettibone will act as... envoy for our journey.
Seriously?
The Pettibones are as famous for their tracking skills...
...as they are notorious for their rather abrasive personalities.
He's cruel, but he's not wrong.

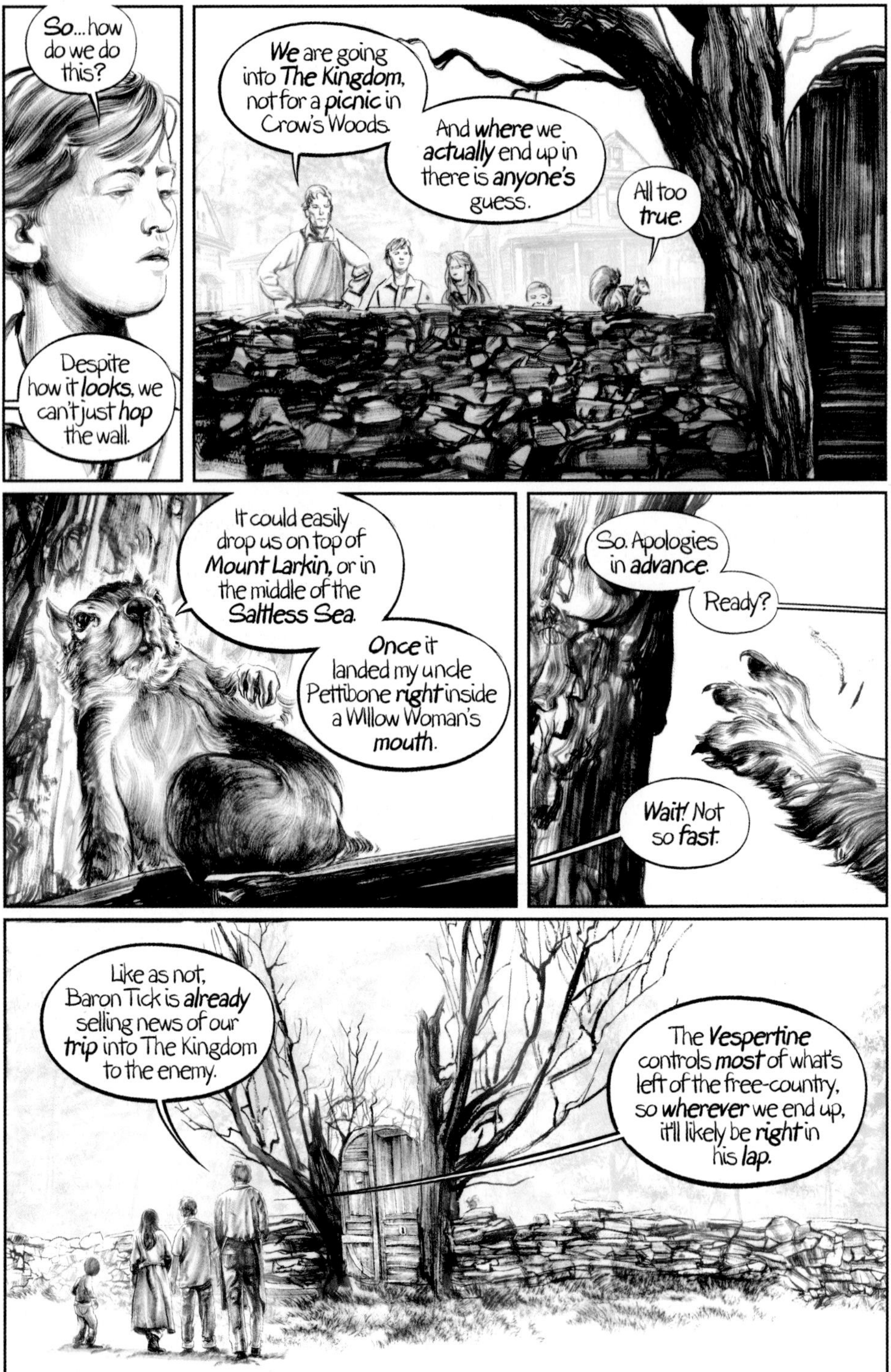

So... how do we do this?
Despite how it looks, we can't just hop the wall.
We are going into The Kingdom, not for a picnic in Crow's Woods.
And where we actually end up in there is anyone's guess.
All too true.
It could easily drop us on top of Mount Larkin, or in the middle of the Saltless Sea.
Once it landed my uncle Pettibone right inside a Willow Woman's mouth.
So. Apologies in advance.
Ready?
Wait! Not so fast.
Like as not, Baron Tick is already selling news of our trip into The Kingdom to the enemy.
The Vespertine controls most of what's left of the free-country, so wherever we end up, it'll likely be right in his lap.

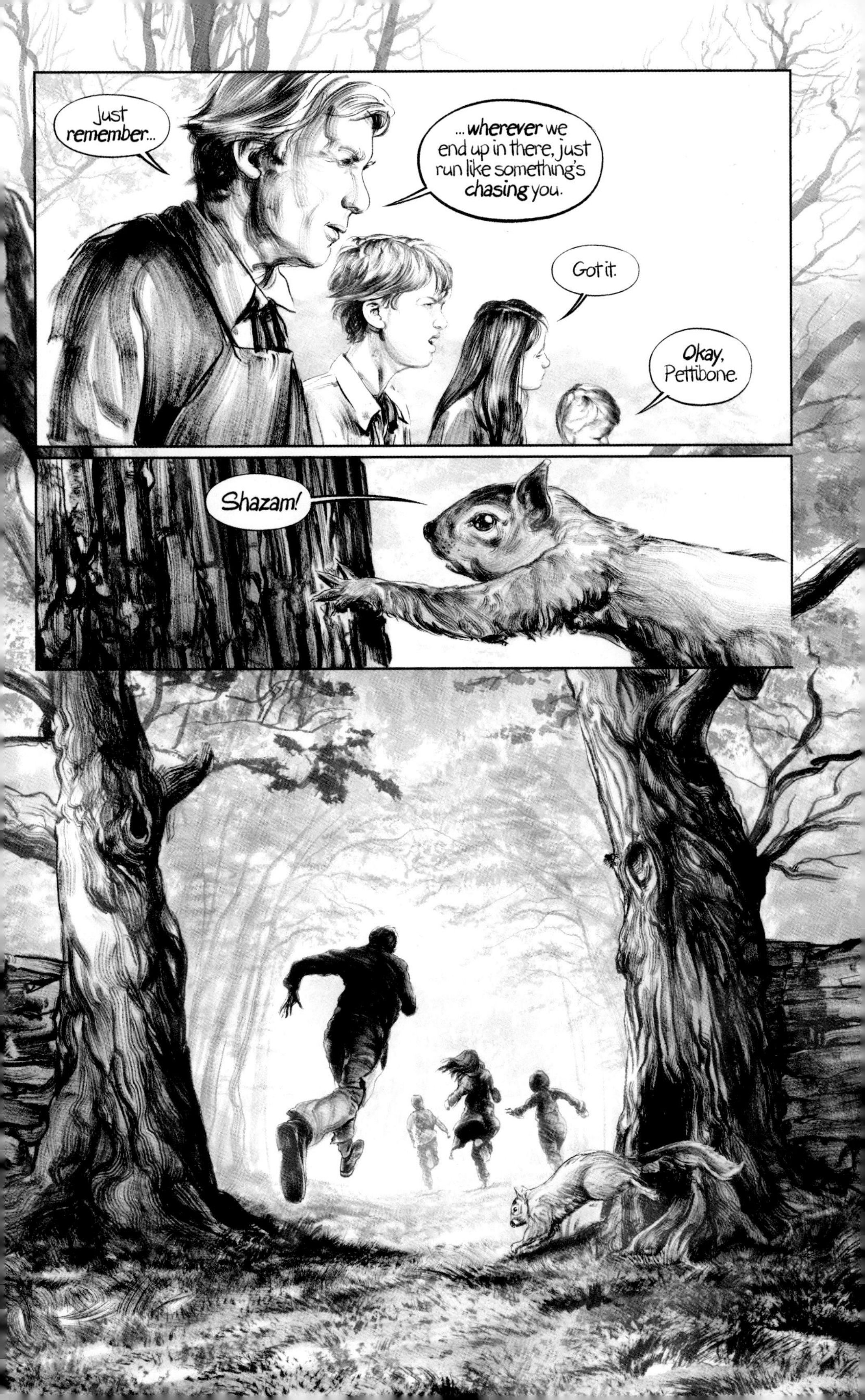

Just remember...
...wherever we end up in there, just run like something's chasing you.
Got it.
Okay, Pettibone.
Shazam!

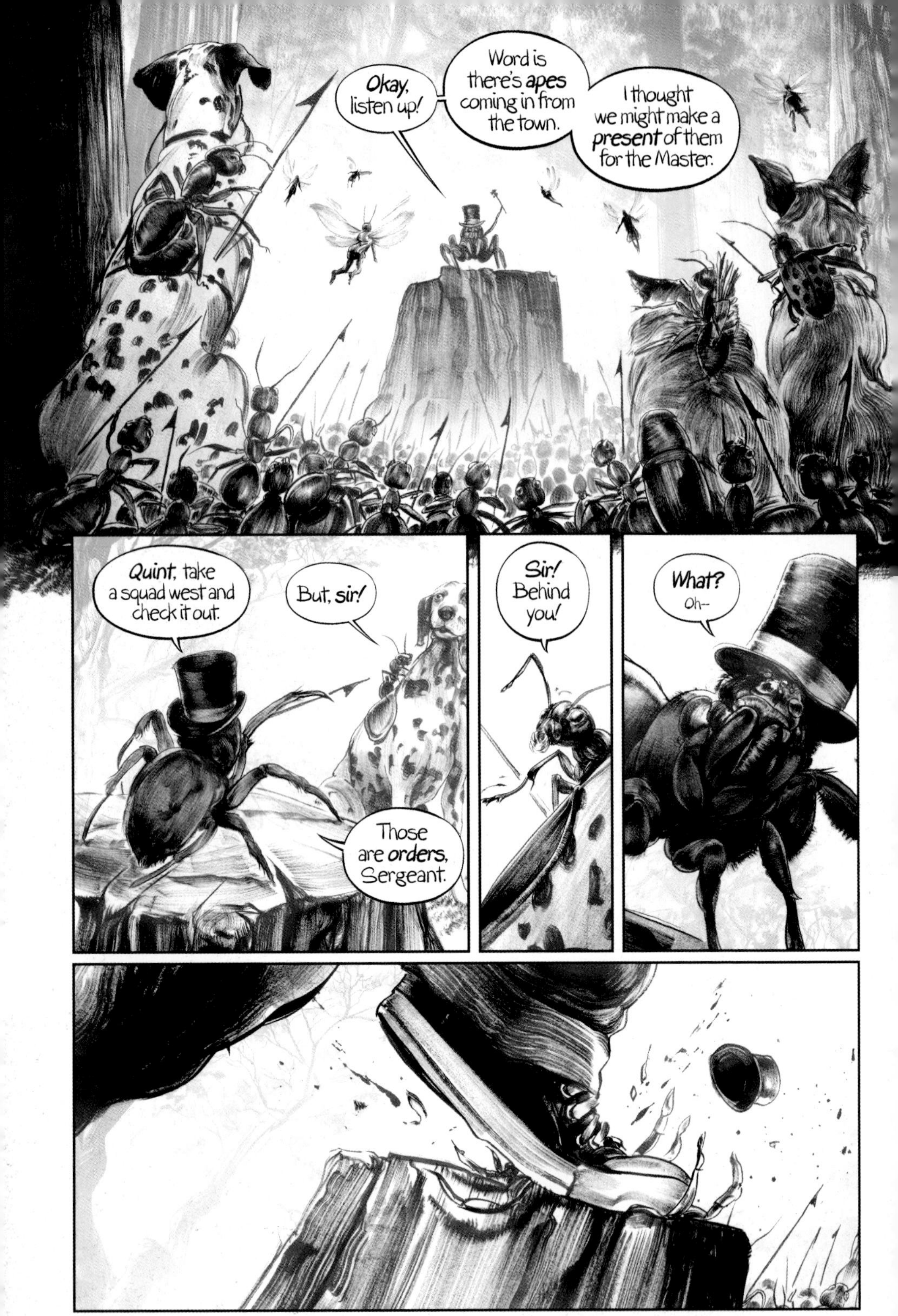
Okay, listen up!
Word is there's apes coming in from the town.
I thought we might make a present of them for the Master.
Quint, take a squad west and check it out.
But, sir!
Those are orders, Sergeant.
Sir! Behind you!
What? Oh--

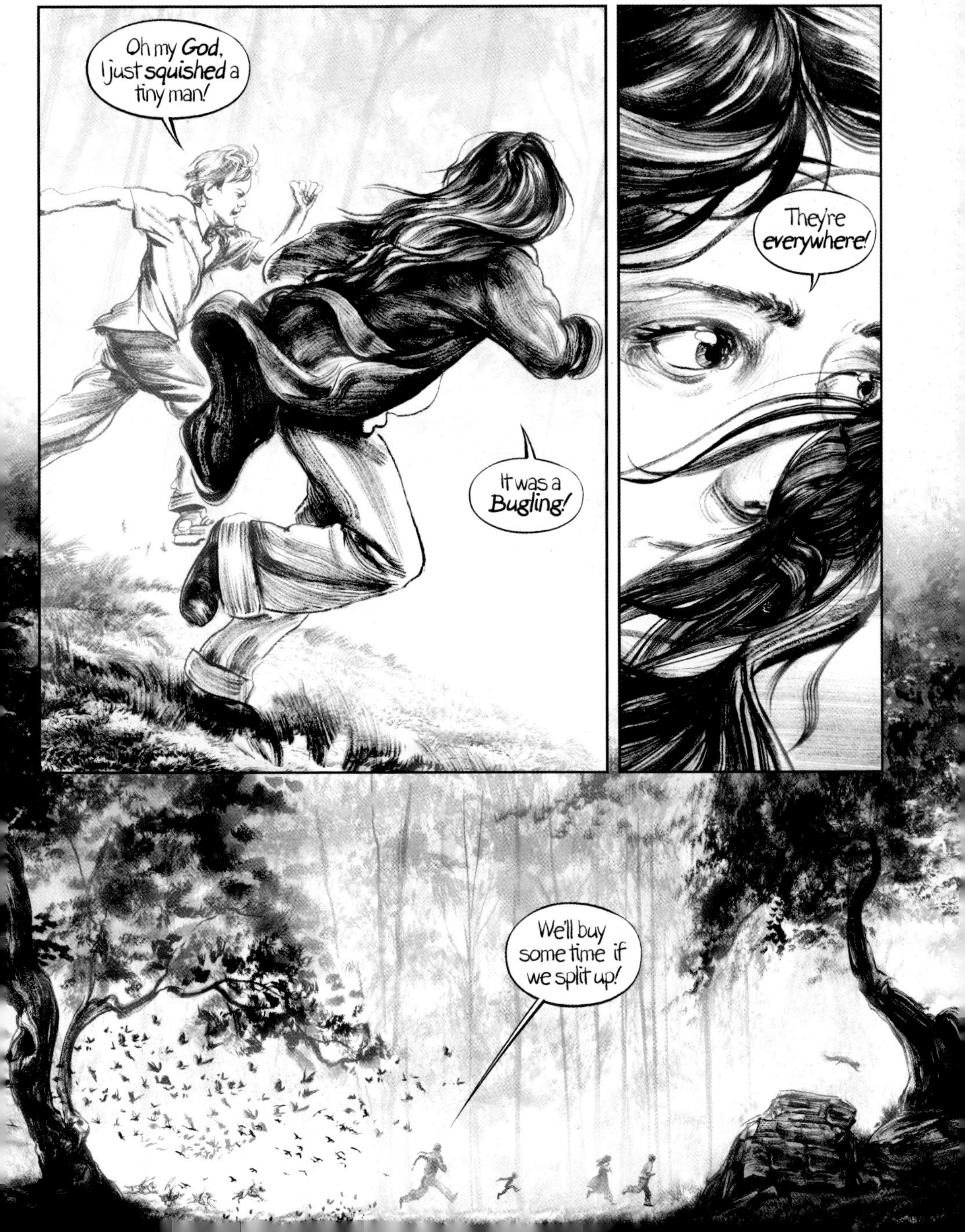
Oh my God, I just squished a tiny man!
It was a Bugling!
They're everywhere!
We'll buy some time if we split up!

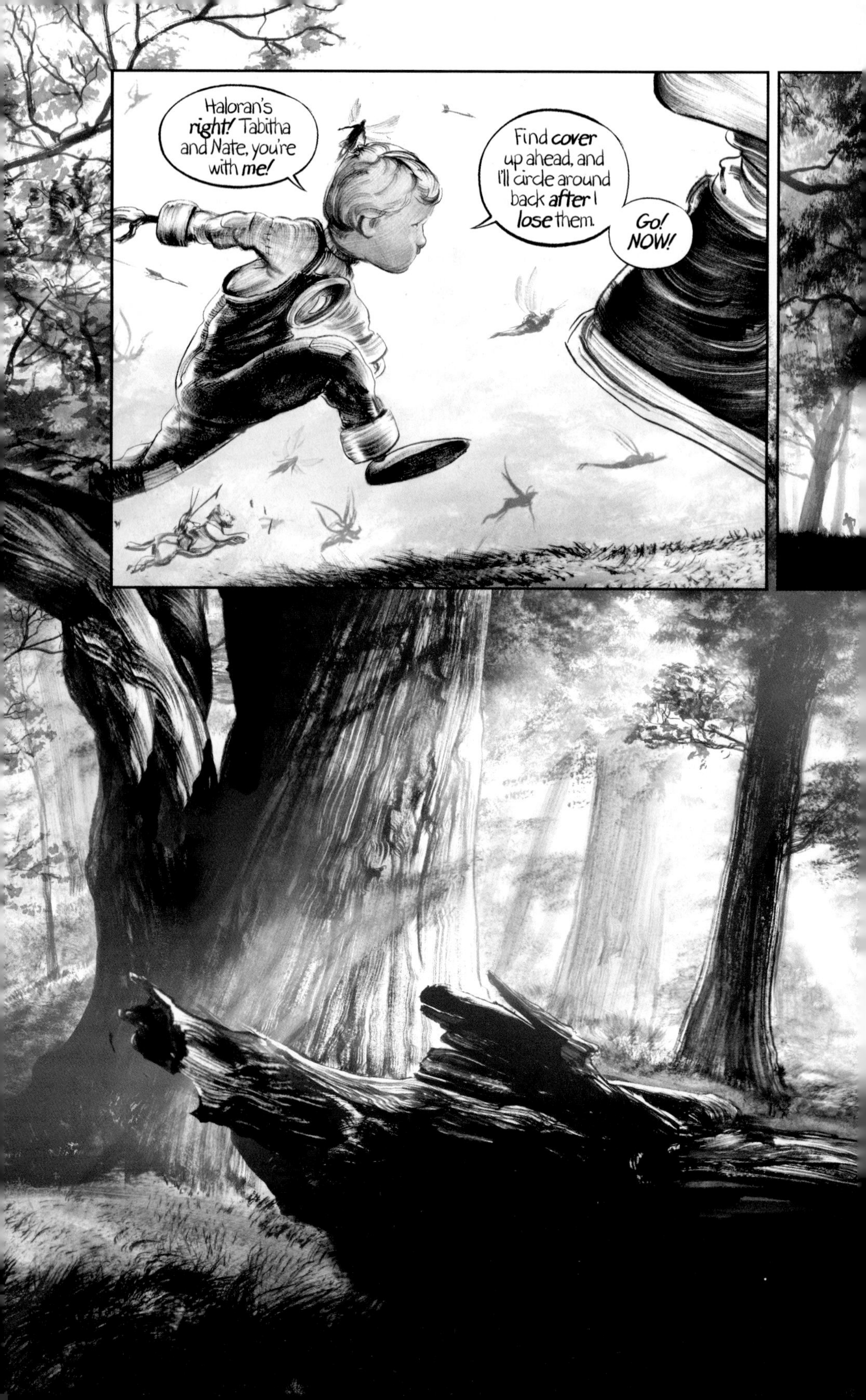
Haloran's **right!** Tabitha and Nate, you're with **me!**
Find **cover** up ahead, and I'll circle around back **after** I **lose** them.
Go! NOW!

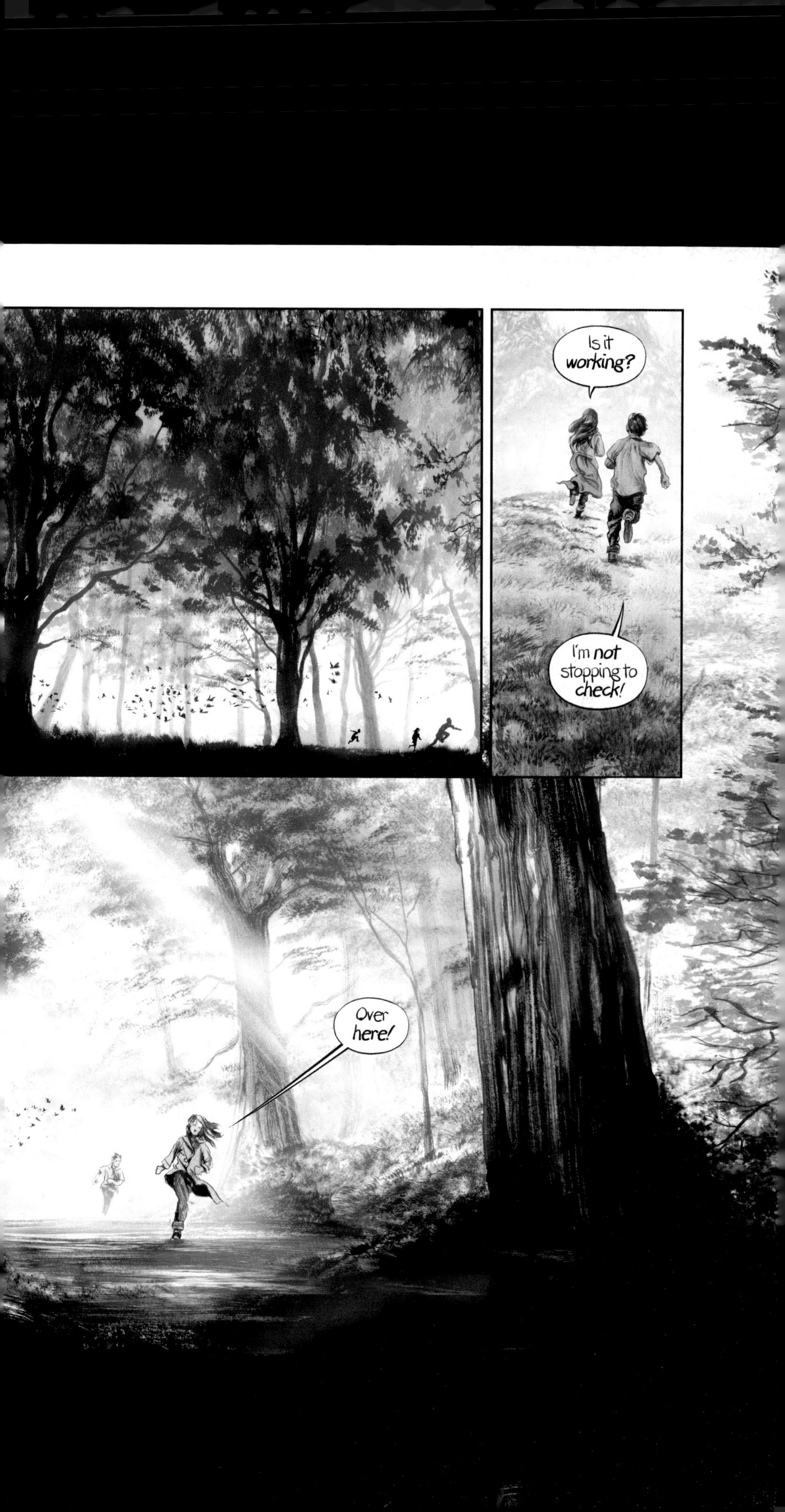
Is it working?
I'm not stopping to check!
Over here!

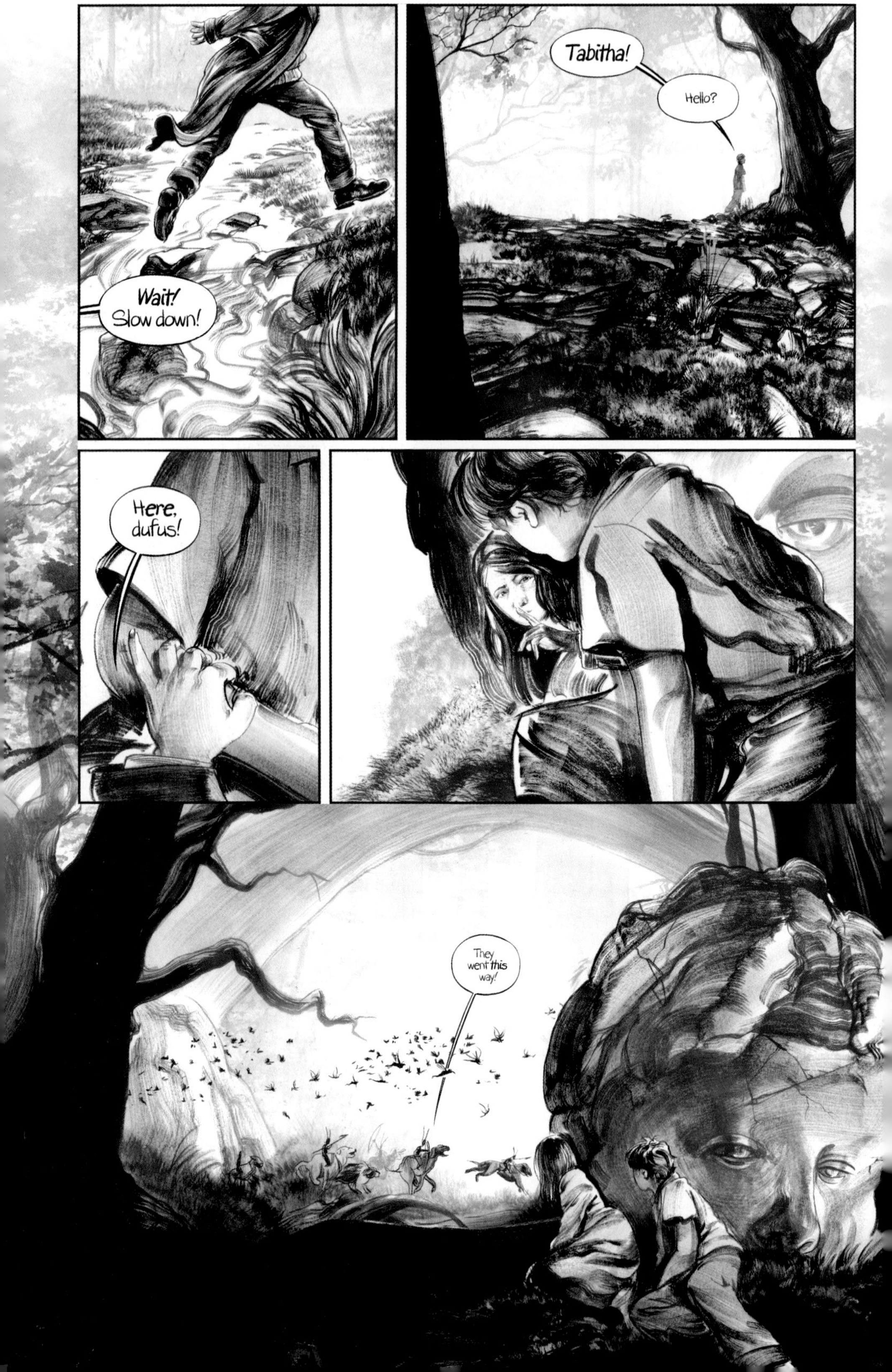
Wait! Slow down!
Tabitha!
Hello?
Here, dufus!
They went this way!

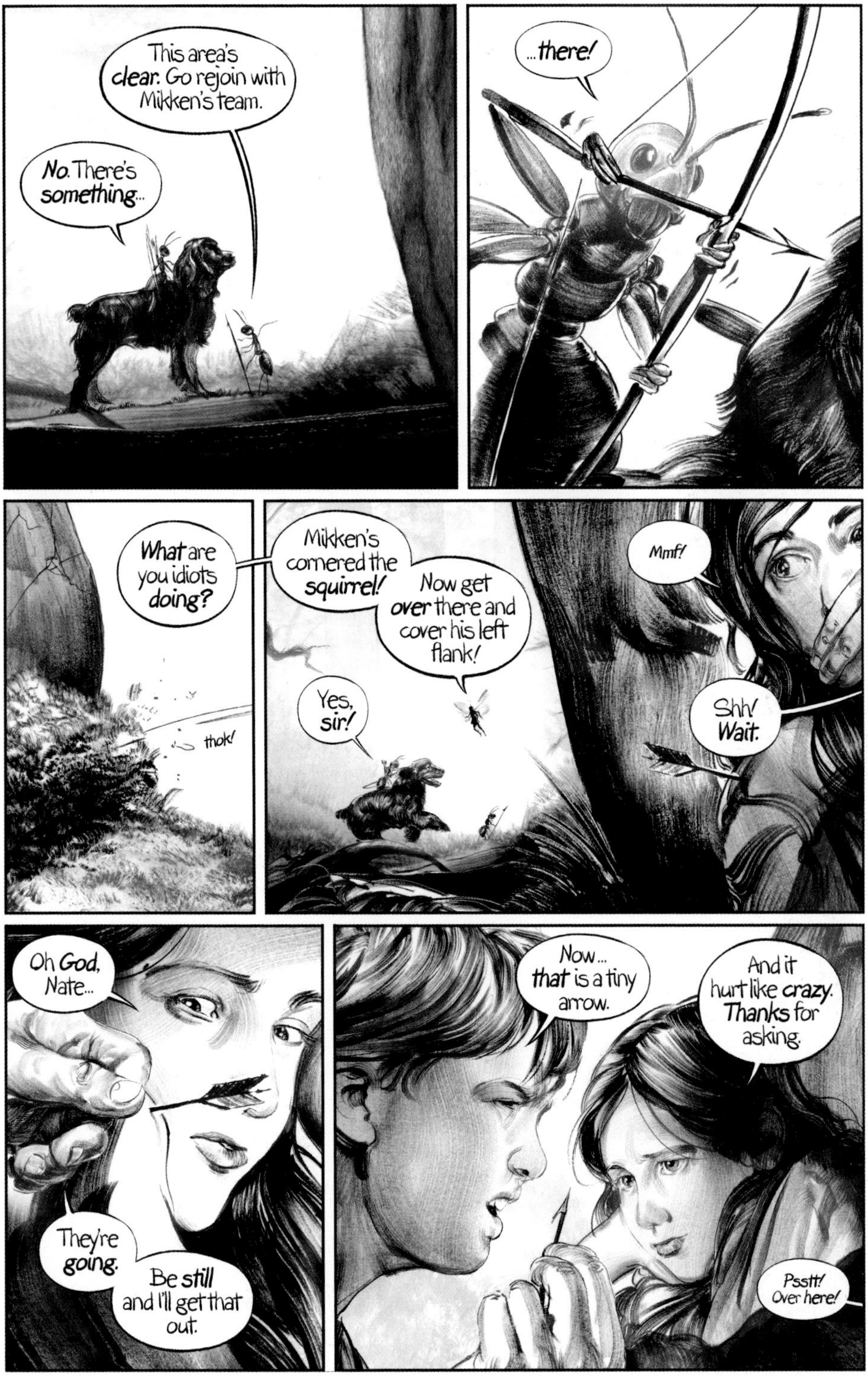
This area's clear. Go rejoin with Mikken's team.
No. There's something...
...there!
What are you idiots doing?
Mikken's cornered the squirrel!
Now get over there and cover his left flank!
Yes, sir!
thok!
Mmf!
Shh! Wait.
Oh God, Nate...
They're going.
Be still and I'll get that out.
Now... that is a tiny arrow.
And it hurt like crazy. Thanks for asking.
Psstt! Over here!

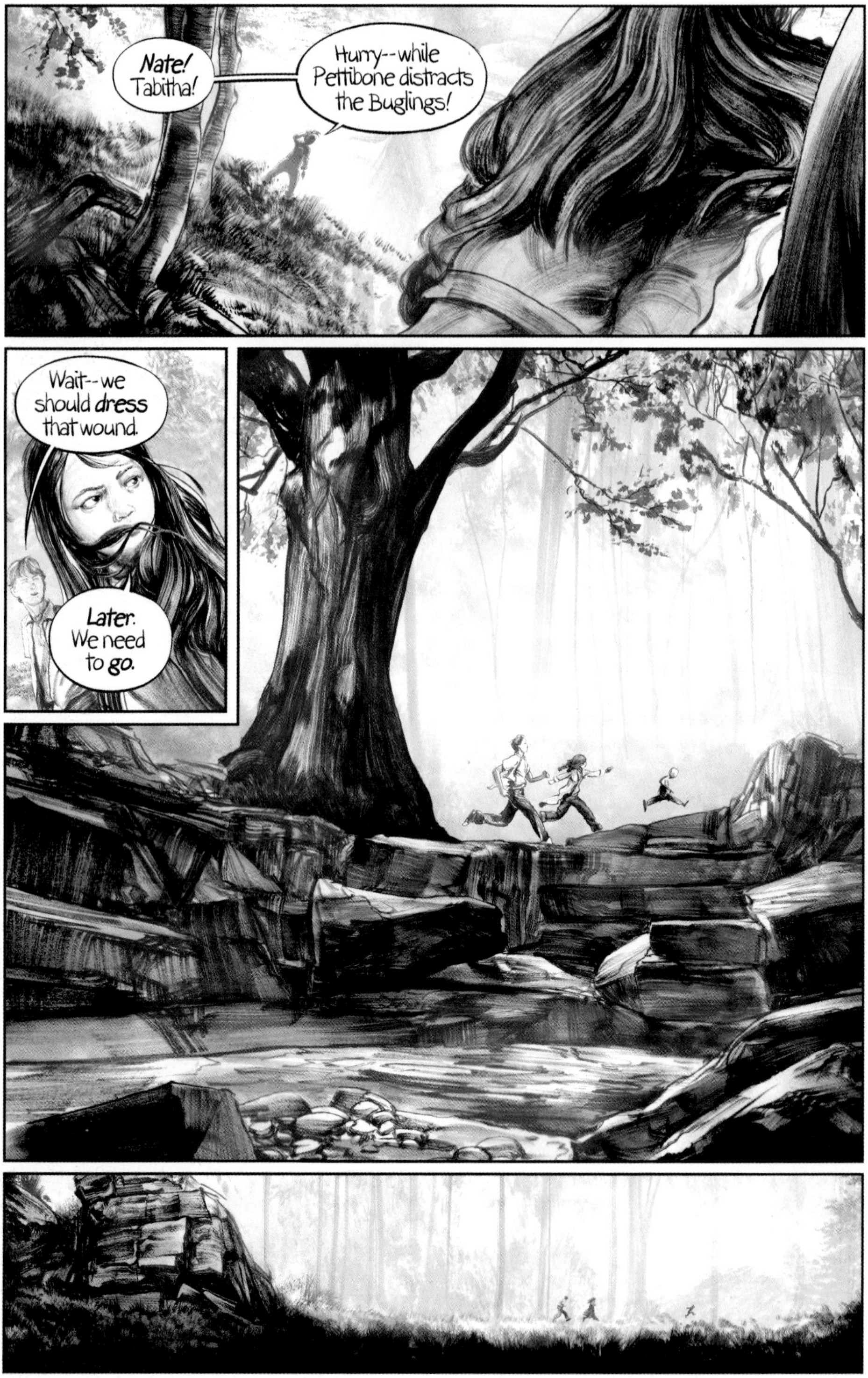
Nate! Tabitha!
Hurry--while Pettibone distracts the Buglings!
Wait--we should dress that wound.
Later. We need to go.

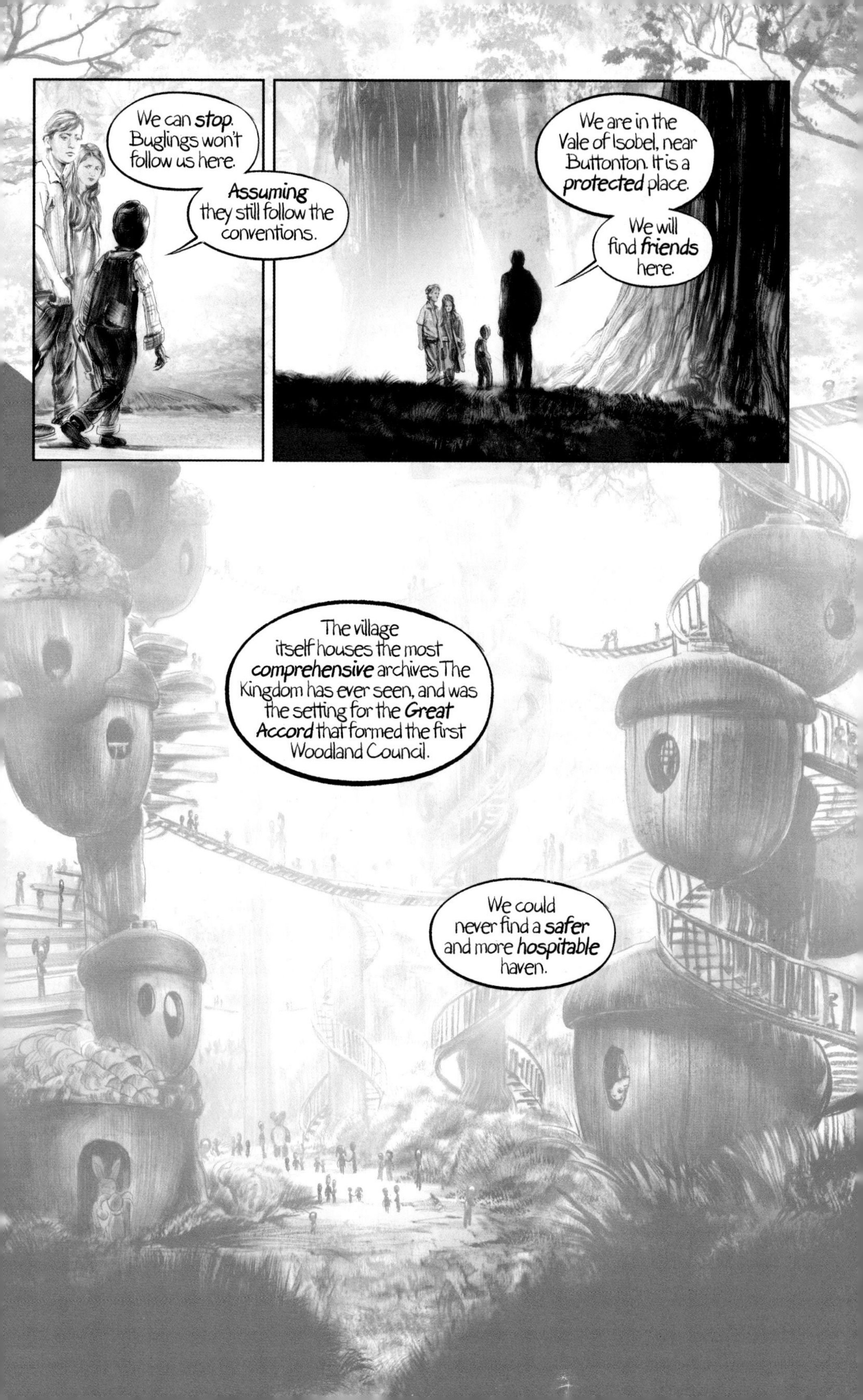
We can stop. Buglings won't follow us here.
Assuming they still follow the conventions.
We are in the Vale of Isobel, near Buttonton. It is a protected place.
We will find friends here.
The village itself houses the most comprehensive archives The Kingdom has ever seen, and was the setting for the Great Accord that formed the first Woodland Council.
We could never find a safer and more hospitable haven.

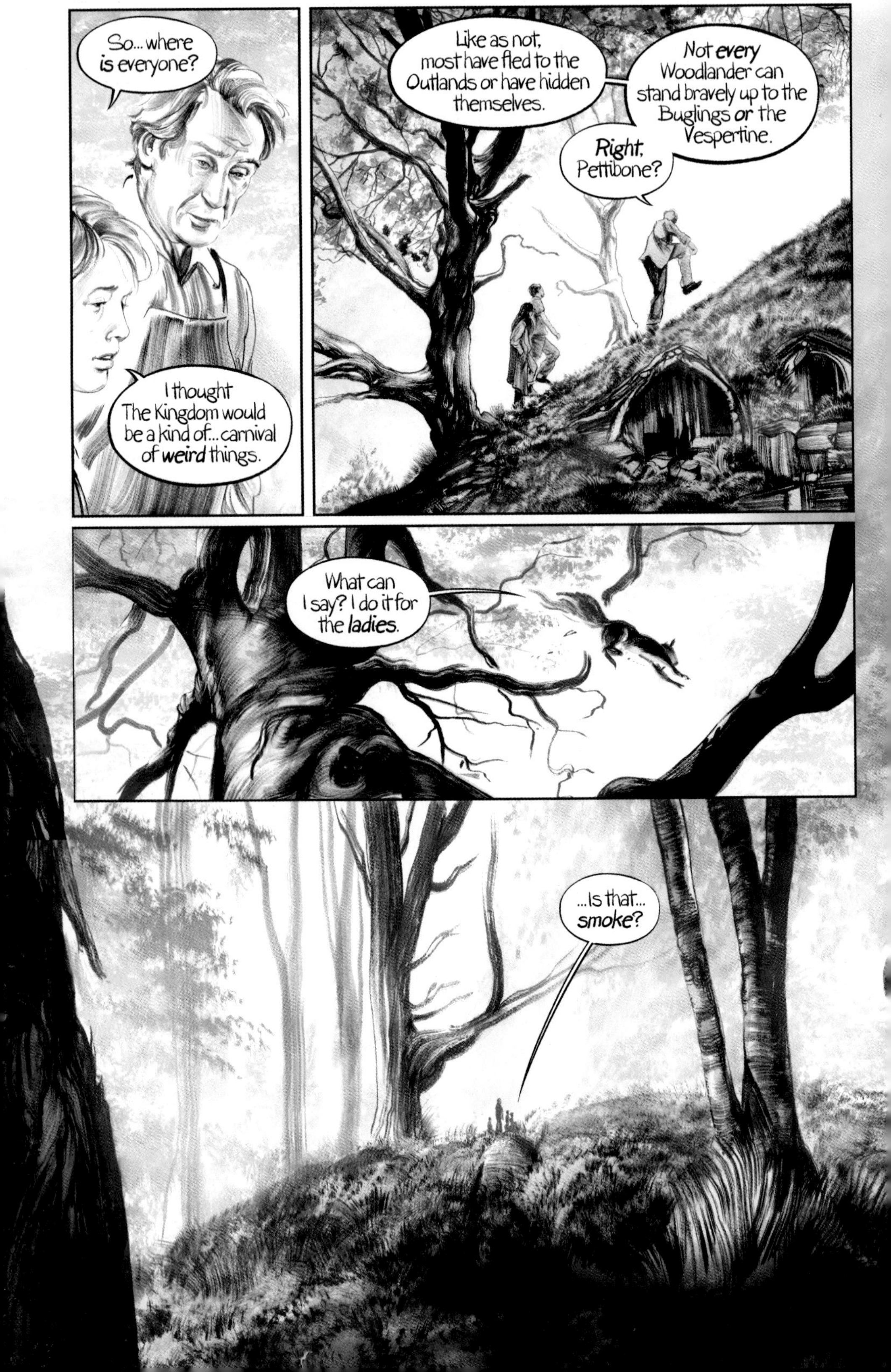
So... where **is** everyone?
I thought The Kingdom would be a kind of... carnival of ***weird*** things.
Like as not, most have fled to the Outlands or have hidden themselves.
Not ***every*** Woodlander can stand bravely up to the Buglings ***or*** the Vespertine.
Right, Pettibone?
What can I say? I do it for the ***ladies.***
...Is that... ***smoke?***

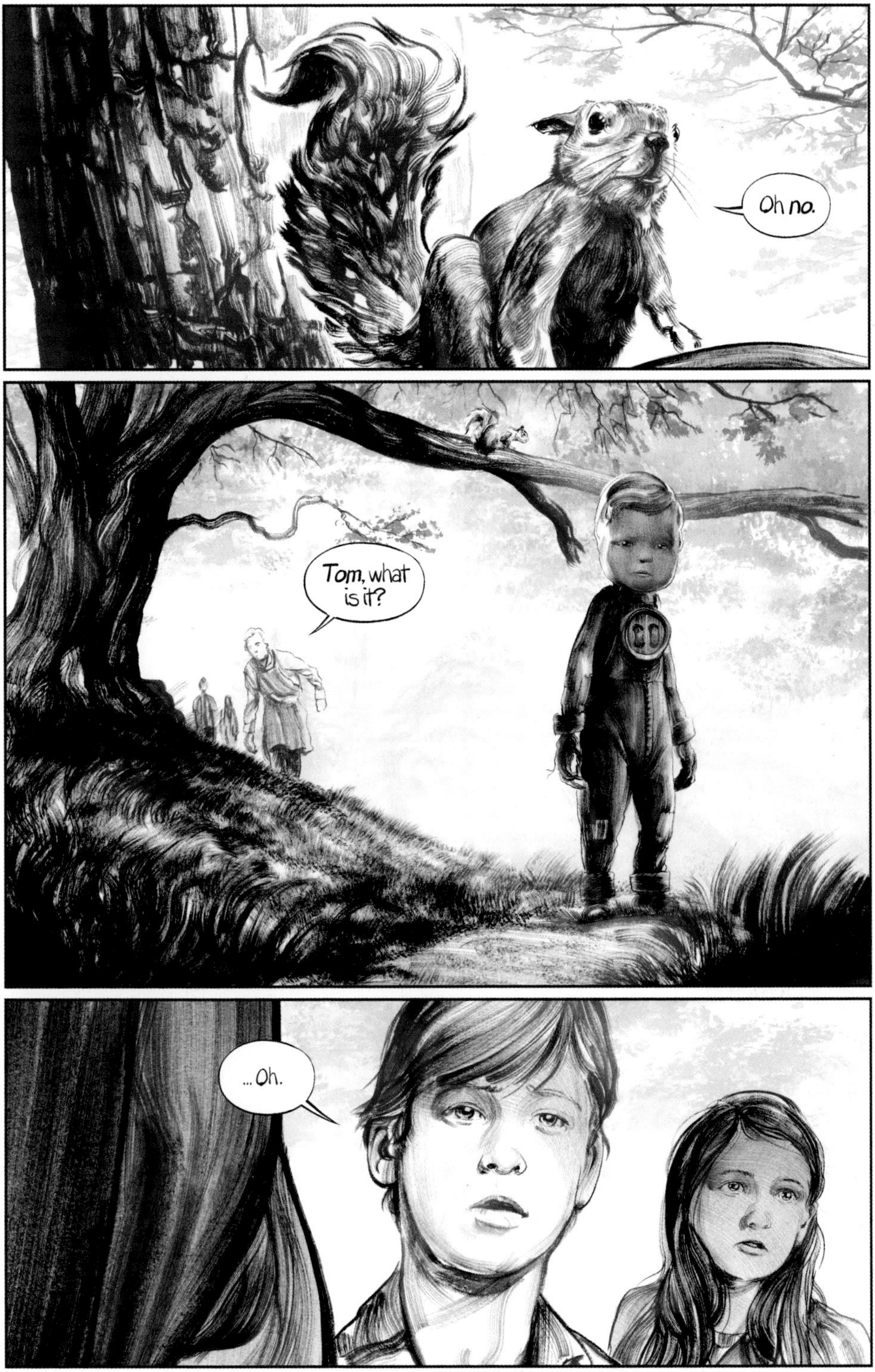
Oh no.
Tom, what is it?
...Oh.

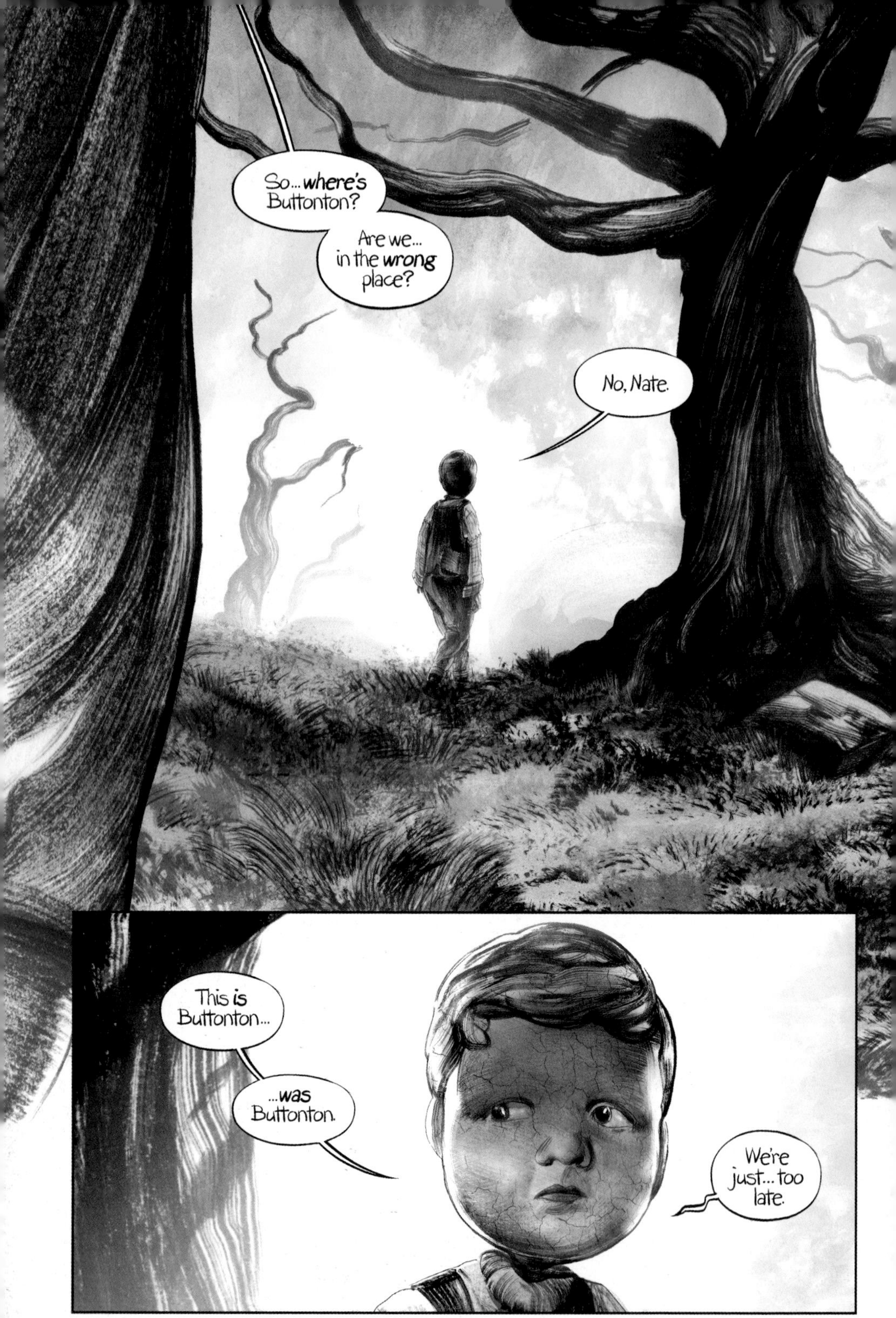
So... where's Buttonton?
Are we... in the wrong place?
No, Nate.
This is Buttonton...
...was Buttonton.
We're just... too late.

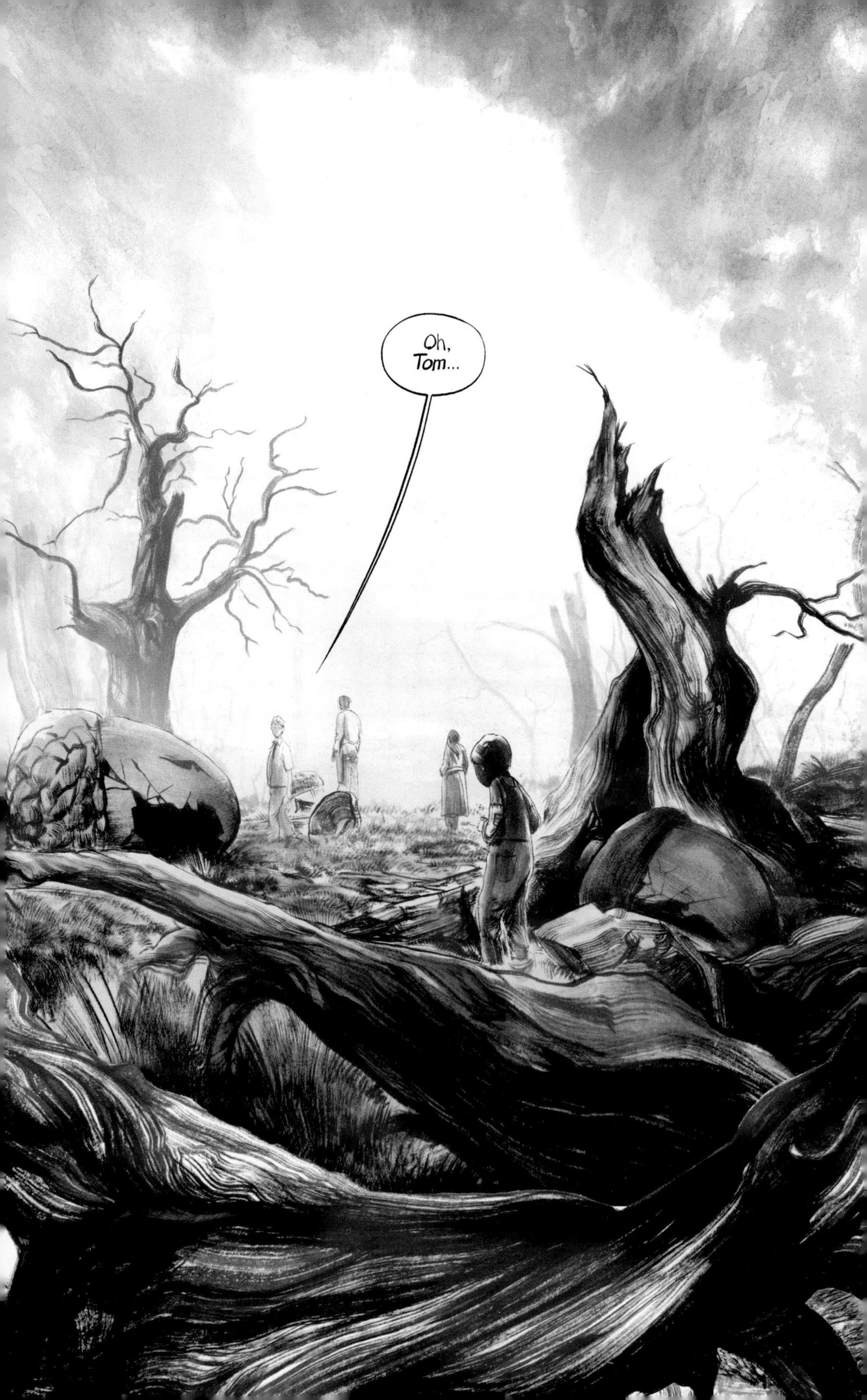
Oh, Tom...

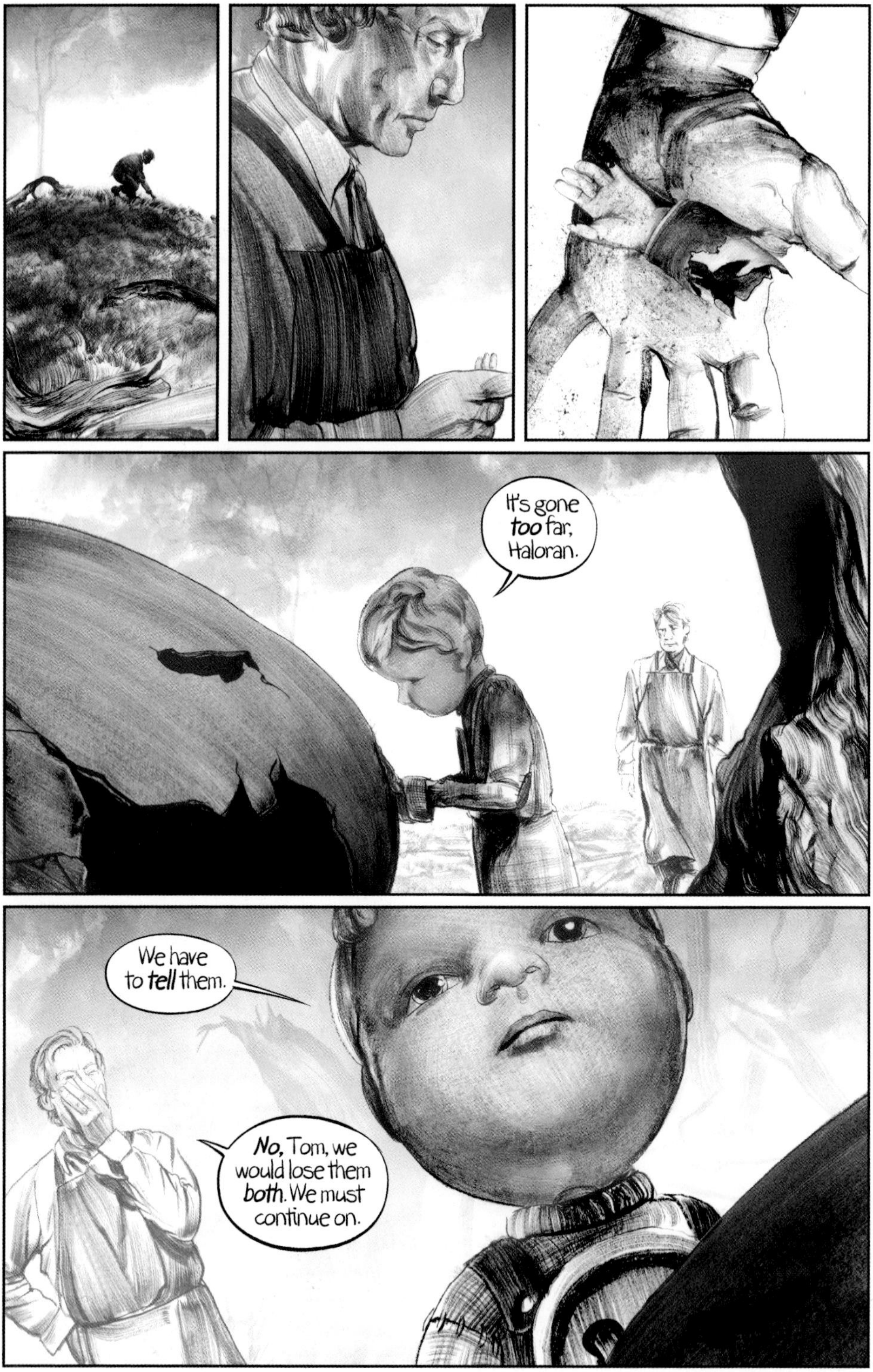
It's gone *too* far, Haloran.
We have to *tell* them.
No, Tom, we would lose them *both*. We must continue on.

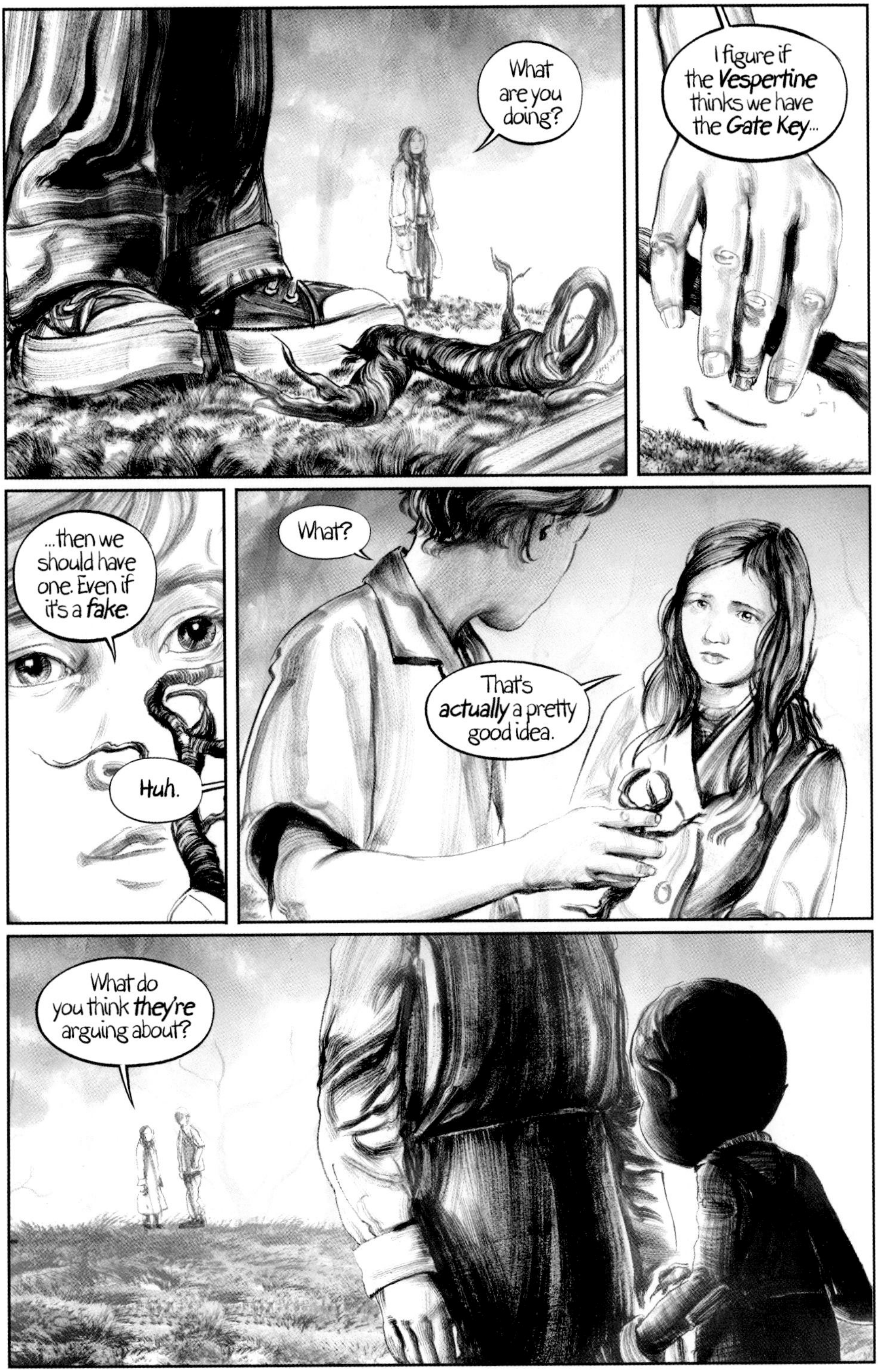
What are you doing?
I figure if the Vespertine thinks we have the Gate Key...
...then we should have one. Even if it's a fake.
Huh.
What?
That's actually a pretty good idea.
What do you think they're arguing about?

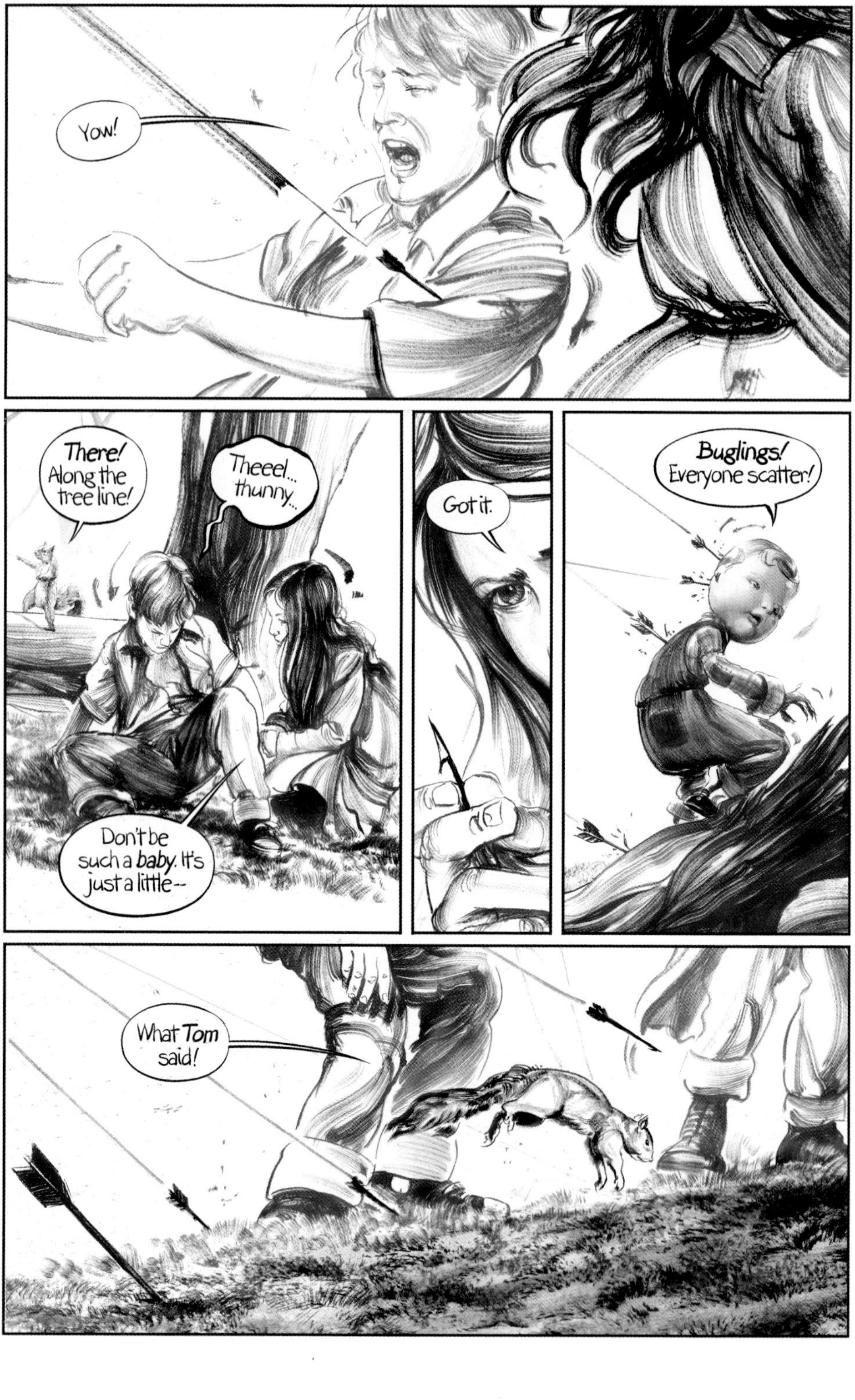
Yow!
There! Along the tree line!
Theeel... thunny...
Don't be such a baby. It's just a little--
Got it.
Buglings! Everyone scatter!
What Tom said!

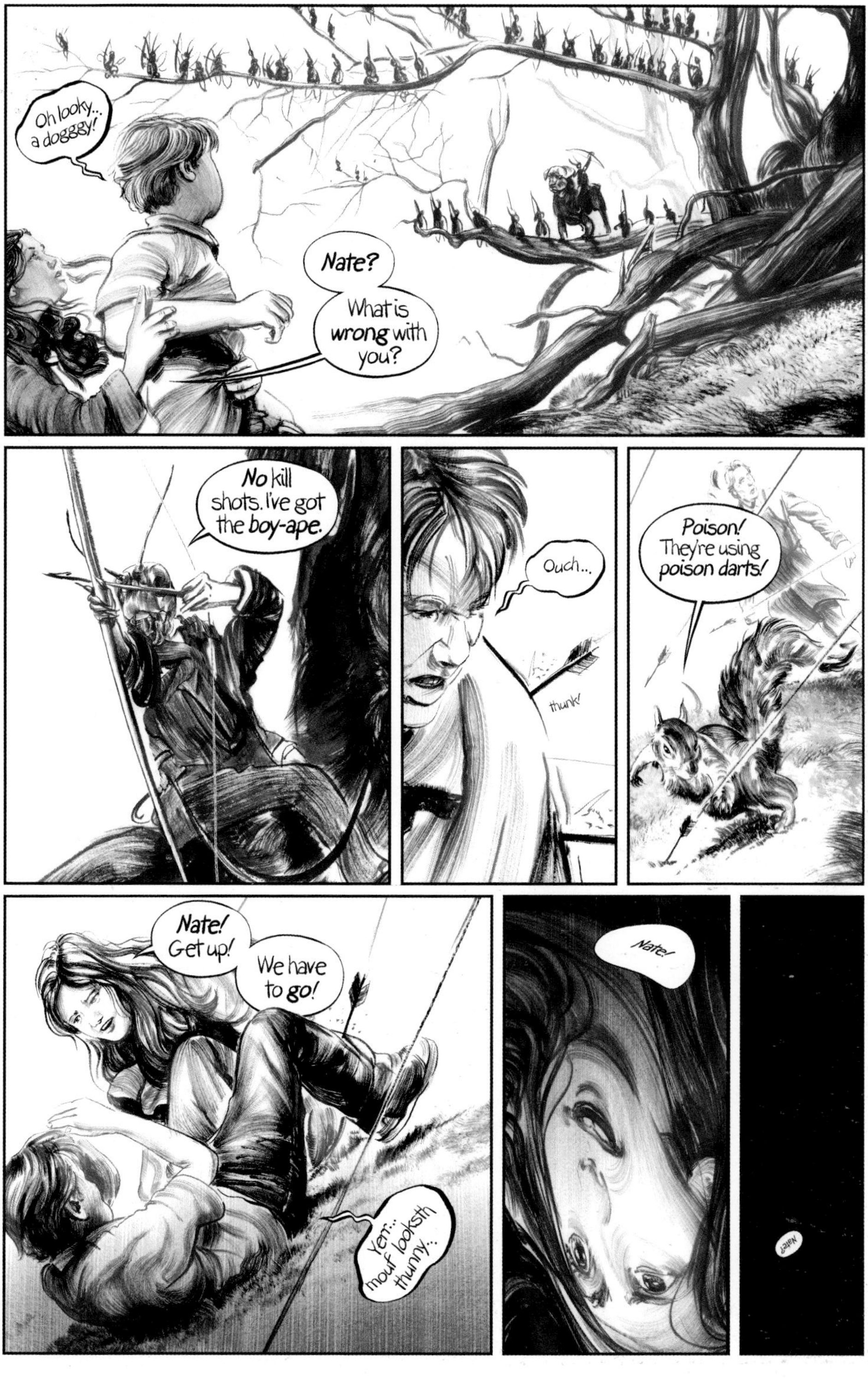
Oh looky... a dogggy!
Nate?
What is wrong with you?
No kill shots. I've got the boy-ape.
Ouch...
thunk!
Poison! They're using poison darts!
Nate! Get up!
We have to go!
Yerr... mouf looksth thunny...
Nate!
Nate?

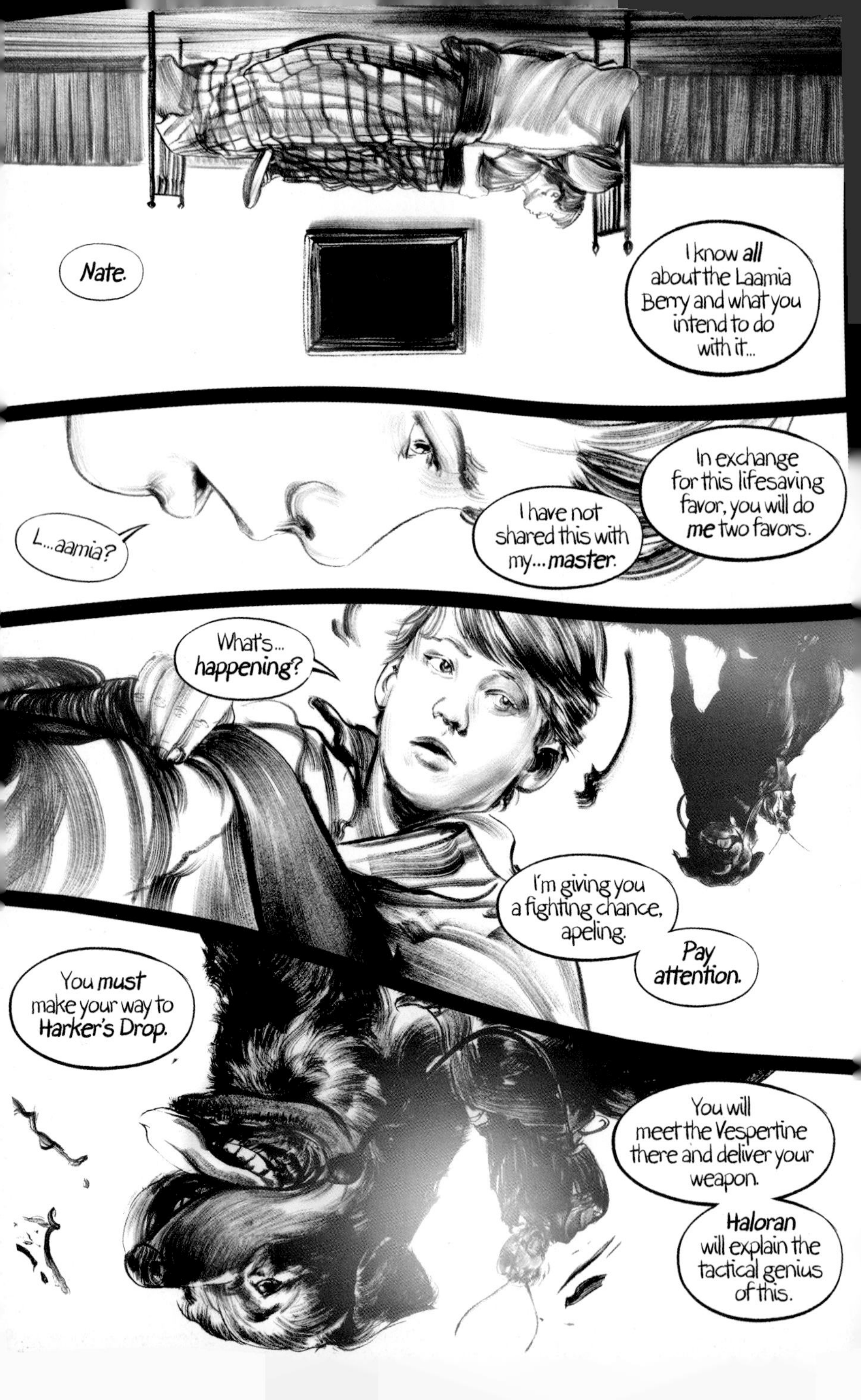
Nate.
I know all about the Laamia Berry and what you intend to do with it...
L...aamia?
I have not shared this with my... master.
In exchange for this lifesaving favor, you will do me two favors.
What's... happening?
I'm giving you a fighting chance, apeling.
Pay attention.
You must make your way to Harker's Drop.
You will meet the Vespertine there and deliver your weapon.
Haloran will explain the tactical genius of this.

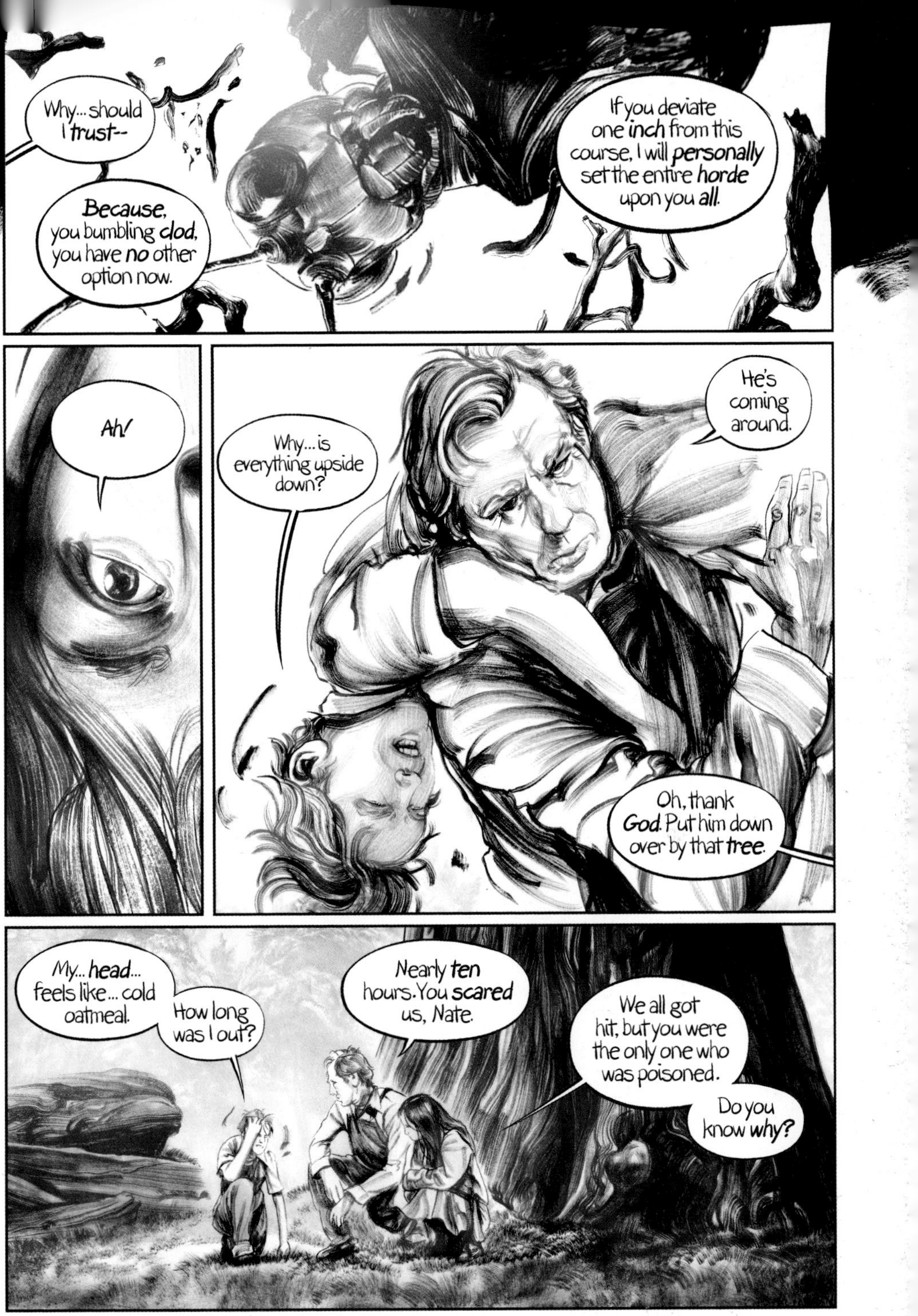

Why... should I trust--
If you deviate one inch from this course, I will personally set the entire horde upon you all.
Because, you bumbling clod, you have no other option now.
Ah!
Why... is everything upside down?
He's coming around.
Oh, thank God. Put him down over by that tree.
My... head... feels like... cold oatmeal.
How long was I out?
Nearly ten hours. You scared us, Nate.
We all got hit, but you were the only one who was poisoned.
Do you know why?

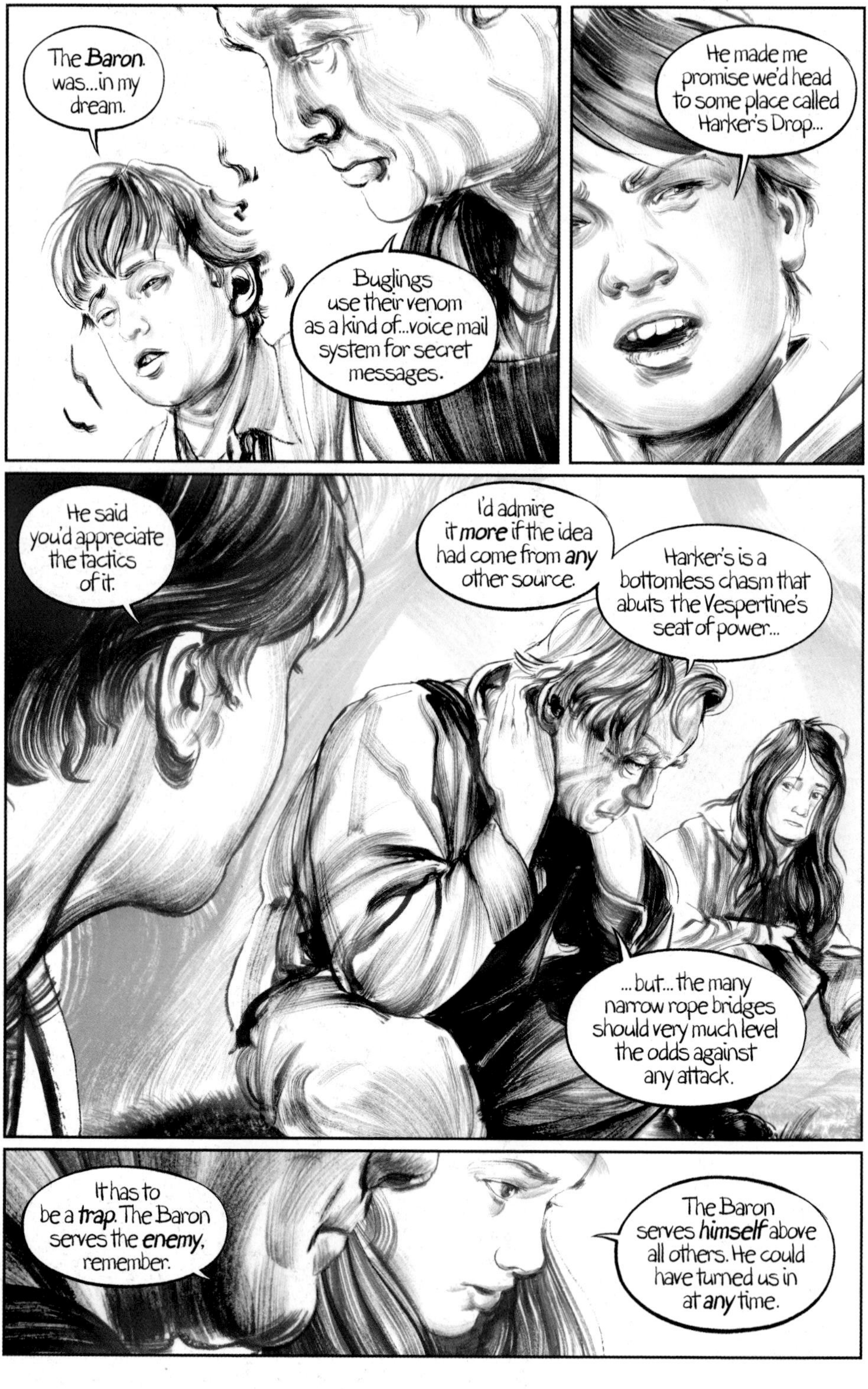

The **Baron**. was...in my dream.
Buglings use their venom as a kind of...voice mail system for secret messages.
He made me promise we'd head to some place called Harker's Drop...
He said you'd appreciate the tactics of it.
I'd admire it **more** if the idea had come from **any** other source.
Harker's is a bottomless chasm that abuts the Vespertine's seat of power...
...but... the many narrow rope bridges should very much level the odds against any attack.
It has to be a **trap**. The Baron serves the **enemy**, remember.
The Baron serves **himself** above all others. He could have turned us in at **any** time.

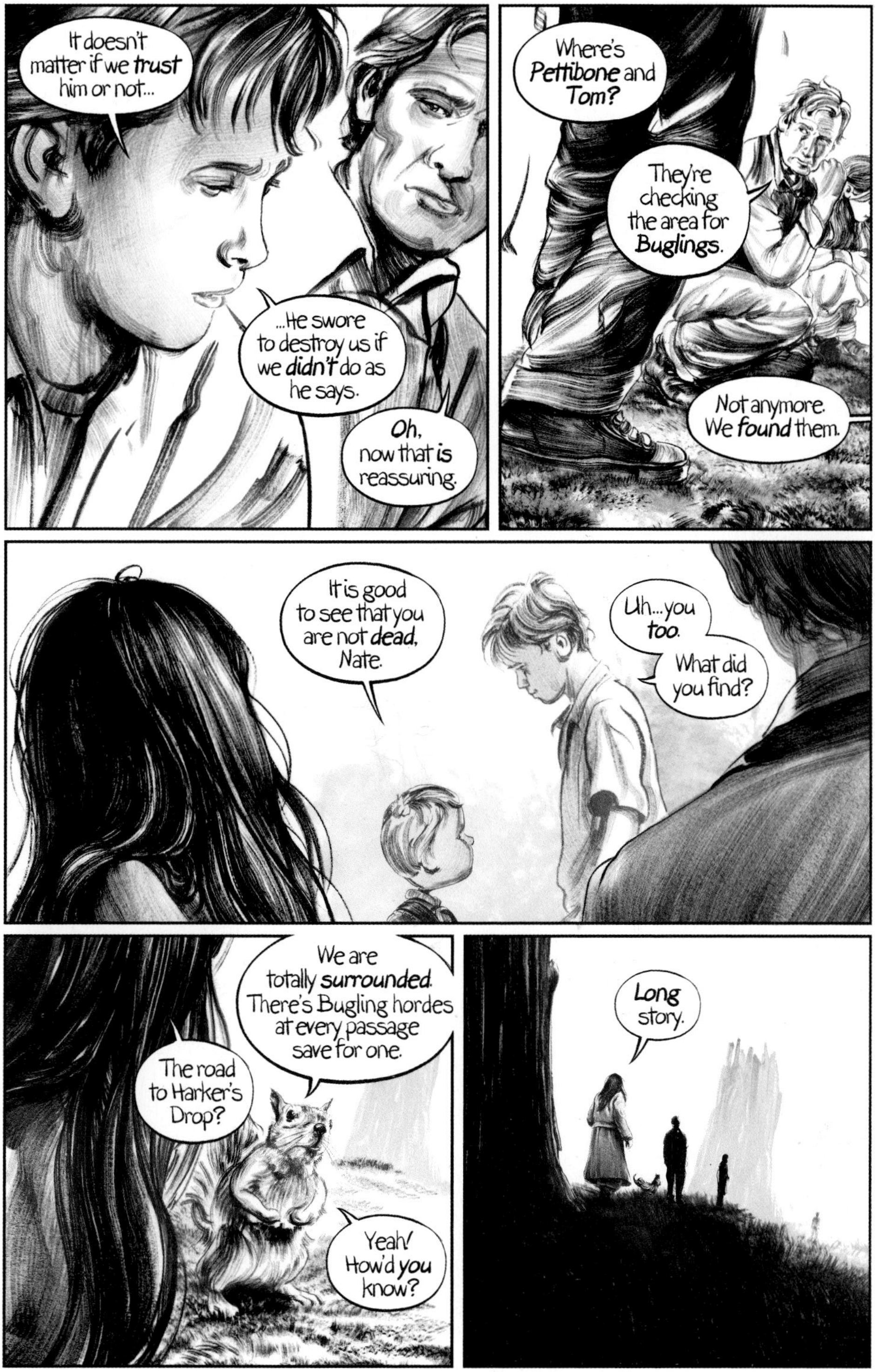
It doesn't matter if we **trust** him or not...
...He swore to destroy us if we **didn't** do as he says.
Oh, now that **is** reassuring.
Where's **Pettibone** and **Tom?**
They're checking the area for **Buglings**.
Not anymore. We **found** them.
It is good to see that you are not **dead**, Nate.
Uh...you **too**.
What did you find?
We are totally **surrounded**. There's Bugling hordes at every passage save for one.
The road to Harker's Drop?
Yeah! How'd **you** know?
Long story.

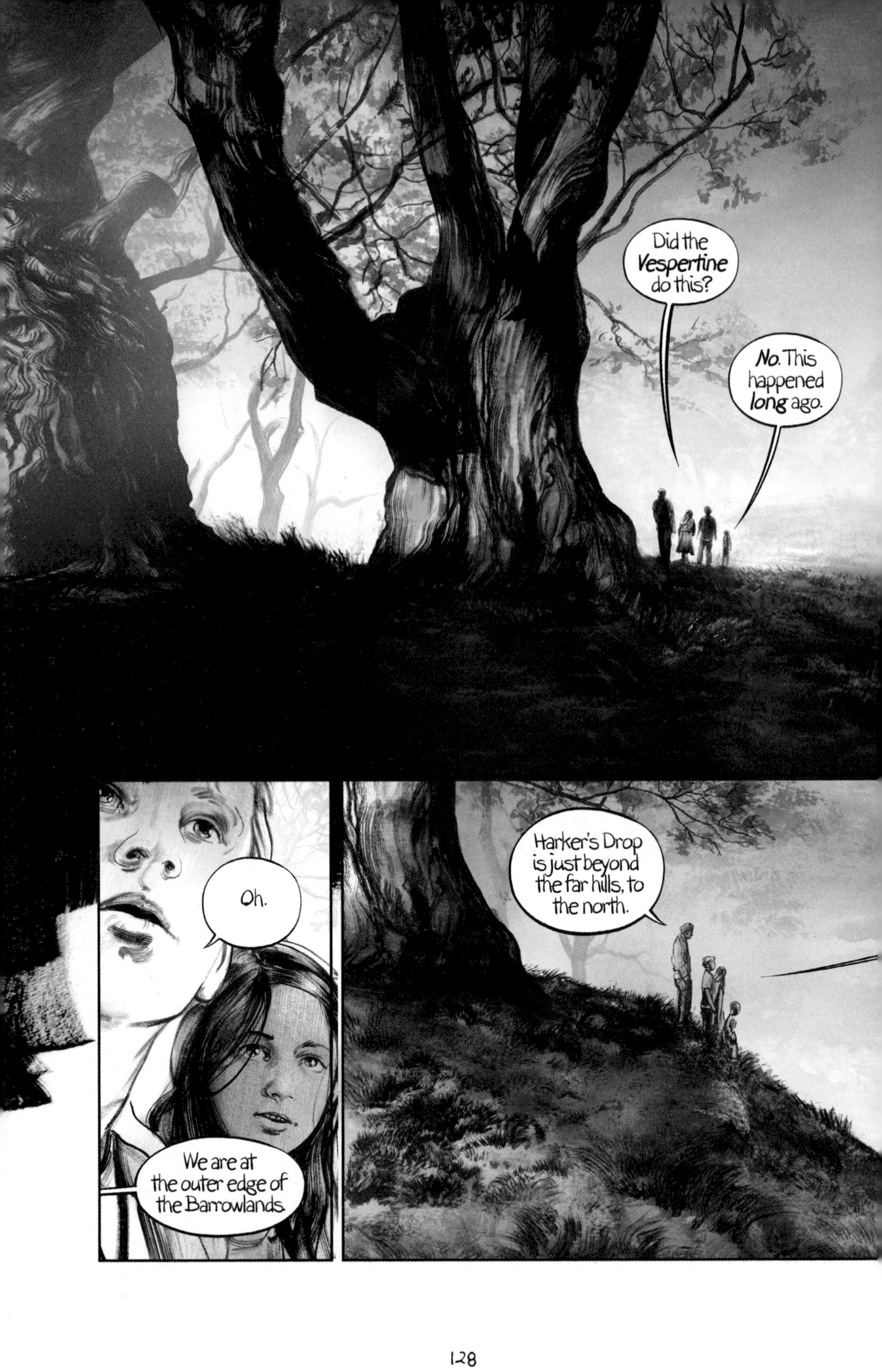
Did the Vespertine do this?
No. This happened long ago.
Oh.
We are at the outer edge of the Barrowlands.
Harker's Drop is just beyond the far hills, to the north.

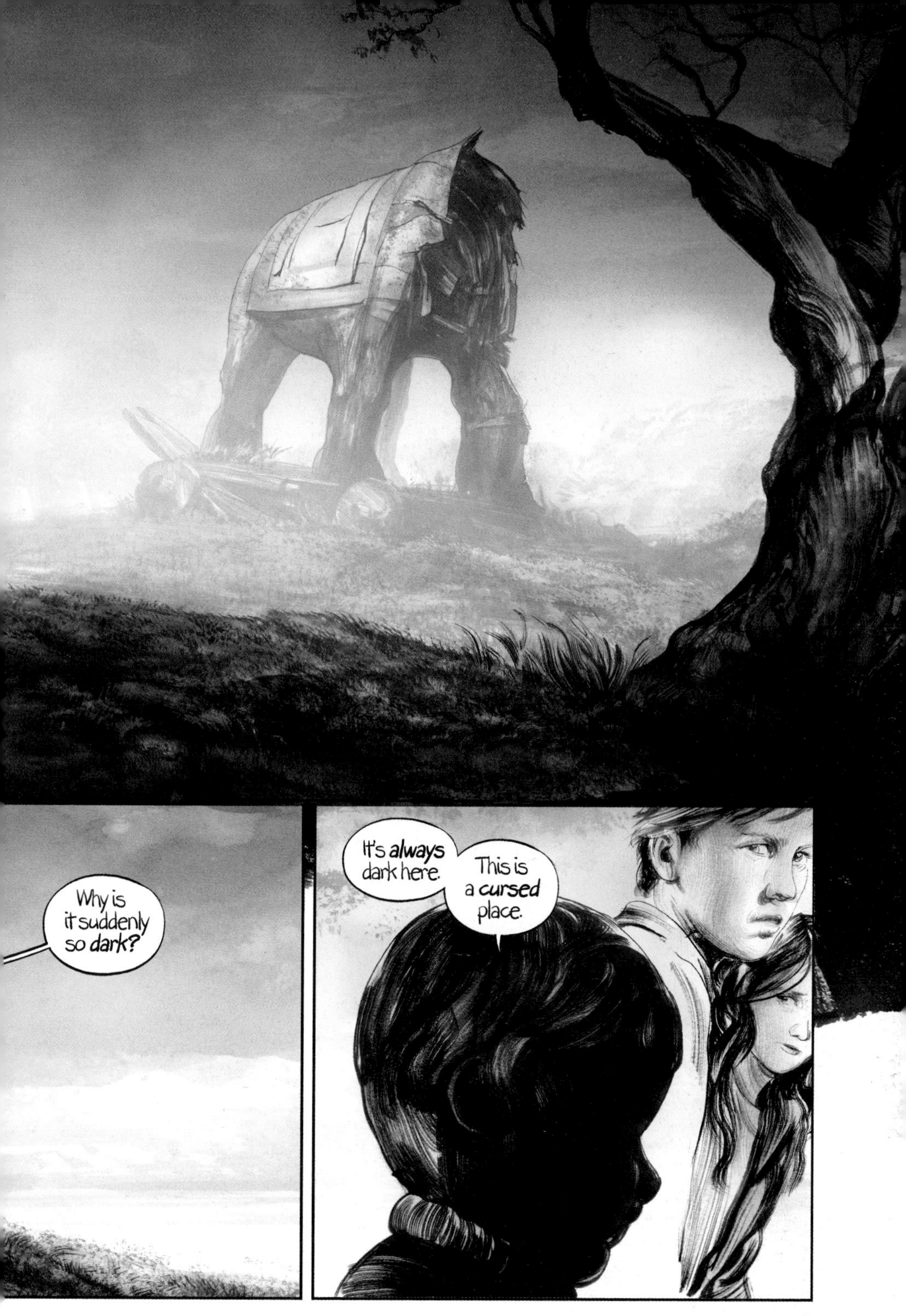
Why is it suddenly so dark?
It's always dark here.
This is a cursed place.

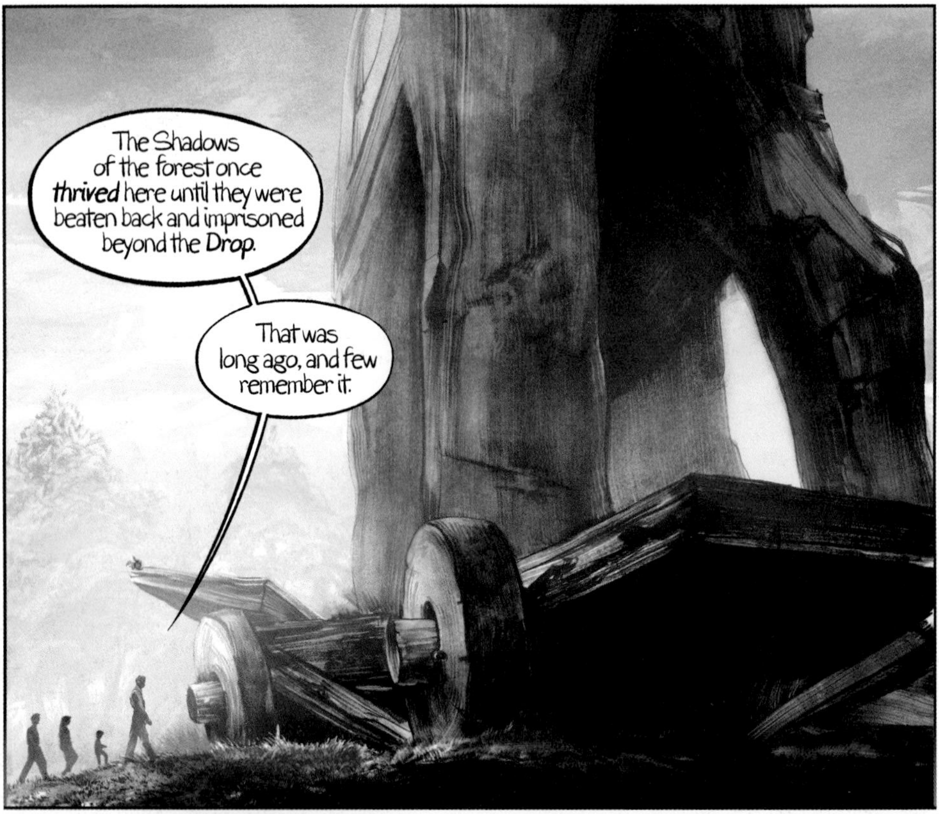
The Shadows of the forest once ***thrived*** here until they were beaten back and imprisoned beyond the ***Drop***.
That was long ago, and few remember it.

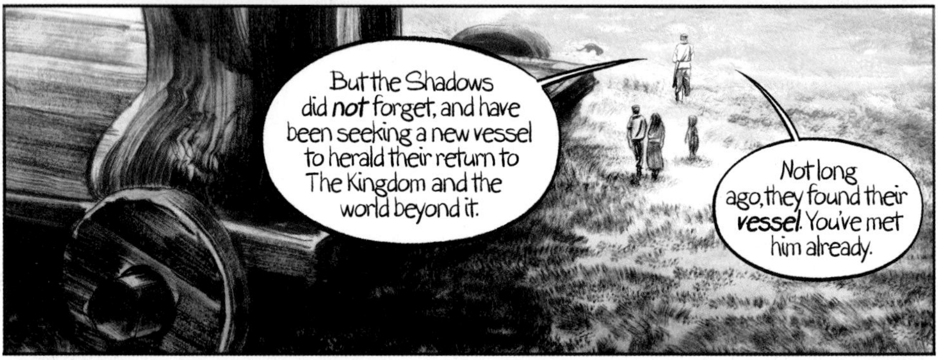
But the Shadows did ***not*** forget, and have been seeking a new vessel to herald their return to The Kingdom and the world beyond it.
Not long ago, they found their ***vessel***. You've met him already.

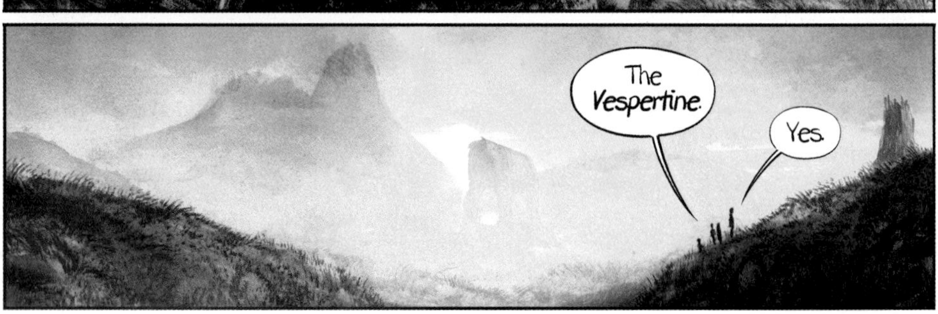
The ***Vespertine***.
Yes.

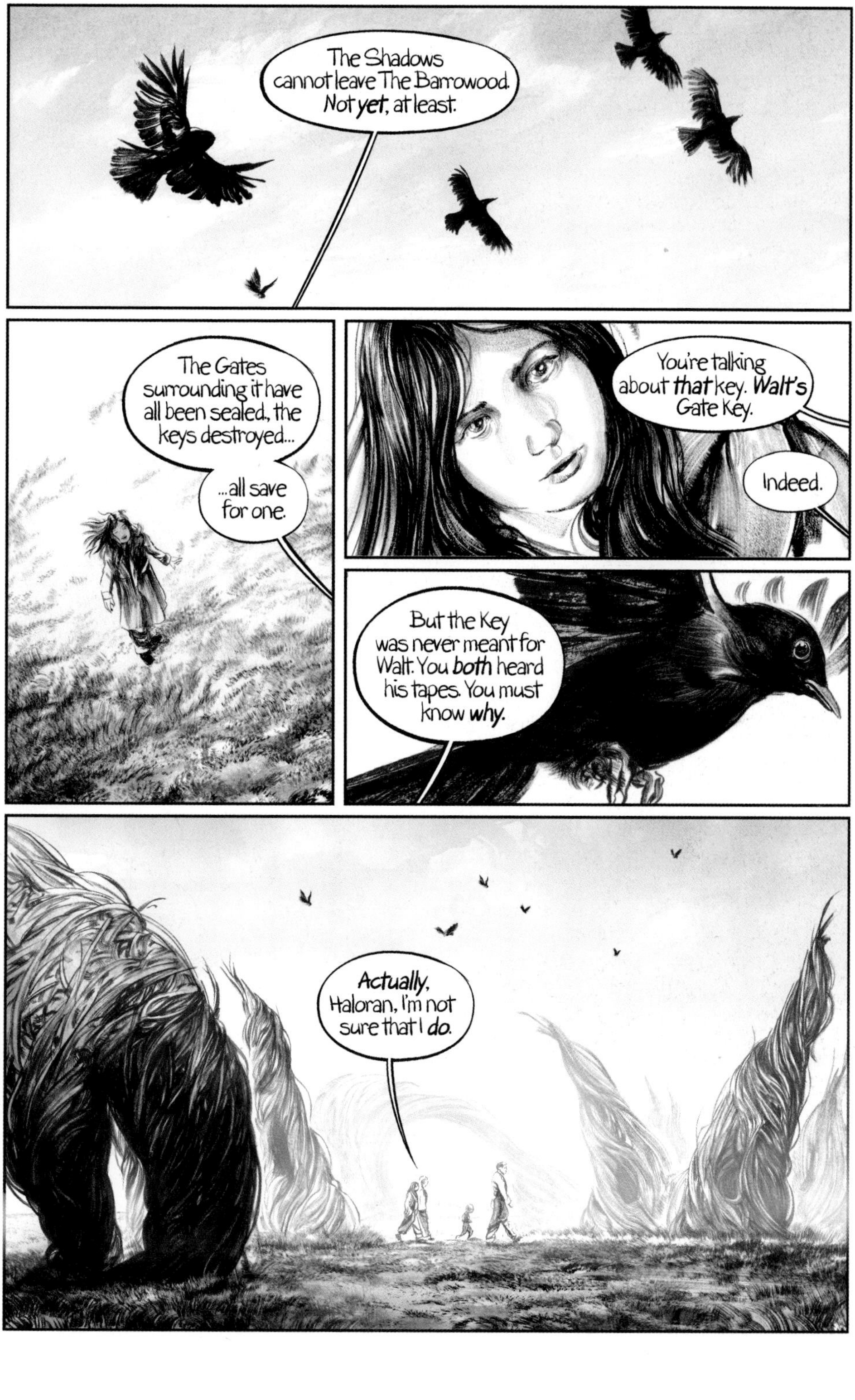
The Shadows cannot leave The Barrowood. Not *yet*, at least.
The Gates surrounding it have all been sealed., the keys destroyed...
...all save for one.
You're talking about *that* key. *Walt's* Gate Key.
Indeed.
But the Key was never meant for Walt. You *both* heard his tapes. You must know *why*.
Actually, Haloran, I'm not sure that I *do*.

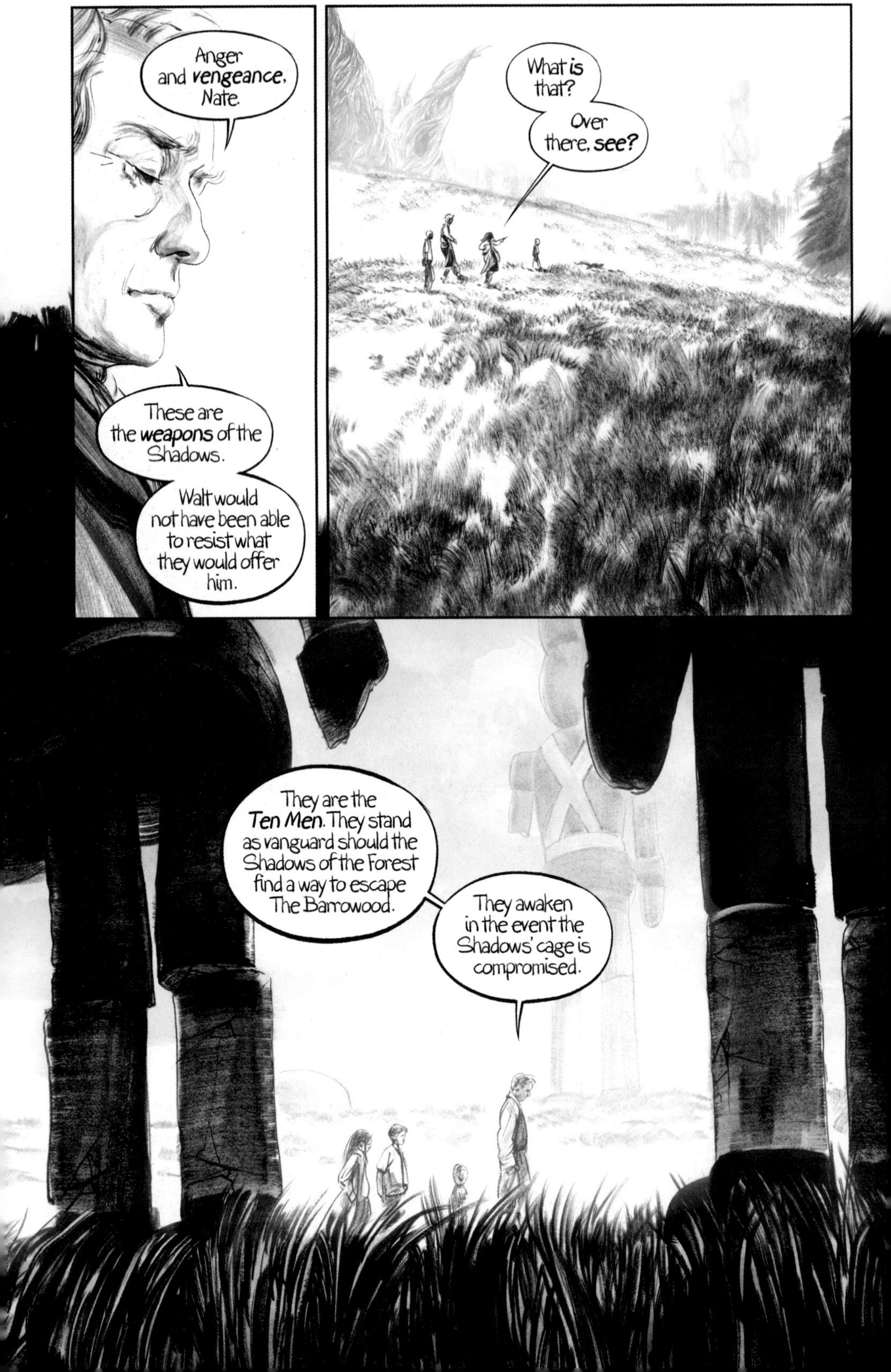

Anger and vengeance, Nate.
These are the weapons of the Shadows.
Walt would not have been able to resist what they would offer him.
What is that?
Over there, see?
They are the Ten Men. They stand as vanguard should the Shadows of the Forest find a way to escape The Barrowood.
They awaken in the event the Shadows' cage is compromised.

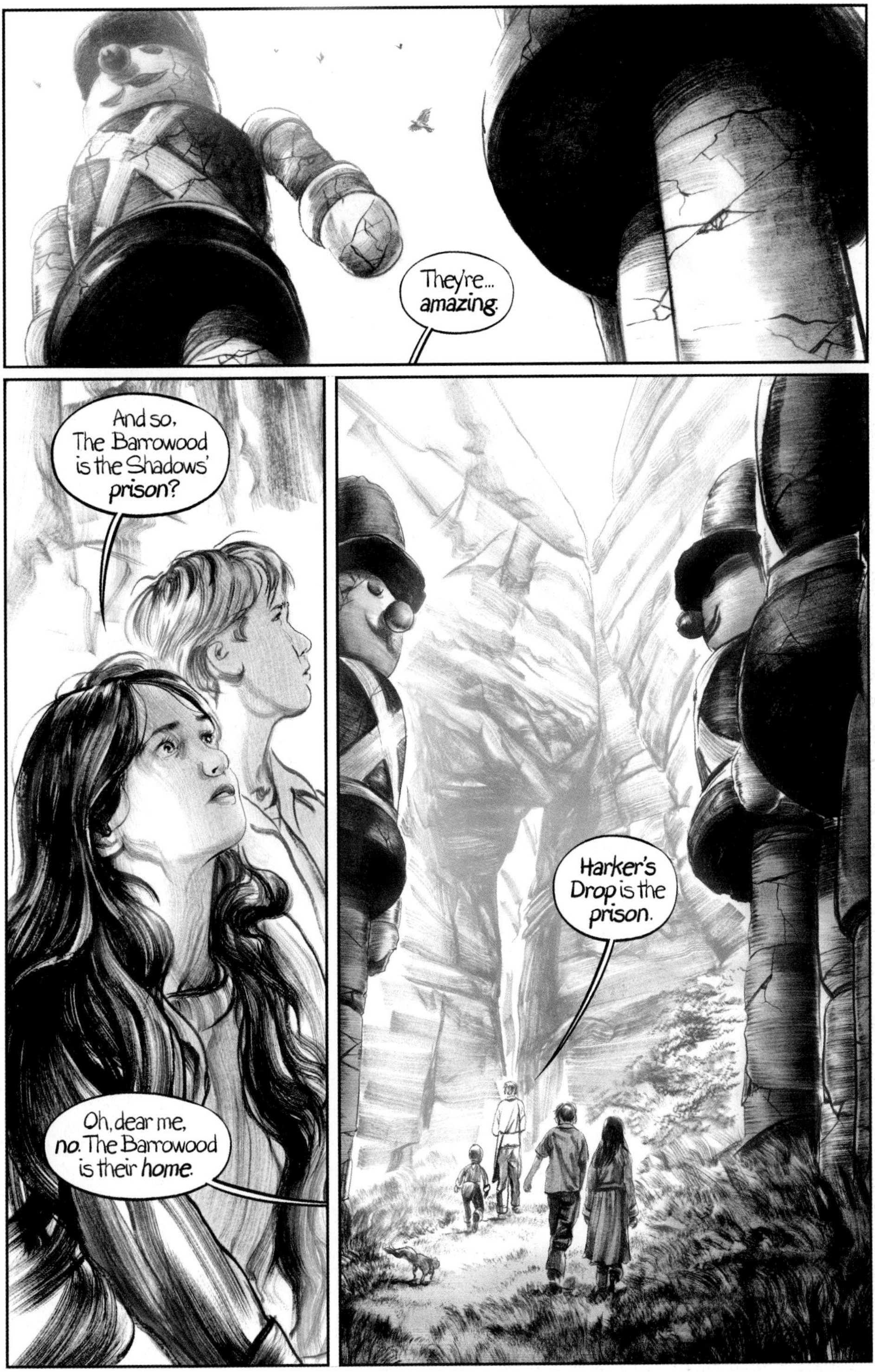
They're... amazing.
And so, The Barrowood is the Shadows' prison?
Oh, dear me, no. The Barrowood is their home.
Harker's Drop is the prison.

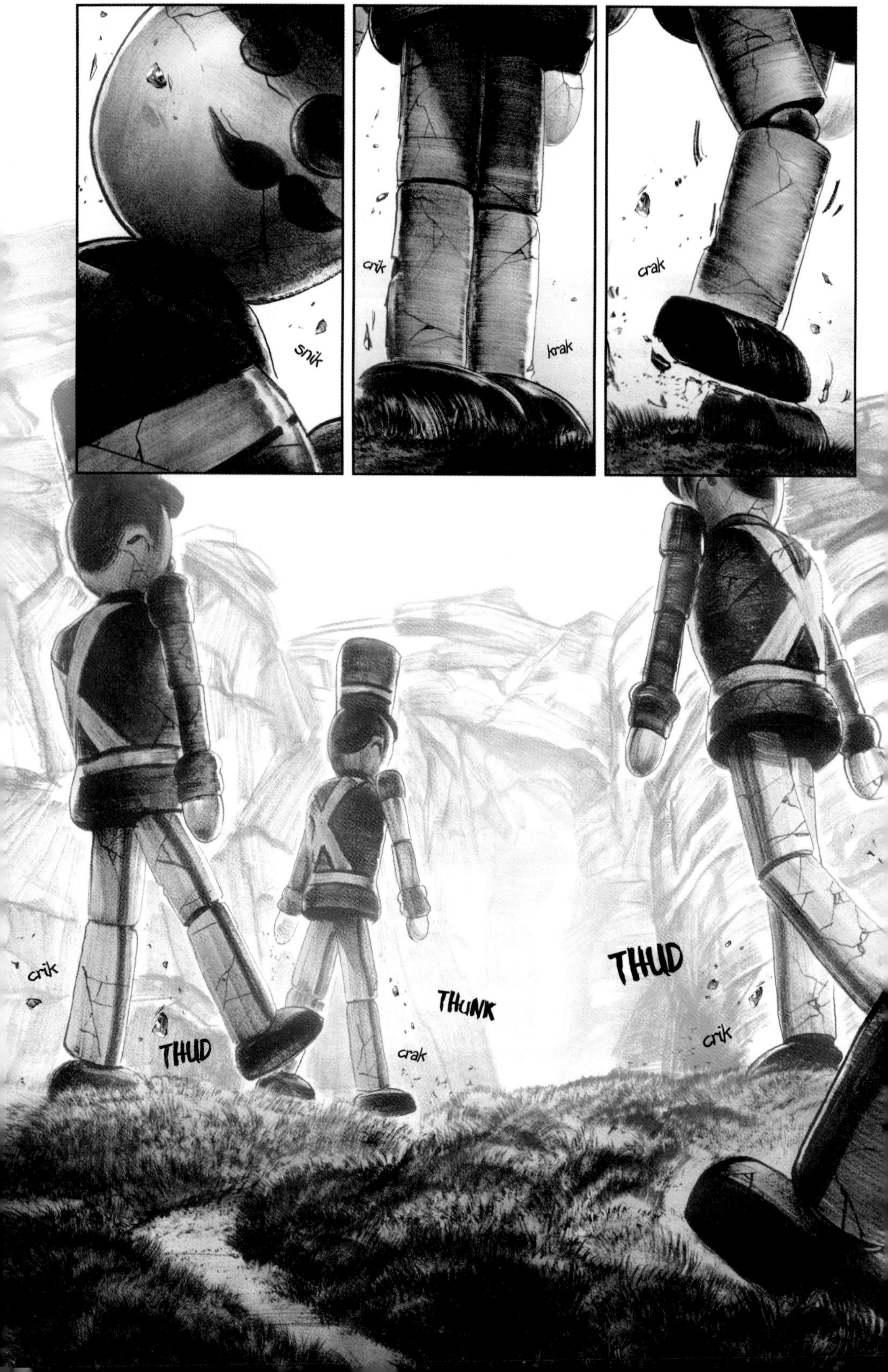
snik
crik
krak
crak
crik
THUD
THUNK
crak
THUD
crik

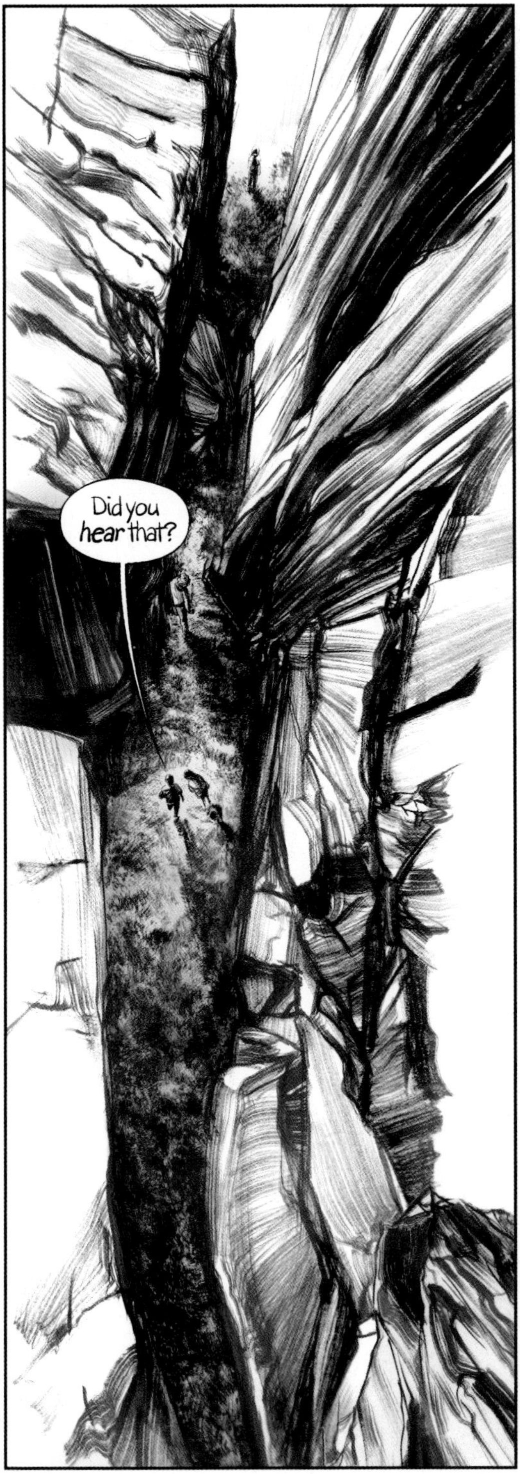
Did you **hear** that?

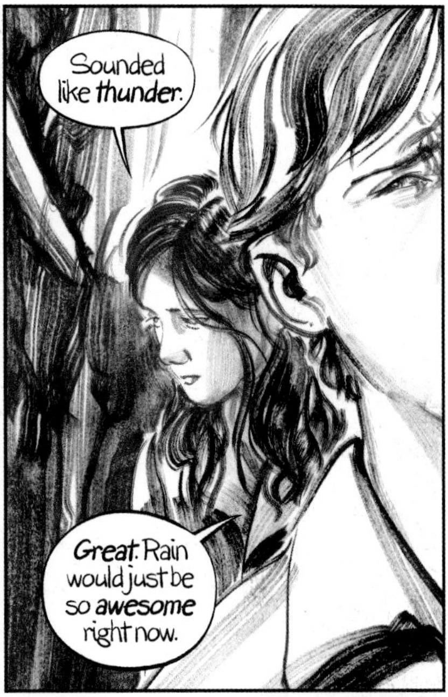
Sounded like **thunder**.
Great. Rain would just be so **awesome** right now.

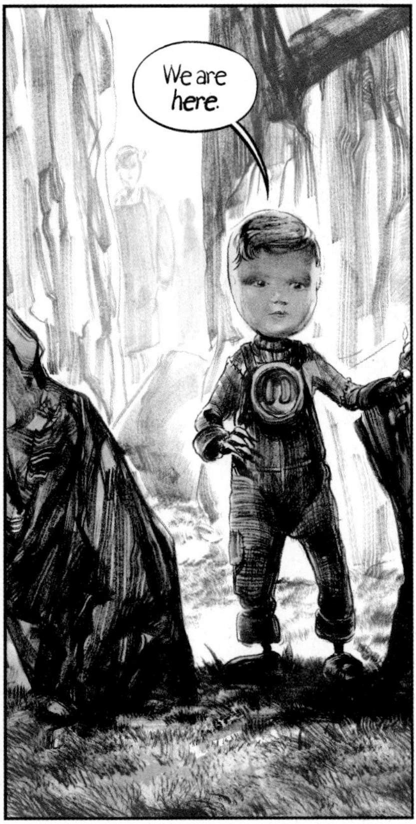
We are **here**.

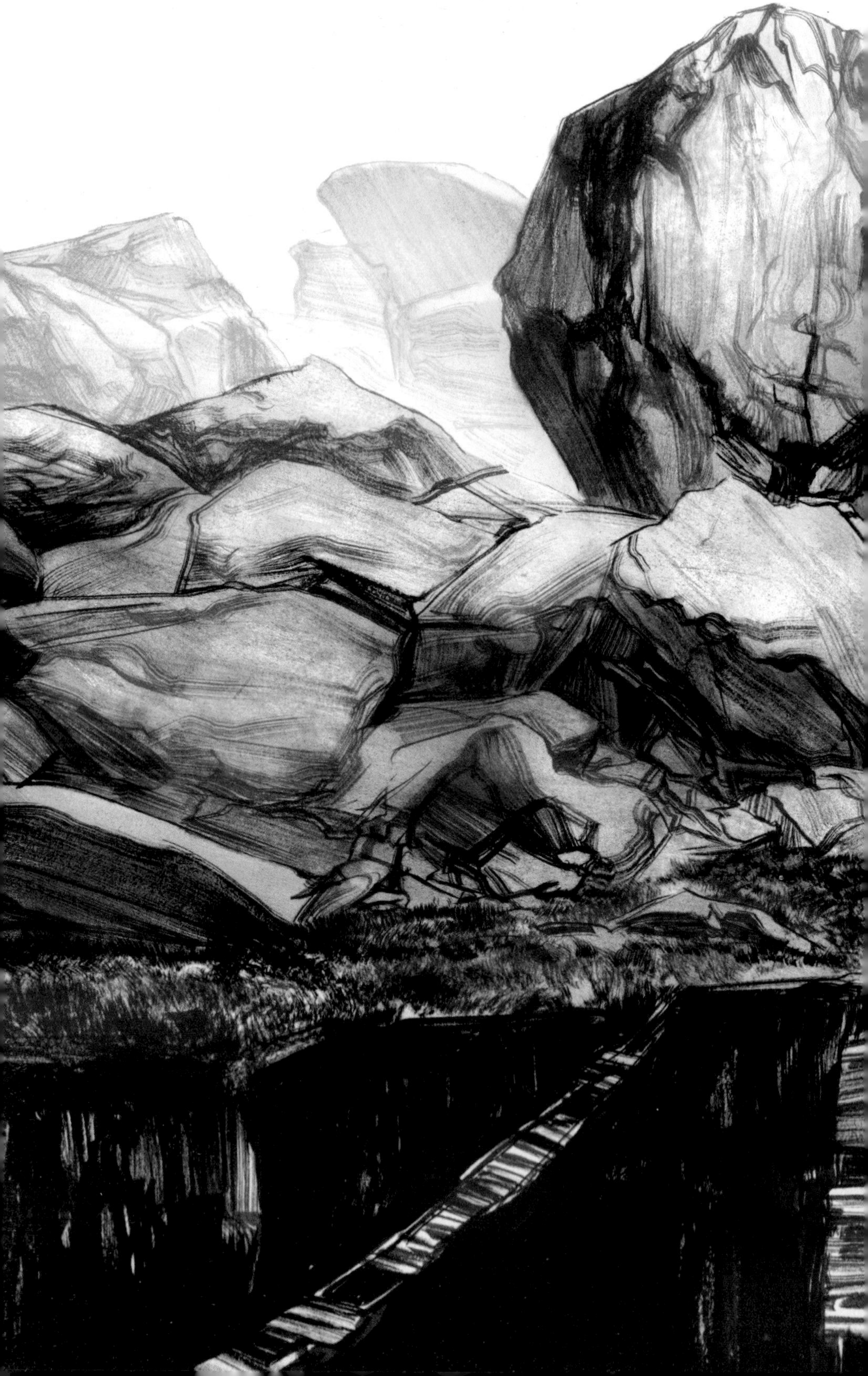

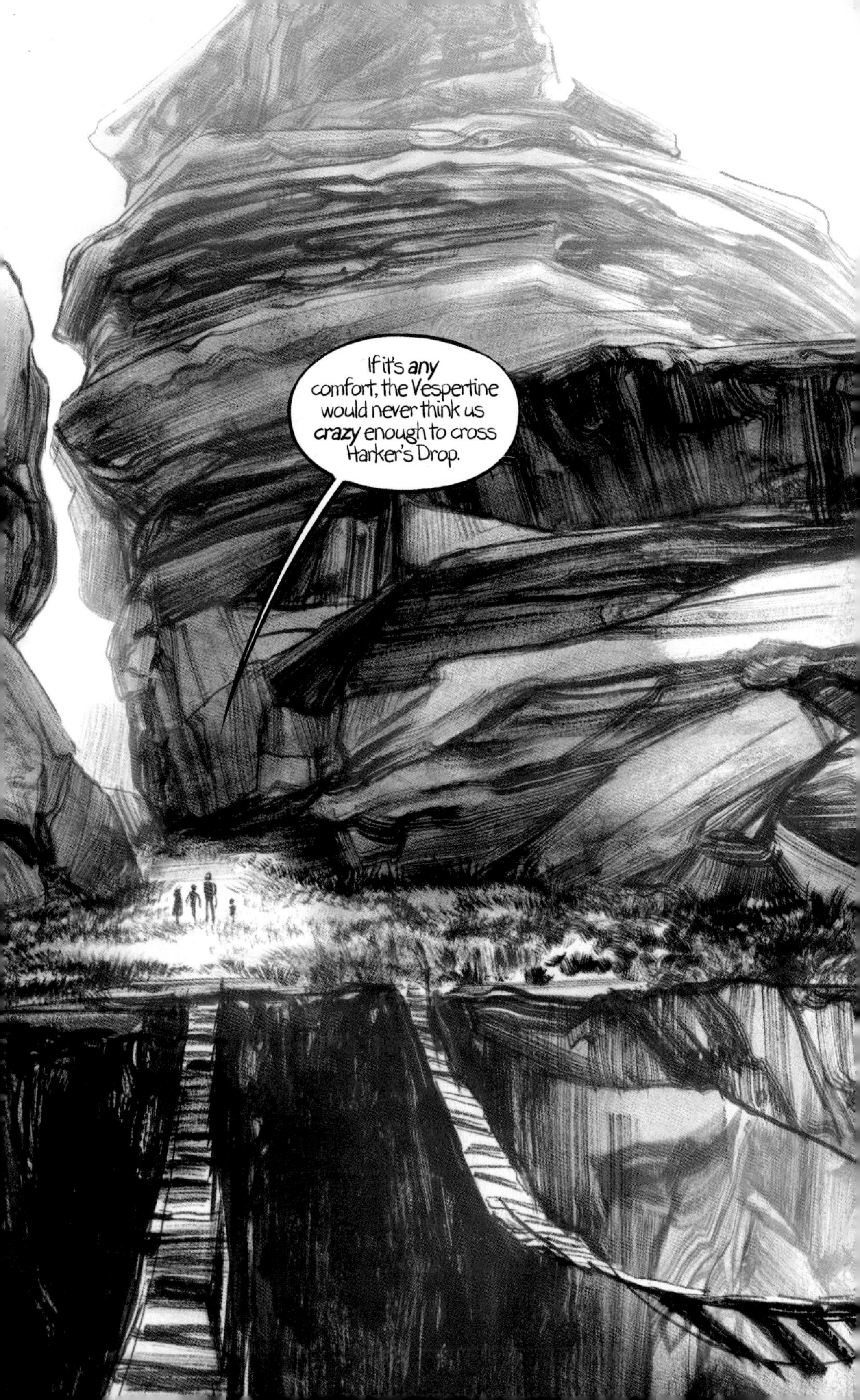
If it's **any** comfort, the Vespertine would never think us **crazy** enough to cross Harker's Drop.

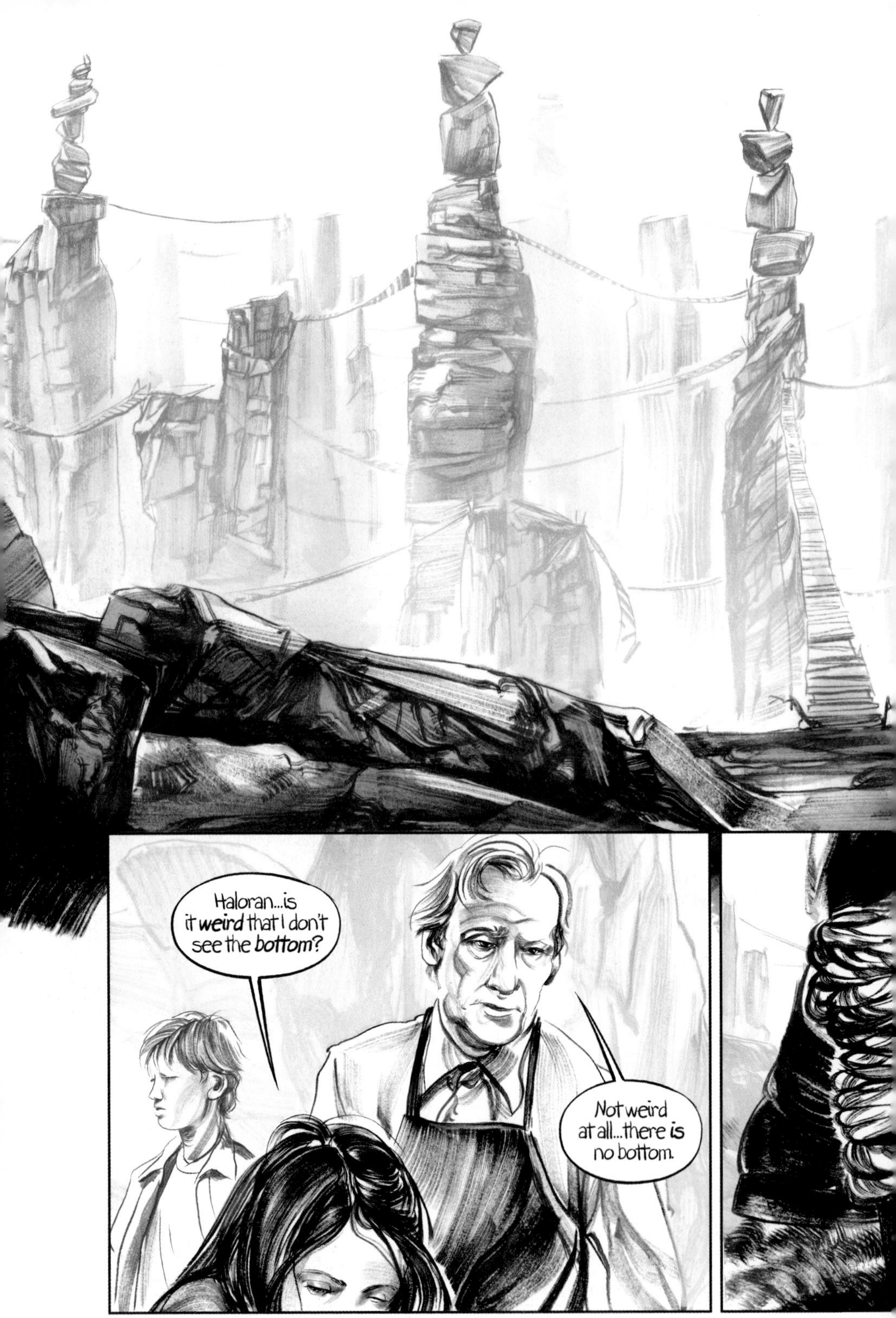
Haloran...is it weird that I don't see the bottom?
Not weird at all...there is no bottom.

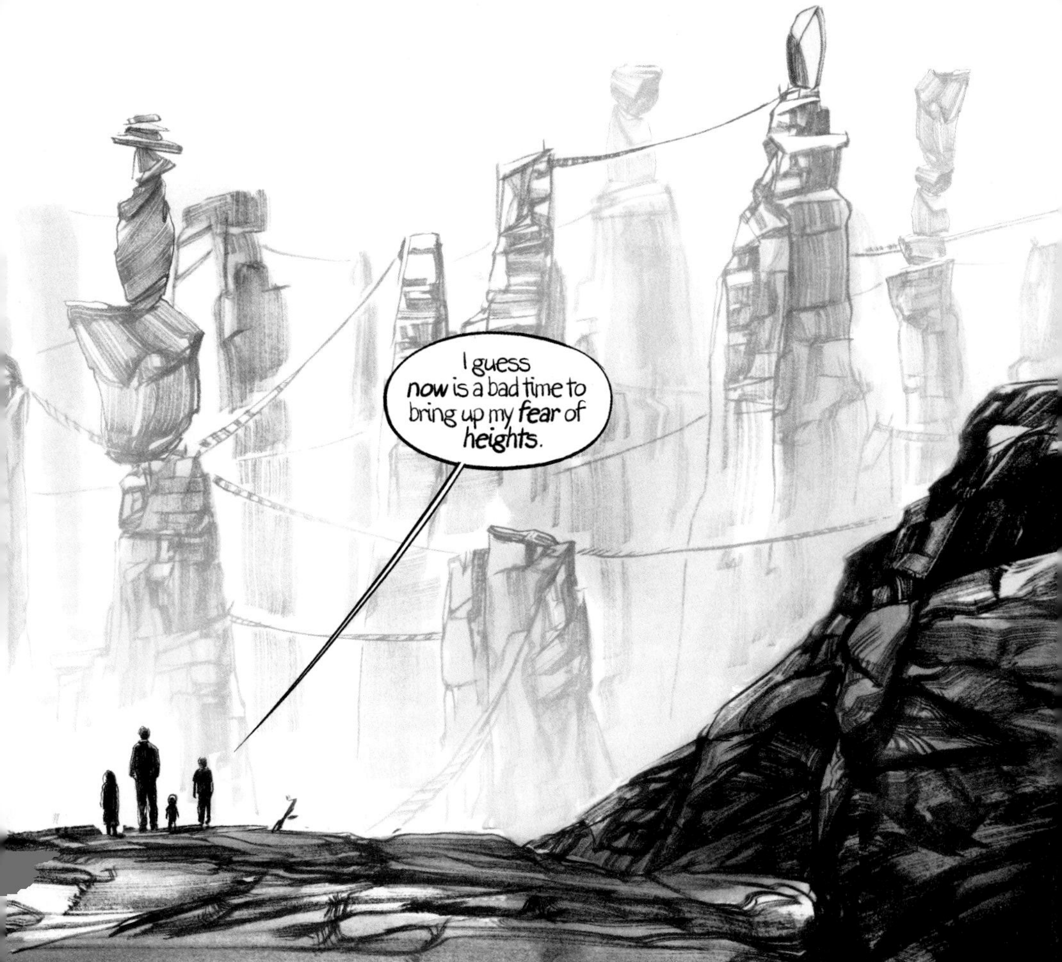
I guess now is a bad time to bring up my fear of heights.

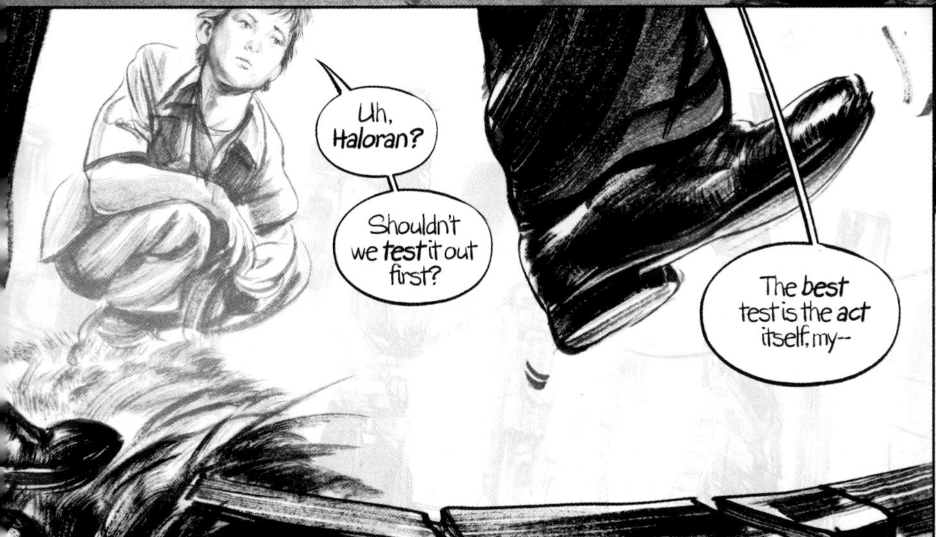
Uh, Haloran?
Shouldn't we test it out first?
The best test is the act itself, my--

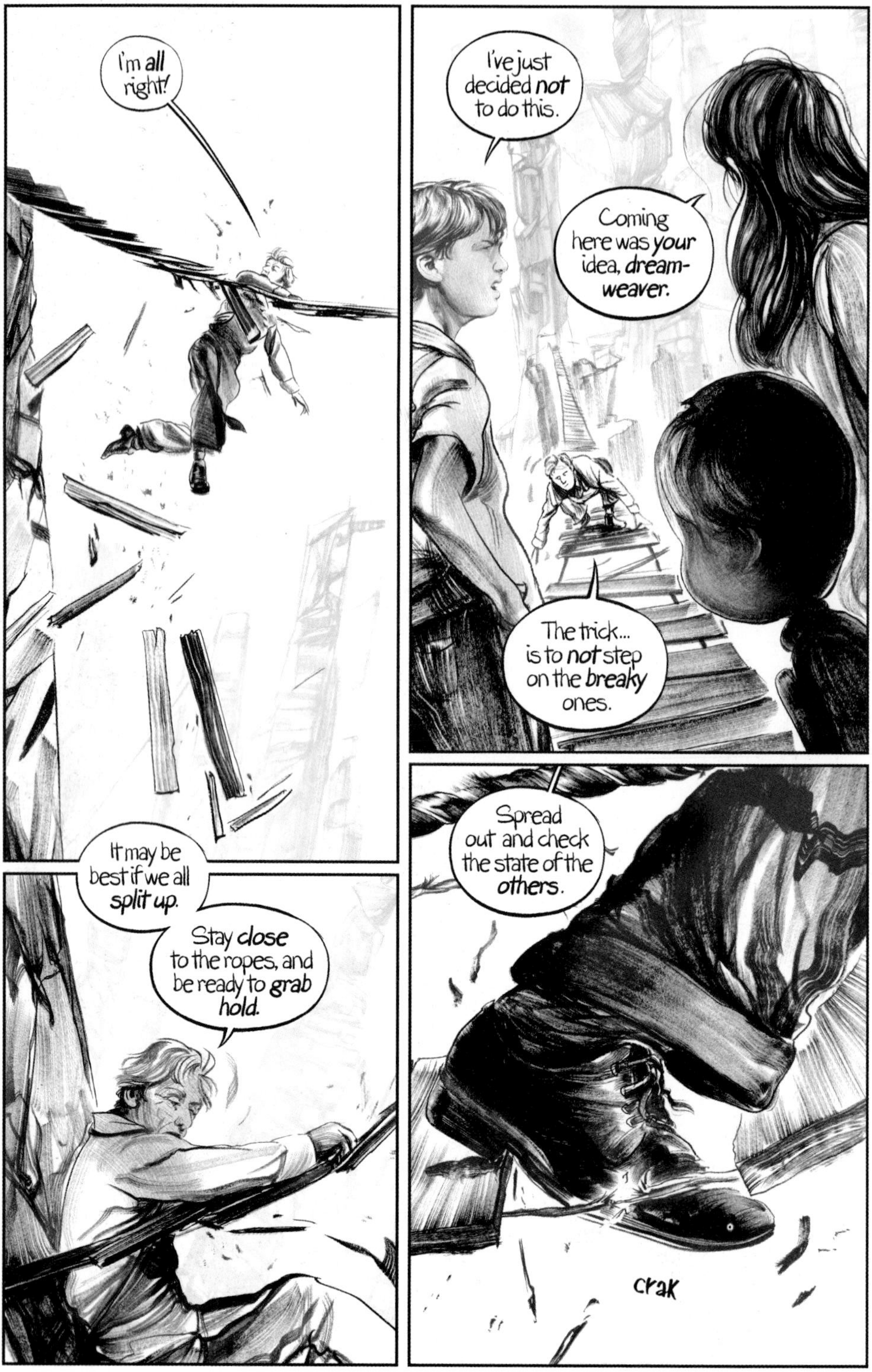

I'm all right!
I've just decided not to do this.
Coming here was your idea, dream-weaver.
The trick... is to not step on the breaky ones.
It may be best if we all split up.
Stay close to the ropes, and be ready to grab hold.
Spread out and check the state of the others.
crak

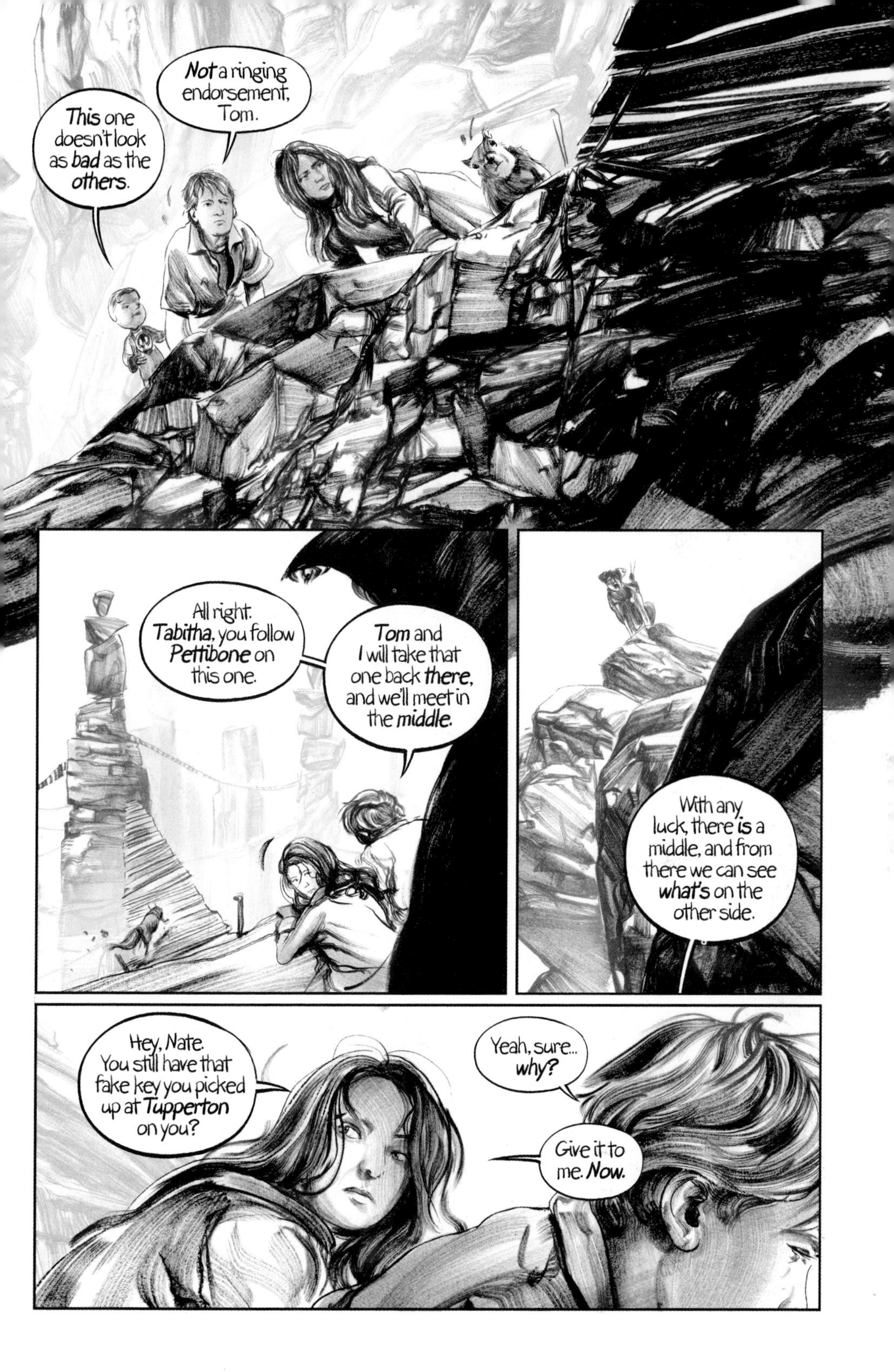
This one doesn't look as bad as the others.
Not a ringing endorsement, Tom.
All right. Tabitha, you follow Pettibone on this one.
Tom and I will take that one back there, and we'll meet in the middle.
With any luck, there is a middle, and from there we can see what's on the other side.
Hey, Nate. You still have that fake key you picked up at Tupperton on you?
Yeah, sure... why?
Give it to me. Now.

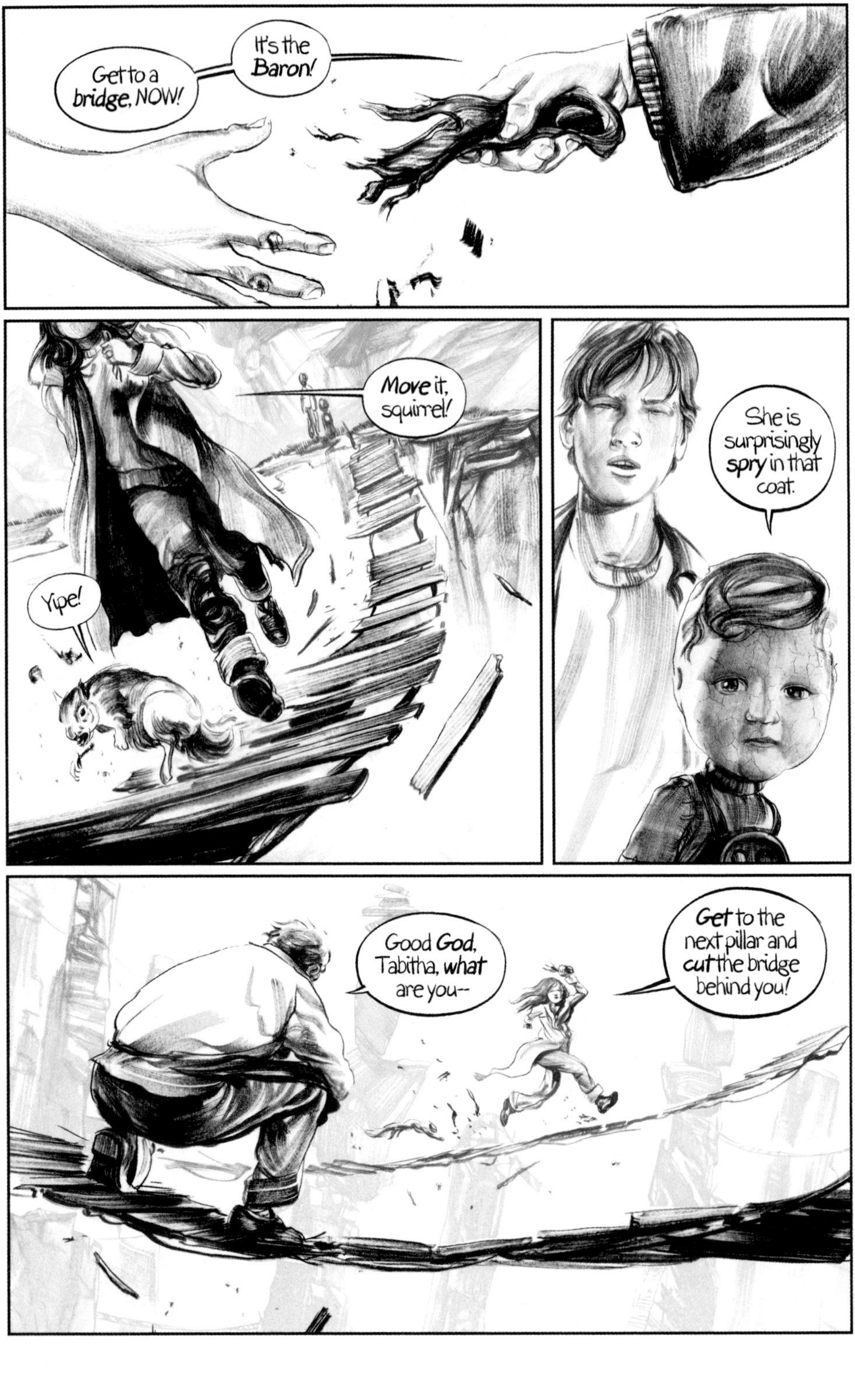
Get to a bridge, NOW!
It's the Baron!
Move it, squirrel!
Yipe!
She is surprisingly spry in that coat.
Good God, Tabitha, what are you--
Get to the next pillar and cut the bridge behind you!

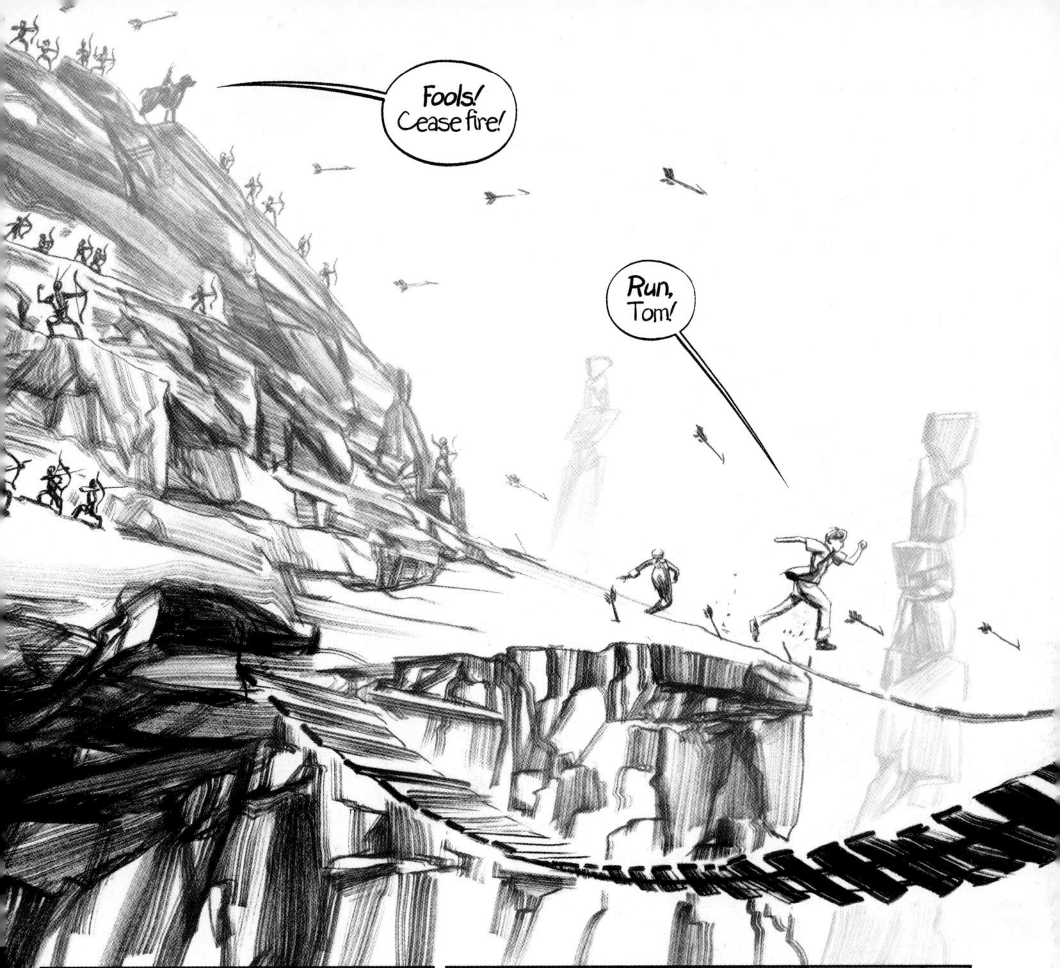
Fools! Cease fire!
Run, Tom!

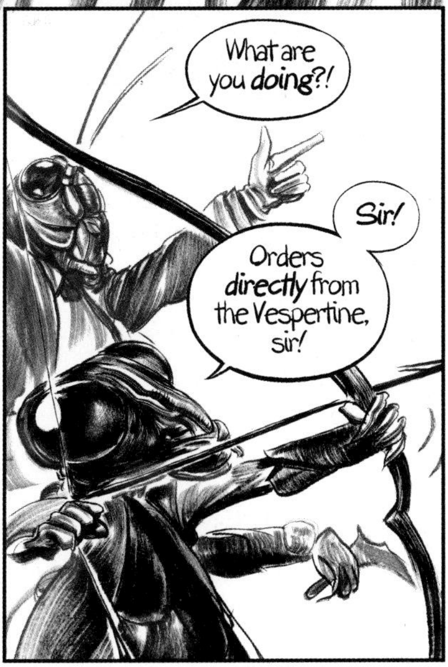
What are you **doing**?!
Sir!
Orders **directly** from the Vespertine, sir!

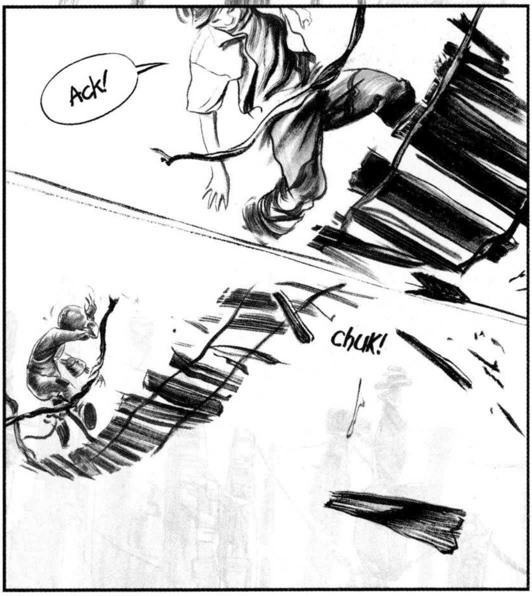
Ack!
chuk!

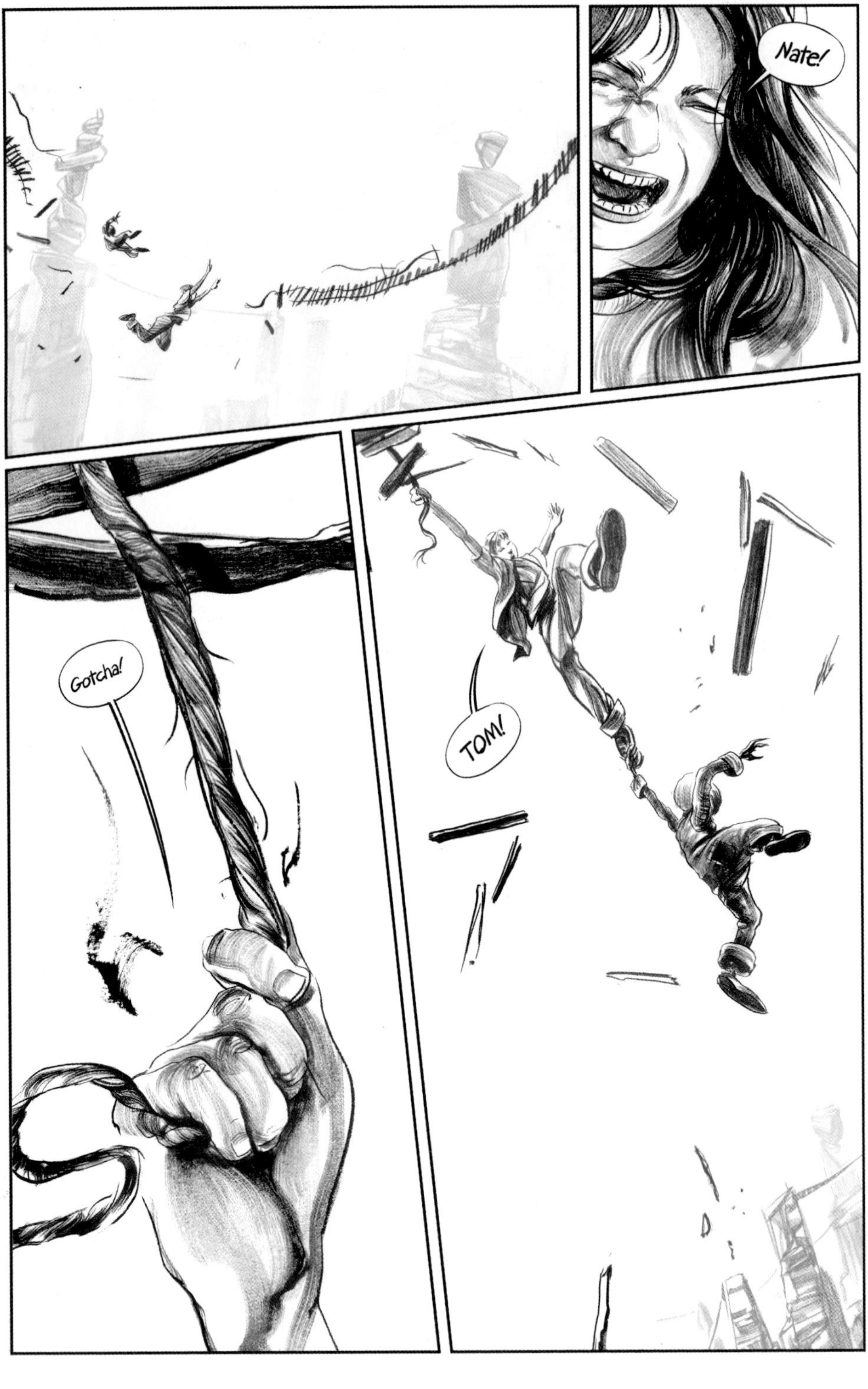
Nate!
Gotcha!
TOM!

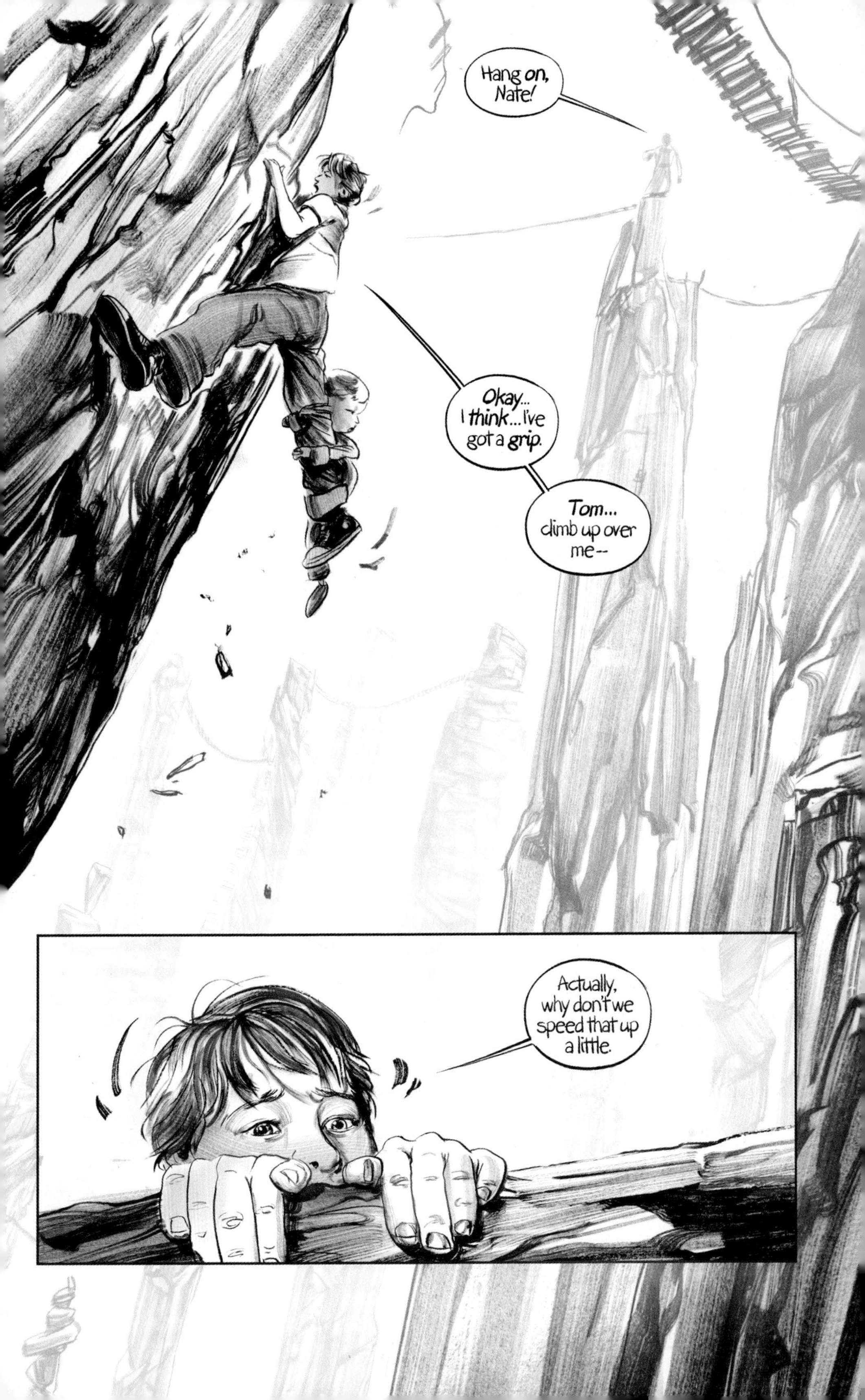
Hang on, Nate!
Okay... I think... I've got a grip.
Tom... climb up over me--
Actually, why don't we speed that up a little.

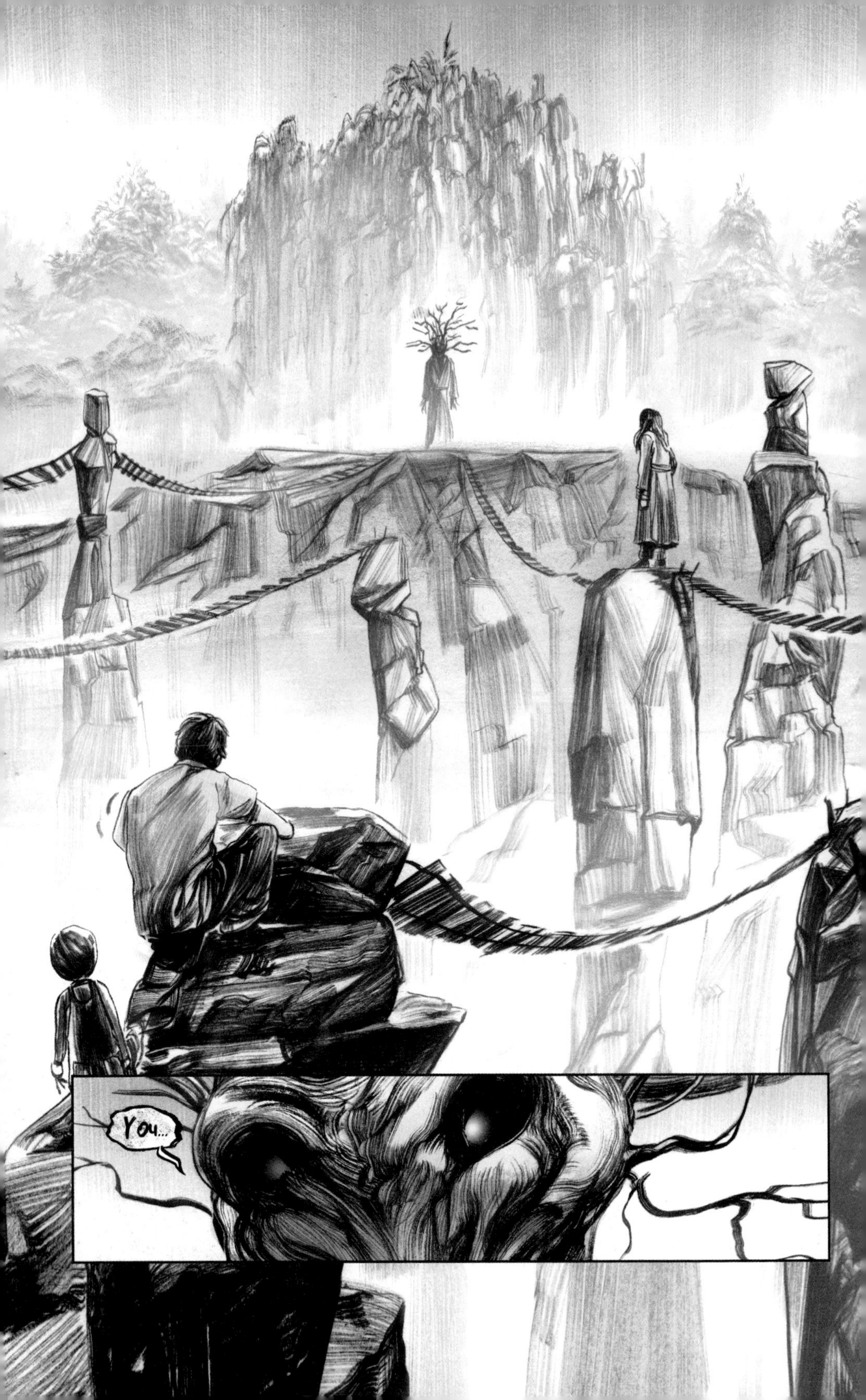
You...

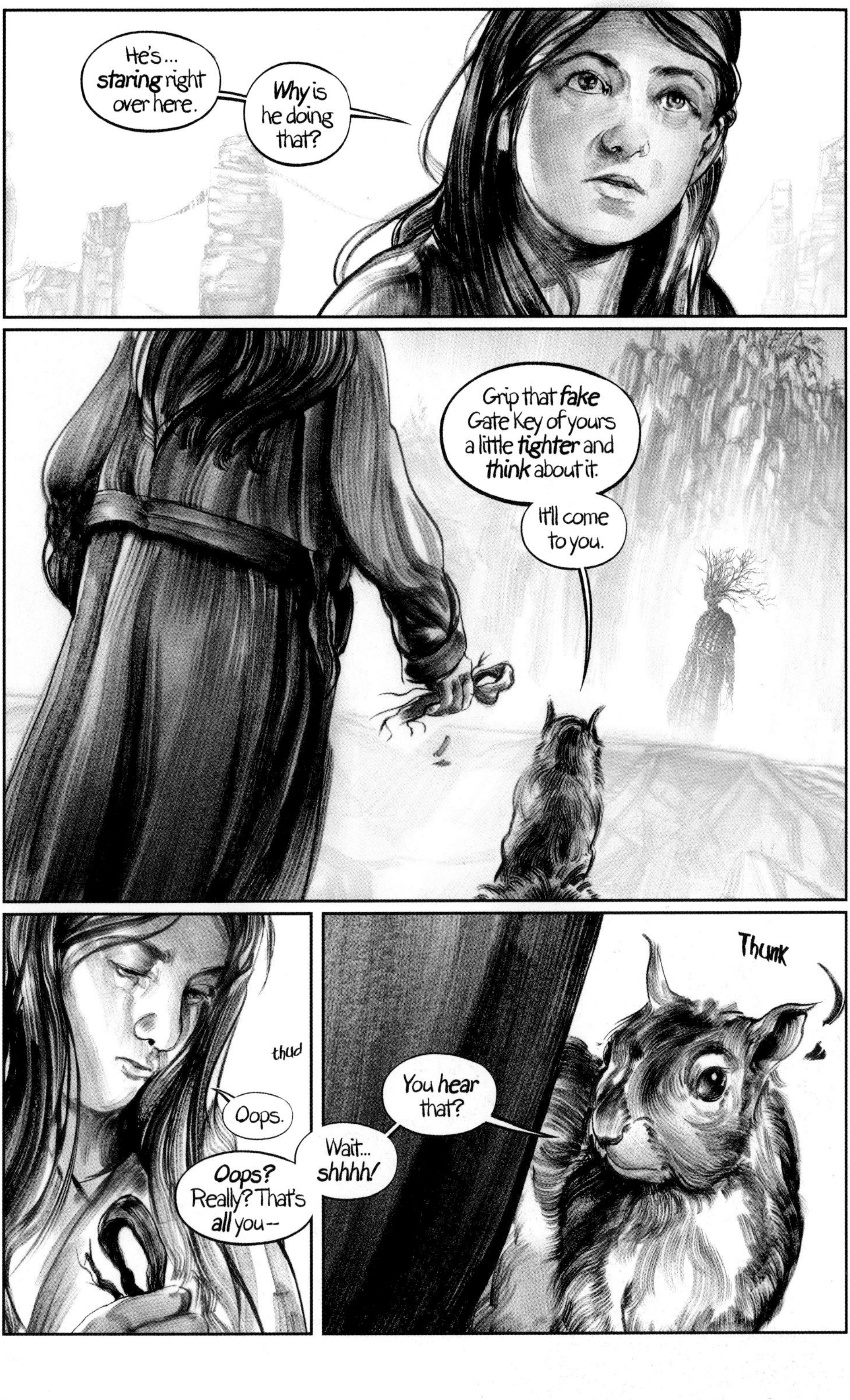
He's... staring right over here.
Why is he doing that?
Grip that fake Gate Key of yours a little tighter and think about it.
It'll come to you.
thud
Oops.
Oops? Really? That's all you--
Wait... shhhh!
Thunk
You hear that?

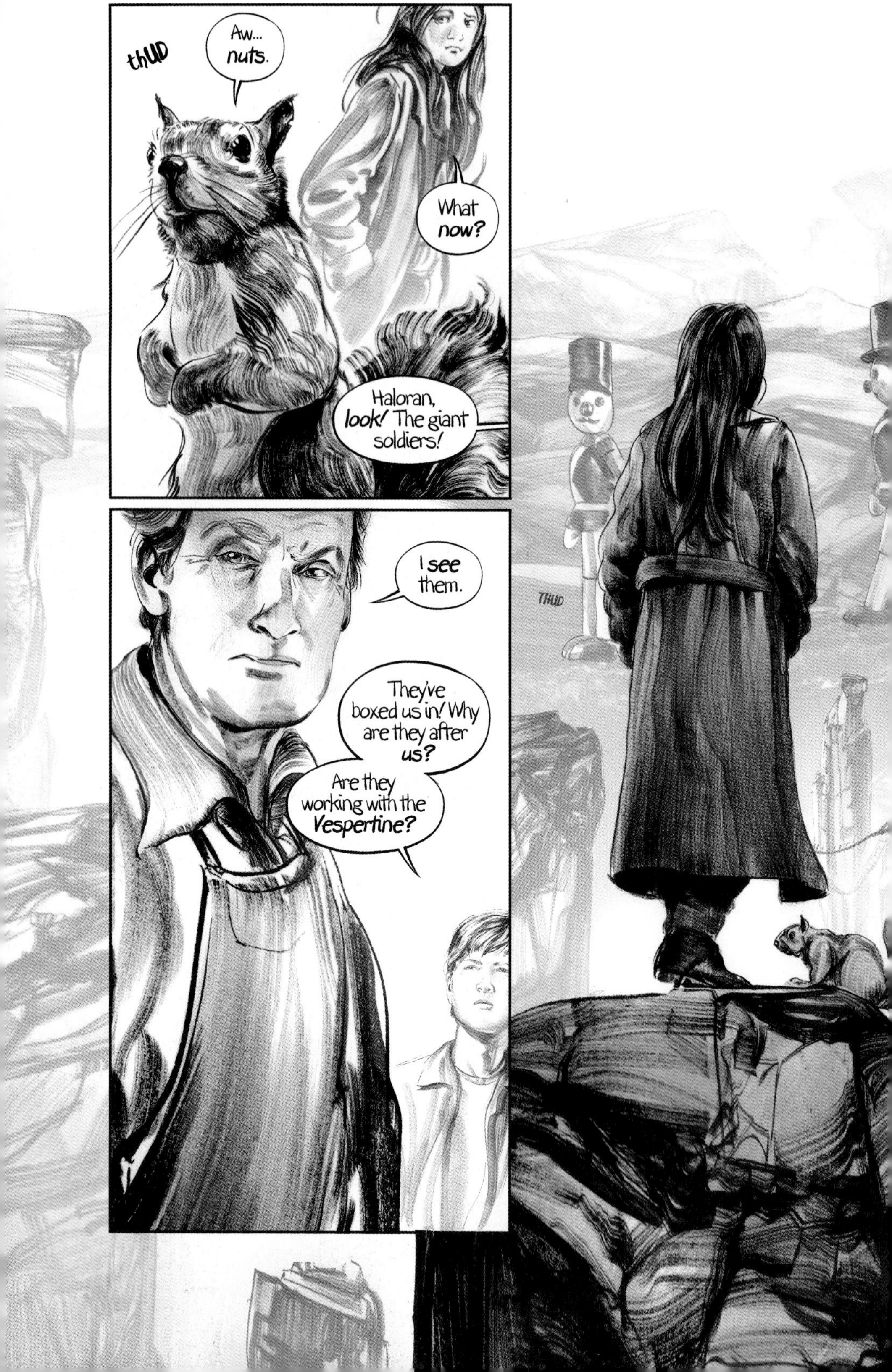
thUD
Aw... nuts.
What now?
Haloran, look! The giant soldiers!
I see them.
They've boxed us in! Why are they after us?
Are they working with the Vespertine?
THUD

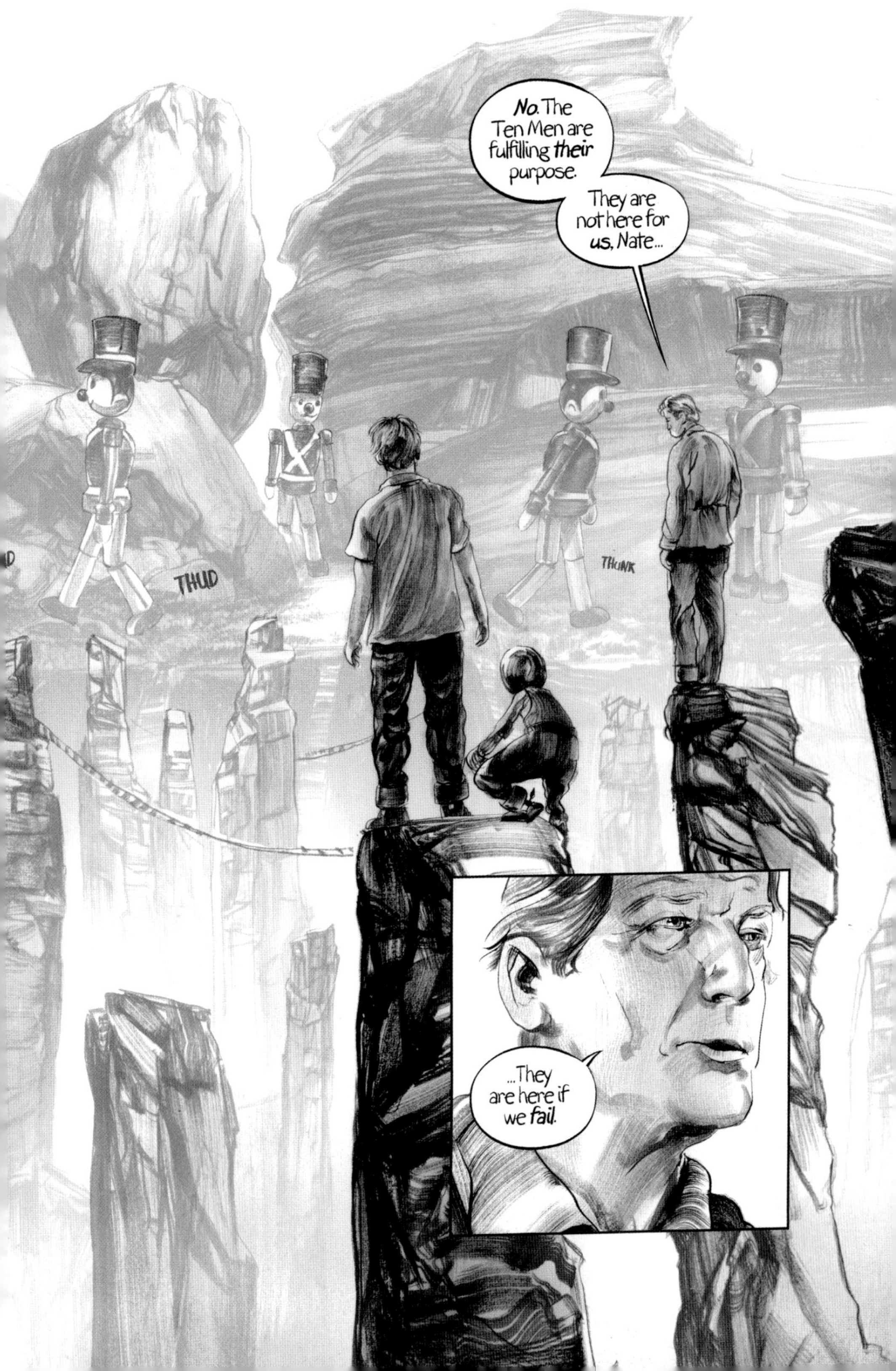

THUD
THUNK
No. The Ten Men are fulfilling their purpose.
They are not here for us, Nate...
...They are here if we fail.

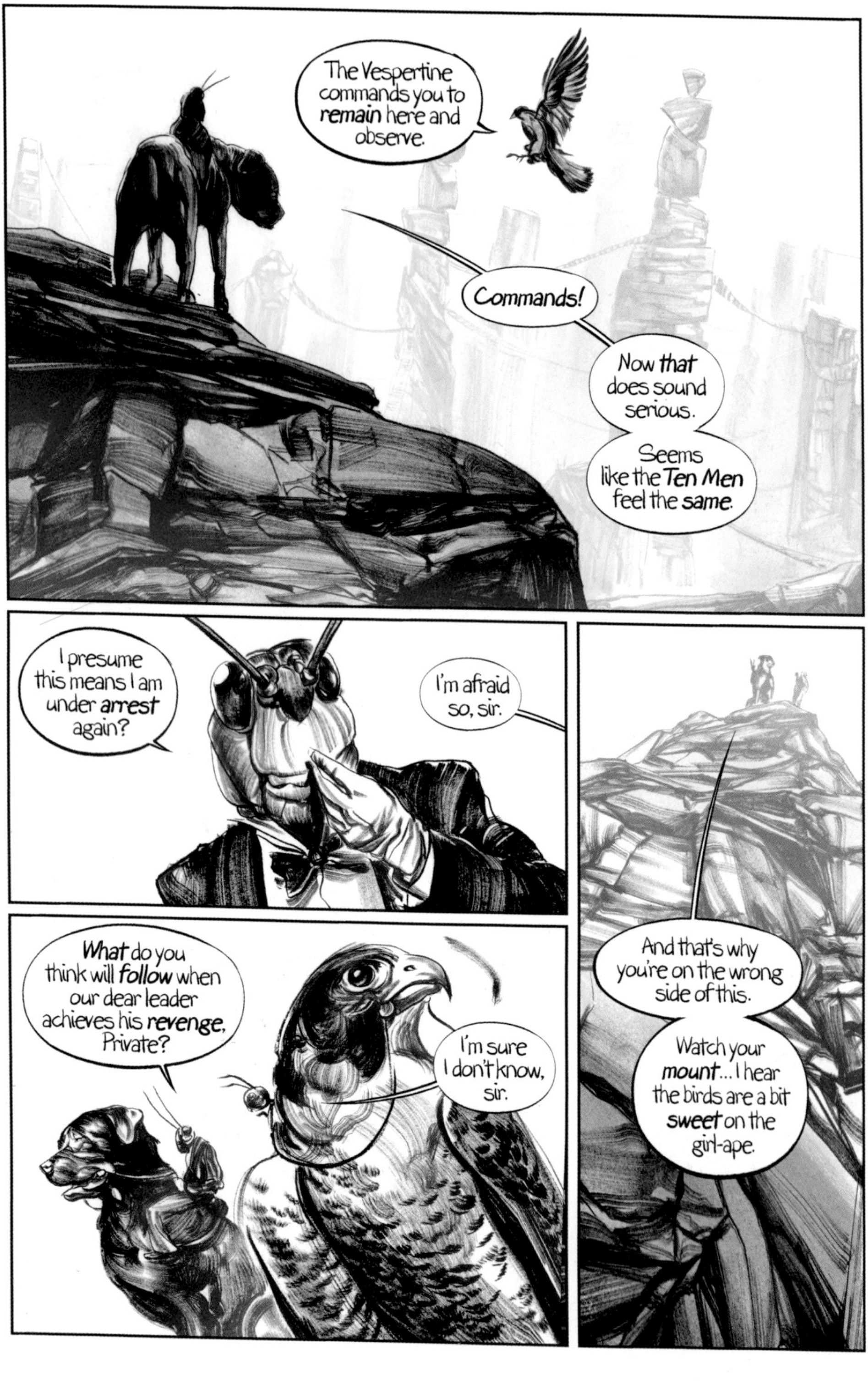
The Vespertine commands you to remain here and observe.
Commands!
Now that does sound serious.
Seems like the Ten Men feel the same.
I presume this means I am under arrest again?
I'm afraid so, sir.
What do you think will follow when our dear leader achieves his revenge, Private?
I'm sure I don't know, sir.
And that's why you're on the wrong side of this.
Watch your mount... I hear the birds are a bit sweet on the girl-ape.

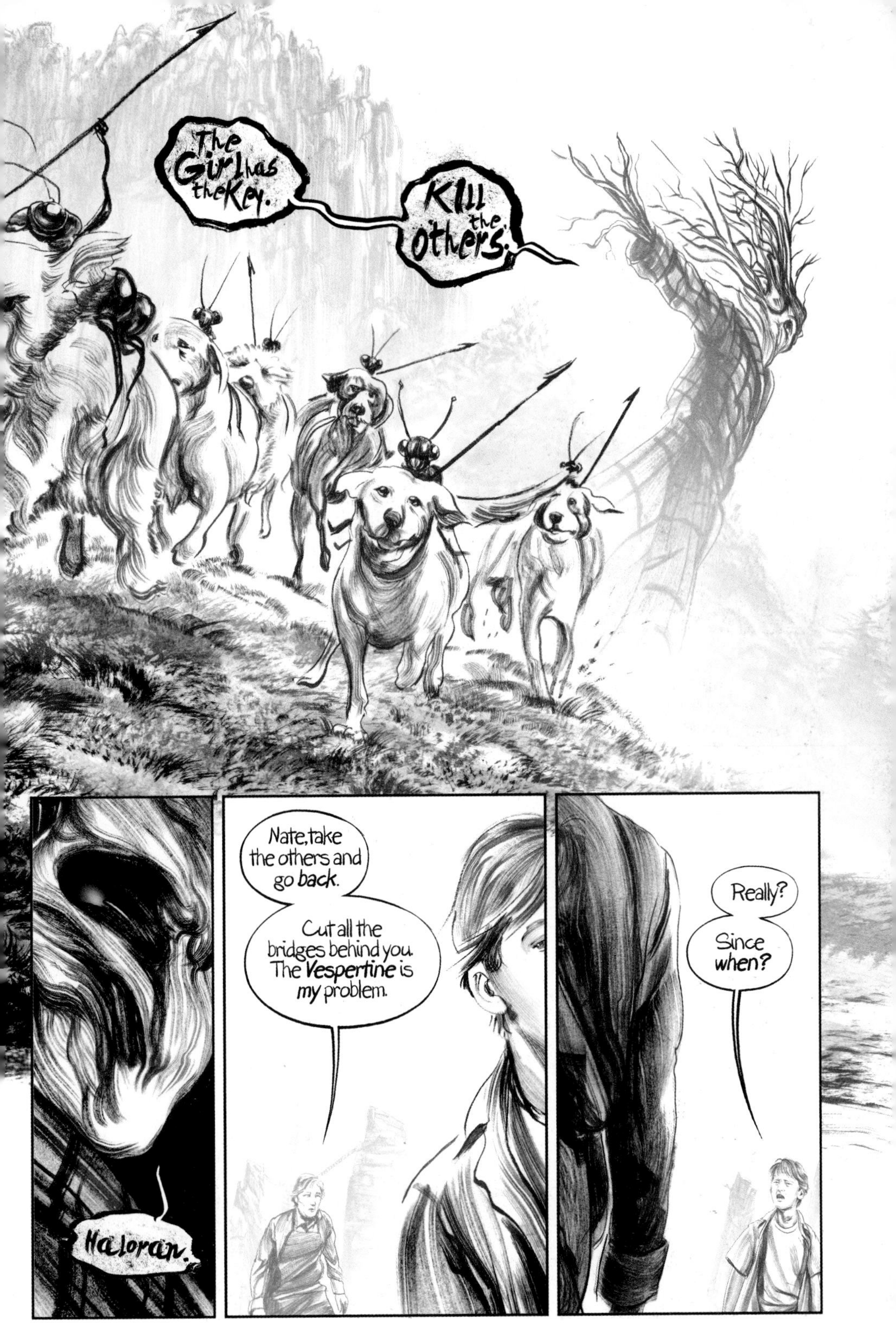
The Girl has the Key.
Kill the others.
Haloran.
Nate, take the others and go back.
Cut all the bridges behind you. The Vespertine is my problem.
Really?
Since when?

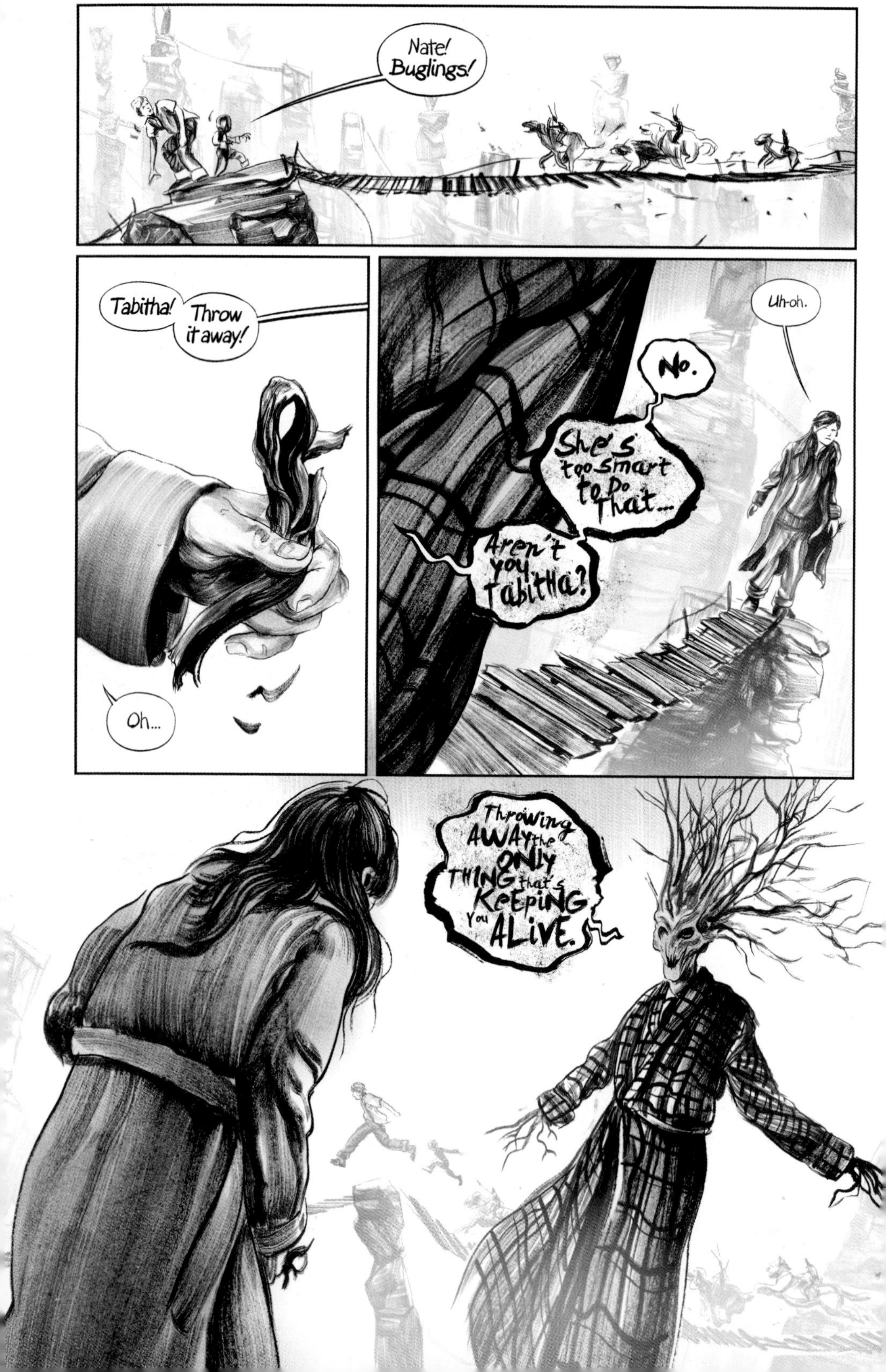
Nate! Buglings!
Tabitha!
Throw it away!
Oh...
Uh-oh.
No.
She's too smart to do that...
Aren't you, Tabitha?
Throwing AWAY the ONLY THING that's KEEPING you ALIVE.

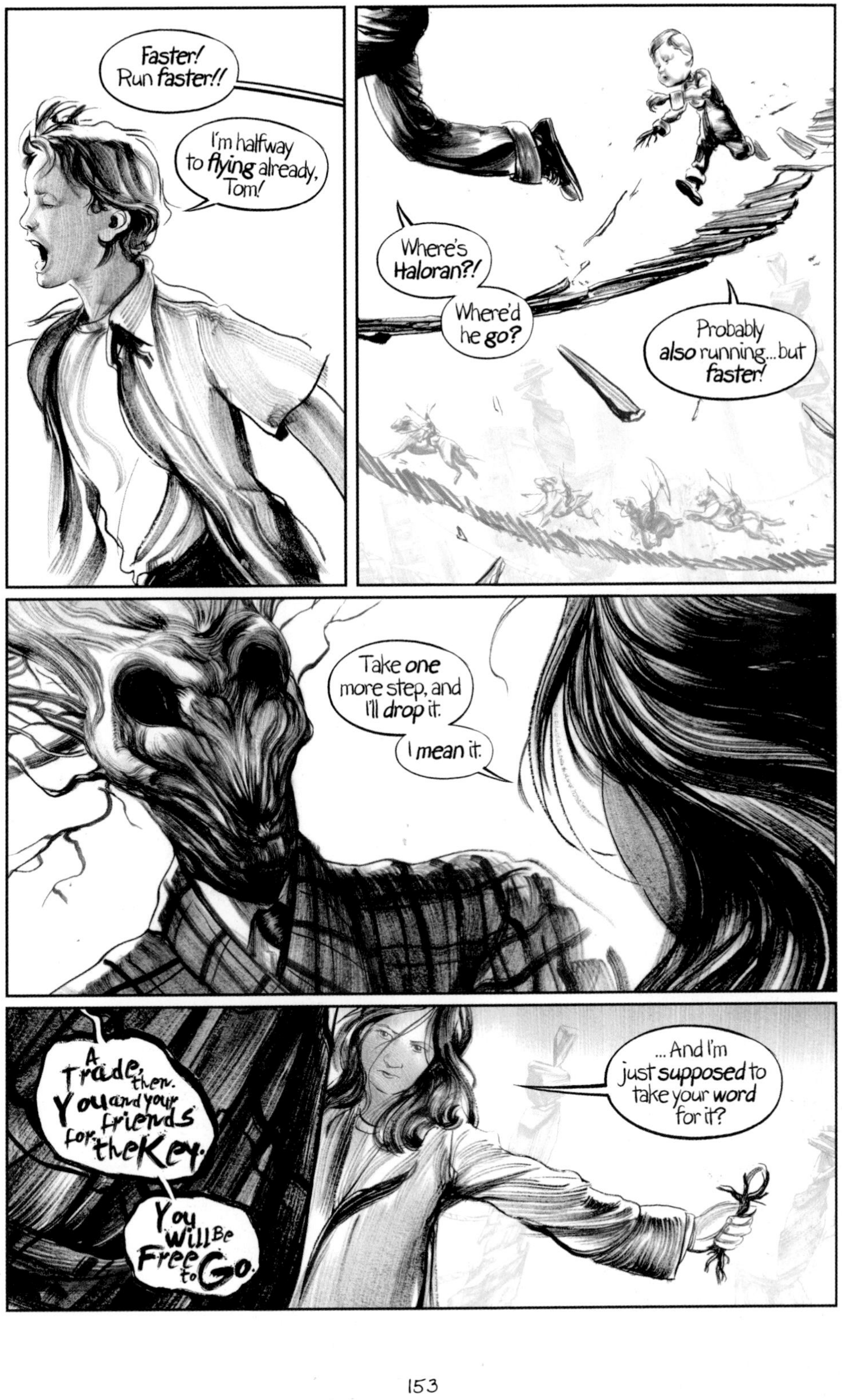
Faster! Run faster!!
I'm halfway to flying already, Tom!
Where's Haloran?!
Where'd he go?
Probably also running...but faster!
Take one more step, and I'll drop it.
I mean it.
A Trade, then. You and your friends for the Key.
You will Be Free to Go.
...And I'm just supposed to take your word for it?

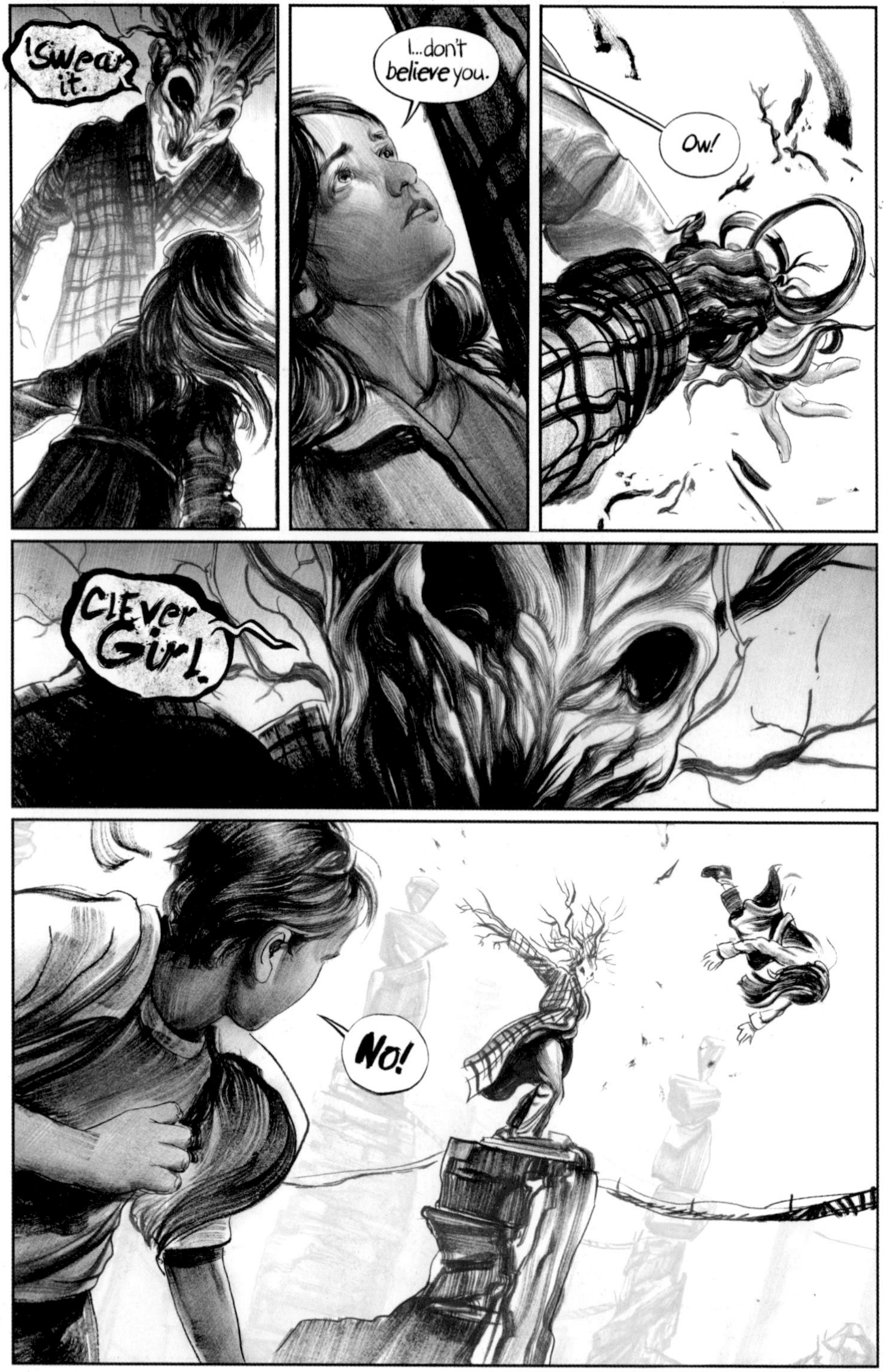
Swear it.
I...don't believe you.
Ow!
Clever Girl.
No!

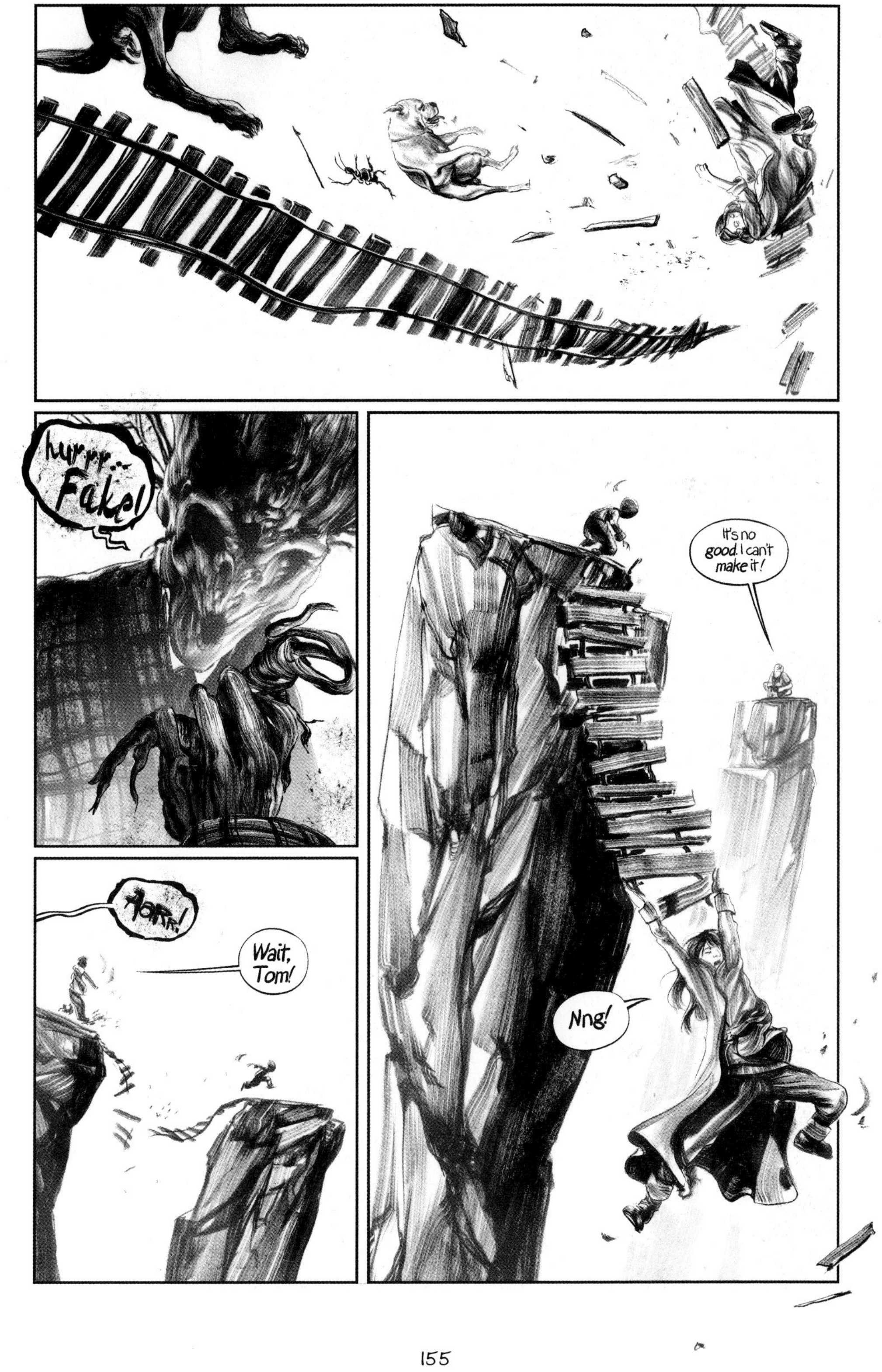
hurrr.. Fake!
RORR!
Wait, Tom!
It's no good. I can't make it!
Nng!

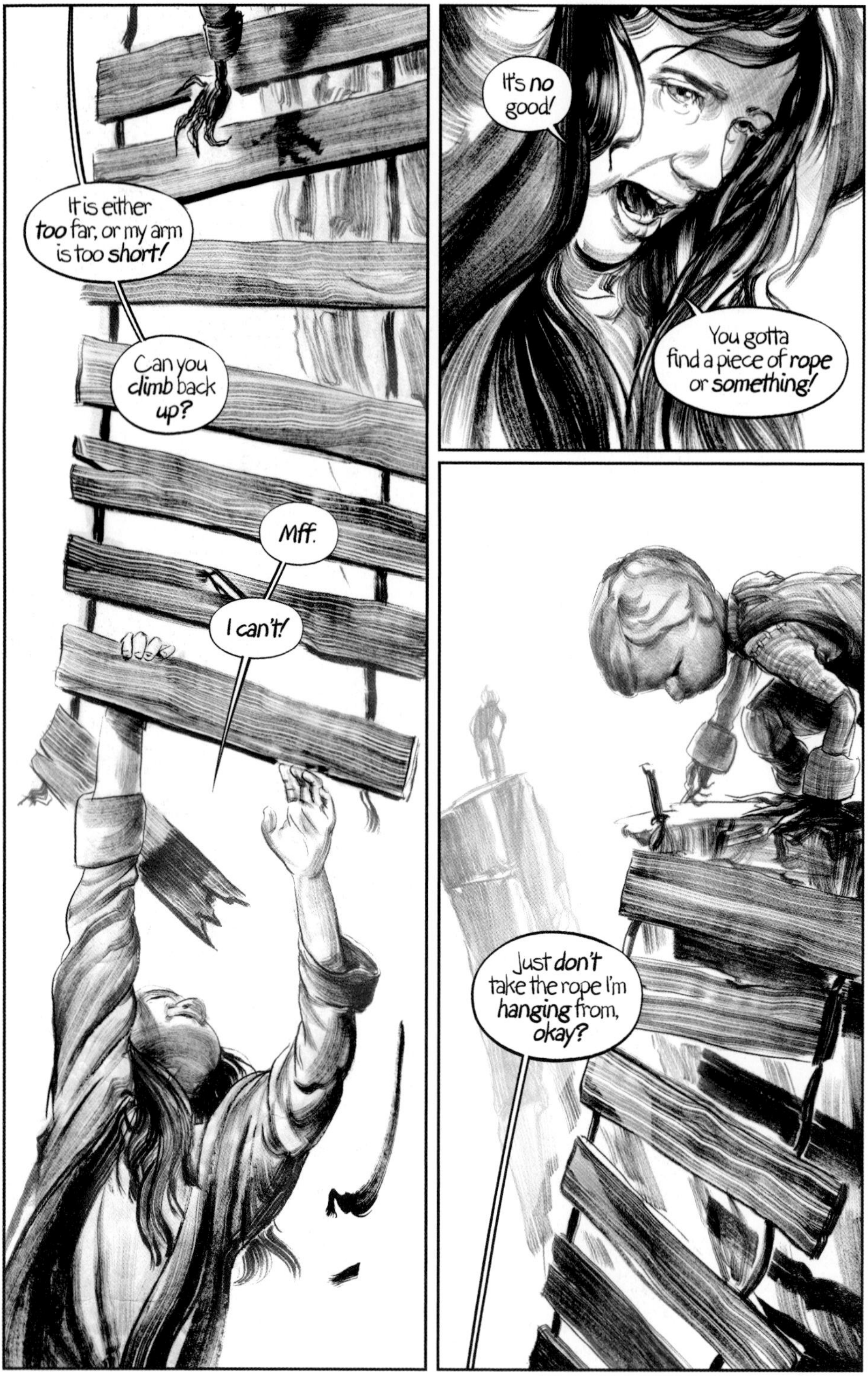
It is either too far, or my arm is too short!
Can you climb back up?
Mff.
I can't!
It's no good!
You gotta find a piece of rope or something!
Just don't take the rope I'm hanging from, okay?

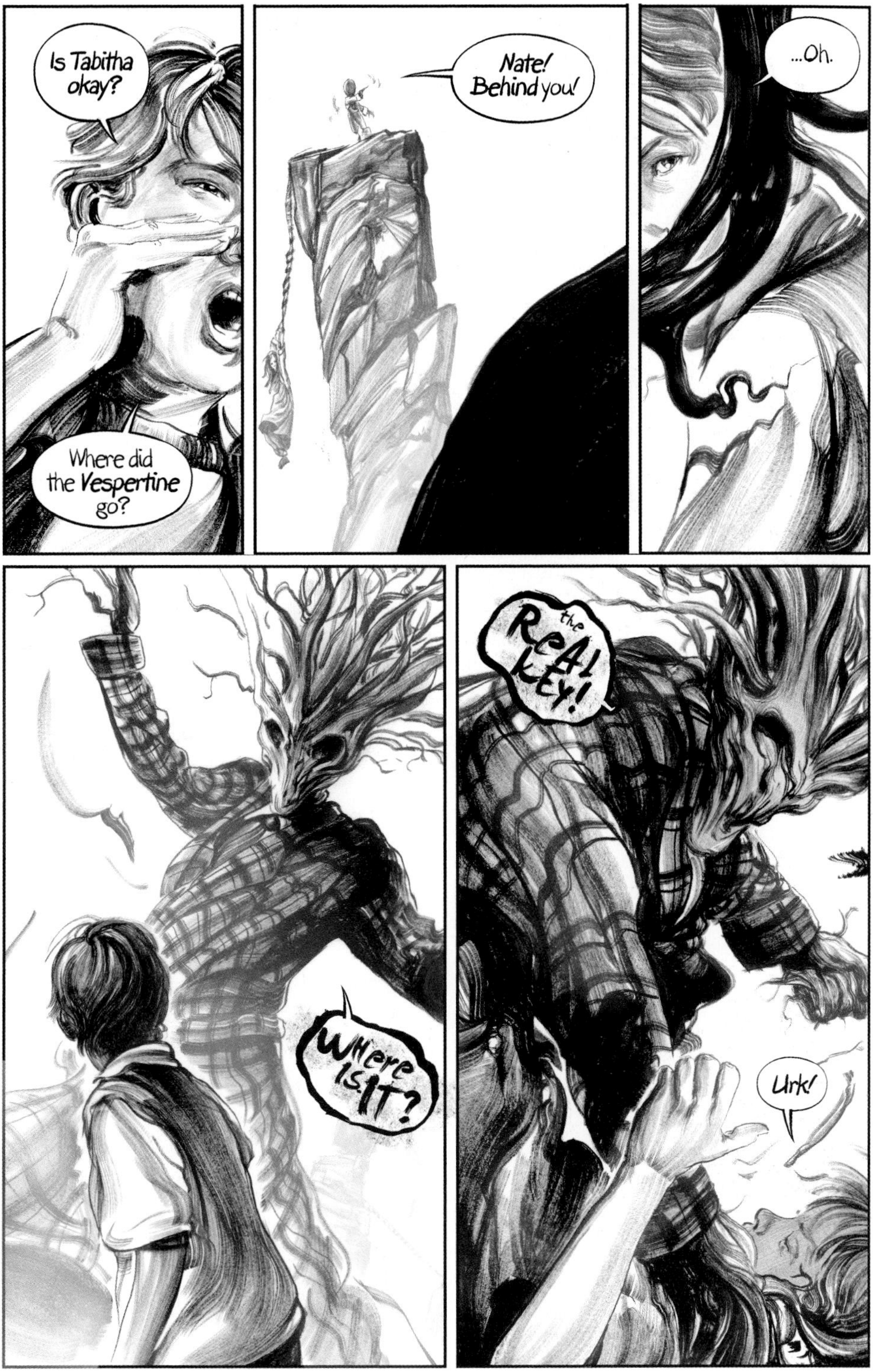
Is Tabitha okay?
Where did the Vespertine go?
Nate! Behind you!
...Oh.
Where is IT?
the ReAl key!
Urk!

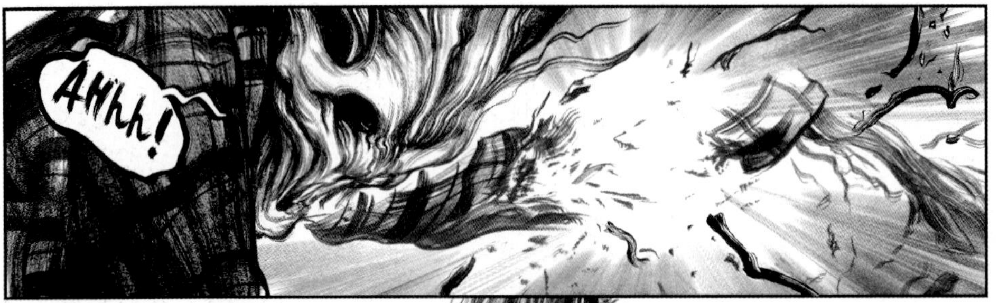
AHhh!

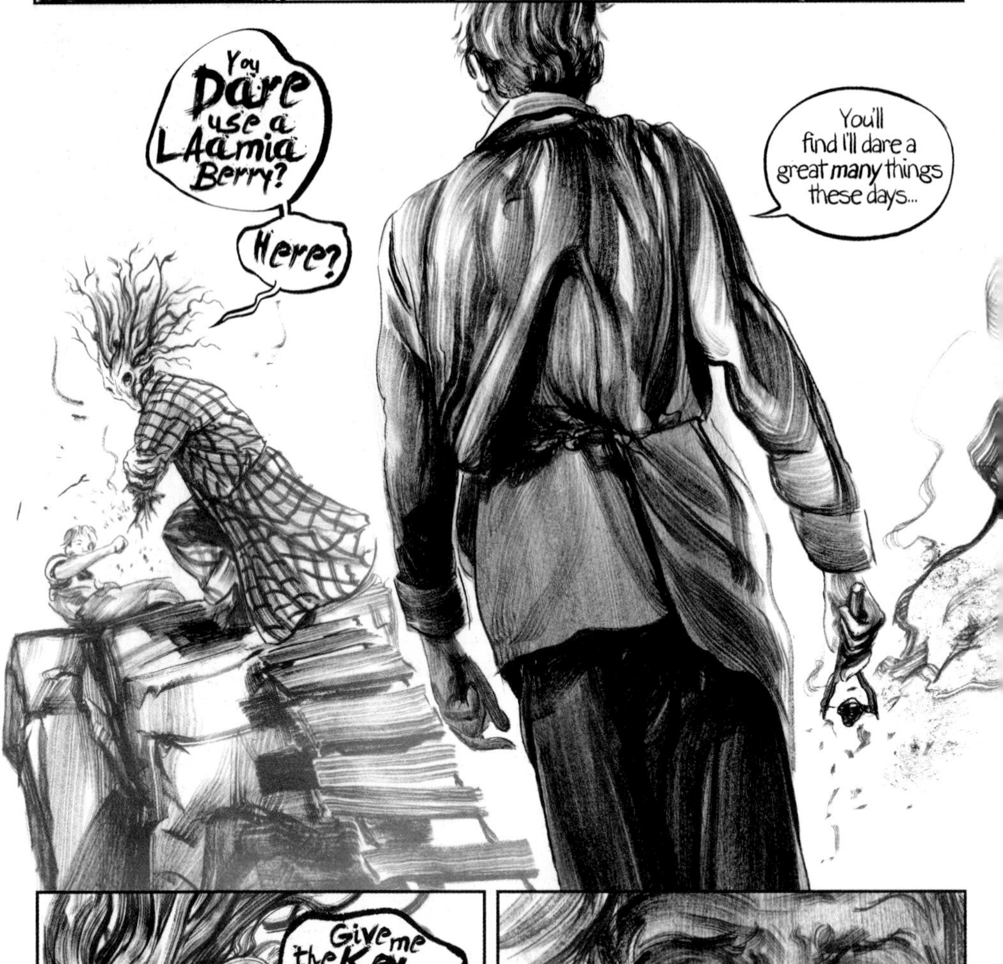
You Dare use a LAamia Berry?
Here?
You'll find I'll dare a great *many* things these days...

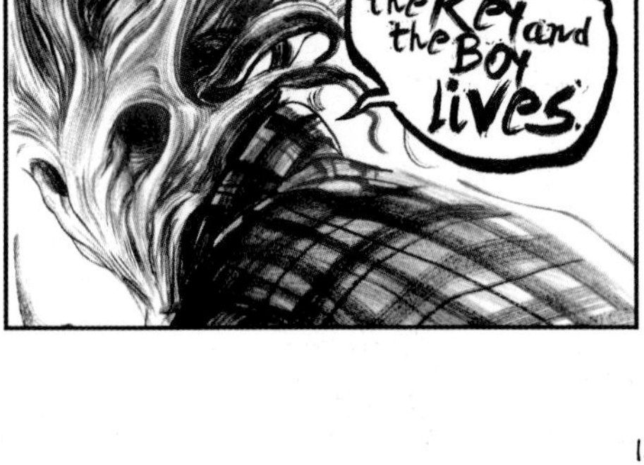
Give me the Key and the Boy lives.

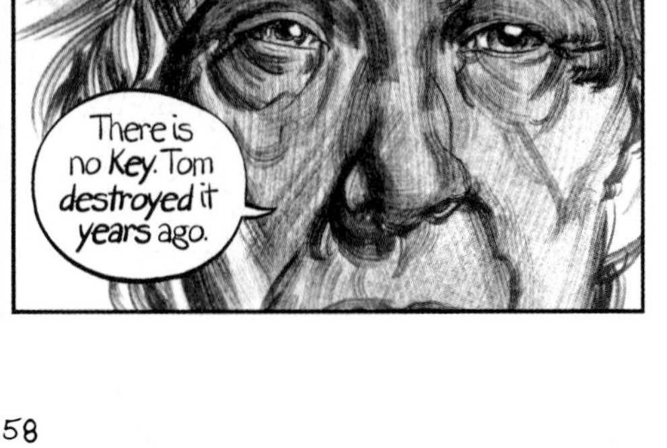
There is no *Key*. Tom *destroyed* it *years* ago.

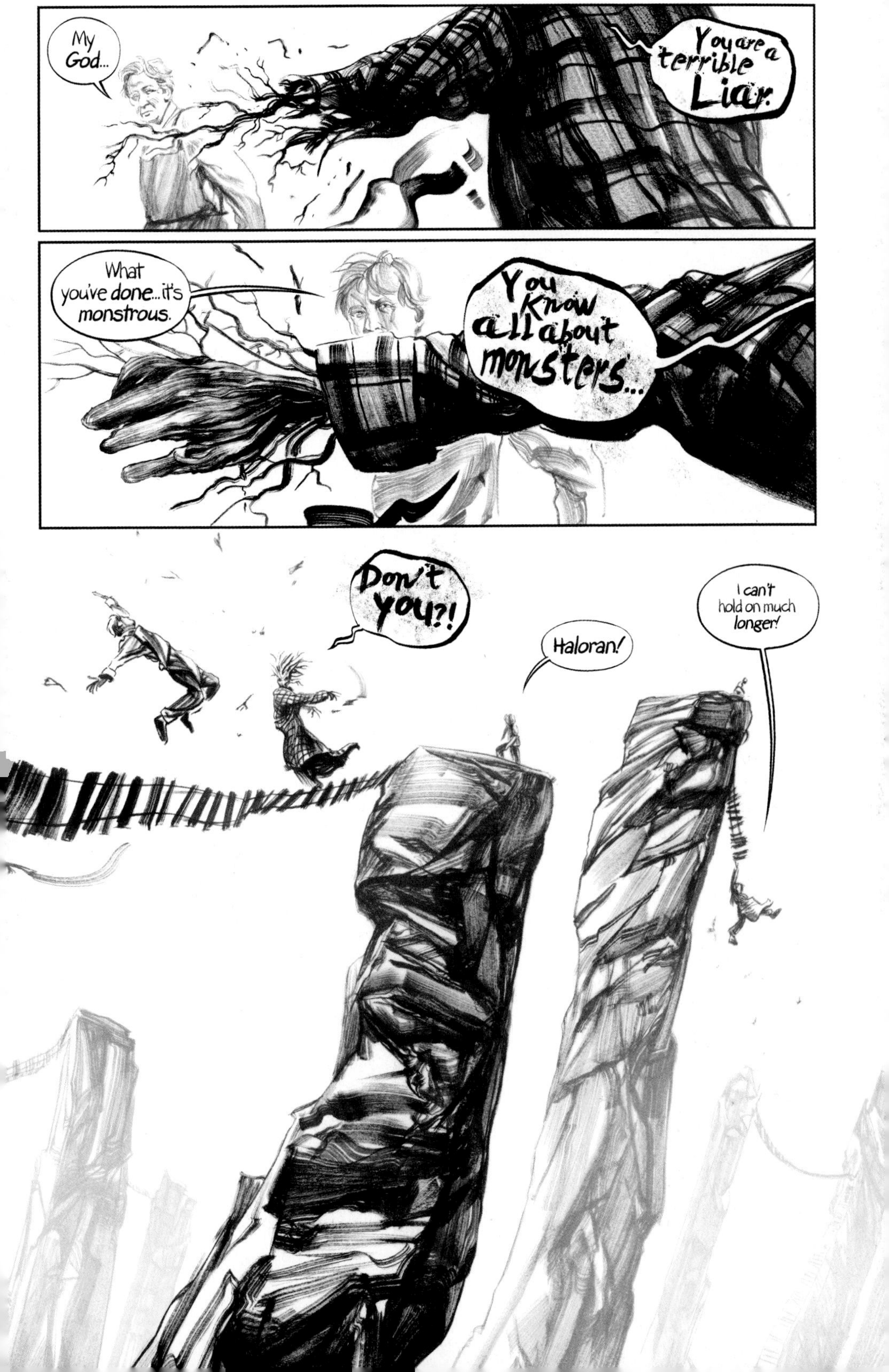
My God...
You are a terrible Liar.
What you've done...it's monstrous.
You know all about monsters...
Don't you?!
Haloran!
I can't hold on much longer!

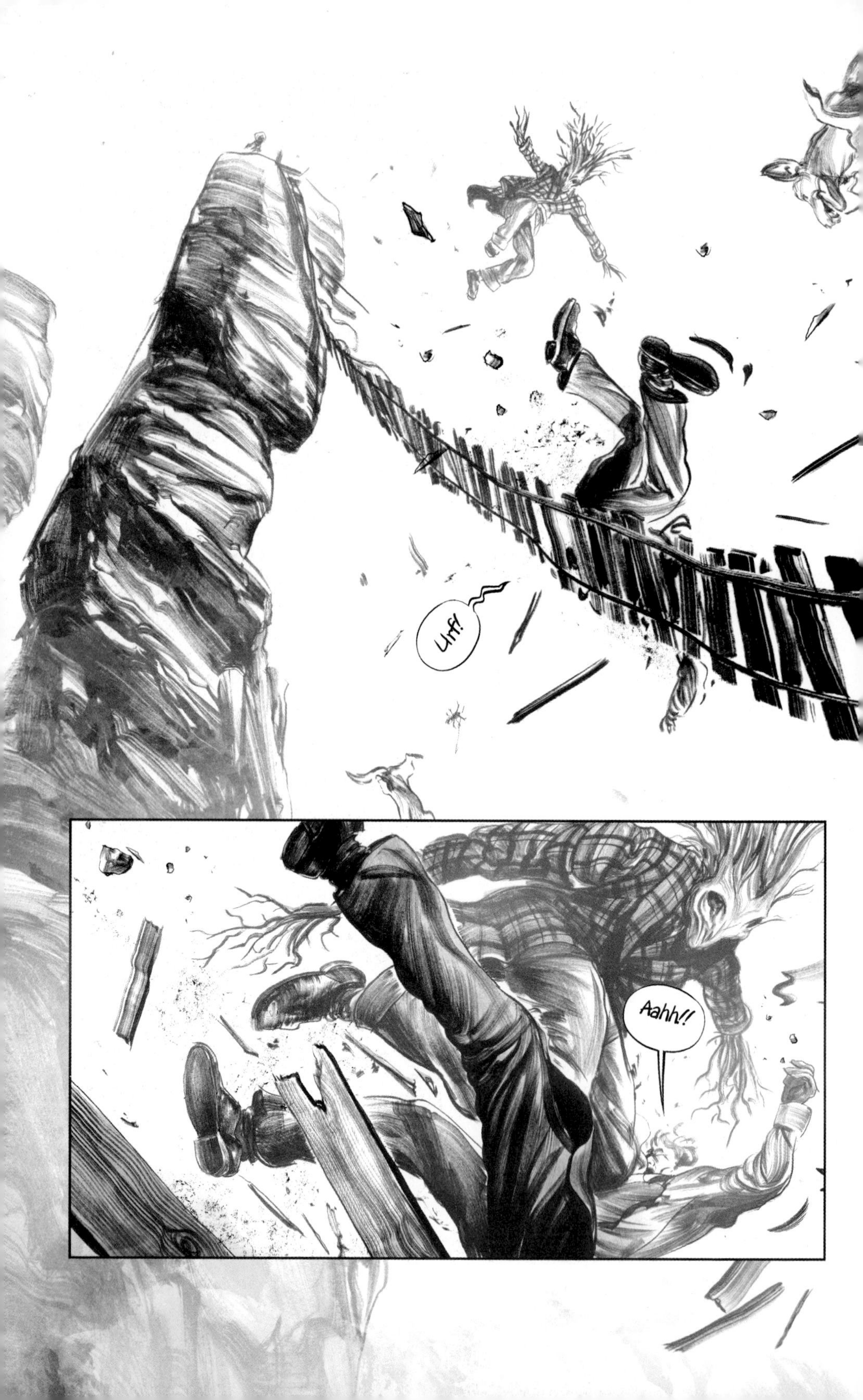
Urf!
Aahh!!

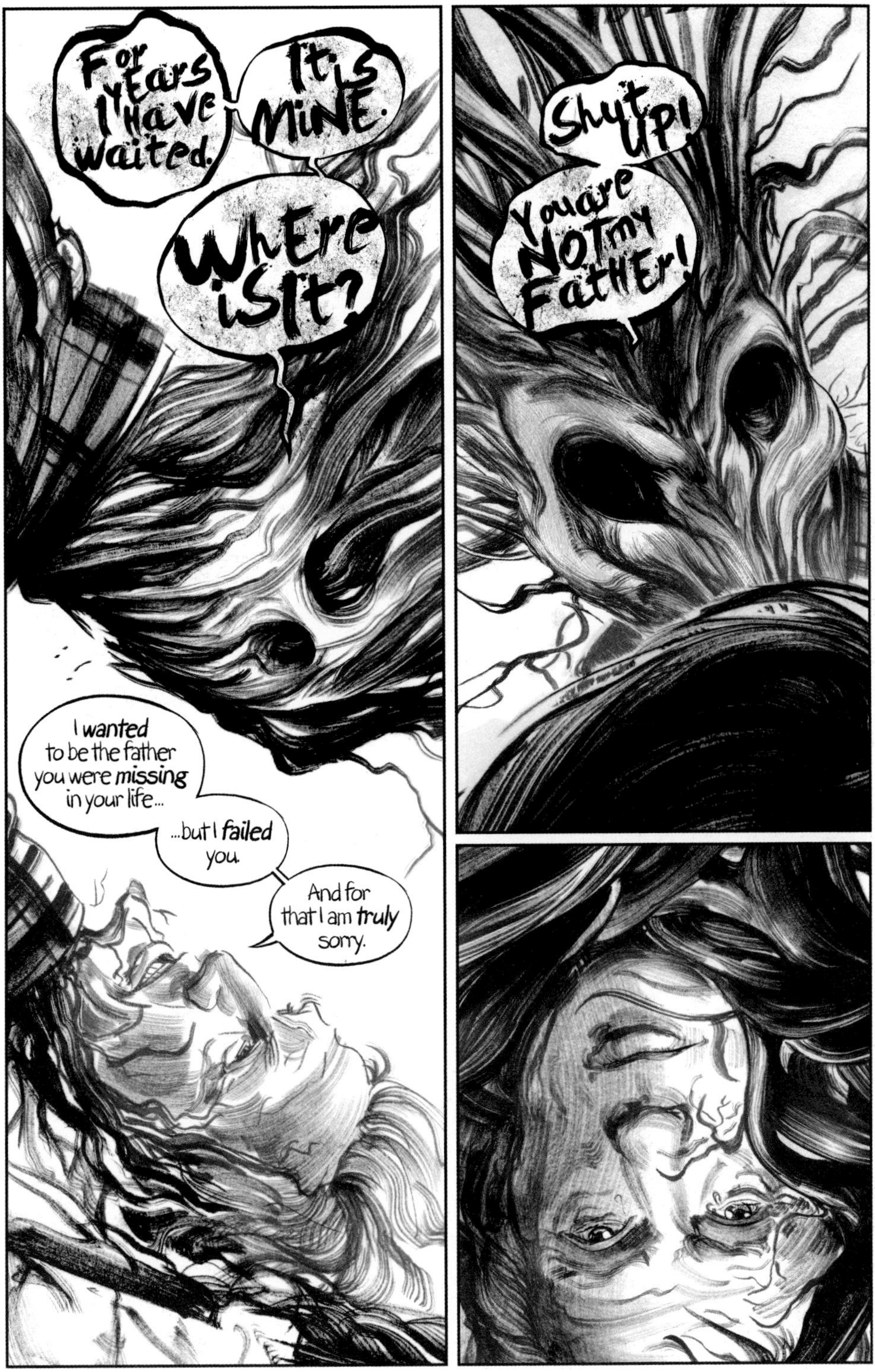
For years I have waited.
It is MINE.
Where is It?
Shut UP!
You are NOT my Father!
I wanted to be the father you were missing in your life...
...but I failed you.
And for that I am truly sorry.

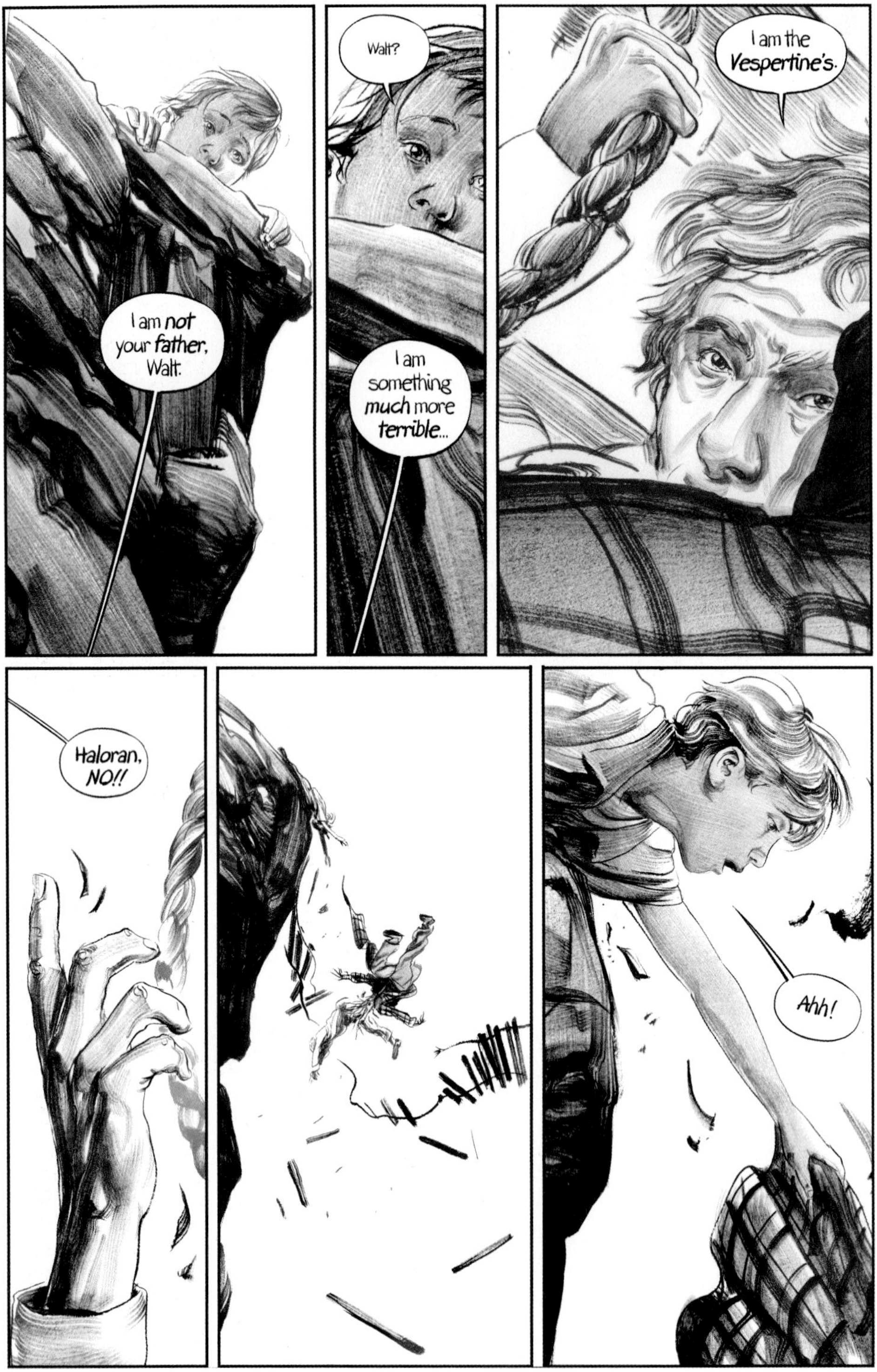
I am not your father, Walt.
Walt?
I am something much more terrible...
I am the Vespertine's.
Haloran, NO!!
Ahh!

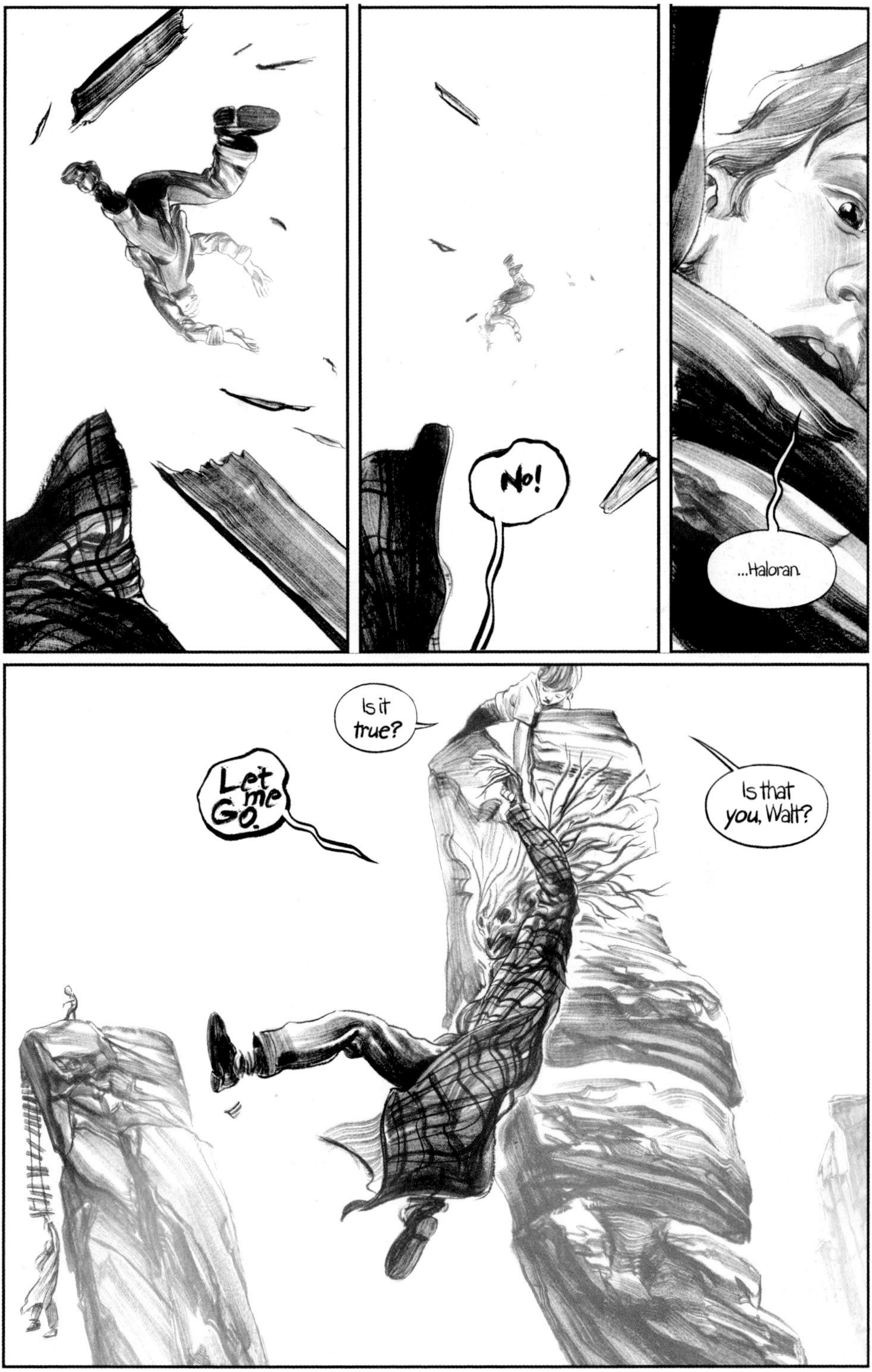
No!
...Haloran.
Is it true?
Let me Go.
Is that you, Walt?

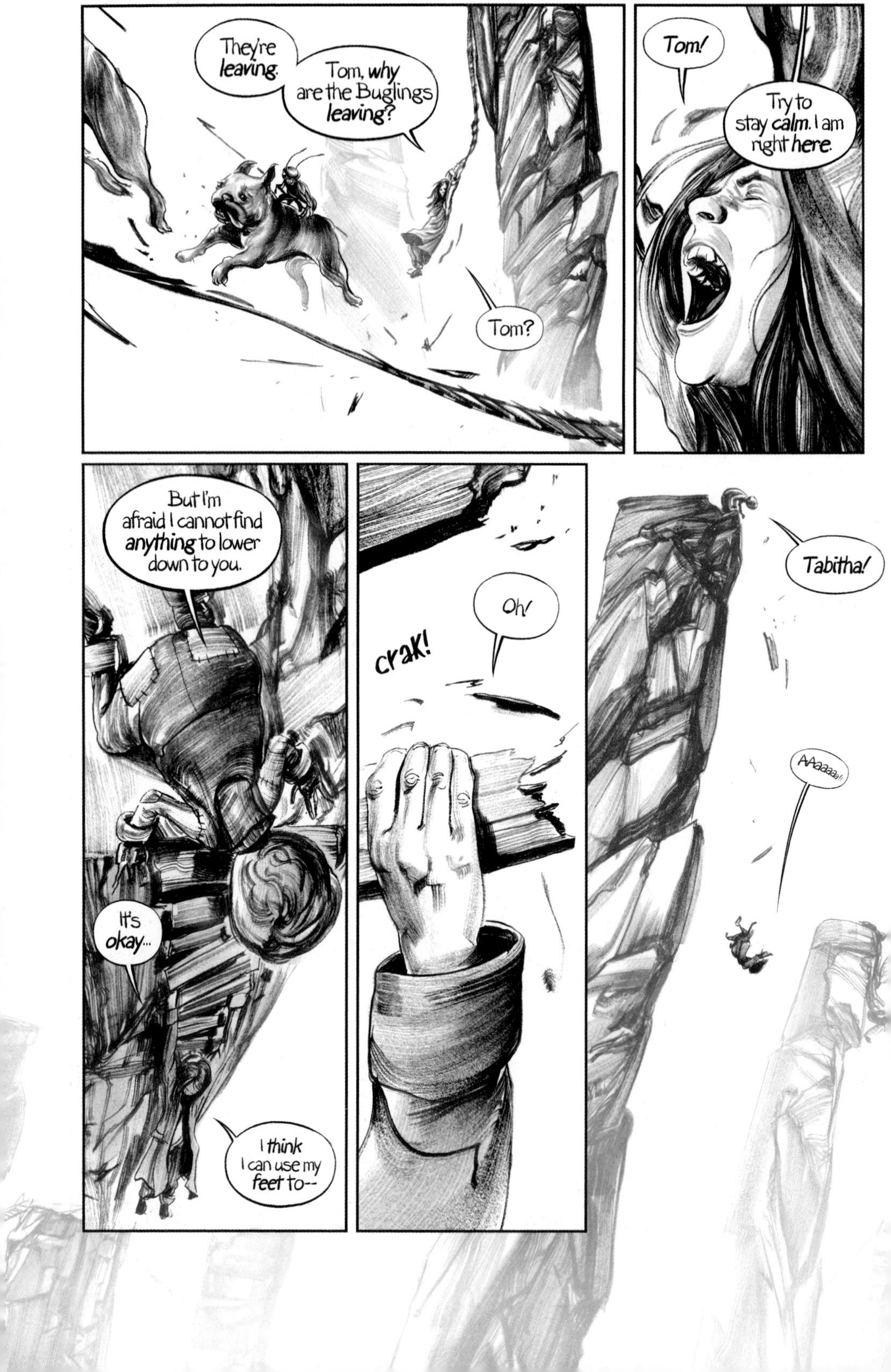
They're leaving.
Tom, why are the Buglings leaving?
Tom?
Tom!
Try to stay calm. I am right here.
But I'm afraid I cannot find anything to lower down to you.
It's okay...
I think I can use my feet to--
crak!
Oh!
Tabitha!
AAaaaaa!!

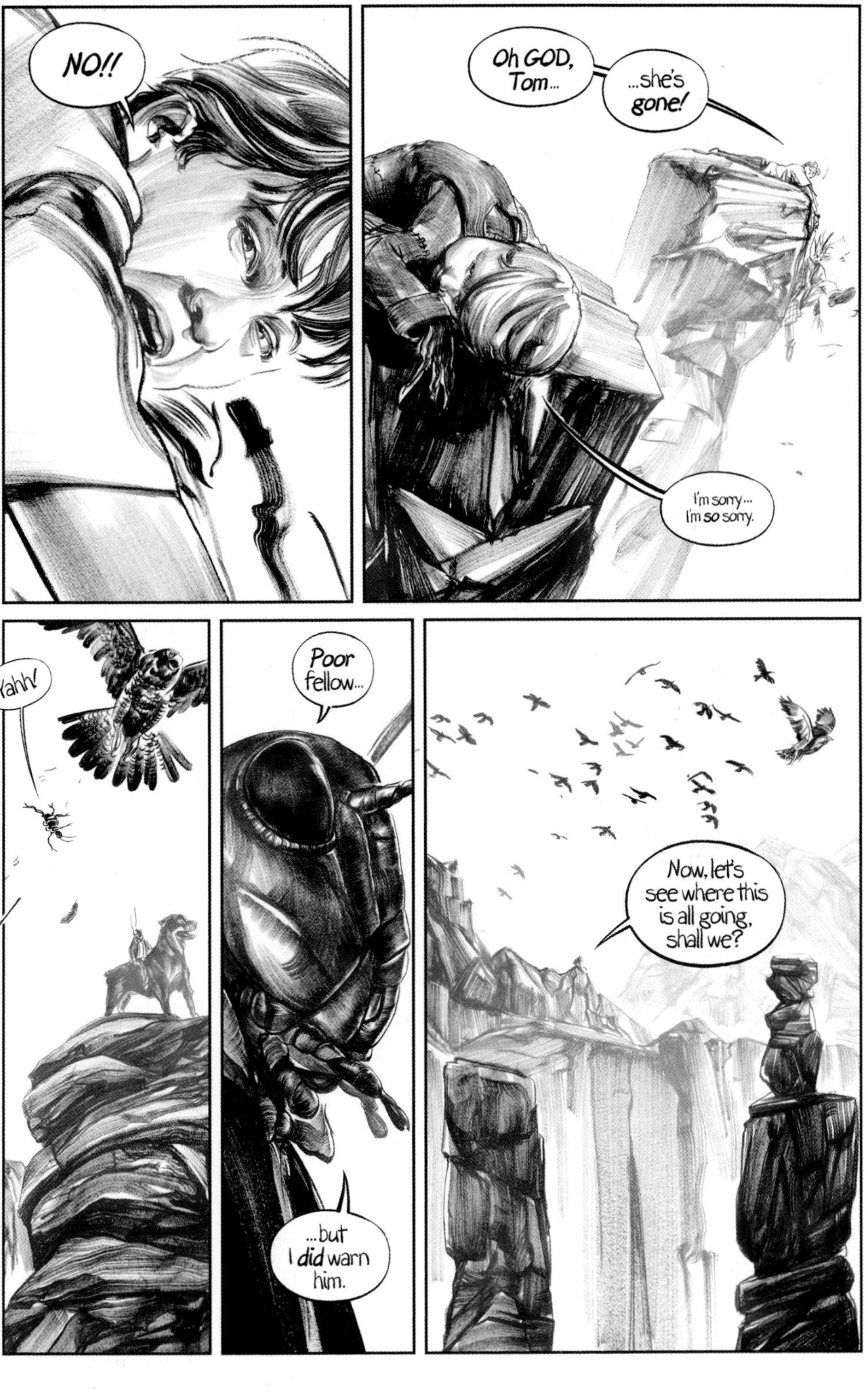
NO!!
Oh GOD, Tom...
...she's gone!
I'm sorry... I'm so sorry.
Yahh!
Poor fellow...
...but I did warn him.
Now, let's see where this is all going, shall we?

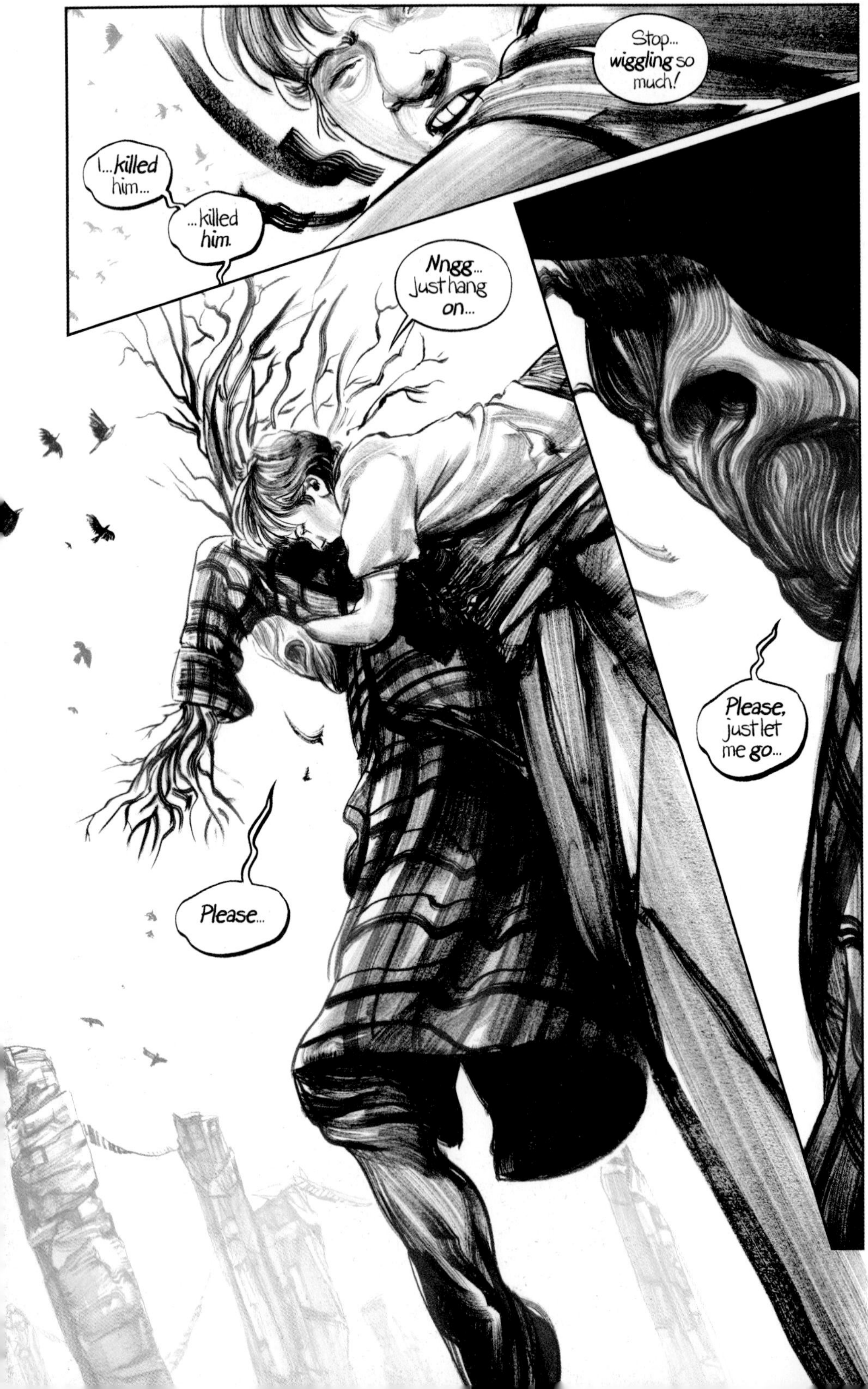
Stop... wiggling so much!
I...killed him...
...killed him.
Nngg... just hang on...
Please, just let me go...
Please...

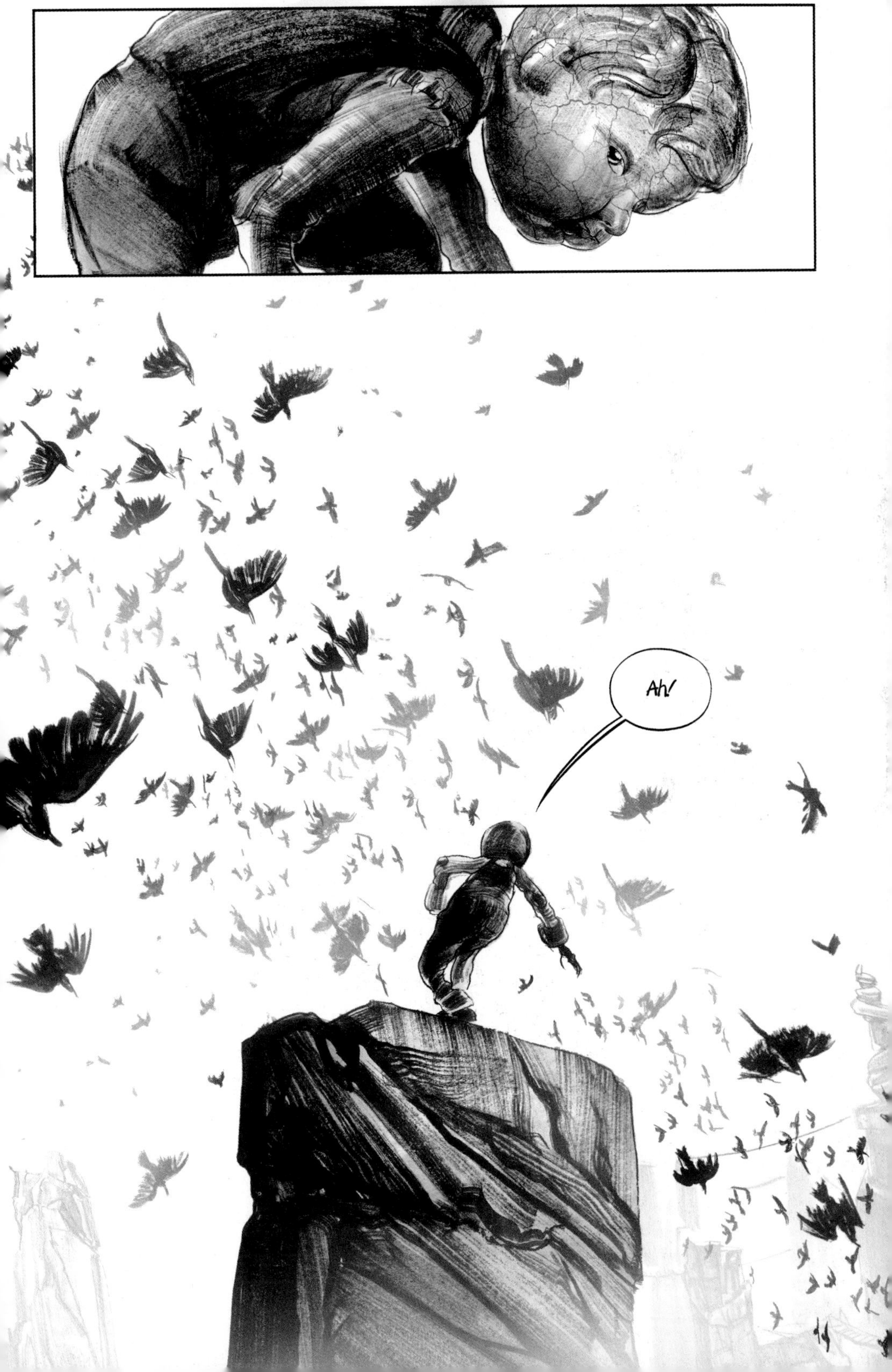
Ah!

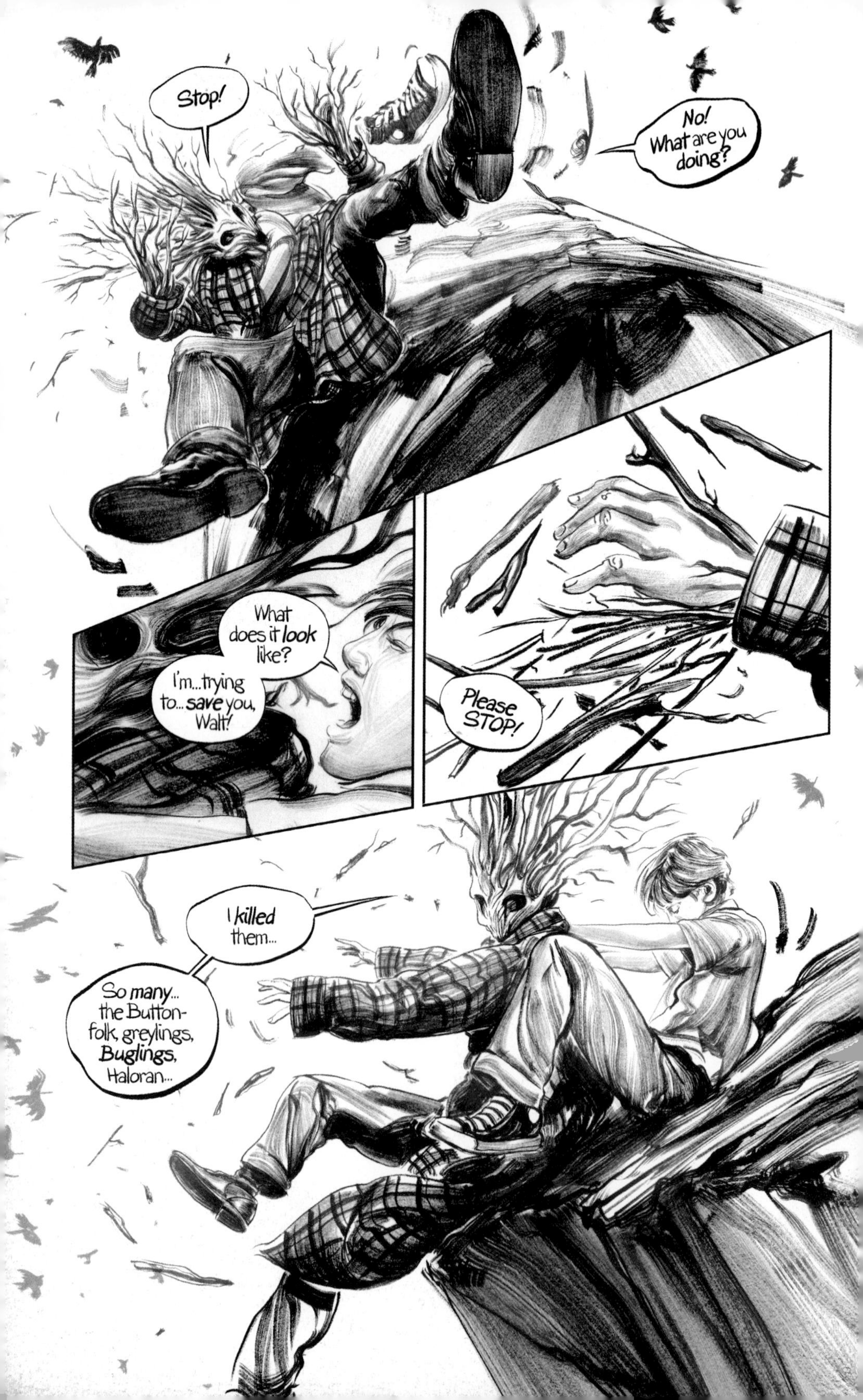
Stop!
No! What are you doing?
What does it look like?
I'm... trying to... save you, Walt!
Please STOP!
I killed them...
So many... the Button-folk, greylings, Buglings, Haloran...

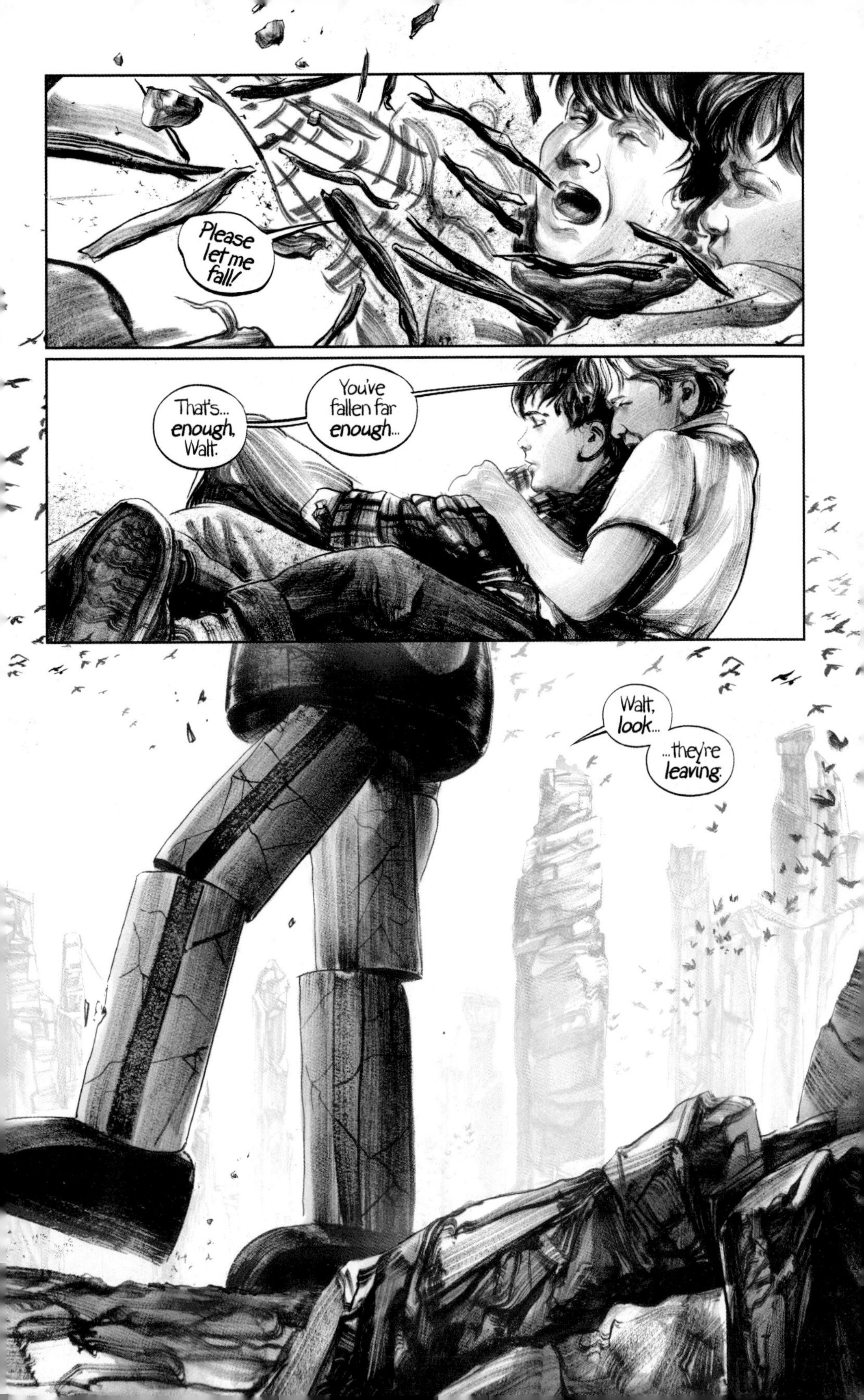
Please let me fall!
That's... enough, Walt.
You've fallen far enough...
Walt, look...
...they're leaving.

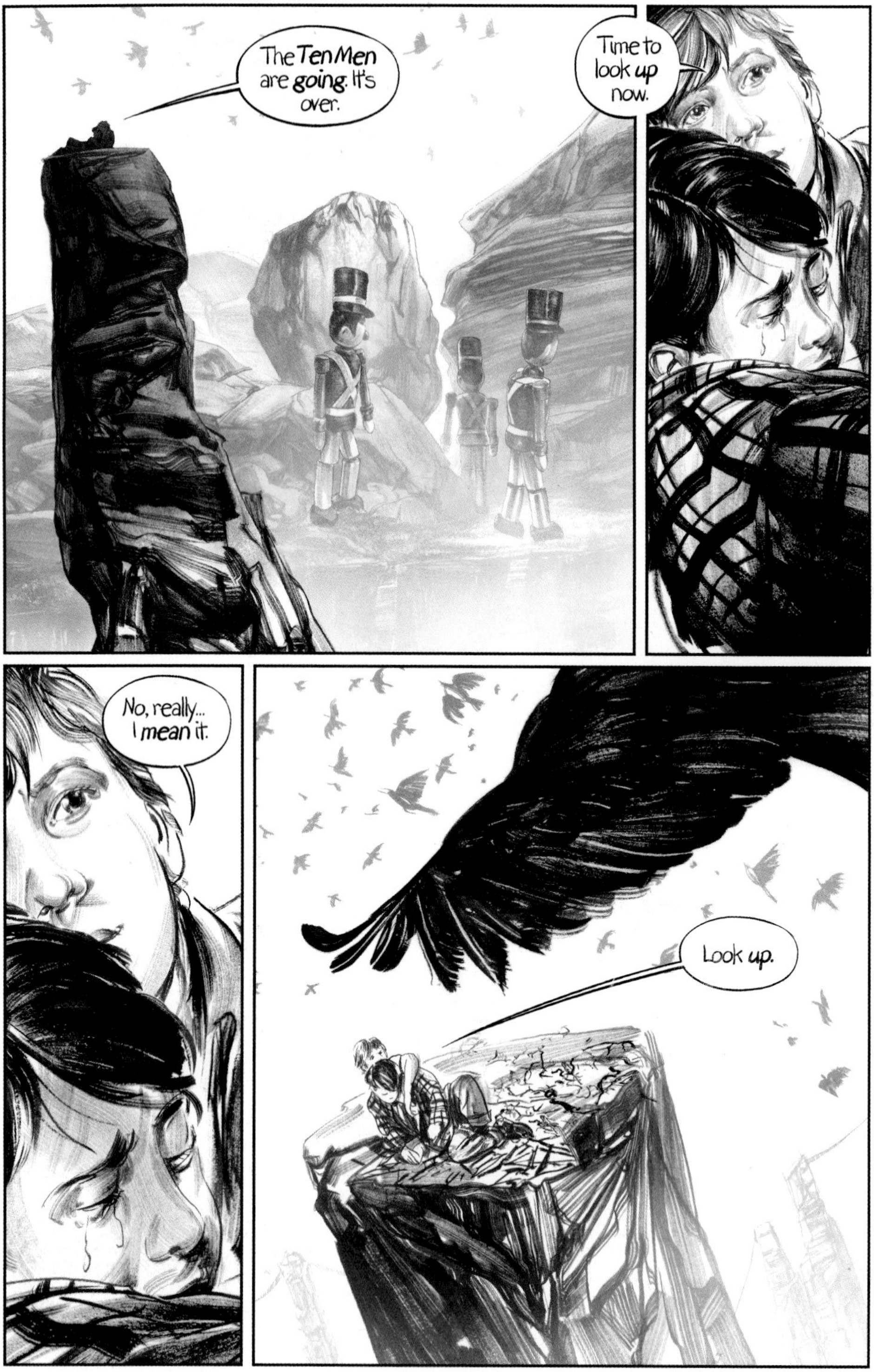
The Ten Men are going. It's over.
Time to look up now.
No, really... I mean it.
Look up.

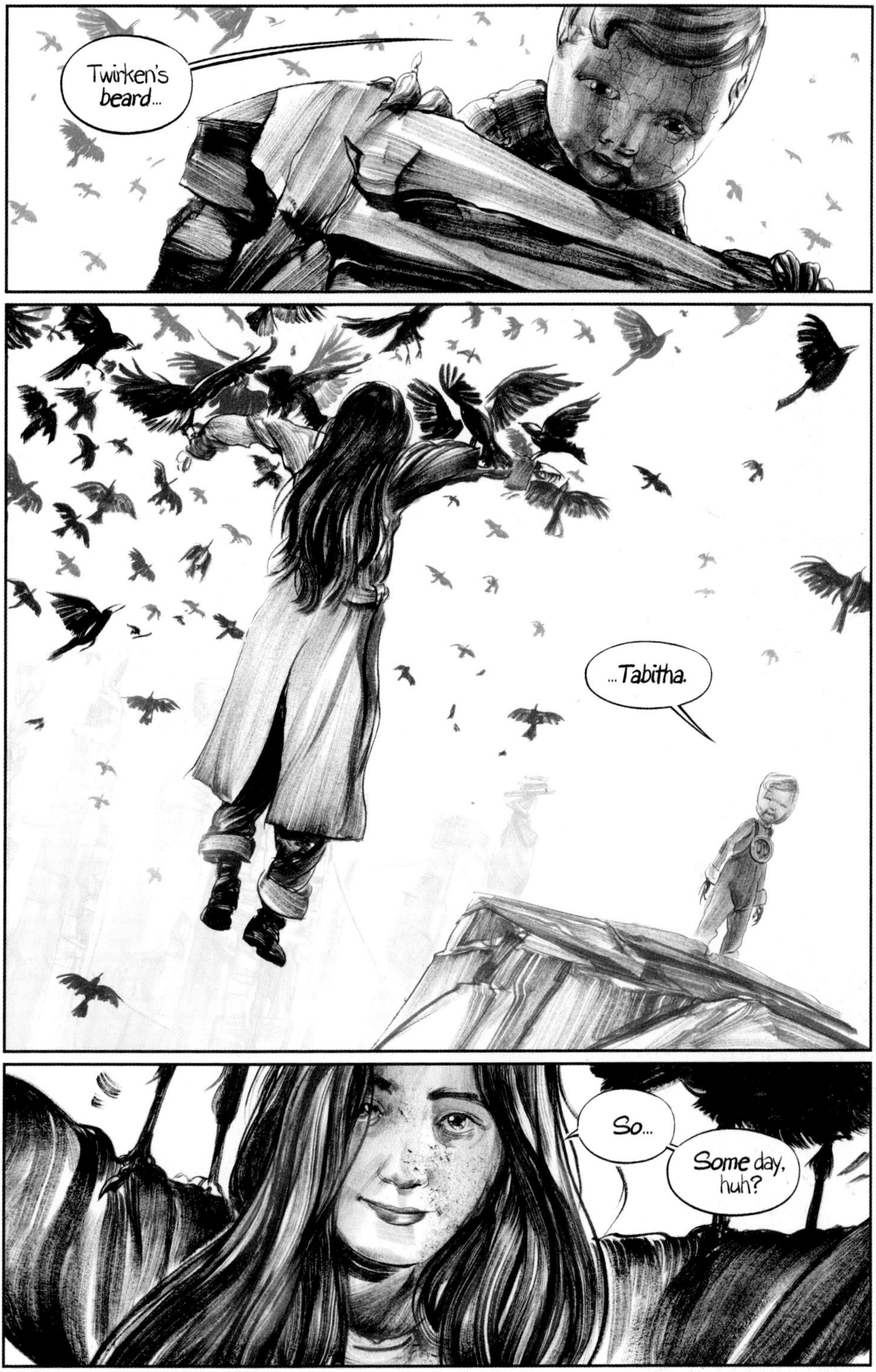
Twirken's beard...
...Tabitha.
So...
Some day, huh?

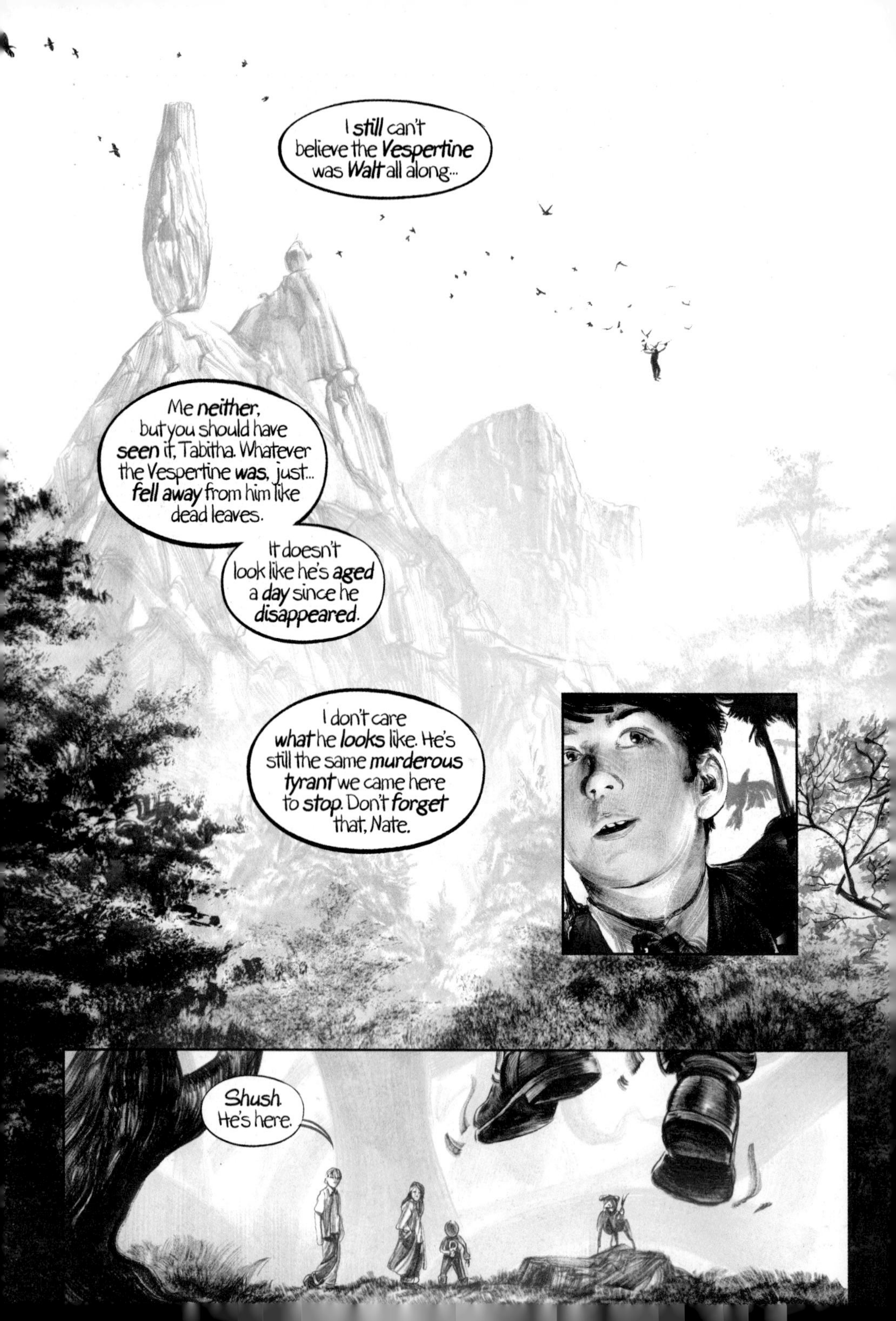
I still can't believe the Vespertine was Walt all along...
Me neither, but you should have seen it, Tabitha. Whatever the Vespertine was, just... fell away from him like dead leaves.
It doesn't look like he's aged a day since he disappeared.
I don't care what he looks like. He's still the same murderous tyrant we came here to stop. Don't forget that, Nate.
Shush. He's here.

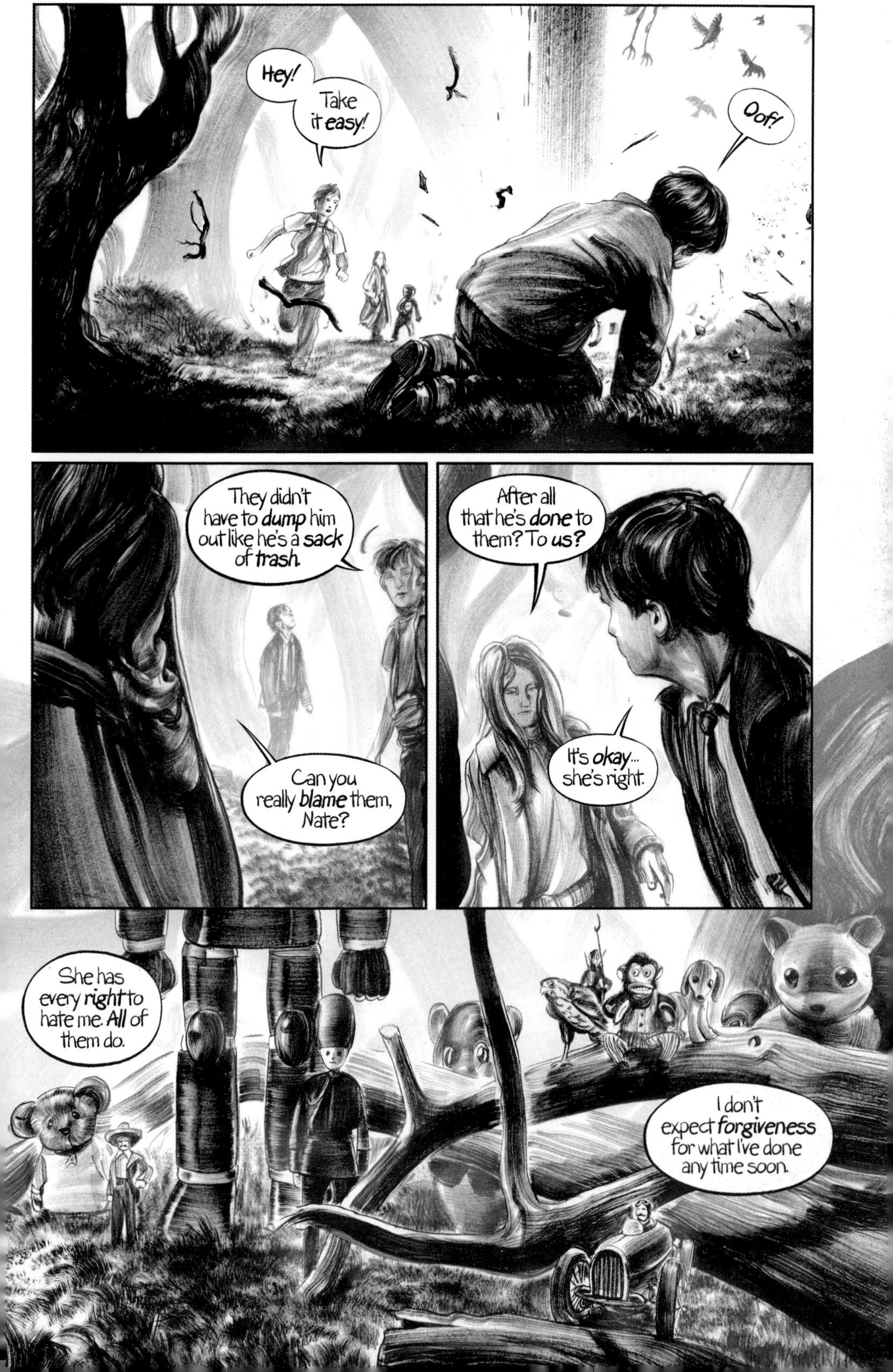
Hey!
Take it easy!
Oof!
They didn't have to dump him out like he's a sack of trash.
Can you really blame them, Nate?
After all that he's done to them? To us?
It's okay... she's right.
She has every right to hate me. All of them do.
I don't expect forgiveness for what I've done any time soon.

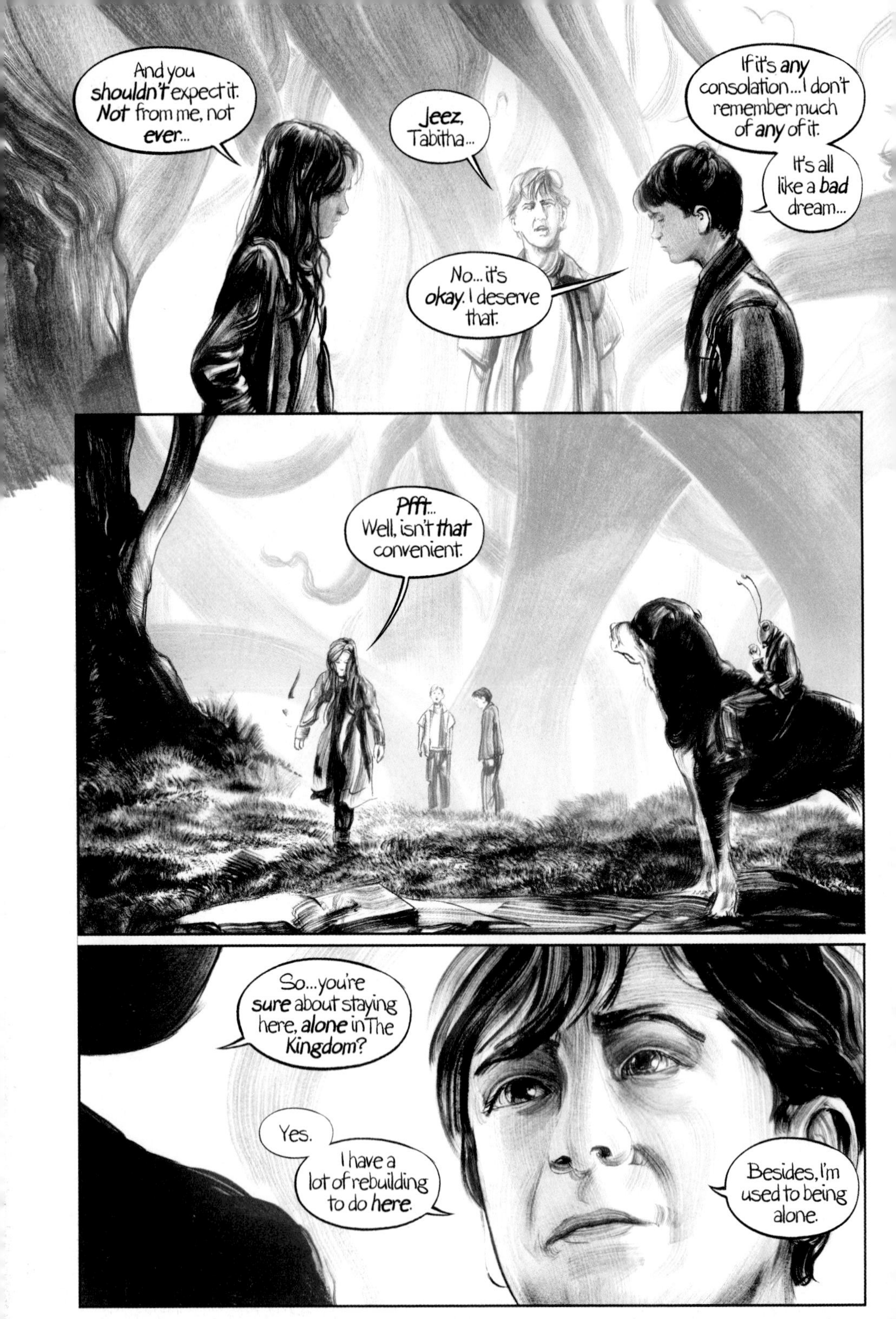
And you shouldn't expect it. Not from me, not ever...
Jeez, Tabitha...
If it's any consolation...I don't remember much of any of it.
It's all like a bad dream...
No...it's okay. I deserve that.
Pfft... Well, isn't that convenient.
So...you're sure about staying here, alone in The Kingdom?
Yes.
I have a lot of rebuilding to do here.
Besides, I'm used to being alone.

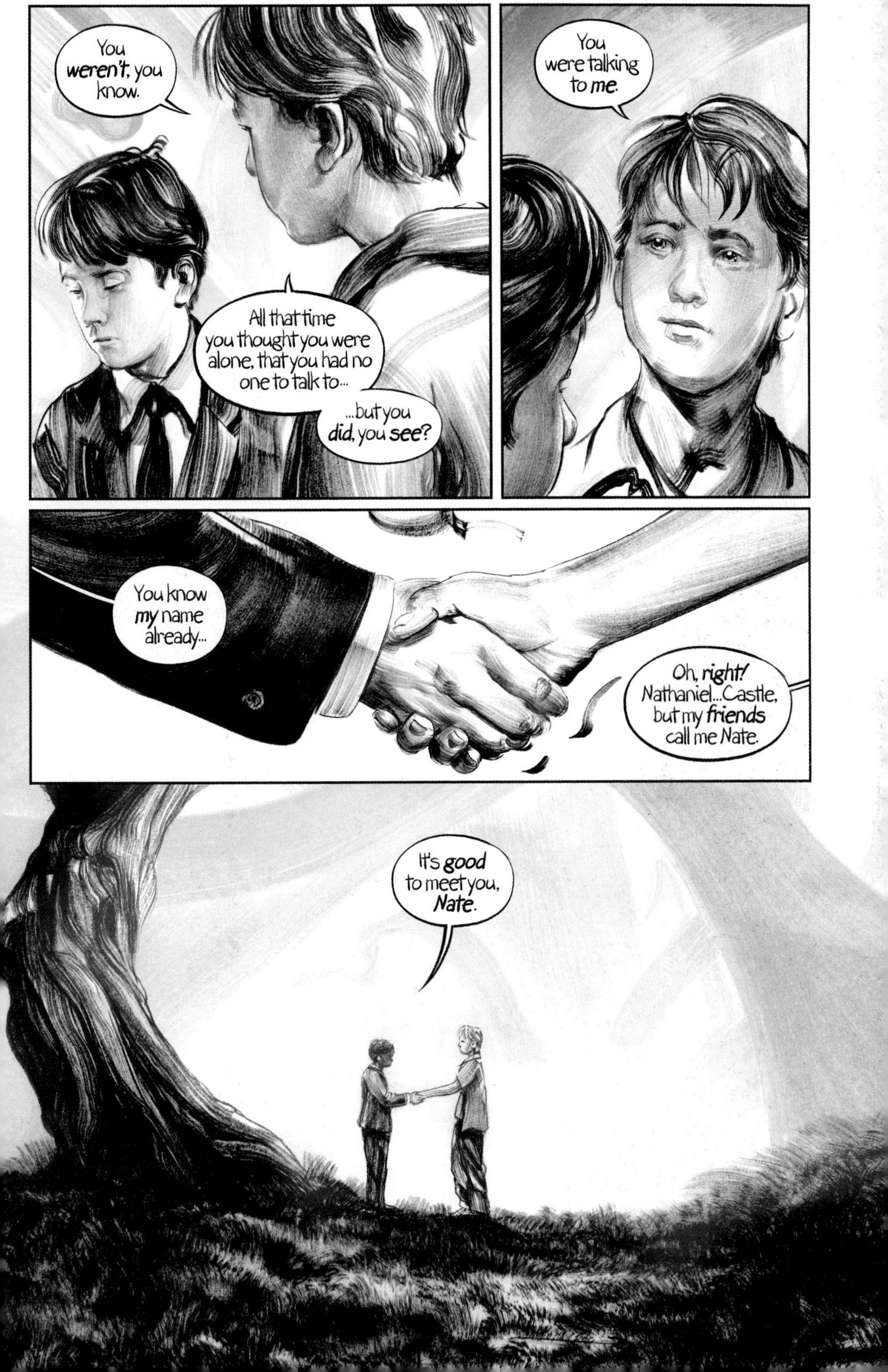
You weren't, you know.
All that time you thought you were alone, that you had no one to talk to...
...but you did, you see?
You were talking to me.
You know my name already...
Oh, right! Nathaniel...Castle, but my friends call me Nate.
It's good to meet you, Nate.

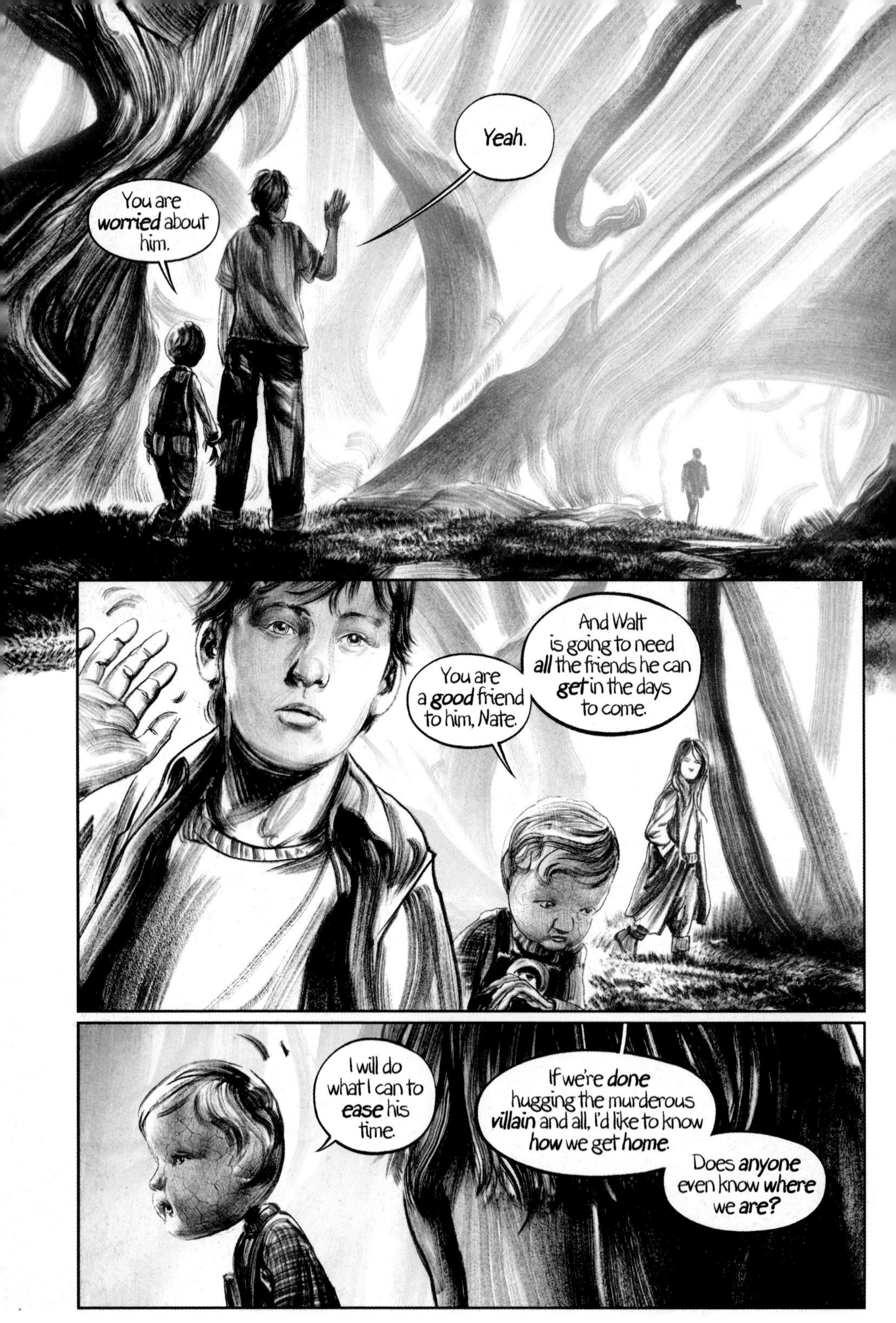
You are worried about him.
Yeah.
You are a good friend to him, Nate.
And Walt is going to need all the friends he can get in the days to come.
I will do what I can to ease his time.
If we're done hugging the murderous villain and all, I'd like to know how we get home.
Does anyone even know where we are?

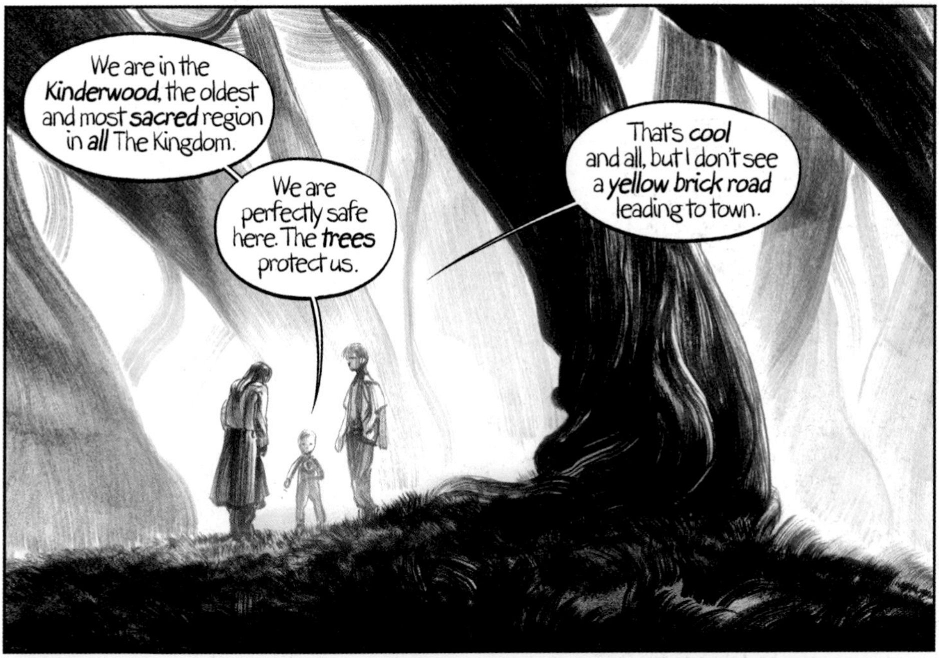
We are in the Kinderwood, the oldest and most sacred region in all The Kingdom.
We are perfectly safe here. The trees protect us.
That's cool and all, but I don't see a yellow brick road leading to town.

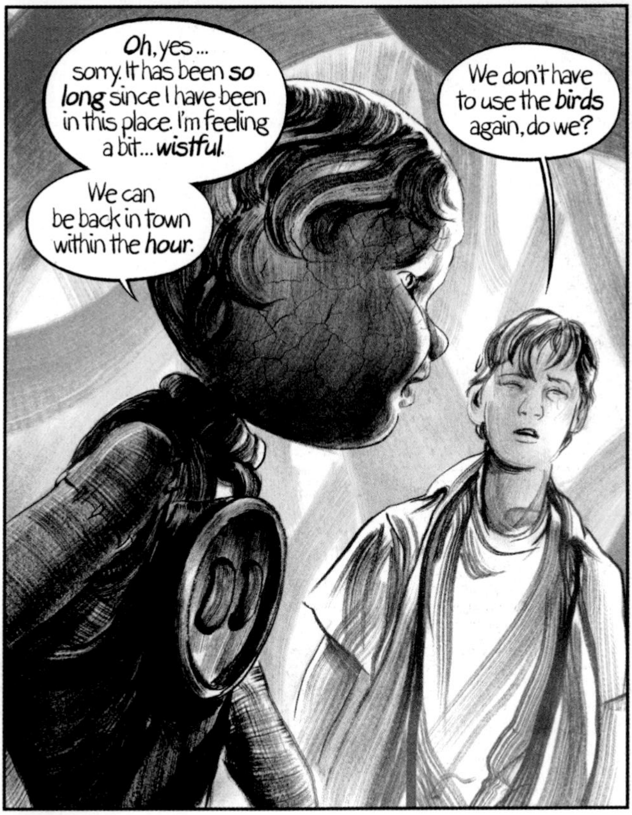
Oh, yes ... sorry. It has been so long since I have been in this place. I'm feeling a bit... wistful.
We can be back in town within the hour.
We don't have to use the birds again, do we?

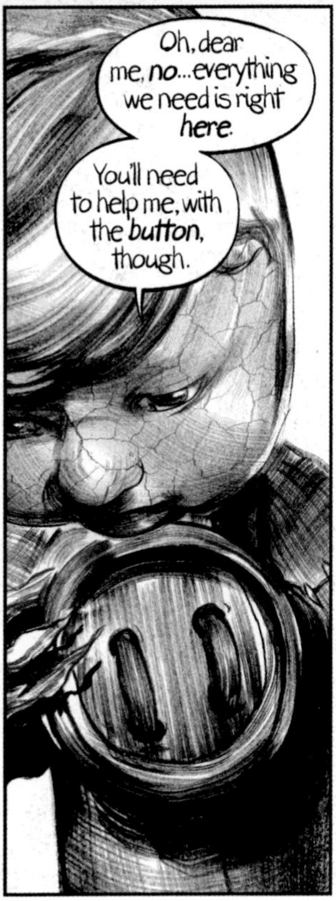
Oh, dear me, no...everything we need is right here.
You'll need to help me, with the button, though.

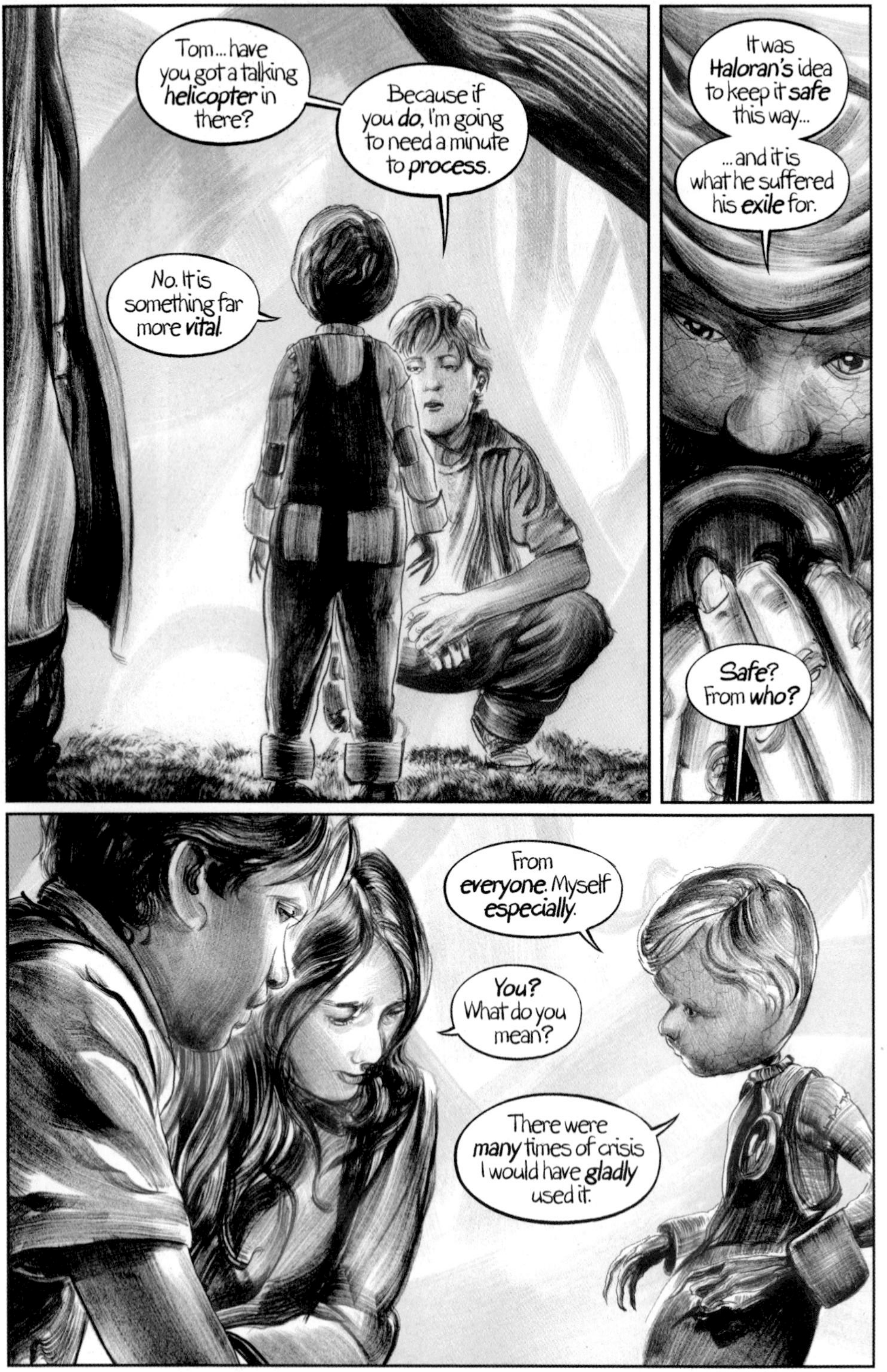
Tom... have you got a talking **helicopter** in there?
Because if you **do**, I'm going to need a minute to **process**.
No. It is something far more **vital**.
It was **Haloran's** idea to keep it **safe** this way...
...and it is what he suffered his **exile** for.
Safe? From **who?**
From **everyone**. Myself **especially**.
You? What do you mean?
There were **many** times of crisis I would have **gladly** used it.

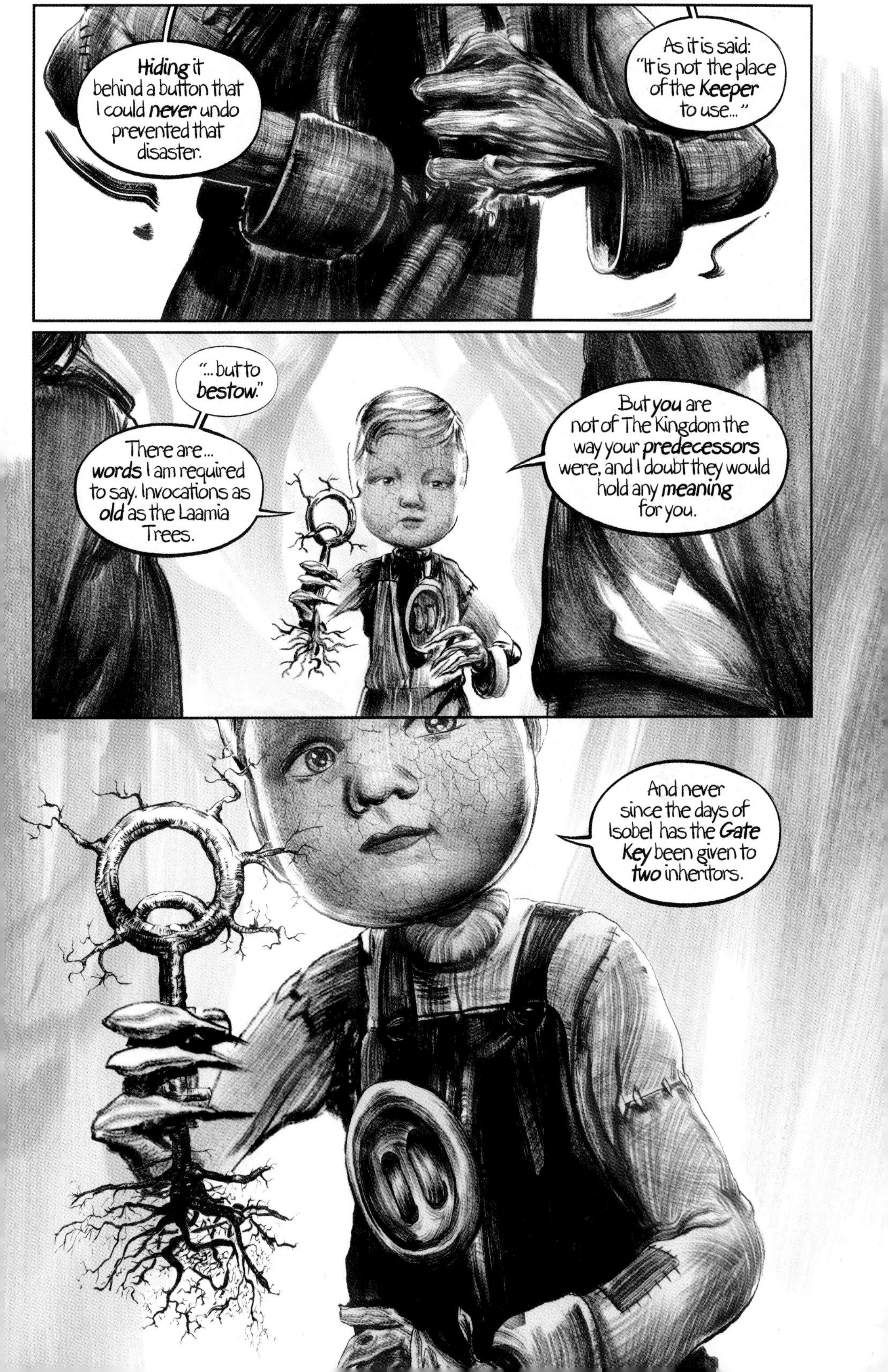

Hiding it behind a button that I could **never** undo prevented that disaster.
As it is said: "It is not the place of the **Keeper** to use..."
"... but to **bestow**."
There are... **words** I am required to say. Invocations as **old** as the Laamia Trees.
But **you** are not of The Kingdom the way your **predecessors** were, and I doubt they would hold any **meaning** for you.
And never since the days of Isobel has the **Gate Key** been given to **two** inheritors.

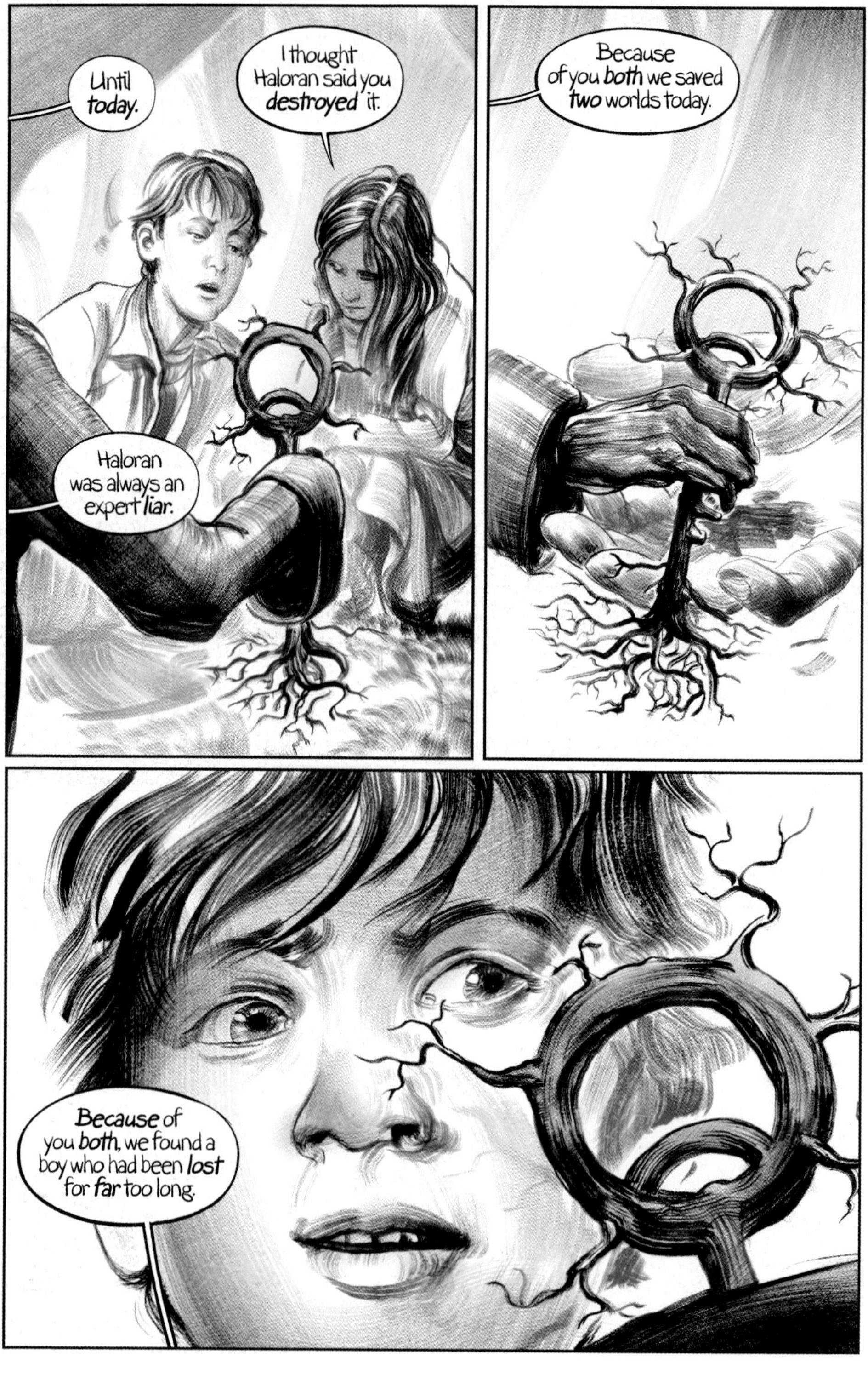
Until today.
I thought Haloran said you destroyed it.
Haloran was always an expert liar.
Because of you both we saved two worlds today.
Because of you both, we found a boy who had been lost for far too long.

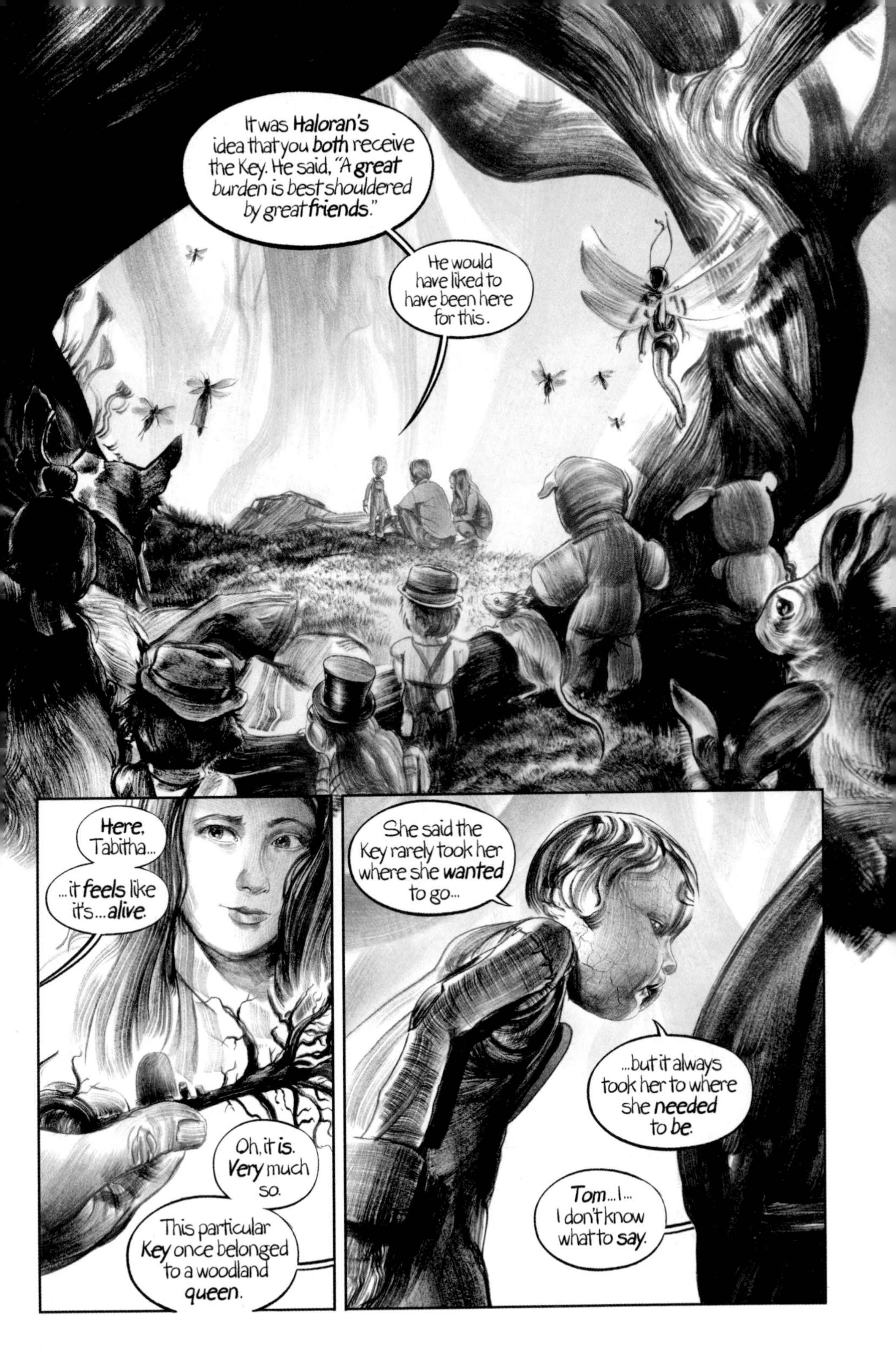
It was Haloran's idea that you both receive the Key. He said, "A great burden is best shouldered by great friends."
He would have liked to have been here for this.
Here, Tabitha...
...it feels like it's...alive.
Oh, it is. Very much so.
This particular Key once belonged to a woodland queen.
She said the Key rarely took her where she wanted to go...
...but it always took her to where she needed to be.
Tom...I... I don't know what to say.

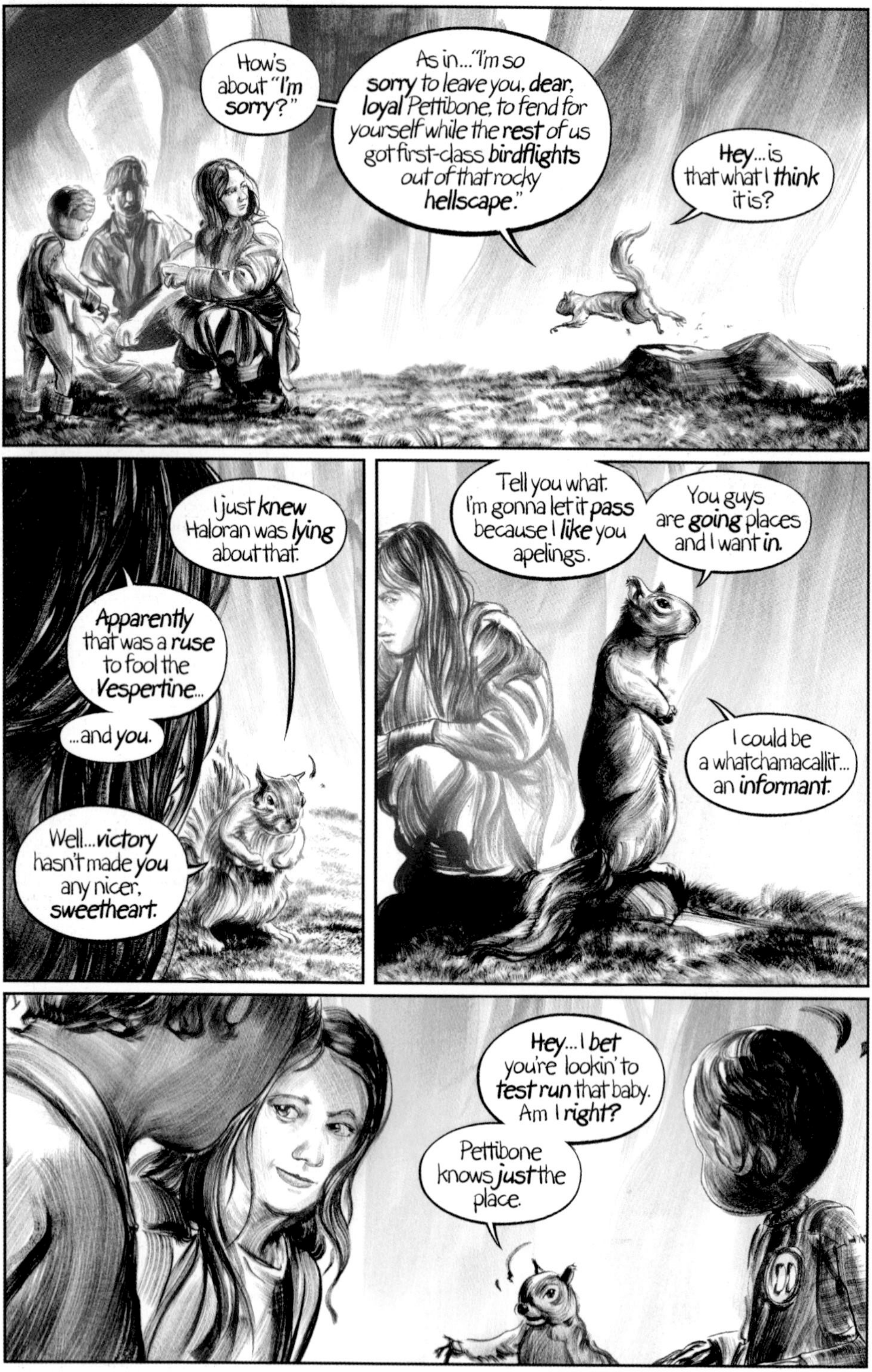
How's about "I'm sorry?"
As in..."I'm so sorry to leave you, dear, loyal Pettibone, to fend for yourself while the rest of us got first-class birdflights out of that rocky hellscape."
Hey...is that what I think it is?
I just knew Haloran was lying about that.
Apparently that was a ruse to fool the Vespertine...
...and you.
Well...victory hasn't made you any nicer, sweetheart.
Tell you what. I'm gonna let it pass because I like you apelings.
You guys are going places and I want in.
I could be a whatchamacallit... an informant.
Hey...I bet you're lookin' to test run that baby. Am I right?
Pettibone knows just the place.

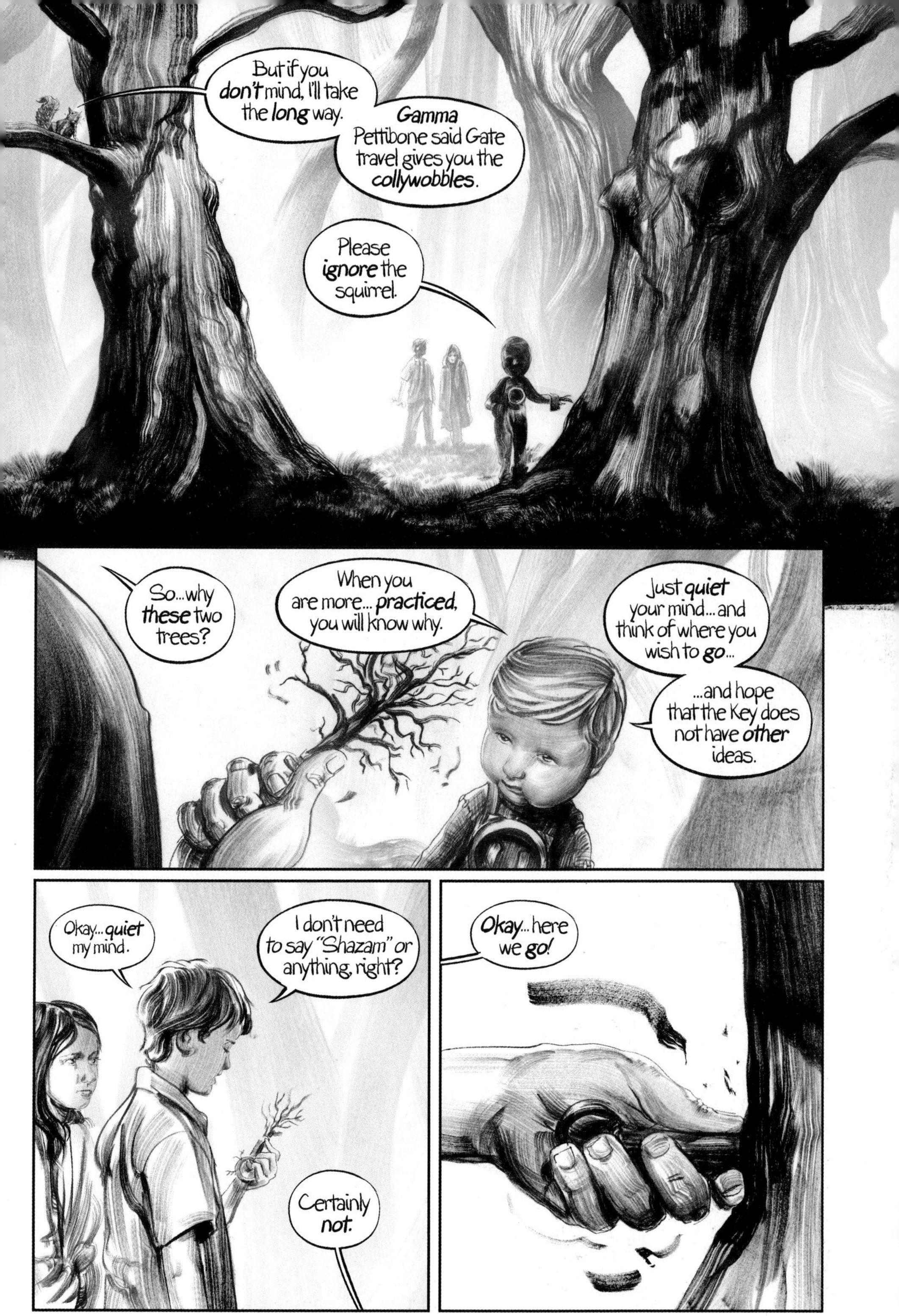
But if you don't mind, I'll take the long way.
Gamma Pettibone said Gate travel gives you the collywobbles.
Please ignore the squirrel.
So...why these two trees?
When you are more... practiced, you will know why.
Just quiet your mind... and think of where you wish to go...
...and hope that the Key does not have other ideas.
Okay...quiet my mind.
I don't need to say "Shazam" or anything, right?
Certainly not.
Okay... here we go!

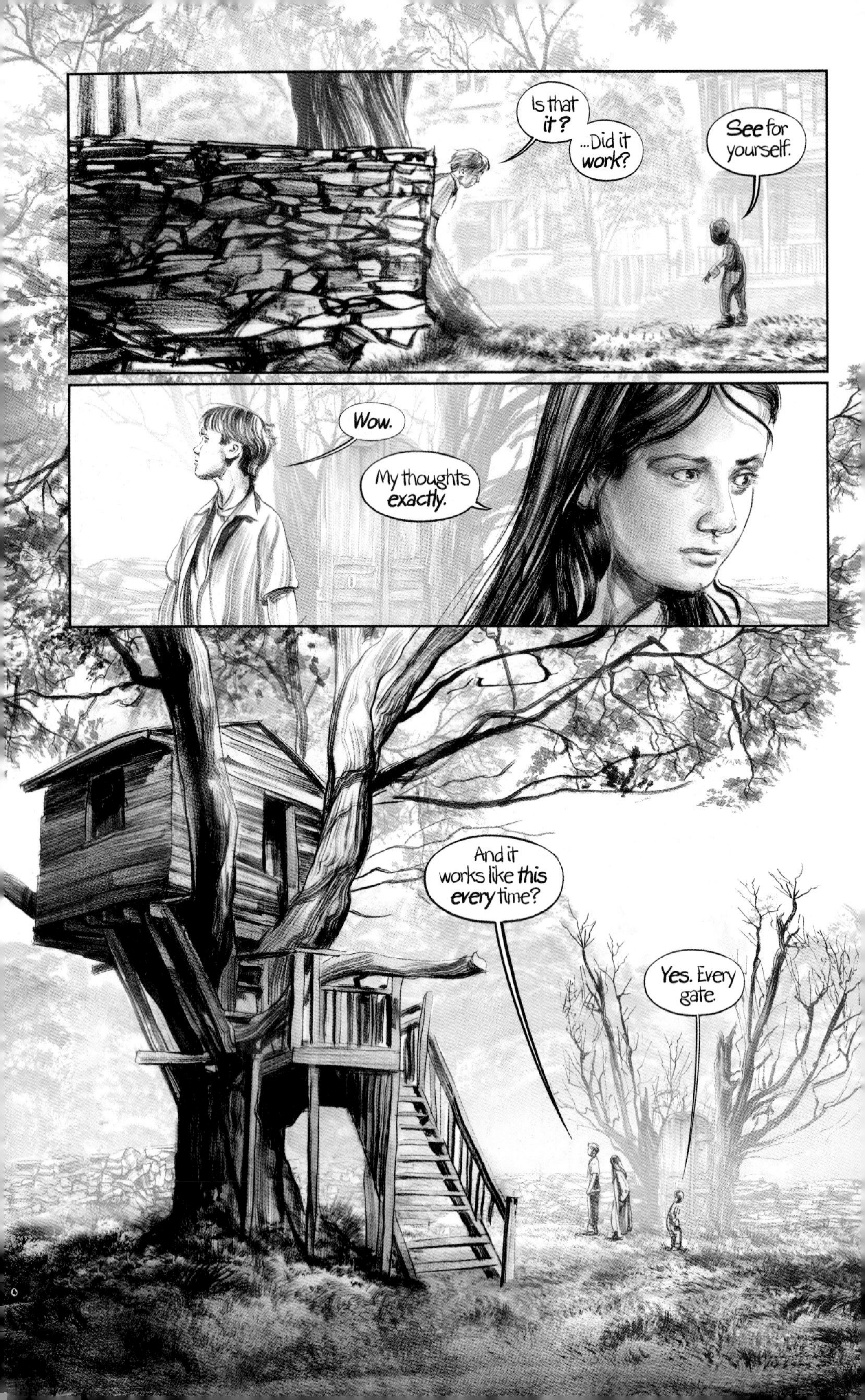
Is that it?
...Did it work?
See for yourself.
Wow.
My thoughts exactly.
And it works like this every time?
Yes. Every gate.

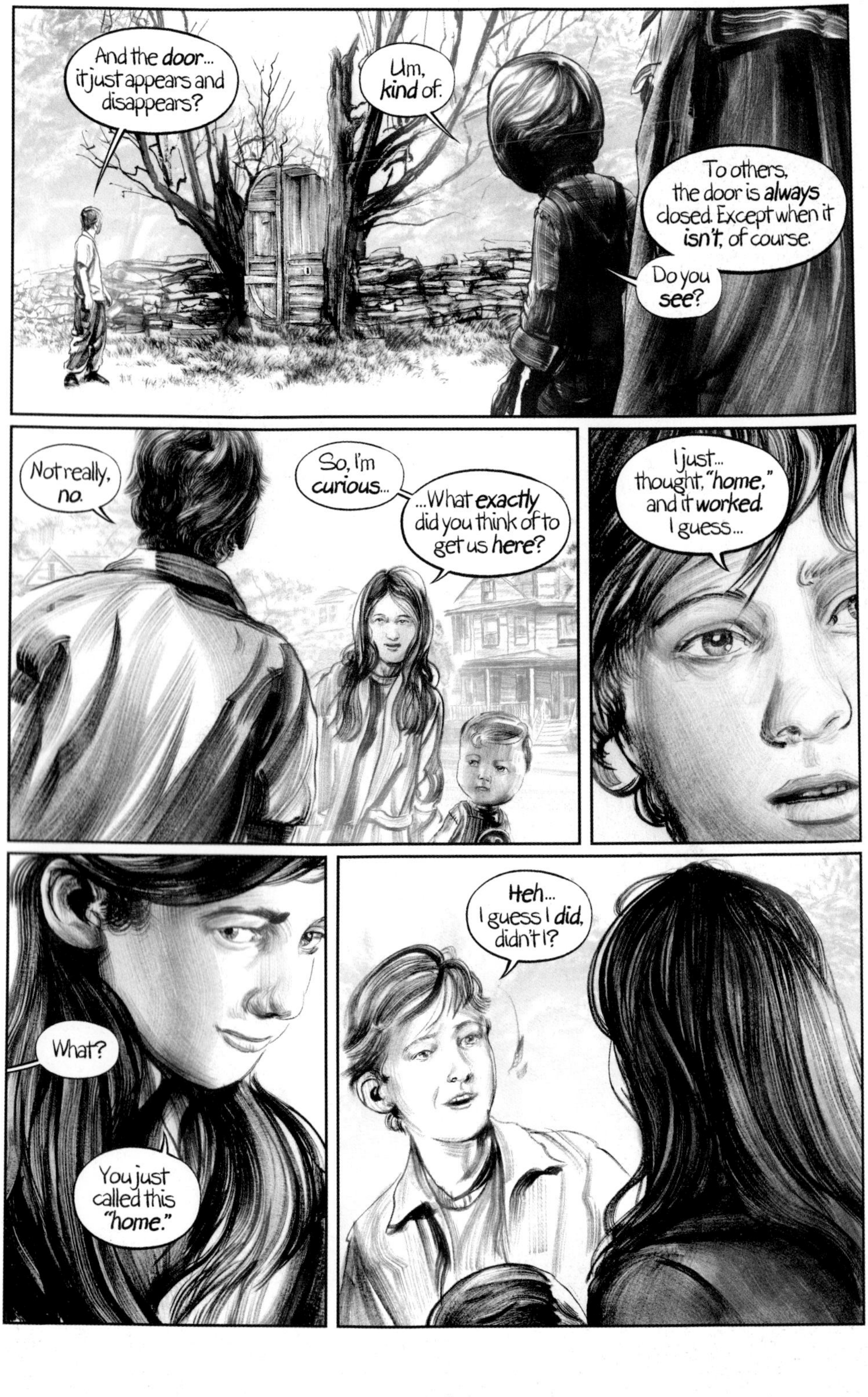
And the door... it just appears and disappears?
Um, kind of.
To others, the door is always closed. Except when it isn't, of course.
Do you see?
Not really, no.
So, I'm curious...
...What exactly did you think of to get us here?
I just... thought, "home," and it worked. I guess...
What?
You just called this "home."
Heh... I guess I did, didn't I?

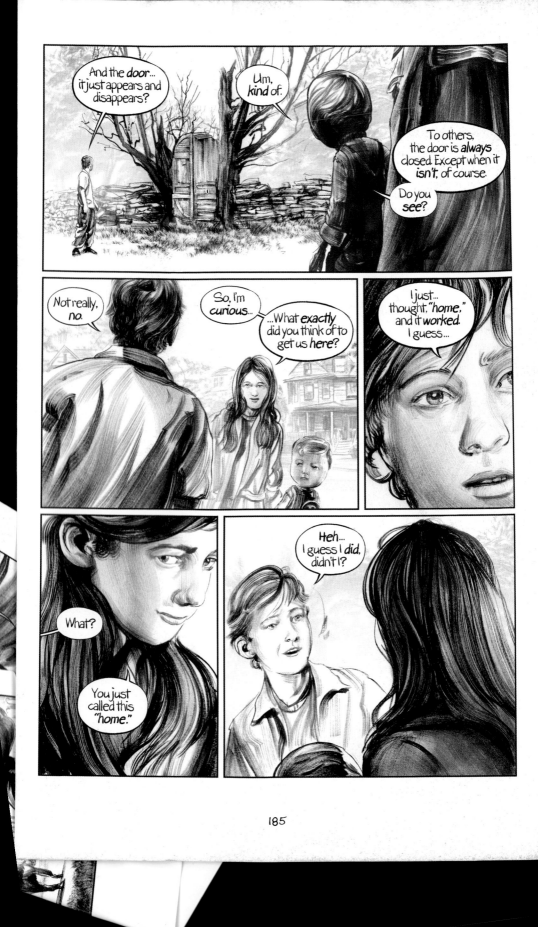

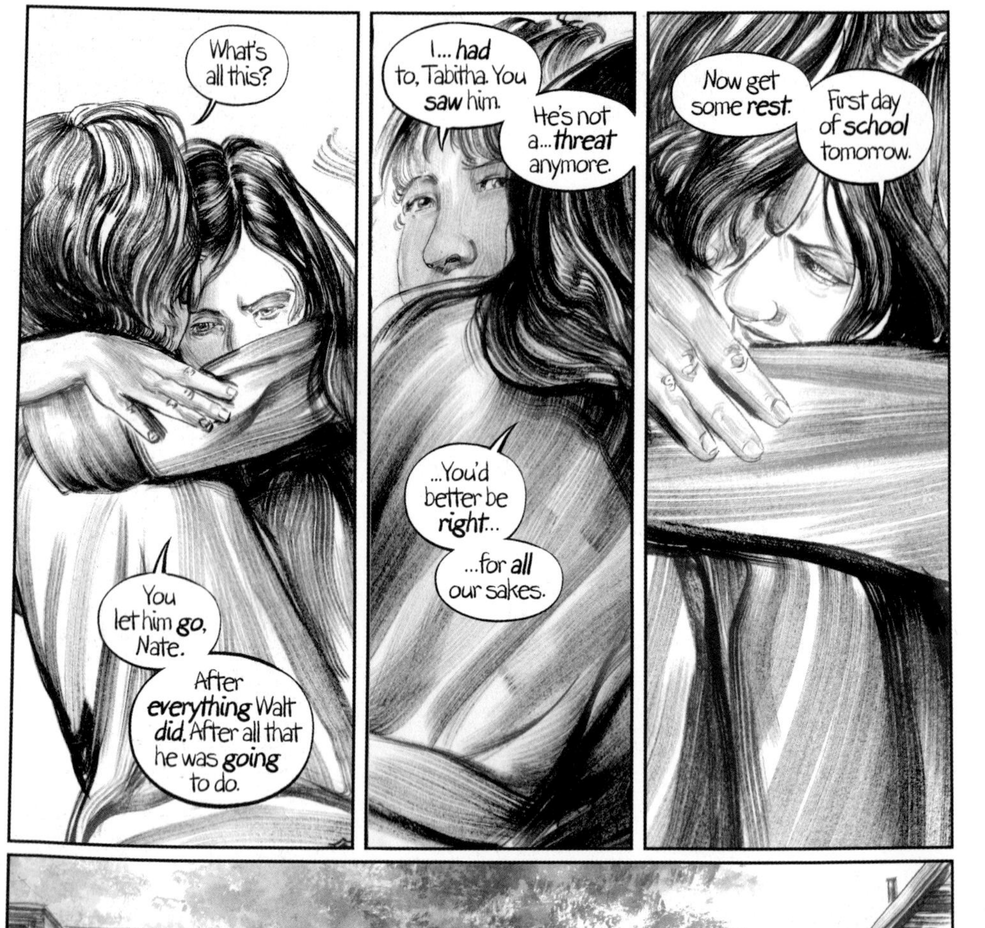

What's all this?
You let him go, Nate.
After everything Walt did. After all that he was going to do.
I... had to, Tabitha. You saw him.
He's not a... threat anymore.
...You'd better be right...
...for all our sakes.
Now get some rest.
First day of school tomorrow.
Jeez... that's right.
Try not to be late. Old Mrs. Choat is a total beast if you're tardy.

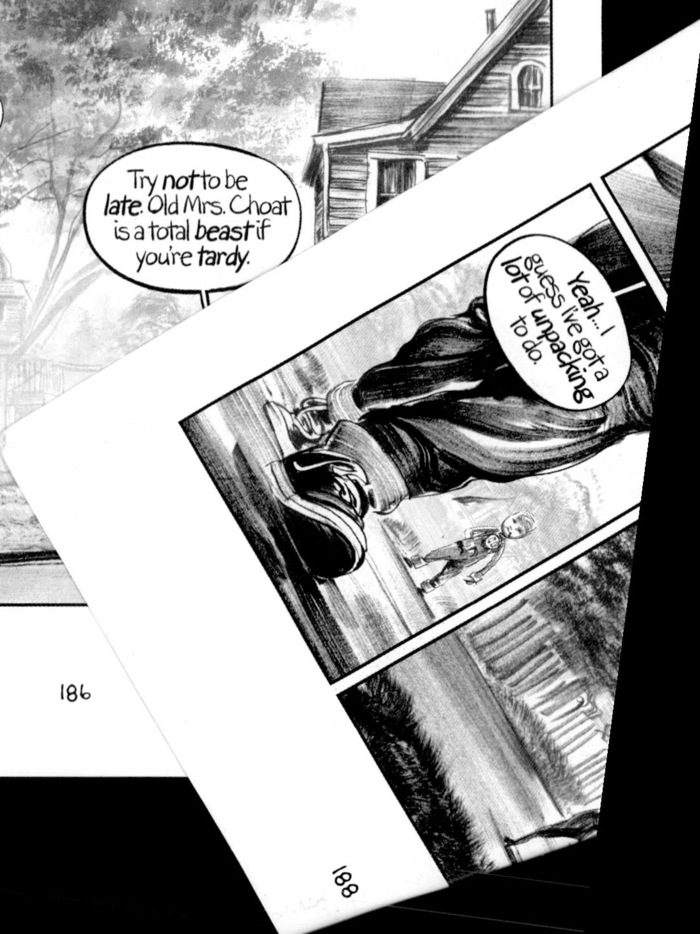

Yeah... I guess I've got a lot of unpacking to do.
188

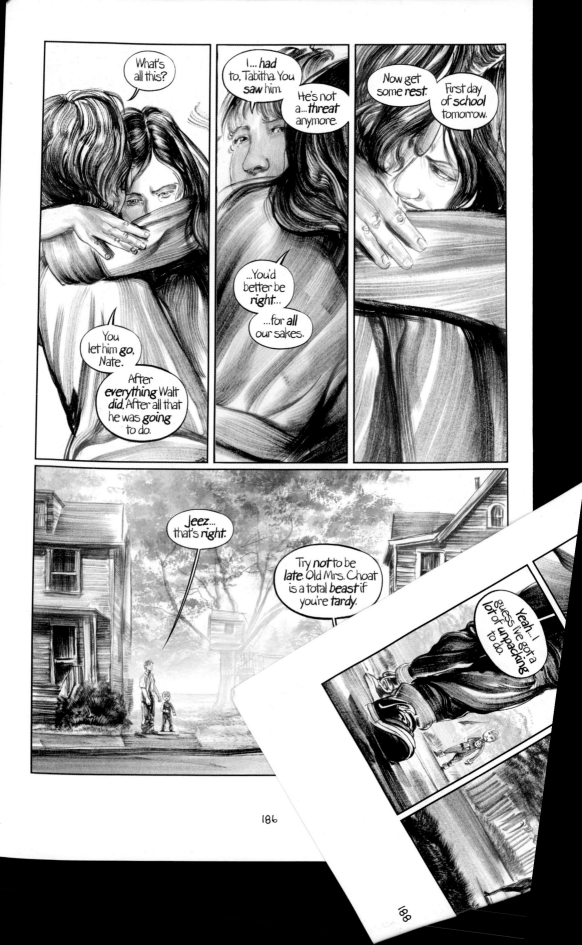

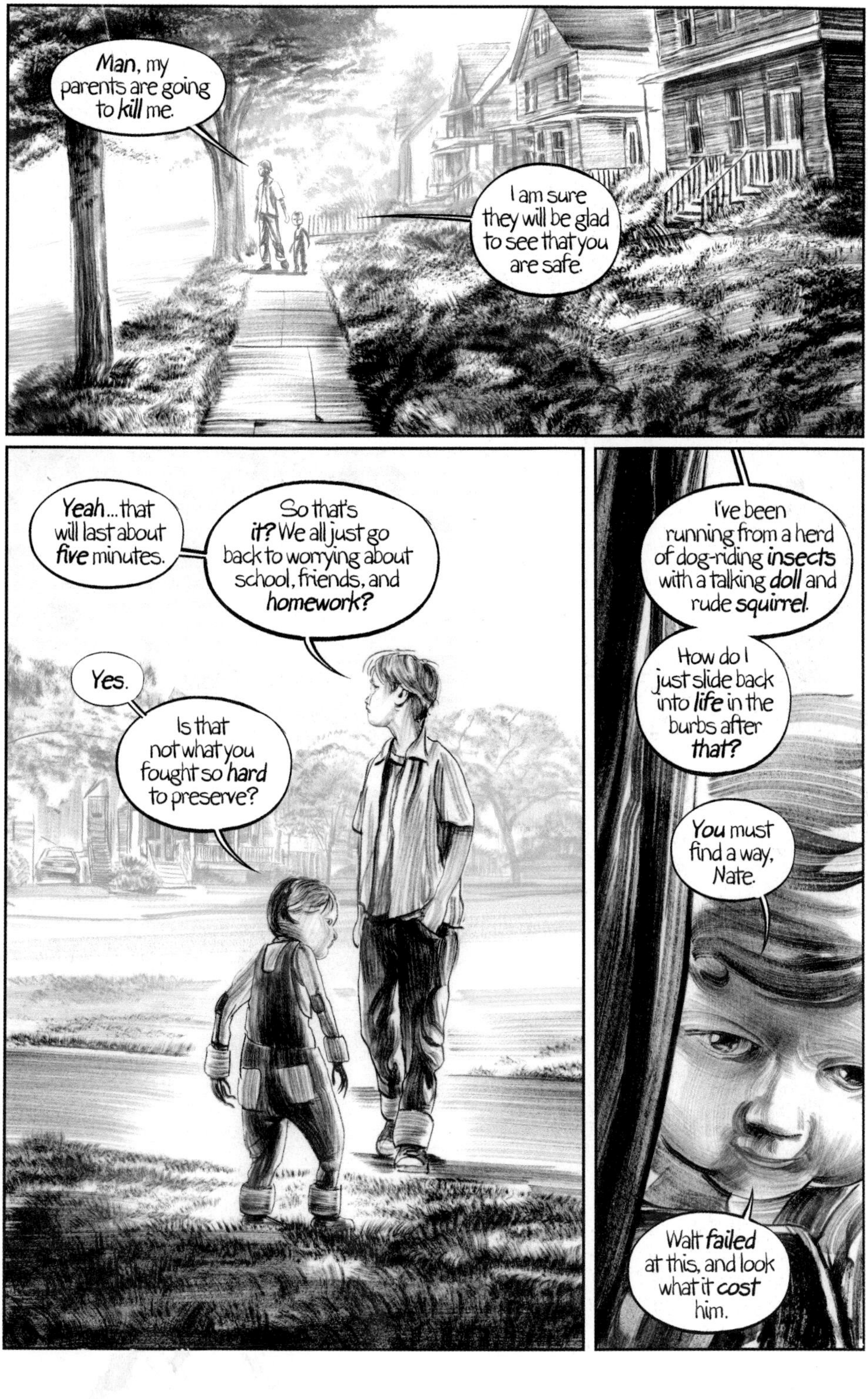
Man, my parents are going to kill me.
I am sure they will be glad to see that you are safe.
Yeah...that will last about five minutes.
So that's it? We all just go back to worrying about school, friends, and homework?
Yes.
Is that not what you fought so hard to preserve?
I've been running from a herd of dog-riding insects with a talking doll and rude squirrel.
How do I just slide back into life in the burbs after that?
You must find a way, Nate.
Walt failed at this, and look what it cost him.

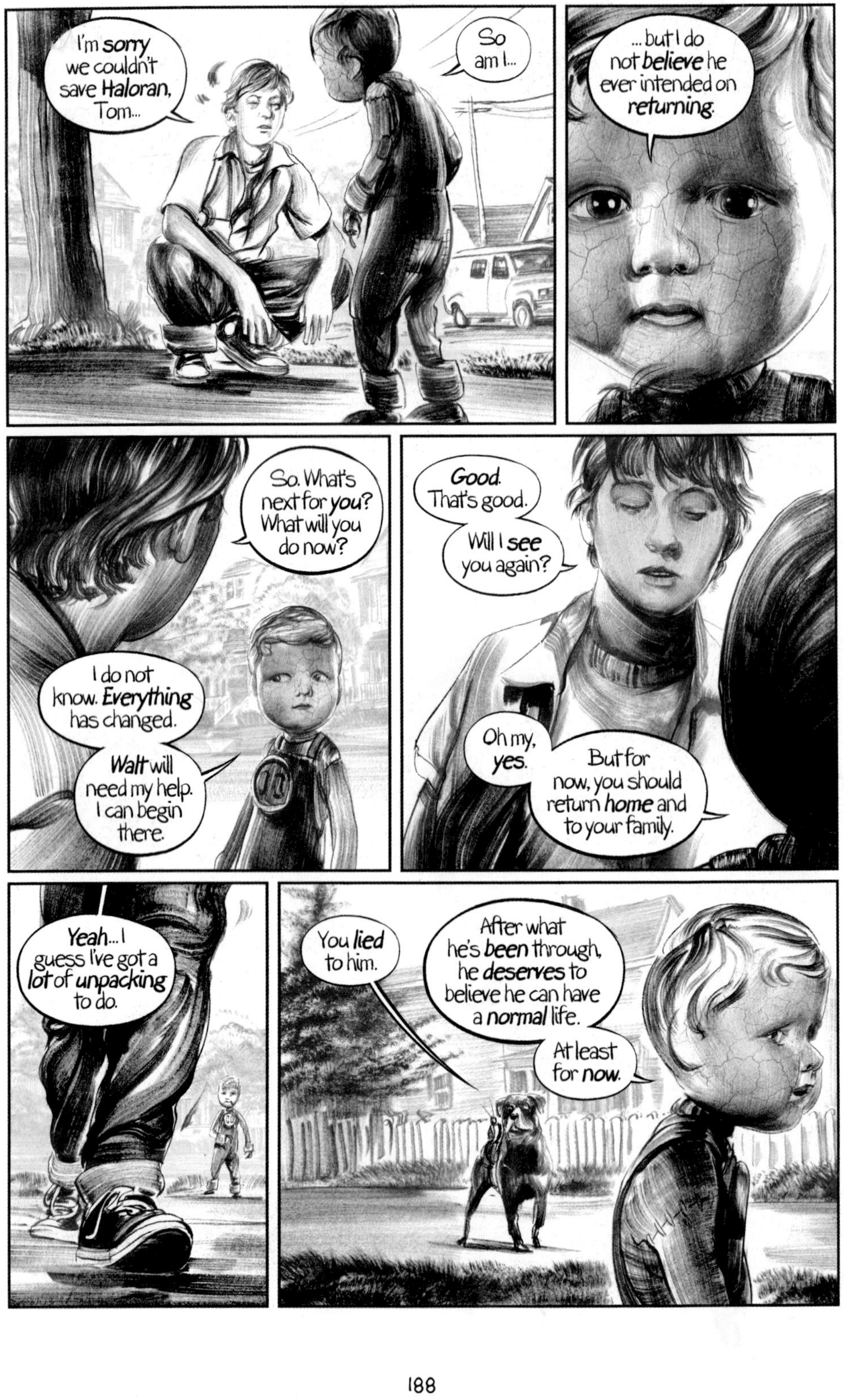
I'm sorry we couldn't save Haloran, Tom...
So am I...
...but I do not believe he ever intended on returning.
So. What's next for you? What will you do now?
I do not know. Everything has changed.
Walt will need my help. I can begin there.
Good. That's good.
Will I see you again?
Oh my, yes.
But for now, you should return home and to your family.
Yeah...I guess I've got a lot of unpacking to do.
You lied to him.
After what he's been through, he deserves to believe he can have a normal life.
At least for now.

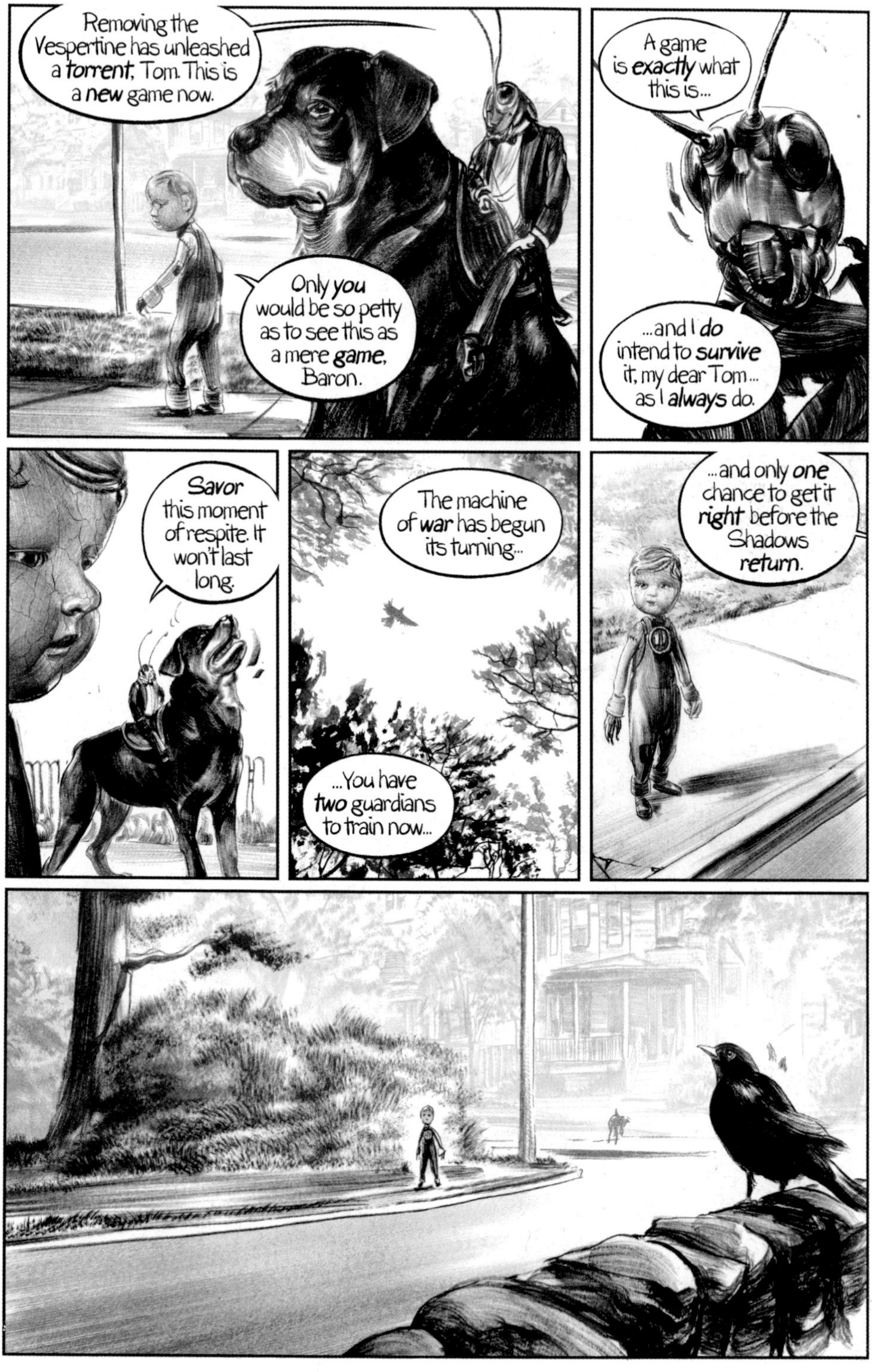
Removing the Vespertine has unleashed a torrent, Tom. This is a new game now.
Only you would be so petty as to see this as a mere game, Baron.
A game is exactly what this is...
...and I do intend to survive it, my dear Tom... as I always do.
Savor this moment of respite. It won't last long.
The machine of war has begun its turning...
...You have two guardians to train now...
...and only one chance to get it right before the Shadows return.

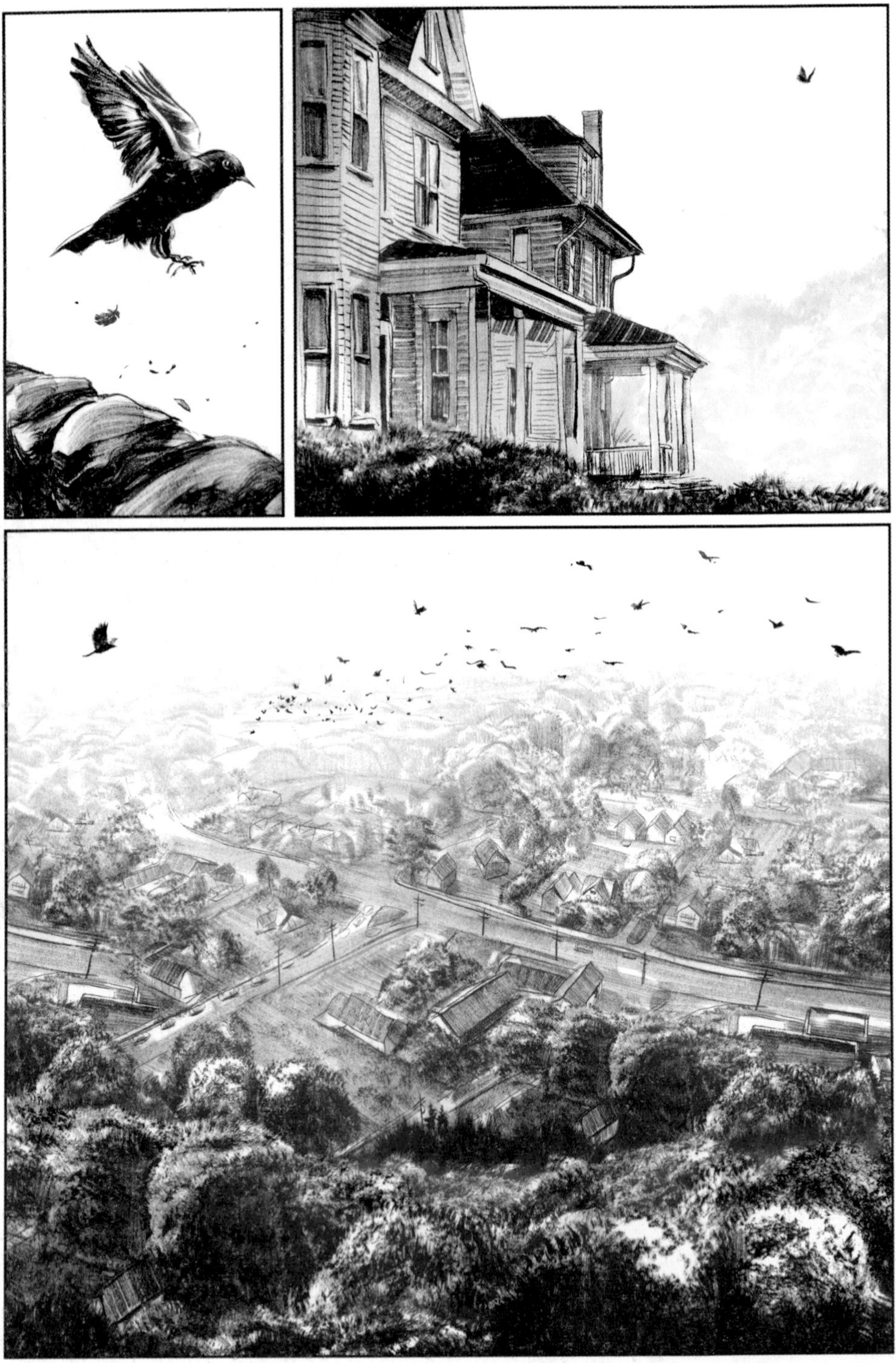

The End